DEAD AMERICA
THE NORTHWEST INVASION COLLECTION
PART 1
BOOKS 1 - 6
BY: DEREK SLATON
© 2020

BOOKS:
1. PORTLAND - PT. 1
2. PORTLAND - PT. 2
3. SEATTLE - PT. 1
4. SEATTLE - PT. 2
5. SEATTLE - PT. 3
6. SEATTLE - PT. 4

FOLLOW NEW RELEASES AT:

www.DeadAmericaBooks.com

DEAD AMERICA: THE NORTHWEST INVASION
BOOK 1
PORTLAND - PART 4
BY DEREK SLATON
© 2020

CHAPTER ONE

Day Zero +22

Zion stepped out of his apartment early in the morning. As the door clicked shut behind him, he looked up the dimly lit hallway towards the stairwell, waiting for his eyes to adjust to the low light. The only source was from a mirror at the end of the hallway that had been positioned to reflect the sunlight from the outer wall.

"Really need to add some emergency lighting to the shopping list," he muttered as he began to walk. A few doors down, he stopped and smacked a door with the palm of his hand a few times. "Yo, Calvin, we got work to do, brother!" he called.

He waited a moment, hearing low groaning and shuffling from inside. When his friend didn't come to the door, he smacked it again loudly, the sound echoing through the empty hallway.

"Don't make me come in there!" he warned playfully. There was more shuffling, and then muffled voices, which made his brow furrow.

Zion turned the knob, cracking the door open. As soon as it was an inch side, Calvin appeared, bracing his body against

it to keep it from opening further. His
hair stuck out in all directions, his face
flushed, looking far more frantic than he
usually was in the morning.

"Hey, Zion, man," he blurted, "can
you give me like, two minutes, and I'll be
out?"

His visitor stared him down
suspiciously. "Yeah… I can do that," he
said slowly. "But first, you gotta tell me
who else is in here with you."

"What?" Calvin asked, voice shrill.
"There's nobody in here."

Zion narrowed his eyes. "I heard
voices."

Calvin opened his mouth, freezing,
presumably going over excuses in his head,
but none that worked post apocalypse such
as *I was just watching TV*. After a few
awkward moments of silence, he sighed and
stepped aside.

"All right, you got me," he admitted.
"But it's not what you think."

Zion smirked. "Which means it's
definitely what I think," he quipped, and
moved into the apartment.

There was paper and empty bottles
everywhere, the picture of a perfect
bachelor pad. As he entered the living
room, he spotted Tori sitting on the
couch, nose wrinkled in embarrassment. Her
sandy hair was askew, sticking up on one

side, and she pushed her glasses up her nose as she avoided his gaze.

"Morning, Tori," Zion greeted brightly.

She chewed a fingernail. "Oh, good morning, Zion," she babbled, still not looking at him. "I was… just… getting ready to join the others in the parking garage."

"Well, we'll be down in a bit," he said gently, smiling and nodding. "Look forward to seeing what you came up with."

She nodded like a bobblehead. "You won't be disappointed." She grabbed some papers from the coffee table and rushed out of the apartment, throwing a wild grin at Calvin on her way out.

He shot her back a goofy smile and watched her leave, closing the door behind her. As soon as it was closed, Zion threw his arm around his buddy, shaking him.

"Hell yeah, get you some player!" he gushed.

Calvin's face flushed crimson. "It's not like that," he insisted.

"Oh, you ain't gotta be shy around me," his friend teased. "Do you have any idea what a relief it is that I'm not going to have to watch my sister whoop your ass for hittin' on her one of these days?"

Calvin bristled. "That's still on the table," he said.

"Come on, man." Zion rolled his eyes. "You can't tell me it ain't what it looks like. Pretty girl waking up in your apartment with hair like that?"

His friend shook his head and motioned for him to follow over to the couch. There were numerous papers strewn about across the coffee table, despite what Tori had taken with her.

"Is it safe to sit on that couch?" Zion asked, eyebrow raised.

Calvin scoffed. "I'm telling you man, it's *not* what you think," he insisted.

They sat down, Zion playfully looking around for any messes he shouldn't be sitting on. As he got situated, Calvin rifled through the papers, and pulled out what looked like engineering schematics of a truck.

"What the hell is this?" Zion furrowed his brow.

His friend held out the paper. "It's what Tori and I were working on last night," he explained.

Zion grabbed the drawing and inspected it, eyes roving over the badass vehicle with a reinforced front end, spikes, and several other bells and whistles. It was the perfect zombie-killing machine for the apocalypse.

"So you're telling me that y'all spent the night drawing *trucks*?" he asked, gaping.

Calvin grinned wolfishly. "Not just any truck," he said, "it's my future battle truck."

Zion blinked at him in confusion. "Battle truck?" he blurted.

"Hell yeah, a battle truck!" his friend exclaimed, throwing up his hands. "We're in the apocalypse, and it's about damn time we went all Mad Max with this." He leaned forward as Zion stared dumbfounded at the drawing, grabbing a joint from a little box on the corner of the coffee table and sparking it up. "I ran into Tori at dinner last night, and we got to talking," Calvin explained as he puffed. "She asked how Fingers was coming along with rebuilding my trucks, and then I made a joke about Mad Max, and then the next thing you know she started throwing out ideas. After that, we came up here and started drawing stuff, and the time kinda got away from us."

Zion chuckled, shaking his head. "Man, I hope to god you aren't that oblivious when you are watching my back out there," he said.

"What do you mean?" Calvin's brow furrowed.

"Come on man," his friend said, tossing the paper on the table, "you have a highly intelligent and cute girl talking about weaponizing your truck, and you didn't make a move?"

Calvin took a long drag on his joint and shook his head. "I really didn't think she-"

Zion cut him off by smacking him on the back of the head. "Lucky for you, we're in the apocalypse so her pickins are slim," he said, pointing a playful finger in his friend's shocked face, "so you might be able to get another chance."

"Wait, you think…" Calvin trailed off, sitting with his joint smoldering away in his hand, forgotten.

"Hell yeah, I think she's into you," Zion confirmed with a nod. "And I'm not just saying that to protect your wellbeing from my sister."

His friend thought back to every moment from the night before, finally remembering his weed and taking another thoughtful few puffs, replaying each bat of Tori's eyelashes and brush of her fingers on his arm as they drew their blueprints.

He finally scrubbed a hand down his face, groaning. "Apparently I need to start having some coffee with dinner," he admitted, "because holy hell, how did I miss those signs?"

"If you're interested," Zion replied playfully, "I do teach a course for a totally affordable amount." He laughed.

Calvin sighed, shaking his head. "I'll keep that in mind."

"Come on," his friend said, smacking his knees and getting to his feet. "Let's grab some breakfast and go see what your girlfriend has cooked up in the parking garage."

Zion and Calvin came out of the stairwell to the parking garage. Every truck and SUV had been moved against the far wall, and the cement floor was a disaster zone. There were car parts and bits of metal strewn around everywhere, tools and bins scattered about.

"This place looks like my brother's room growing up," Calvin declared. "If my momma were here, somebody would be getting yelled at for sure."

Zion opened his mouth to respond, but a loud metallic clang startled them.

"What in the holy hell was that?" Calvin demanded, and they rushed into the thick of things, looking around. As they came around a large van, Jack, Missy, and Harold exchanged high fives while standing beside a tall metal structure on rollers.

Zion raised an eyebrow. "Looks like they built something fun," he said. He and Calvin wandered over, studying the contraption.

It was six feet tall, with roughly welded patches of metal in the center. The top two feet had a dozen metal bolts about four feet long, points on the ends. At the back was a giant lever connected to the bolts, with five wheels along the bottom,

like heavy duty versions of office chair
wheels.

"My my," Zion piped up as they
approached, "what do we have here?"

Jack grinned, brushing his sweaty
hair off of his forehead. "Hey guys, you
like what you see?" he asked.

"That depends," Zion replied, cocking
his head. "I'm not exactly sure what I'm
looking at."

Missy spread her hands, presenting
the object as if she were on a game show.
"I like to call this the Impaler Three-
Thousand."

"Patent pending," Harold added.

Calvin scratched the back of his
head. "Why do you call it three-thousand?"
he asked.

"Because each spike is capable of
reaching three-thousand psi, assuming you
have someone strong enough to work the
lever," Missy replied.

Zion eyed his companion with a smirk,
"Guessing she isn't talking to you," he
joked, and there was a ripple of laughs
throughout the group, Calvin included.
"So, walk me through it," he said,
motioning to the contraption.

Jack stepped forward, demonstrating
as he spoke. "It's simple enough," he
explained, "you just push it up to the
concrete barrier, and pull the lever as

hard as you can." He pulled the lever slightly to the right before slamming it down, and all twelve metal bolts rocketed in between the metal railing above the concrete, all of them hitting around head height with a deafening *CRACK*.

Calvin crossed his arms. "Didn't look like you pulled the lever that hard," he said. "Hell, I'm pretty sure I can hit three-thousand myself."

Jack smirked and shook his head, grunting as he strained to lift the lever back up to the top. As he moved up, it clicked into place in the notches. He gave up a few from the top.

"Need a hand with that?" Zion asked.

Jack shook his head and stepped back from the machine. "Nah, it's all good," he replied. "We still need to make a few minor tweaks to the springs."

"So it's a spring-loaded death machine?" Zion asked, a wide grin forming on his face.

"I was wondering why you had those on the shopping list yesterday," Calvin mused, wagging his finger at the students.

"You guys found a lot of them," Missy declared, smiling triumphantly. "Enough to build four or five more of these."

Harold rubbed the back of his neck. "But we still need a few smaller parts to complete them," he admitted.

"Just put them on the shopping list, and we'll see what we can do this afternoon," Zion suggested.

Missy cocked a brow. "I thought you were doing a run this morning?" she asked.

He shook his head. "Sorry, but Wendy called in last night, and we have to go help them out first," he replied.

"Oh, okay," she said, nodding, "that gives us time to work out everything we're going to need for the lopper."

Zion and Calvin exchanged a glance, saying in unison, "The lopper?"

The college kids grinned, and Jack motioned for them to follow him. They walked to the far corner of the garage, next to an area completely bathed in sunlight. Tori sat on the ground tinkering with a small weed-eater sized engine connected to a long six-foot handle that jettisoned out from the base. Above the engine was a metal post that was six feet high, with a trio of plastic arms sticking out of the top in a four-foot radius.

"Okay, I'm intrigued," Zion said, gaping at the machine.

Tori looked up and regarded them, smiling warmly at Calvin. "Hey guys," she said, "give me just a minute and I can give you a demonstration."

Zion nudged his companion playfully as she looked down again, and Calvin blushed, wrinkling his nose. They approached the machine, and Zion flicked one of the thin plastic arms jetting out from the center.

"Not sure if this is gonna do a whole lot of damage," he mused.

Tori shook her head. "Well, this is more of a proof-of-concept prototype," she replied. "Wanted to make sure the concept was sound before we sent you two out shopping."

"All right," Zion agreed, "so what does it do?"

The blonde held up a finger, signifying she needed a minute. She finished tinkering with the engine and then primed it. "You may want to take a step back," she warned. "It won't kill you, but might leave a mark."

The duo took a few steps back, waiting with bated breath. Once they were clear, Tori pulled the ripcord and the engine sprung to life. She moved back to the handle that stood at her waist, with a motorcycle throttle attached to the right side.

"You ready?" she asked.

Zion gave her a thumbs up, and she hit the throttle. The center metal rod began to spin rapidly, and the plastic arms whirled like a helicopter. It started to move so fast that they were barely visible.

The audience nodded appreciatively, impressed.

"Jack, the can!" Tori called over the loud engine.

Jack looked down and grabbed an empty soda can from a pile on the ground next to his feet and then lobbed it at the blades. The machine shredded it into pieces, sending debris flying against the back wall. Tori grinned as she flicked the power off and turned back to the duo.

"If that can was any indication, I'd say your little test worked," Zion declared, holding up a hand.

The blonde nodded vigorously. "Yeah, I'm pleased with it," she agreed, pushing her glasses back up her nose. "Although I think the impaler three thousand should be our priority."

"Why?" Zion asked, brow furrowing. "This thing looks like it could tear those bitches to shreds."

Tori tilted her head back and forth. "Don't get me wrong, this thing will do the job when the time comes," she assured him. "However, it's going to be heavy. Like it will take three of us to move it into position heavy."

"Which means," Harold added, "for it to be effective, we're going to need a horde to be headed in our direction."

"And even then, it's just going to thin some of them out," Missy piped up.

Zion crossed his arms thoughtfully. "Still, if you make it heavy duty enough it could help out."

"What would you need to make a real one of those?" Calvin asked.

"We have most of the main components," Tori replied. "The metal and blade components, anyway. We even have the gas."

Zion cocked his head. "But…"

"We need engines," the blonde finished. "The weed eater engine I used on the test isn't going to pack enough punch."

Calvin pursed his lips for a moment. "So what are you thinking?" he asked. "Go karts?"

"I was thinking," Tori replied, "riding lawn mower engines?" She held up her hands as the duo shared a concerned look. "I would have thought those would be plentiful," she quickly added. "I can't imagine too many looters targeting those."

Zion nodded. "Problem is, they're out of season, so a lot of smaller stores stopped carrying them," he pointed out.

"There's always that super garden center in the mall," Calvin suggested.

His companion shook his head. "That mall is a clusterfuck and a half," he replied.

"I thought you were luring zombies away," Jack piped up. "Why not just do the same there?" he asked.

"We tried," Zion explained, "and we were only able to get the ones outside to follow. The ones inside just didn't want to come out the doors, and I sure as shit wasn't going to play doorman for them. So we just locked them up inside."

Tori nodded, pushing her glasses back up on her nose. "It's okay," she assured him. "I'll see if I can come up with a workaround."

"Although when we're out raiding, I'll keep and eye out for some," Calvin said quickly. "Never know what we're gonna find."

She smiled, eyes lighting up as she regarded him.

"Just write down everything you need," Zion said. "We'll take care of it as best we can."

"Thanks, Zion," Tori said, and then her eyes flicked back to his companion. "Thanks Calvin." She shot him a little wink, and a goofy grin broke out on his face.

"We'll be back this afternoon, so have your shopping list ready," Zion said, and led his swooning friend away. "We need to get going."

"Yeah," Calvin added, "you know how Wendy gets when we don't show up on time."

"Monique ain't much better," Zion added, and they shared a chuckle as they headed back across the garage.

"Oh good, you two haven't left yet," Cheryl called as she emerged from the stairwell.

Zion waved to her. "What's up?"

"Just got a call from the cattle drivers," she replied, "and they landed a big one."

"How many?" he asked.

She tucked a stray lock of hair behind her ear with a pencil. "Their best guess was eight to ten thousand."

"Well damn." Zion crossed his arms and smirked at his companion. "Looks like they beat our record."

Calvin clenched a fist in front of his face. "We'll get 'em next time."

"Was there anything else?" Zion asked. "We were about to head out to Wendy's."

"I've already taken the liberty of letting her know you're going to be running a bit late due to the mob," Cheryl assured him.

He nodded. "They hittin' the crossroads, I take it?" he asked.

"They're approaching the front edge of the crossing now," Cheryl informed him, checking her clipboard.

"The crossroads?" Missy asked, the students having clustered behind them to listen.

"Where our roads meet the interstate," Cheryl explained. "It's only a few miles down, so we pull everybody back from it to make sure it's as quiet as possible."

Calvin grinned. "Those critters are like lemmings," he added. "You get one of them going one way, and the rest of them follow."

"Oh okay," Missy said, nodding. "I get it. Thank you."

"How long until we can hit the back road?" Zion asked.

Cheryl held up a finger. "Give them one hour and you should be good."

"Well," Zion said with a sigh, "since we have all this time on our hands, Calvin maybe you can take Tori out for some breakfast."

His companion raised an eyebrow. "But we already…" He stopped at Zion's wide-eyed stare, and then continued, "...Told them we didn't have time today. So Tori, we might have to wait a few minutes for

them to make us something fresh," he
stumbled over his words nervously. "I
mean. Um. Assuming you're free and all."

She pushed her glasses up her nose
and seemed amused by his nervousness. "I
would like that."

Calvin's face lit up as she joined
him.

"Just be down here in forty-five so
we can get prepped," Zion reminded him as
they sauntered off together.

Calvin didn't even break stride,
giving a thumbs up over his shoulder as
they left.

Zion shook his head and chuckled
under his breath. "I swear, that boy
wouldn't get anywhere if he didn't have a
wingman like me." There was a smattering
of chuckles and he turned to the remaining
trio of students. "So, what other sorts of
crazy zombie-killing gadgets you guys come
up with?"

Harold rubbed his hands together in
excitement. "Come on, let us show you our
idea book."

Zion sat in his truck, loaded up and ready to go. He glanced in the side mirror, watching one of the guards fill up the tank with a gas can before setting the half-full can in the back. After a few moments, the passenger door opened and Calvin slid into the seat.

"There's the playboy!" Zion declared with a grin. "How'd your breakfast date go?"

His companion simply threw him a smirk.

"Just remember that Christmas isn't too far away, and your wingman likes weaponry," Zion said.

Calvin winked at him. "Tori and I will whip you up something nice, then."

"Well, buckle up so we can get on the road," his friend replied with a laugh. "Gotta get you back quick so your girl doesn't yell at me for keeping you out so late."

Calvin chuckled as the truck roared to life, and Zion peeled out of the parking garage, heading out down the driveway and towards the interstate.

"So, you gonna give me some details?" Zion pressed.

His friend blushed and shook his head, pulling out a joint from his pocket.

"Not much to tell, man," he admitted, and sparked it up. "We just sat in one of the garden areas and drank coffee. Honestly, spent a lot of time just sitting quietly and enjoying the peacefulness."

"Uh oh," Zion said.

Calvin blinked at him, choking on his inhale. "What do you mean, uh oh?" he asked through a fit of coughing. "I really enjoyed myself."

"I don't know, man," his friend replied, drawing out his words. "You sure she was having a good time too? My sister has told me some horror stories about guys who couldn't hold a conversation."

Calvin's eyes were wide as saucers. "I mean, she put her head on my shoulder while we were sitting there," he said. "I'd say that was a good sign, wouldn't you?"

Zion burst out laughing and smacked his friend on the arm. "Man, look at you giving me the ole okey-doke," he teased. "You know exactly what you were doing, didn't you?"

"Gotcha!" Calvin replied with a grin and took a smaller puff from his joint.

"Well, I'm happy for you, man," Zion said. "Glad you got you a little romance brewing there."

His companion let out a happy sigh on the exhale. "Me too," he said wistfully.

"I know this is gonna come as a shock, but even when times were good, I was never much of a ladies' man."

"No!" Zion gasped dramatically. "You don't say?!"

Calvin rolled his eyes, fighting a smile. "Shocking, I know."

"Well, make sure you treat her right," his friend instructed, "because it's not like you can avoid her."

Calvin chuckled and shook his head. "No shit, right?"

When they reached a mile within the interstate, there were half a dozen men standing in the road, and Zion sobered as one of them flagged him down. He pulled up and unrolled the window.

"What's going on?" he asked.

"That mob of dead fuckers are still shambling by," the guard replied, jerking his thumb over his shoulder.

Calvin leaned over. "What did they do?" he asked. "Stop and have a picnic? They should have passed by now."

The guard shrugged. "It's been moving steady for a while now," he said. "So either those boys can't count, or they picked up another group along the way."

"Either way, it's good that they're getting so many of these things outta here," Zion said with a sigh. "Less we gotta deal with, right?"

The guard nodded stoically. "Yes sir, mister Zion."

"So, any idea how much longer we need to camp out here?" he asked. "Because we got stuff to do."

The guard pulled out his walkie talkie, holding up a hand. "Hang on, let me check." He lifted the radio to his lips. "Hey bubba, you copy?" he asked.

"Yeah, I'm here, what's up?" Bubba came back.

The guard raised a hand over his eyes, peering towards the interstate. "How's the tail end of this thing looking?"

"Last of them passed by the exit about five minutes ago," Bubba replied.

The guard nodded. "All right, you keep sitting tight till I tell you otherwise," he instructed.

"Ten-four," Bubba replied, and the line clicked off.

"So, what's the verdict?" Zion asked.

The guard lifted a hand and tilted it back and forth. "He's a ways down south, so you're probably looking at another hour or two before the last of the stragglers come through," he replied.

"Wonder if Tori is free for lunch?" Calvin joked.

The guard pursed his lips and cocked his head. "If you don't mind a bumpy ride, I got an alternative for you."

"I'm listening," Zion replied, leaning out the window.

The guard pointed past him. "Go back up the road about half a mile until you see a dirt clearing in the trees," he said. "It looks like at one time they were trying to put in a mountain bike path for all those healthy fuckers that could afford to live in these parts. They didn't get much past the clearing stage, however."

"Is it drivable?" Zion asked.

The guard shrugged. "As long as you got four wheel drive, you're good. Anything else and you're going to get stuck." he replied.

Zion patted the steering wheel. "Covered."

"It's gonna wind around a bit in spots," the guard admitted, "but if you keep going, you'll hit a road just after a few miles. Just hang a left and you'll hit the interstate."

Zion smiled and extended a fist. "Appreciate the info."

"Anytime, mister Zion," the guard replied, returning the smile and bumping his fist with his own. "You two be safe out there."

Zion nodded and rolled up the window, executing a quick three-point turn and heading back up the road.

"Here's hoping we got the bad out of the way today," Calvin said with a sigh as he stubbed out the end of his joint.

His friend shook his head. "Don't go jinxing us now," he said, and they shared a chuckle.

Zion slowed to a crawl as they looked for the trail entrance. After a few moments, Calvin pointed to an opening in the trees.

"That's gotta be it," he said.

Zion turned onto it, stopping at the entrance. Before them stretched a bumpy dirt path that was barely wider than the truck.

"Buckle up," he said, "this ain't gonna be fun."

Zion and Calvin pulled up to the camp less than a mile from the bridge over the river. As they approached the neighborhood, there were a few groups of armed guards about, both men and women, patrolling the streets on foot. They waved at the vehicle as it rolled up towards the entrance.

"Man, they're really expanding down here," Calvin said as he waved back to the guards.

Zion nodded. "Talked to Monique last night for a bit, and she said they've taken over another two blocks since we were last here," he said.

"That's a hell of an expansion," Calvin mused in awe.

Zion shrugged as he pulled in. "Kind of necessary with the survivors they've been taking in," he explained. "She said they found a family of ten yesterday and brought them in."

"Let me guess," his friend drawled, "they have a shopping list for us?"

Zion cocked his head. "She didn't say, she just said come down," he said, and drove through the eight foot tall iron gate across the center of the road.

One of the door guards leaned in. "Wendy and Monique are waiting for you at

the house on the corner," he said, waving
them through and then helping to close the
giant gate.

Zion nodded and drove on, parking the
truck outside a large two-story brick
house. As he killed the engine and they
got out of the car, Wendy and Monique
emerged from the house.

"You're late, little brother," his
sister quipped.

Zion shook his head. "Cheryl said she
let you know we were running behind," he
said.

"You're nearly half an hour late
outside of that," Wendy added, crossing
her arms.

"We had to off-road it a bit to get
around the interstate horde," Calvin
explained. "Feels like I'm still bumping
up and down even though I'm not moving."
He shook out his arms a bit.

"So what you got for us?" Zion asked.

Wendy turned towards the door and
waved for them to follow. "Why don't you
come inside?" she asked. "We got some
people we'd like you to meet."

The duo headed up the porch steps,
and Monique and Zion embraced before they
headed into the house. There was a Latino
family sitting in the main foyer, looking
like they were several generations of
people ranging from four to eighty-four

years old. A couple of the children were playing together in the corner under the watchful eye of a grandmother, while several adults sat around a table in the center playing a card game.

"Wow," Calvin said, blinking at the guests. "Where in the world did you find them at?"

"At their restaurant about ten miles south of here," Wendy replied. She waved at one of the men, who looked to be in his mid-twenties. "Mateo, can you come over here, please?" she asked.

He got up from the table. He was physically fit, but no body builder, with dark hair and determined eyes. He extended his hand to Zion and Calvin in turn with a warm smile.

"Hello gentlemen," he said with a slight accent, but a confident tone that said he'd been speaking English his entire life. "I am Mateo."

Zion nodded as they shook. "I'm Zion, and this is my friend Calvin."

"Tell them what you told us," Wendy prompted.

"Okay," he began, taking a deep breath. "My family, we have had this restaurant for years, and we got all of our supplies from a, um, family friend. He really wanted to help out people like him, so he would only sell to people he knew.

Because of this, his place of business wasn't listed. No signs, no nothing."

"When you say supplies, you mean…" Calvin prompted.

"Food," Mateo replied with a nod. "Dried beans, masa flour, other staples with a long shelf life."

Zion cocked his head. "Where is this place?"

"About ten miles south of here," Mateo replied.

Calvin nodded. "Could be worth checking out," he said, and grinned at the corner inhabitants. "Especially with some old school grandma cooks."

"That's why we called you," Wendy piped up. "We could send some of ours from here, but they're worn out from clearing the block over the past few days."

Monique winked at her brother. "And we know how much you love bashing in skulls," she said. "What kind of sister would I be if I didn't look out for my kid brother?"

Zion chuckled. "Thanks, sis."

"So you'll go?" Mateo asked, hope in his eyes.

"Yeah, we'll go check it out," Zion replied.

Their new acquaintance clapped his hands. "Wonderful!" he exclaimed. "Let me get my things and I will join you."

"Slow down, bud," Zion said, putting up a hand. "Calvin and I can handle this. Just tell us where to go."

Mateo's brow furrowed. "You can use my help," he insisted, "and my guidance to the warehouse."

"Can you fight?" Calvin asked.

"Look around this room," Mateo said, and spread his arms. "Do you see anybody that looks capable of handling themselves against the dead? Other than myself?"

The duo scanned the room, scrutinizing the rest of the family, not seeing anyone they would really want to put out in battle.

"Guess not," Zion admitted.

"I am the reason my family is alive," Mateo declared. "And I would like to be a part of the reason the people who took us in make it through the winter."

Calvin held up his palms in surrender. "I have one very important question for you, buddy," he said.

"Yes?" Mateo cocked his head.

"If we get this stuff," Calvin began, taking a deep breath, "can someone here make me some tamales? I've had a craving for weeks." He patted his belly.

The group chuckled, and Mateo grinned.

"I guarantee it will be the best you ever have," he assured him.

Calvin nodded. "All right, I'm sold."

Zion chuckled. "Go on, get your stuff and meet us outside."

Mateo nodded and ran off, and Monique took Zion's arm, pulling him out onto the porch. He looked around the street, seeing dozens of people milling about in the open, looking casual, happy even.

"Amazing the difference a few weeks makes, huh?" she asked.

Zion nodded, but took a deep breath. "Those things coming over the bridge still concern me, but I think you're in a great spot here, sis."

"We wouldn't be anywhere close to this built up if it wasn't for what you're doing, little brother," she said, running a hand over the back of his neck.

He wrinkled his nose. "Really wish you wouldn't call me that," he muttered.

"Baby brother it is, then," Monique teased.

He put up a hand. "Little brother is fine," he said.

She chuckled. "So are things going well at the complex?" she asked.

"Everybody seems to be happy," Zion said. "And we got those college kids ramping up our defenses."

She smiled. "Well, tell them once they get you squared away, we wouldn't mind borrowing them for a bit."

"I think that can be arranged," Zion replied with a nod.

Calvin, Wendy, and Mateo emerged from the house, the latter wearing a makeshift holster with two blades dangling on either side.

Zion raised an eyebrow. "Those are your weapons?" he asked.

Mateo pulled out one of the glittering blades, at least a foot long with a slight curve. "Butcher quality, cuts through bone like butter," he declared. "Especially those of the dead that have begun to rot."

"If it works for you, I'm all for it," Zion replied with a nod. "Let's load up." He gave Monique's shoulder a squeeze and led his men to the truck. He opened the door and let Mateo clamber in to the middle seat.

"If you want to clear it out and do a brief inventory," Wendy said from the steps, "I can send some of my guys down tomorrow to finish clearing it out."

Zion nodded. "We'll also load up what we can and bring it back," he assured her.

"Appreciate your help," she replied.

He gave her a little salute. "It's what I do." He threw his sister a smile who beamed back at him with pride.

The trio drove to a rundown neighborhood. There were bars on the windows, overgrown grass, and broken-down cars in the driveways. As they crawled along the street, there were a few zombies around the houses that shambled out from the side yards, attracted to the engine noise.

"It's about three more blocks up to the right," Mateo instructed. "Just a regular brick building."

Zion nodded. "Shouldn't be too hard to find." He coasted up the road, a few zombies reaching the asphalt and beginning to tail them. When they passed a few more intersections, Mateo pointed to a building at the end of the block.

"That's it!" he exclaimed.

There were a few dozen zombies around the building, a few pawing at the front door lazily like a kitten against a fish tank.

"Looks like someone was alive in there at one time," Zion mused.

Mateo pursed his lips. "Could be the owner and his family," he said.

"So how do you want to play this?" Calvin asked, rubbing his hands together.

Zion glanced in the rearview mirror and watched the dozen or so zombies spread out and lumbering after them, though still about fifty yards away. "Mateo and I will clear out the zombies in front," he said. "Anything behind us gets to that last intersection, you put it down."

"Not a problem," Calvin replied.

"All right," Zion said, glancing at Mateo, "let's see what you can do." He cut the engine, and they slid out of the truck, quickly surveying the immediate area for threats. Other than the pack to their friend and the stragglers behind, there was nothing else coming out of the woodwork.

Zion reached into the back seat, pulling out his makeshift two-by-four that Tori and her friends had crafted for him, the handle covered in duct tape, still covered in dried blood on the business end.

Calvin walked to the back of the truck, hopping up into the back. He knelt behind the tailgate, resting his rifle on top of it. He looked through the scope, getting a read on the closest zombie, what had once been a woman missing an arm.

"Looks like a zombie got a to-go order," he muttered to himself, and then shook his head at the groaner of a joke. He refocused, dialing in his sights, waiting for the zombie to cross the threshold up the block. As soon as its foot touched the intersection, he squeezed the trigger.

Its head exploded in a satisfying array of blood, sending the body to the ground in a heap. He chambered another round and continued to wait, the next zombie about fifteen yards behind her.

"Easiest detail I've had in a while," he murmured, and then he pulled back from his scope, checking his immediate left and right just to back up his claim. Nothing appeared to be drawn to the noise of his gun. "Guess they're all at the warehouse," he said to himself.

Meanwhile, the other two moved towards the horde, Mateo flinching as Calvin's first round went off.

"Don't go getting soft on me, now," Zion said, and it was a joke, but the undertone had a hint of worry.

Mateo shook his head. "Sorry," he replied, "just been a while since I've heard gunshots going off close by."

"It's all good," Zion assured him. "Just don't let it break your concentration."

His companion nodded and pulled out his two blades from the holsters at his sides. One was the foot-long curved blade, and the other was a meat cleaver, both of them shiny and unbelievably sharp.

As they walked up, a few of the zombies broke away from the building, attracted by the gunshots. The trio made it within fifteen yards before another shot cracked, and more zombies turned towards the truck.

"Which one do you want?" Zion asked.

Mateo inclined his head. "I'll take the trio," he said.

Zion nodded, impressed at the bravado. "Have at it," he said, waving his companion forward.

Mateo walked up confidently to the trio of zombies, and the lead of the triangle lunged at him, clad in designer jeans and a tattered polo shirt. The living man went into a flurry of slashes, the cleaver taking off both of the creature's arms and the long blade slipping up through the ghoul's chin like butter.

He pulled back on the blade and fell into a crouch as the two behind came forward, shoulder to shoulder. Mateo slashed at throat level, cutting deep into their necks but not quite far enough to sever their heads. He flipped the cleaver around and attacked with the blunt end, coming across his body and catching the left zombie on the side of the head.

The impact sent the head clean off its body from its weakened severed neck, and slammed into its partner, partially knocking the second zombie's head off. It fell to the ground and continued to moan and gnash its teeth as the head held on by a few tendons. Mateo jabbed down into its eye socket with the long knife, silencing it.

Zion began a slow clap, shaking his head. "My apologies on doubting you, sir," he said sincerely.

"A lot of people underestimate me," Mateo admitted, tossing him a smirk. "Always fun to prove them wrong."

Zion chuckled as he readied his weapon and stepped up next to his companion. Two more zombies approached, still a little ways ahead of the main horde of twenty or so that had broken off due to Calvin's firing.

"Hang tight," he instructed, holding up his weapon. "I wanna show you who you are partnered with."

Mateo playfully extended his hand, presenting the duo of ghouls to Zion, who headed forward. He stopped about five yards away from the two monsters, who kept stride with one another.

Zion put the large weapon on his shoulder like a bat, playfully pointing to left field like he was Babe Ruth calling his shot. When they got close, he swung with all his might, catching the creature on the side of the head and driving it through its partner.

The blow partially disintegrated the zombie's head, sending a splatter of blood through the air. The corpse crashed down on top of its partner, trapping it for a moment. Zion stood over it and drove the tip of the weapon into its face, crushing it.

Mateo playfully tapped his two metallic weapons together, praising his new friend. "Impressive," he declared. "However, I need to remember to keep a few feet back so I don't get caught in the backswing."

"Good call," Zion agreed.

They looked towards the warehouse, seeing twenty-five or so creatures moving towards them, easily twenty yards away. The pack was fairly thick, with only a few feet between each group.

"So, what do you think?" Zion asked, wiggling his weapon. "I knock 'em down, and you slice 'em up?"

Mateo readied his blades, flashing and glinting in the sun. "Batter up, my friend," he said.

Zion grinned and rushed forward towards the right flank of creatures. He quickly reared back and swung hard, catching a zombie in the ribcage and sending it tumbling back into several

others. He darted to the left, extending
the two-by-four in front of him and
ramming it into the center of a ghoul's
chest and sending it back, staggering
several more of its brethren and giving
him room to tee up another swing.

Meanwhile, Mateo ran up, his cleaver
swinging upward and catching a fallen
zombie struggling to sit up in the face.
The blade created a thin slit all the way
up through the skull, cutting the brain
clean in half. He stabbed down with the
long blade into the forehead of another
fallen ghoul, and then immediately slashed
the head off of another with the cleaver
in a deadly dance.

As he stepped up to the next group,
Zion swung mightily one more time,
knocking down another four creatures. He
stepped back and tugged on his companion's
arm, pulling him lightly back towards the
truck.

"Something wrong?" Mateo asked.

"Nah," Zion replied, shaking his
head. "Just giving them a chance to break
up a bit. We are a two man wrecking crew,
but there's no sense in risking getting in
over our heads."

His partner nodded and backed up
about ten yards. They waited patiently as
the eight or so zombies on the ground
staggered to get back to their feet,

tripping up a few of their friends in the process. A few moments later, the horde of twenty had been broken up into smaller, more manageable groups.

"Let's clear this batch and do the same retreat," Zion suggested. "You ready?"

Mateo nodded. "Beat 'em down," he replied.

The two of them worked in tandem for several minutes, systematically dispatching the threat. Zion stepped up to the last creature that was trying to pull itself off of the ground after falling. He swung the hunk of wood like a golf club, catching the ghoul underneath the chin and ripping the head clean off. As the head landed several feet away, he let out a cheer and threw up his arms, celebrating the decent chip.

"Good distance there, my friend," Mateo said with a grin.

Zion returned it as he turned around. "Yeah, golf was never really my game," he admitted, "but my sister did take me to the driving range a few times before all this."

"Did you enjoy it?" Mateo asked.

"Oh yeah," Zion said, nodding, "great way to let out frustration while still being competitive with the guy next to you."

His companion chewed over the words. "Never thought of it like that," he admitted.

A few more shots rang out from behind them in rapid succession, and they turned towards the truck just in time to see Calvin hop down and head towards them.

"Okay, that's the last of the stragglers," the sniper announced. "Doesn't look like anything else is too close by, at least not in numbers we need to worry about."

Zion clapped him on the shoulder. "Then let's hurry up and get what we need before that changes," he suggested.

They headed briskly towards the building, hopping over corpses, and Calvin checked the front door first. He tried the knob, but it was locked. He shook the door a few times, a clanging metallic sound coming from the inside.

"Locked up tight," he said, stepping back. "And sounds like it's chained, too."

Zion turned to Mateo. "Is there a back entrance?" he asked.

"There's a small loading dock in the back," his companion replied.

Zion nodded and led the trio around the side of the building, slowing at the corner. He peeked around to make sure there was no gaggle of undead back there and saw the area empty.

There was a four-foot high concrete
slab against the back of the building, and
a metal rolling door that opened to the
side.

Calvin tried the door, but it was
also locked. "Ideas?" he asked.

Zion looked up at the horizontal
windows above and motioned for the others
to get out of the way. Once they were
clear, he swung up with his weapon,
smashing one of the panes of glass.

"Okay," he said, "which one of you
wants to go?"

Mateo holstered his blades and raised
a hand. "I'll do it," he said. "I know the
layout in there, so if there is company, I
know where I can go."

"Hell, I'm not gonna argue that,"
Calvin quipped.

Zion smirked at him. "You just don't
wanna go."

"And?" Calvin shrugged.

Zion chuckled and laced his fingers
together, creating a step for Mateo to
vault upwards through the window. "Get in
and get the door open," he instructed.
"We'll sweep it together."

His companion nodded and placed his
boot into Zion's cupped hands. As the
strong man boosted him up, he grabbed on
to the edge of the window, careful to
avoid jagged glass, and hooked a leg up

into the frame. He rolled his body inside and then landed with a thud on the floor.

"You okay?" Zion called from outside.

"Yeah, I'm good," Mateo replied, and looked around to make sure there were no threats in the immediate area. When he was sure he was alone, he clicked the lock on the sliding door and dragged it open. After about eighteen inches, it snagged, and he noticed a chain along the ground. "Looks like it's secured with a padlock," he reported.

Mateo bent down to unlatch it, taking a knee.

"Stay down!" Calvin suddenly cried from the other side of the opening and raised his weapon through the hole. He fired once, taking out a zombie that had been lumbering out of the shadows. He scanned the area. "I don't see anything else."

Mateo quickly popped open the lock and tossed it aside, opening the door. "Got it!" he said and then clapped Calvin on the shoulder. "Thank you, friend."

"No problem," the sniper replied, and he and Zion crossed the threshold.

The trio turned towards the main part of the warehouse, staring wide-eyed at pallets and boxes full of goods.

"Jackpot," Calvin breathed.

Zion raised a hand. "Clear first, then shop," he reminded them.

The trio moved quickly but carefully through the space, checking every corner of the building and stacks of boxes. As they reached the other side, they all yelled out that they hadn't found anything, and converged together on the far end.

"Calvin, keep watch on the door while Mateo and I see what we got," Zion instructed.

"On it," the sniper replied, and headed back off towards the sliding door.

Zion studied the labels on the nearest boxes, seeing everything was in Spanish. "So," he drawled, "you tell me, did we do good?"

Mateo studied one stack of boxes and then moved on to a few others. "Dried beans," he murmured, "this one os masa flour… this one is canned tomatoes…"

"At the very least we should get a few weeks of meals out of these," Zion said.

His companion nodded. "Without a doubt," he replied. "My grandmama grew up dirt poor and knows how to stretch every bean. You're in good hands, my friend."

Calvin reached the door and scanned the area, keeping watch on the back lot for movement. There was none, but in the distance he heard a low, metallic roar, and his ears perked up.

"What in the hell is that?" he muttered to himself, as the sound grew louder. It soon became clear that there were multiple roars, competing with each other for noise. "Zion!" he called.

"What is it?" Zion asked, heading to the doorway.

"Something's up, man," Calvin replied.

His friend reached him, brow furrowing. "Well, what is it?" He stopped at the noise and glanced at Mateo with a questioning gaze.

"Where's it coming from?" Mateo asked as he approached.

"Can't tell," Calvin replied.

A moment later, the roar was so loud it was almost deafening. They looked up and their eyes widened at the sight of several tomahawk missiles flying overhead.

"What the fuck?!" Calvin screamed.

Seconds later there were several loud, ferocious explosions in the distance, rattling the building. The men shared looks of panic and concern. Several more explosions went off, mostly to the north, and Zion pushed the sickening feeling out of his gut to take control.

"Lock this bitch up tight, we'll come back for it later," he barked. "We gotta get back up to Wendy's camp."

Calvin slammed the door shut behind them, opening it up just enough so that he could secure the chain inside. After that, they sprinted back around to the truck, hopping in.

As Zion fired up the engine, several plumes of smoke rose to the north. "Mother of god, what the fuck is going on?"

CHAPTER SIX

Zion sped towards the camp, seeing
huge pillars of smoke rising ahead. His
eyes were intense and focused as he
seethed with rage.

Mateo was nervous, worried about his
family in the camp, and Calvin simply sat
dumbstruck, staring in every direction,
still in shock from the explosions.

"Jesus christ man, it's everywhere,"
he breathed, seeing several columns of
thick smoke around the city.

Zion clenched his jaw. "I know," he
said.

Calvin leaned forward to look at the
approaching plume, stretching hundreds of
feet into the air. "What the hell were
those things?" he demanded. "Fucking
missiles?"

"Sounded like it," Mateo replied.

"But from who?" Calvin asked. "Why?
What the fuck?" He scrubbed his hands down
his face.

Zion gripped the steering wheel with
white knuckles, punching the gas. His
stomach sank lower and lower as they grew
closer to the camp. What if the missile
had hit it? Of course, even if it didn't,
hitting close enough would be just as
dangerous as the noise would attract
zombies towards whatever damage was done.

They were still a few miles away when they came around a bend and Zion slammed on the brakes, skidding to a stop in front of a horde easily several hundred zombies strong. They shambled in the direction of the camp.

"Now what?!" Calvin cried.

Zion revved the engine several times, staring straight ahead. "Buckle up," he demanded.

Calvin swallowed hard. "Oh, shit," he muttered, and then squeezed up against the door. He motioned for Mateo to get closer to him. He did, and Calvin managed to buckle the seatbelt around both of them. Zion clicked his own belt on, and then gunned it, tires squealing as the truck peeled out.

As he picked up speed, he drifted to the right side of the road, getting into the shoulder where the zombies weren't as thick. The first creature smacked hard, flying off into the horde and vanishing as it fell into the sea.

Several more cracked off of the front of the vehicle, jostling everyone inside. As the horde thickened, Zion drove almost completely off of the road into the grass. Tree branches bounced off of the right side of the truck while zombies bounced off of the left.

The constant sound of wood and bone crunching against the truck was sickening, and damaging to the truck. Numerous cracks appeared in the windshield, blood and leaves sticking to it. Zion didn't let up, speeding even faster.

The front passenger tire hit a deep divot in the grass, sending the right side lurching up. Mateo and Calvin held on for dear life as Zion gave the gas one more push. As they approached the other side of the horde, he steered back onto the road, plowing through another batch of creatures as he broke through, leaving them in the dust.

Calvin whirled around and looked back at the horde they'd just broken through, lumbering after them, arms outstretched. "How close are we?" he asked.

"A mile at most," Zion replied.

"That gives us, what," Calvin stammered, "thirty minutes at most before those things get here?"

Zion nodded firmly, not taking his eyes off of the road. "Then you'd better start coming up with a plan."

"What the hell are *you* gonna do?" the sniper demanded.

"Destroy," Zion replied. He made a hard right turn onto the road where Wendy's camp was. As he approached, his chest tightened as he saw a missile had landed a block away from the edge of the gate. The impact had ripped through the fencing, creating a gaping hole where several zombies were already working their way through.

Gunshots filled the air in the distance, popping off one right after the other. The trio sat in stunned silence for a moment before Zion snapped back to action and punched the gas again.

The truck made it up to speed quickly, heading straight for the hole in the gate. Calvin gripped the handle above his head to brace for impact as the vehicle hit some debris just short of it. They launched slightly into the air, crashing through the handful of zombies at chest level, demolishing them.

They skidded into the heart of the camp, four square blocks of utter chaos. Debris was everywhere, a house on fire in the corner, several people trying to escape from the second floor. Bodies littered the ground, indiscernible between zombies or civilians who'd been near the blast.

Then, a terrifying sight sprinted towards them. A runner.

The freshly minted zombie tore across the street, heading towards the burning house. Without hesitating, Calvin unbuckled himself and dove from the car, slinging his rifle into position in a fluid motion. He raised it and looked through the scope, tracking the sprinting monster as it grew closer to its roasting dinner.

A split second later, he squeezed the trigger and the ghoul's head exploded. The creature flopped to the ground, sliding to a stop a few feet away from two people escaping the house. The gunshot startled them, and they whirled around to see Calvin, who waved at them.

"Get in!" Zion barked. "We gotta find Monique!"

Calvin jumped into the back, getting situated and standing against the back of the cab, smacking the roof to let him know he was ready to go.

"Please, can we go to my family?" Mateo pleaded.

Zion nodded. "They'll probably be in the same place," he replied, and hit the gas. They tore off down the road towards the family house, one block up and over. As they came to the first intersection, they saw that the chaos wasn't just relegated to the front entrance.

There were several runners roaming the area, chasing down people and responding to any noise. Gunshots rattled in the distance at a panicked pace. Zion sat for a moment, letting Calvin pop off a shot, taking out a runner. After the sniper smacked the roof again, Zion sped off towards the house.

When they got there, several zombies were clustered out front, slapping and clawing at the door. Calvin aimed, but Zion honked the horn to get him to stop. The two men jumped out of the cab, Zion turned to the sniper.

"Cover our six, we got this," he barked, and Calvin nodded, turning to survey the area, waiting for zombies to emerge from any direction.

The honking had alerted the four ghouls from the porch, and they turned, shambling down the stairs.

Zion's brow furrowed. "They're not runners," he said.

"Which means there's another breach somewhere," Mateo added, eyes wide.

Zion clutched his weapon tightly, readying himself to strike. "One problem at a time." He rushed forward, swinging his blunt weapon over his head, crumpling a teenage zombie into a heap.

Mateo stepped past him with his dual blades, delivering a series of precise strikes that incapacitated two creatures. Zion gave another vicious swing, sending the final ghoul to the ground.

Mateo rushed the door, banging on it and yelling in Spanish. After several tense moments, the deadbolt clicked open and a middle-aged heavyset woman appeared. They embraced tightly, exchanging rapid dialogue in Spanish.

"Ask her where Monique and Wendy are," Zion demanded.

After a quick exchange, Mateo turned to him. "She says they ran off to the main gate."

"Come on, we gotta get over there," Zion replied.

Mateo tried to break away from his mother's grip, but she held on tight. He leaned back in, saying something urgently, and she began to cry, but let go of him. She disappeared back inside and bolted the door shut.

"We have to hurry," Mateo gushed as they trotted down the steps.

Zion threw himself back into the truck. "What did you say to her?" he asked.

"That I'm not her little boy anymore and I'll be okay," his passenger replied as he slammed the door. "People need my help."

"Hate to break it to you," Zion said, "but no matter how old or big you get, you'll always be some lady's little boy or brother."

Mateo smiled thinly, and Calvin squeezed off another round before ducking and looking in the back window.

"Where are they?" he asked.

"Main gate," Zion replied as the gunfire continued to increase in the distance.

Calvin went pale and took a knee. "Shit, that can't be good."

Zion made the turn onto the outer road of the camp, speeding towards the main gate. As they approached, they witnessed a frantic scene.

Eight guards perched up on makeshift platforms made of cars and dumpsters, frantically shooting, aiming at targets perilously close to the gate. Several people on the ground stood directly in front of the gate, swaying under the pressure from the zombies on the other side of it.

Others used whatever they could to reinforce the fence, some holding tree branches, one holding a twisted car bumper. A few others used knives and machetes to strike the creatures reaching through.

Dozens of arms stretched out, grasping at the people who darted forward to deliver strikes before jumping back to relative safety. As Zion pulled the truck up just short of the gate, one of the stabbers, a young woman in her twenties, managed to take out a ghoul, but another grasped her wrist in a death grip.

She screamed for help, but it was drowned out in the noises of the fray. Mateo spotted her and lunged forward, bringing his cleaver down hard on the ghoul's forearm, severing it completely.

The woman staggered backwards, shaking the severed limb from her wrist and falling to the ground. Mateo quickly helped her up, and she stared at him with wide, panicked eyes.

"You're okay now, you're okay," he assured her, and she finally took a deep breath, nodding jerkily.

"Thank you," she replied, and then headed off to find another weapon.

The top right hinge on the gate cracked open, breaking away from the frame.

"Right side, sight side!" Wendy barked from her position at the fence.

The top began to lean and buckle, and the man holding the car bumper shifted to the side, trying to hold it up. As he struggled with it, Zion darted up, taking the makeshift support and jamming it up into position, putting his weight into it to briefly stabilize the barrier.

As he held it in place, he stared through the fence, swallowing hard at the couple hundred ghouls pressed up against it.

"Zion, thank god you're here," Wendy gushed as she joined him.

"Where's Monique?" he demanded.

The redhead jerked her thumb over her shoulder. "She's with a couple others checking the perimeter," she said.

Calvin approached, his face white as a sheet as he surveyed the sea of zombies on the other side of the gate. "Where the hell did they come from?" he breathed.

"When that bomb went off next door," Wendy explained, "it alerted every fucking thing in a ten mile radius."

"Are they from the bridge?" Zion asked.

She shook her head. "I don't think so," she replied, and took a deep breath. "We gotta send somebody down there. We have to know what we're up against."

Zion and Calvin shared a look, and the former said, "There's hundreds more coming up from the south, too."

Wendy's expression changed from determined to defeated, and she stared at the sky for a moment before clenching her jaw and snapping back into alpha mode. "Jackie, Stevie," she barked at a few of the shooters on the wall, "get to the south wall and start patching it up. Grab whoever and whatever you need to make it happen. And hurry up, because we're on the clock!"

The men leapt down and hurried off, and the redhead turned to Zion and Calvin.

"We still need to know what's coming on the bridge," she said.

The sniper glanced over at Mateo, stabbing wildly through the gate. "Mateo, you're with me!" he called.

The butcher downed one more creature before stepping away from the line and heading over.

"Go out, see what you can see and report back," Wendy said.

"No," Zion said firmly.

She jutted out her chin, glaring at him. "No?"

"If there are zombies on the bridge, we need to find a way to slow them down," he replied.

Calvin scratched the back of his head. "How do you propose we do that?"

"Burn 'em," Zion replied.

Wendy shook her head furiously. "No, no, no," she insisted. "We need the gas that's in those cars if we're going to be able to-"

"Wendy," Zion cut in, "I know you don't want to hear this, but we need to get people out of this camp, and now."

Her eyes went wild, and she pointed a finger at him. "No!" she yelled. "This is our home and I'm not going to abandon it!"

"Look around!" Zion yelled back, waving his free arm. "We can barely hold this group back and we have a fucking gate. What do you think is going to happen if zombies from the bridge join them? Or the hundreds that are about to come through the hole in the wall on the other side of town?"

She screwed her fists into her eyes for a moment. "Fuck, fuck, fuck!" she snapped, but she knew that he was right. She pulled out her walkie-talkie. "Monique, come in," she said, defeat in her voice.

"What's up?" came the reply.

Wendy took a deep breath. "What's your status?"

"Two blocks up on the western wall," Monique reported. "Found a hole caused by some debris so we're patching it up."

"Keep it open," the redhead instructed. "I'm sending some people your way."

"My brother get back?" Monique asked.

Wendy nodded. "Yep."

"Feel safer already," the other woman came back. "We'll be waiting."

The redhead pocketed her radio and raised her chin. "What do you need?"

Calvin and Mateo shared a glance, and then the latter spoke up. "I need a lighter and a shirt or rag or something."

"And we need to know how far down to go before we find a car with gas left in the tank," Calvin added.

Wendy turned and shoved two fingers in her mouth, letting out a sharp, loud whistle. One of the gunmen jumped down from the wall and trotted up to her like a trained dog.

"Yes, ma'am?" he asked.

She motioned to him. "Give Mateo here your lighter," she instructed. "And your shirt."

The man didn't miss a beat, peeling off his stained t-shirt, and handing it over to Mateo with his lighter. "Anything else?" he asked.

"Do you recall how far you have made it on the bridge getting gas?" she asked.

The man nodded. "Yes ma'am," he replied. "We left a pizza delivery sign on top of the last car we drained."

"So we need to go one past it?" Mateo asked.

The gunman nodded again. "Yep, the next one up should be full," he said.

"Thank you," Wendy cut in, "now get back to the fire line."

He turned quickly and rushed back up to his post to resume shooting, now shirtless.

"If you boys are good, get going," the redhead urged.

The duo glanced at each other and then tore off in a sprint towards the hole in the wall.

Wendy turned to Zion. "We have to figure out how to get these people out of here," she said firmly. "I only have enough vehicles to get a little more than half of them out."

He motioned for one of the nearby stabbers to come take his spot holding the gate up. Once he was sure it was secure, he stepped away and faced her. "Then we need more vehicles," he said. "How many more do we need?"

"Five, maybe six if they're big," she replied.

He pursed his lips for a moment. "What if we get the shuttle buses from the park and ride a few blocks over?"

She sighed. "Assuming that bomb didn't destroy it," she muttered.

"That's a chance we're gonna have to take," Zion replied.

Wendy turned and whistled at the fence crew. "Joan, I need you to start getting people from the houses to the center of town," she barked. "Use my house as the base. Then get every vehicle you can over there."

The young woman that Mateo had saved nodded from the fence and turned to head off.

"And watch yourself!" Zion called. "We've seen some runners."

Joan swallowed hard, face terrified, but nodded firmly and rushed off.

"It's close enough that we can get to the park and ride on foot, right?" he asked, turning back to Wendy.

The redhead nodded. "Just a few blocks."

"Yo, shirtless dude," Zion called to the half-naked gunman, "get my truck in front of the gate. That should hold them off!"

The man nodded and hopped down, getting to work as Zion and Wendy broke away from the gate.

She waved for him to follow her. "Let's go."

Calvin and Mateo tore down the street, looking to the west for the hole in the fence. The latter was the first to skid to stop as he spotted Monique and two others standing guard.

"Hey guys," Monique greeted as they jogged over, "how bad is it up there?"

Calvin shook his head. "Real bad," he admitted. "How's it looking on the street?"

"Looks clear at the moment," she replied. "Everything that's coming up joins up with the horde at the gate."

He nodded. "Watch yourself on the south," he advised, "we have another horde coming up. Maybe twenty minutes away if we're lucky."

She wrung her hands. "This isn't looking good, is it?" she asked.

"It's not," he admitted. "Zion and Wendy are getting transportation to evacuate."

Monique blinked at him, stunned. She knew that if Wendy was giving up the camp, it showed how serious the situation was. The redhead was not so easily swayed.

"You two better get going then," she said, snapping back into action. She pointed out the hole. "Cut through the yard across the street, go up a couple of blocks, and then go over to the main road of the bridge. Should keep you out of trouble."

Calvin rubbed his forehead and offered her a reassuring smile. "Might be the first time I've ever avoided trouble in my life," he said.

"Explains why you and my little brother get along so well," she quipped, and they shared a quick chuckle. She squeezed his shoulder and then the duo hopped through the hole.

They darted across the street, reaching the first house and moving slowly along the wall to the corner. Calvin peered around it, seeing a few creatures about forty yards up near the road, wandering towards the noise at the gate.

The sniper tapped his companion on the arm, motioning for him to follow across the street to the next house. As they reached the corner, Calvin looked to the left, seeing a couple of creatures lumbering towards them.

"Mateo," he murmured.

His partner stepped up, cleaving the side of one ghoul's skull before quickly stabbing the other one in the face. As quickly as it had begun, the fight was over and they were both down, without a single peep or snarl.

Calvin blinked with appreciation. "We live through this," he said, "and you're gonna have to teach me how to do that."

"With pleasure," Mateo replied with a grin. "Just don't ask for my grandmother's tamale recipe."

Calvin scoffed. "Shit man, I'd be like a teenage boy with a porn star," he said. "Wouldn't know what to do with it even if I had it!"

They reached the next corner and peered down the road, seeing several zombies coming up from the bridge.

"Hope we're not too late," Calvin murmured. He crept across to the next street and into the yard, coming up to the next house. They did a quick sweep, not seeing any zombies in the immediate area. Across the street was a dead end, thick woods that would eventually lead to the river.

The two took a deep breath in tandem, simultaneously hoping that the coast would be clear to the bridge. They broke out from cover and ran up the road, staying just off of it on the grass, hoping to muffle their footsteps.

As they approached the main road, they ducked down behind a tree as another group of a dozen or so zombies lumbered past towards the camp. They stayed silent, hoping and praying that nothing else followed them up. Luckily, once the lumbering throng moved out of their line of sight, nothing else appeared to be following them.

They rushed out onto the main road, pausing at the corner to scan the area. To the right towards the camp were several groups of zombies, moving up, attracted by the noise. To the left it was mostly clear to the bridge, where a makeshift blockade of cars kept a lot of creatures at bay. It was about four blocks away, and easily fifteen creatures stood between them at the front edge of the cars.

Wendy's camp had tried their best to barricade the bridge using the cars at one point, but it was only minimally successful. There were still some gaps that were filled with sheet metal, but those had been broken through, presumably by some of the horde at the gate. From their vantage point, they couldn't see how many were waiting for them on the bridge.

"Let's blow past these fuckers, knock them down if you have to, and we'll deal with them on the way back," Calvin whispered.

Mateo nodded in agreement, and the sniper looked through his scope towards the bridge. About forty yards past a bread delivery truck in the center of the road, he spotted the target vehicle with the pizza delivery sign on top. He moved over to let his companion have a look.

"That's your target," he said quietly. "I'm going to get up on that delivery truck and provide you cover. You get in there, light it up, and get the fuck out. You with me?"

Mateo gave him a thumbs up, and they readied themselves to spring. The duo darted out into the road, running full speed ahead towards the bridge and the zombies standing in their way.

They split up, each taking one side of the road, ducking and running past the creatures that clumsily reached out for them. Calvin approached two of the ghouls near the delivery truck, and lowered his shoulder, plowing into one of them, sending it to the ground.

He used the butt of his rifle to smash the second one in the face, and when it fell he leapt onto the trunk of a sedan next to his target. He clambered up onto the roof and threw his rifle over his shoulder, jumping and grabbing the top of the delivery truck. He struggled to pull himself up, but with a heaving groan, managed to haul his body on top of the truck.

He didn't waste any time dropping a knee, drawing his weapon, and refocusing on the pizza sign. As he scanned, he saw three zombies huddled around the car, so he took careful aim and fired. One by one, the creatures' heads exploded, splattering nearby windshields with crimson goo. After taking out the immediate threat, he looked past the vehicle, and his blood ran cold.

"Mother of god," he breathed.

Between the bomb going off and the constant stream of gunshots, thousands of zombies had been attracted to the noise. Slowly, they navigated their way across the densely packed bridge, breaking through the makeshift barricades just from their sheer numbers. The weight of their mass was too great.

The front edge of the horde was close to thirty yards from the target car. Calvin immediately took aim at one of the lead creatures, hoping that if he dropped enough of the rotted undead they'd stumble up their brethren and buy Mateo precious seconds.

"You're gonna have to haul ass, brother," he muttered to himself.

Meanwhile, Mateo did just that. He ran as hard as he could towards the delivery car, picking one of the center aisles and pumping his legs. He could hear Calvin firing at a rapid pace, and the situation worried him.

Oh god, what am I running in to? He thought, and managed to push himself even harder. As he reached within twenty yards of the car, several zombies emerged from behind a truck, cutting over from another aisle. Rather than waste time fighting them, Mateo climbed up onto the hood of the next car, running over the top of the vehicles.

Calvin saw this and readjusted his sights to focus on the new threat that had caused the change in course. He quickly took aim, firing several times and taking out the creatures that had surprised his companion. He paused quickly to reload as fast as his fingers would work.

Don't worry brother, I'll have you covered, he thought frantically.

Mateo ran over the cars, keeping his focus on the delivery vehicle ahead. The higher vantage point gave him a view of the mass of ghouls in the distance, which terrified him. He didn't stop moving, though, pushing forward until he reached his target.

As he leapt down beside the delivery vehicle, he rushed up to the car just in front of it, a late model luxury sedan. He did a quick check around it, making sure he was alone, at least for the time being, before concentrating on the gas tank.

Shot continued to ring out over his head, but he didn't waste time looking up to see how close they were getting. He

knew he needed to trust Calvin to cover
him. He glanced on the driver's side,
seeing no gas tank, and then rushed around
to the other side, relieved to see the
tank door flush against the body of the
car. That meant it was likely it still had
fuel inside.

Mateo ran over and pried at the flap,
but it was latched tight. He jammed the
tip of his long blade into the locking
mechanism, but it was no use, it didn't
budge.

"Time to get tough on you!" he
growled, and reared back with his cleaver,
slamming it as hard as he could into the
center of the flap, slicing it right in
two. He pried both halves off and revealed
the gas cap, which he quickly unscrewed
and threw aside.

He was unable to stop himself from
pausing and glancing at the coming horde
as the gunfire ceased, seeing that the
zombies were only about twenty yards from
him. He froze for a moment in fear, but
snapped back to the moment as Calvin
resumed firing, presumably having
reloaded.

Mateo quickly pulled out the shirt
and stuffed it as far down into the gas
tank as he could. He pulled out the
lighter and flicked it several times until
a flame was born. He lit the shirt,

pausing for a second to make sure it took root. When it began to blaze, he took off like a shot back towards Calvin.

The sniper shifted his aim towards his companion's escape, scanning the area between him and the running man. When he didn't see any stragglers, he turned his attention towards their escape, seeing about twenty creatures had begun making their way towards the bridge.

Rather than focus on the closest creatures, he aimed towards groups that were clustered together. He fired several shots into them, thinning them to the point where two running humans could break through if they needed to. After several shots he was forced to reload, and Mateo banged on the side of the large vehicle.

"Come on, let's get out of here!" he yelled.

Calvin slammed in a few more bullets before hopping down onto the car next to him and hitting the road. As he gathered himself, Mateo lunged at a few close by zombies and carved them up with his blades.

With the immediate threat cleared, the two men ran hard back towards the camp, darting and weaving around the ghouls they'd dodged on the way in. It didn't take long for them to get clear of the creatures and back to the first road.

They stopped in the middle of Main Street, clear of any undead for at least twenty yards.

They looked back at the bridge, chests heaving from the hard running.

"Do you think you got it good enough?" Calvin huffed.

Mateo nodded. "If that shirt was any deeper in there, I wouldn't have had anything to light," he replied.

They stood for another moment, and then the telltale *boom* of an exploding car went off in the distance. A fireball shot into the sky, sending flaming liquid spreading in every direction on the bridge. They exchanged a relieved fist bump.

"With any luck, a few more cars will catch fire," Calvin said with a grin.

Mateo nodded. "At a minimum, though, we bought everyone a few extra minutes."

"Come on, let's get back," the sniper said, breaking into a jog. "Pretty sure we don't want to miss the last bus out of town."

Zion and Wendy exited out of the south hole in the wall, walking past the two men she'd sent to patch it up. They seemed to be struggling to find stuff big enough to make much of a difference.

"Forget trying to patch it up," Wendy barked. "Just focus on clearing the debris right in front of it so we can get through, and shoot anything that gets within fifty yards of the hole, you got it?"

The two men nodded and immediately went to work moving the debris that Zion had jumped with his truck earlier. They moved at a brisk jog, knowing their time was short.

"You really got your people whipped into shape," Zion said as they moved, eyes scanning for ghouls all the while.

Wendy chuckled gruffly. "Years of being a fitness instructor paying off," she replied. "Nothing like getting paid to yell at people, am I right?"

"You are correct, ma'am," Zion replied as they ran down a few more blocks. They looked side to side down the streets as they went, seeing several zombies emerging from the neighborhood. They were slow moving and far enough away that they didn't pose any immediate threat.

When they reached the corner of the park and ride lot, they saw a few of the shuttle buses in the distance, parked across from the main office building. Dozens of zombies had poured into the lot, seemingly attracted by the noise of the camp.

"Best guess is that the keys are in the building," Wendy said.

Zion nodded. "If not, I can hot-wire those vehicles, but I'll need some time," he admitted.

"We'll give it two minutes inside," she said in her no-nonsense tone, "and if we can't find the keys, we'll go that route."

He gave her a little salute. "So how do you want to play the zombies in the lot?" he asked.

She looked over his massive wooden weapon, which still sported bits of brain and blood all over the business end.

"Guessing you're pretty handy with that thing?" she asked.

Zion grinned. "Hundreds of crushed skulls can't be wrong," he replied with a smirk.

"In that case, if you want to hold them off, I'll get the keys," the redhead suggested.

He winked at her, giving his weapon a swing. "Let's do it," he replied, excited at getting to crack more zombie heads.

The two of them raced towards the small building on the other side of the lot, Zion taking the lead. He ran up to the first corpse, a middle-aged looking man in a tattered and bloody business suit. He swung hard, sending the zombie careening into a nearby car, crumpling to the ground with a wet smack.

There were several rows of cars parked closely together, a throng of creatures in the aisles.

"Run over the cars, I'll handle them," he suggested, and Wendy nodded, clambering up onto the first car she saw and darting over the tops of them. Some of the creatures reached up in vain, drawn by her footfalls on the fiberglass, giving Zion an easy time in dispatching them while they were distracted.

With a single blow he caved in the heads of two ghouls, crushing them against the top of a sedan. He looked up the aisle, seeing six more monsters lumbering his way. The moans grew in strength as zombies from the flanking aisles came his way, attracted by the noise of their comrades being crushed.

Zion rushed towards the six in front of him, using his blunt weapon like a

jousting lance. The front edge cracked the
sternum of the lead zombie as he drove it
back into the others. With three creatures
on the ground, he quickly delivered an
overhead strike, killing one.

He quickly whipped around when he
heard moans coming from behind him, seeing
zombies coming in between cars from the
other two neighboring aisles. He ran back,
swinging his weapon like a bat, smashing
the face of the creature on the left
before spinning around with the weapon
held high to avoid the tops of the cars
and bringing it down with vicious force
onto the next one.

With zombies pouring into his aisle,
he hopped up onto the hood of a car. As he
scrambled, a zombie grabbed his ankle, and
he kicked back with his free leg to
deliver a heel strike to the creature's
nose. The sound of snapping bone was loud,
but didn't free him from the death grip,
so he punted the corpse again. Finally,
the zombie's skull cracked, and he
wrestled his leg free from the defeated
ghoul.

He looked around as he sprung up onto
the roof of the car, seeing zombies coming
at him from all angles. With a wild grin,
he began to play whack-a-zombie, bringing
his weapon down hard with gleeful overhead
strikes. One after another, the zombie

heads smashed, bodies crumpling all around the car.

The mass of ghouls grew so thick that the vehicle began to sway back and forth, causing Zion to widen his stance to regain his footing. He stepped back onto the trunk and leapt over outstretched rotting arms, whirling with his weapon on the downswing to catch a creature in the side of the head.

He looked back and spotted creatures heading into the lot from the neighborhood, heading towards the door of the building. "Shit," he muttered, and then glanced back at the twenty or so left around the vehicles he'd been whacking. He shook his head in frustration, knowing he didn't have time to deal with them at the moment.

He hopped down from the car into the aisle, a foot away from the group, and ran as hard as he could towards the building. As he reached the end of the aisle, within fifteen yards, the leader of the neighborhood zombies was almost at the door.

Zion raised his weapon to shoulder height, straight out so it led with the blunt end. He rammed it into the side of the ghoul's head, crushing it against the wall, sending a splatter of blood against the brick. He turned to the next creature, swinging like a baseball bat, severing its head from its body to sail back towards the cars.

The zombie conga line branched out a bit, going from single file to three or four wide in spots. He swung wildly, taking out a few more zombies, killing another, and knocking one to the ground. He glanced back at the group he'd run away from, only to find that they'd begun to follow him, thirty yards and closing.

"Wendy!" Zion yelled into the door. "You gotta hurry the fuck up!"

Inside, the redhead heard him, and ran around a desk, narrowly avoiding a grasping zombie. She stumbled over the corpse of the first one she'd put down just seconds earlier.

"Don't worry," she declared as she grabbed a glass paperweight from the desk, "I got something for you too, just like your friend here." She lunged forward and smashed the paperweight onto the zombie's forehead. The glass cracked, as did the skull as she hit it a few more times for good measure. After the third strike it fell to the ground, and she tossed the bloodied instrument to the side.

Chest heaving, she looked around at the four ghouls she'd put down before staring as Zion bellowed in the door again.

"You got fifteen seconds before we have to go!"

The timeline frightened Wendy, who quickly began looking on the desk, throwing papers around to find the two sets of keys she'd dropped during her zombie encounter. With the rings finally secure in her fist, she raced to the front door, skidding to a stop at what had her companion so worked up.

Straight ahead, a horde in the aisle quickly gained on them. There was a sickening crack to her left, prompting her to look over and see Zion delivering another skull-cracking blow. He glanced over his shoulder and spotted her.

"Finally," he said.

She jingled the key rings. "Sorry, had company."

"Same here," he replied, putting his weapon in lance mode and ramming it into the chest of the next zombie, driving it back into the ten or so remaining creatures. He thrust hard, knocking several of them to the ground before darting back to Wendy.

"Follow me," she said, and handed him a set of keys before they ran towards the shuttle buses. They were moderately large, enough to hold thirty people comfortably, or forty uncomfortable if need be. They each took a bus, getting inside quickly and closing the doors behind them.

Zion sat behind the wheel, watching as the zombies staggered to the door, smearing blood on the windows as they tried to get to him. He looked forward when Wendy honked her horn, prompting him to start up his engine.

It took a moment for the large vehicle to rumble to life, and they sat there for several seconds, letting the buses warm up from their long slumber. A few moments later, Wendy honked again before popping the vehicle into gear.

Zion followed suit, and they slowly rolled out to head off back to camp.

The two vehicles raced down the road towards the camp, at least as fast as buses could go while still navigating the streets. As they came around the last corner, Zion saw that the road horde had arrived at the hole in the wall.

The two guards fired as quickly as they could, dropping zombies thirty yards away from the entrance, but it did little to stem the tide. Wendy put the pedal to the metal, gaining speed and honking the horn as she led the charge to the hole. The two gunmen dashed out of the way, allowing the buses to zoom on by.

Wendy sped off towards the meeting spot, but Zion screeched to a halt. He dove out and pointed to one of the gunmen.

"You, drive!" he barked, pointing at one. "You, with me!" He pointed to the other one, and then glanced at the man clambering up into the bus. "And don't leave us behind," he said.

The driver nodded and took off, while Zion and the other man stepped out through the hole in the fence, staring down at the hundreds of zombies bearing down on them.

"Start shooting!" Zion bellowed, and the man complied, picking his targets carefully and delivering headshots with his hunting rifle. The lead creatures fall, causing some stumbling, but really only buying them mere extra seconds.

Zion, meanwhile, looked around the area at the debris the two men had moved out of the way. He eventually focused on a large piece of sheet metal, that if turned sideways could cover the gap in the fence, but only up to waist height.

"Help me with this!" he yelled.

The gunman slung his rifle over his shoulder and rushed over to his companion, and they picked up the large piece of metal together. They pulled it inside the camp, and Zion motioned for him to set it up against the wall.

He looked to his new friend. "Do you trust me?" he asked.

The man blinked at him and shrugged. "Sure, why not?" he replied.

"Good!" Zion declared and pointed to his feet. "Lay down on the ground in the middle and press your legs against this!"

The man blinked at him again, and then it dawned on him what Zion was going to do. "You'd better be swinging that thing like a goddamn madman," he said, motioning to the wooden weapon.

"Oh, you ain't gotta worry about that," Zion assured him.

The man begrudgingly laid on his back and pressed as hard as he could against

the sheet metal that plugged the gap in
the wall.

Zion gripped his weapon tightly,
watching as the ghouls approached,
spreading out across the line. "Here they
come, get ready," he warned.

The man gave a thumbs up as he
focused on keeping pressure on the wall
with his considerably muscular legs.

As soon as the first creature touched
their makeshift barricade, Zion brought
his weapon down in an overhead strike,
dropping it. Then he flew into a flurry of
swings, two-by-four *whooshing* and *cracking*
and delivering death.

The man grunted on the ground as he
strained to hold the wall in place,
looking up in terror as he saw zombies
grasping down at him, fingers coming
within inches of his feet on the waist-
high wall.

Zion rushed to the center, crushing
blow after blow to the creatures closest
to his partner on the ground. They slumped
over to the side, adding weight but also a
bit of a corpse barrier to the creatures
reaching for the blockade.

He looked to his left, seeing that
the flimsy material was starting to give
way on the edge. A creature was able to
push its way through, flaying the rotted
flesh from its legs as it did. He rushed

over and smashed its face in, and then
dropped his weapon, grabbing the slumped
corpse by the shirt and belt and flinging
it into the crowd, hoping to trip up some
of the creatures and relieve the pressure
on the wall.

As soon as he picked up his weapon, a
few zombies began to push through on the
right. His stomach sank, knowing his plan
was busted. The man on the ground saw the
incoming ghouls and began to scream
incoherently.

Zion rushed over and gave the first
zombie a hard shoulder hit before kicking
the other one back. He tossed his weapon
down the street away from the wall before
running over to the man on the ground.

"Get ready to run!" he cried, and
wrapped his hand around the gunman's
collar. He dragged him back with a hard
jerk, using every bit of his strength to
get him clear of the barrier as it
collapsed under the zombies. He yanked him
to his feet and shoved him forward, and
the two of them ran full tilt from the
throng of ghouls.

Zion grabbed his weapon as he passed
it, and they skidded to a stop twenty
yards away to glance back at the horde
pouring into the camp.

"Where's the meeting spot?" Zion
asked.

The man pointed. "Two blocks over," he replied.

"Let's move, then," Zion said, and took off running in the direction indicated.

They ran down a side street, zombies in lumbering pursuit. As they came to the second intersection, they saw the two transport vehicles loading up, as well as several trucks with armed men standing guard.

Zion looked around, seeing Calvin and Mateo having returned, and let out a sharp whistle to get their attention. He waved and then jogged over to Wendy and Monique.

"We need to leave," he demanded.

The redhead nodded tersely. "We're almost there."

"So are those things," Zion urged.

She nodded and ran back towards the house, pointing at a few guards in the process that followed her. A few moments later, some of the guards began firing in multiple directions. Zion stepped out to the road, looking in the direction of the main gate, and saw dozens of creatures coming around the corner. Just up the side road he'd come down, the group he'd tried to hold off from the hole in the fence was already working their way towards them.

Monique approached, patting his shoulder affectionately. "Don't worry

little brother," she said gently, "we will
rebuild this place."

"I know," he growled, "just pisses me
off that we're losing all this hard work
because some dumbass military bastard
decided to launch a couple missiles our
way." He clenched his fists.

She swallowed hard at the look in his
eyes, the anger brewing within him. He'd
already had to deal with rogue military
elements when the apocalypse had begun.
She leaned over and hugged his shoulders,
talking softly into his ear.

"Stay calm, little brother," she
cooed. "Still a lot to get done today."

Her voice calmed him, and he took a
deep breath, knowing that she was right.
They still had to get these people out and
to the safety of the apartment complex. At
least, he hoped that was still a viable
plan.

"Thanks, sis," he said, and patted
her hands.

She let go, and they turned to see
Wendy and her guards carrying an elderly
woman from the house and into the
transport.

"This is the last of them!" the
redhead barked. "Let's roll!" She raised a
hand and whirled it above her head.

Calvin and Mateo approached Zion, and
the trio jumped into their truck that

someone had pulled away from the front gate.

Calvin patted the passenger door as he got in. "This thing is gonna need a new paint job," he quipped as he noted the blood and guts all over it.

Zion stood up, planting his foot on the driver's seat to gain height so everyone could see him. "Follow me out of here!" he bellowed, and everyone honked their horns in acknowledgement.

He ducked back inside and stared up at the truck, doing a one-eighty in the road and heading for the hole in the wall.

"Where we going?" Calvin asked.

Zion raised his chin. "Gotta hope that the hole in the wall is clear," he said.

"And if it's not?" the sniper asked.

Zion just glanced at him while grabbing his seatbelt and fastening it with one hand.

"Aw, hell," Calvin groaned as he tapped Mateo, squishing over so he could belt them both in.

Zion made the turn on a side street before turning on the main road towards the hole in the fence. He was relieved to see that the road was mostly empty, with just a few badly damaged ghouls shambling behind the main horde.

The corpses bounced off the front of the truck as they approached the hole, and Zion punched the gas to make sure they cleared the way in case anything was just outside the hole. As they cleared it, he made a left, away from the camp. The road in front was clear, so they paused to let the rest of the caravan get out. He honked his horn before resuming the journey, hitting the gas.

"Homeward bound!" Calvin declared.

Zion pursed his lips, anxiety thrumming through him. "Assuming it's still there…"

Zion led the caravan towards the apartment complex along the interstate. Several zombies dotted the road, but they were spread out enough that they posed no threat. As they drove up, there was a huge plume of smoke in the general direction of the apartment, putting the men on edge.

"We're still a ways away," Calvin said hopefully, clutching his knees. "It doesn't look like it's that close."

Zion took a deep breath. "Calvin."

"I'm just saying man," the sniper babbled, "I can see that look on your face and-" He stopped short at the hard glance from his friend, and clamped his mouth shut.

As they got close to the exit, an overpass over the road to the complex, and saw a guard standing there that waved them down.

"Oh thank the good lord you're back!" he gushed as they pulled up.

"Calm down man, what's going on?" Zion asked, holding up a hand.

The guard scrubbed his hands down his face. "It's home, man!" he cried. "One of those bombs got dropped a mile or so past us and it's drawing a whole mess of those things towards 'em!"

"How many?" Zion asked.

The guard shook his head, eyes wide in fear. "Hundreds at least," he replied. "We were leading a small group up the interstate, some that broke off from that big horde from this morning when that boom happened. They just stopped paying attention to us and started going up the road!"

Zion's gaze darkened. "Why the hell didn't you do anything?"

"We tried, but this was a group of trainees on their first highway detail," he explained, shaking his head. "They were in way over their heads, so I sent the one competent person I had as a runner to go around them in the woods to give the complex time to prepare. And I did the only thing I could, which was stand here and hoped to god you came back before it was too late."

Zion looked to his passengers. "Mateo, this ain't your fight, so don't feel obligated to tag along."

"You stuck your neck out for my family," Mateo replied firmly. "I'm happy to repay the favor."

Zion nodded in appreciation and put the truck in park. "Hang tight, I'll be right back," he said, and got out. "You, come with me," he said to the guard.

He led the man to the transport vehicle a few cars back. The door opened and Wendy appeared on the steps.

"What is it?" she asked.

Zion motioned to the guard. "I need you to take this man with you and head out towards White Salmon," he said.

"What are you talking about?" Her brow furrowed.

"You're gonna backtrack a couple miles to the interstate eighty-four connection and head east," Zion continued. "It's about sixty miles. When you get there, just ask for Fingers, he'll introduce you to the right people."

Wendy crossed her arms. "Where are you going?" she asked.

"Gotta go save our home," Zion replied.

She nodded as the doors shut. As Zion walked back to the truck, the vehicles began to turn around. He saw Monique staring at him from the back window of one of the buses, eyes wide. He gave her a thumbs-up, letting her know that it was going to be okay.

He hopped back into the truck and popped it into gear, speeding off the exit towards the complex. The cab was silent as they drove, everyone focused on the shitshow they were about to walk into. As they reached the half-mile point, there were zombie stragglers on the road.

Zion drifted the truck over just enough to clip them with the edge of the bumper, which at the very least crippled them. After hitting five or six, there was a large gap between them and the tail end of the horde.

He slammed on the brakes as they came around the bend, a few hundred yards from the complex. They stared in shock at the four to five hundred creatures pressed up against the building, trying to get in.

"With that weight," Calvin said hoarsely, "that garage door isn't going to hold for long."

Gunshots rang out in the distance, and they looked up to see a few people hanging out of third and fourth story windows, aiming and firing down.

"What can we do?" Mateo asked helplessly.

Zion took a deep breath, eyes like steel. "I want you to go back and clear those things we hit on the way up," he instructed. "Calvin, I want you to start firing, draw as many of them towards you as possible and get them down the road as far as you can."

"Man, I only got about fifteen shots left," the sniper replied.

Zion shook his head. "Doesn't matter, just use them to draw them to you," he said. "We gotta relieve pressure on that gate."

"Well, once you do, then come save my ass, will ya?" Calvin asked with a smirk, though it was strained.

"Don't I always?" Zion shot back easily.

Mateo slid over as Calvin unbuckled the seat belt. "What are you going to do?"

Zion cracked his knuckles. "I'm gonna get in there and help 'em."

As Mateo walked back to clear the way, Calvin got up in the back of the truck for an elevated view. He looked over at Zion, who had darted into the woods for cover before beginning to fire.

He honed in on his first target, squeezing the trigger and blowing its head wide open. He quickly bolted in another round and fired quickly, not really taking the time to aim properly since the goal was noise, not precision. Rapid fire was a great way to draw attention.

"Yeah that's right, come and get me!" Calvin declared loudly. The noise peeled off several zombies, a dozen or so. He fired a few more times, catching a couple of creatures in the face and neck.

By the time he had to reload, there were eighty or so corpses shambling his way, easily one fifth of the crowd. The leading edge of the group was about twenty yards away from the front of the truck. As he began to hop down, he fired one more shot, in hopes that it will pull a few more.

"That's the best we're gonna get," he muttered, and jogged down the road, putting some distance between them, while remaining in view. As he did so, Mateo walked back from his mission.

"Route is clear," he said, and then nodded in the direction of the zombie horde. "Good turnout."

Calvin shook his head. "Not as good as it could have been, though," he admitted. "Hopefully it's enough."

The duo began to walk down the road, whistling and shouting and leading the mass of rotted flesh along behind them.

Meanwhile, Zion looked on from the woods, deep in cover and staying silent, pleased with how many they'd been able to draw away from the complex. He stood there, weaponless, looking at the horde in front, pressing on the parking garage door.

Once the horde had passed, Zion went on the move, rushing through the woods towards the building while moving away from the horde. As he got close, a straggler lunged out from behind a tree. He grabbed it by the neck without breaking stride, slamming it into another trunk, dropping it.

Zion ran alongside the wall towards the back, the noise attracting a few creatures from the horde. He glanced over his shoulder as he went, muttering curses to himself for not being quieter. He came around to the back end, past the emergency exit, and over to the first opening in the parking garage. He peeked through and saw

the college kids struggling with the
Impaler 3000.

They had it lined up with some
zombies to the right of the door, throwing
the switch and taking several out with the
rebar bolts. As Jack and Harold struggled
to rearm it, Zion let out a whistle.

"Over here!" he called, and Tori
whipped around, spotting him. As she got
close, he inclined his head back to the
door. "Emergency exit!" he said.

She adjusted course, and he tore for
the emergency door, reaching it just as
his pursuers ambled around the corner. He
leapt into the air, giving the lead zombie
a powerful jump kick to the chest, driving
it back into its buddies.

Tori opened the door. "Glad you're
back," she said.

Zion rushed inside and slammed the
door shut. "Me too," he said.

"We need help!" Missy screamed, arms
flailing wildly at the garage door, which
was beginning to buckle on the right side
from the weight pressing up against it.

Zion raced over, throwing his entire
weight into it.

Jack and Harold released the impaler
and struck a trio of creatures in the
face, the zombies convulsing and falling
back as the duo rearmed the weapon.

"Welcome back, Zion," Jack huffed as he slowly peeled the rebar.

"Thanks," he replied, as if he wasn't holding up a buckling garage door. "I miss anything?"

Jack aimed the impaler and shrugged. "Just an impromptu block party," he replied, and fired, taking out two more zombies.

"It's hard to see from here," Tori piped up, pushing her glasses up her nose. "How many are out there?"

Zion cocked his head. "Few hundred by the door, another hundred or so chasing Calvin down the road," he replied, and at her concerned look, he continued, "Don't worry, your boyfriend is fine. There's nothing between him and the interstate."

She nodded, glancing at the impaler as it fired off again.

"How's that thing working?" Zion asked.

She clenched and unclenched her fists. "It's slow, but effective."

The door popped a rivet on the left side, and the students jumped.

"Slow ain't gonna cut it," Zion said. "Any of you have any bright ideas?"

The girls shared a look, seeming unsure.

"Well spit it out," he urged. "Don't care how bad it is."

"Firebomb," Tori blurted.

Zion shook his head. "Okay, I stand corrected, that is a bad idea," he replied. "We're fucked if the building catches on fire."

"We can make up some high powered fire extinguishers in case things get out of control," Missy assured him.

Tori nodded. "Just need a ton of vinegar and baking soda and some containers," she added.

The left side of the door creaked open a little more, and an arm reached in, flailing about.

"Fuck it, I'm in," Zion grunted, "make it happen. Harold, go with the girls and do what you need to do," he inclined his head sharply. "Jack, get on the other side of this door!"

Everyone sprung into action, the others rushing off as Jack pressed up against the left side of the door to reinforce it a bit.

Tori led the trio racing up the stairs, stopping at the second floor where the cafeteria was. "Missy, you're on baking soda," she said. "Harold, find something we can use for firebombs, I'll get the vinegar."

The two followers yelled in the affirmative and burst into the lunchroom. There were a few people cleaning up, apparently trying to keep themselves busy as the battle raged outside, distracting themselves from the carnage.

"Where's the pantry?" Tori demanded.

One of the works pointed to the back room, and they ran off towards it, ripping through the shelves to find the goods they needed.

"Got the baking soda!" Missy cried and then spotted several plastic gallon milk containers. "And our delivery system!"

Harold pored over the area, looking for something flammable, before finally finding some cheap booze in glass bottles. "Fire bomb is a go," he declared. "How many do we need?"

"Grab as many as you can carry," Tori replied, and he grabbed four, cradling them in his arms.

Missy grabbed a stack of dishtowels from the counter, and Tori finally found a couple large canisters of vinegar.

"Got it, let's move!" she cried, and they ran back out, carrying their goods. The workers gazed after them with confusion, but didn't say anything as the trio rushed back to the stairs.

They thundered up another flight to the lowest level with exterior windows, finding the first open apartment facing the horde. There were a few older men

shooting out the window that startled as
the kids entered.

"You two, they need help down in the
basement and we need the windows," Tori
gushed, setting down the vinegar.

One of the men furrowed his brow.
"Who the hell are you?" he demanded.

"We're scientists," she replied,
pushing her glasses up her nose.

He scoffed. "Does this look like a
situation that needs science?" He rolled
his eyes.

The blonde stepped up, eyes blazing.
"Yeah it does," she snarled, "now get the
fuck down to the basement or everyone is
going to die!"

He blinked at her, surprise all over
his face, and then glanced at his buddy,
who shrugged and headed for the door.

Missy gaped at her friend with
amazement. "I've never seen you like
that," she breathed.

"Don't have time to be polite," Tori
snapped. "Let's get to mixing."

The three of them spurred to action,
creating the firebombs and makeshift fire
extinguishers. When they had everything in
order on the coffee table, Tori handed a
few extinguishers to Harold.

"Get these down to Zion, and help
them out," she instructed. "We'll launch

some from up here if it starts getting out
of control."

He nodded and took the jugs, running
from the room.

Missy pulled a lighter from her
pocket as Tori lifted one of the molotov
cocktails. They looked out the window at
the mass of creatures below, stretching
back along the road about forty yards.

"Where are you thinking?" Missy
asked.

Tori pointed. "Figure I will aim
towards the back, away from the building,"
she replied. "Let's see how that goes and
adjust from there."

Before they could throw the first
one, the window next to them exploded in
gunfire. Tori leaned out the window and
spotted an older man aiming a hunting
rifle. She waved her arms.

"Hey, hey!" she called.

He blinked at her in surprise and
then raised an eyebrow. "Yes, ma'am?" he
asked politely.

"You any good with that?" she asked,
pointing to the rifle.

"Oh, yes ma'am," he replied.

She reached back in and grabbed a
milk jug, showing it to him. "If I throw
one of these, you think you can hit it?"
she asked.

He shrugged. "No different than skeet shooting," he replied.

"Hang tight," she said, "we may need you." She motioned for Missy to go. Her friend nodded and lit up the first molotov.

Tori leaned out the window, and underhand tossed the firebomb. It flew through the air, landing about five yards behind the end of the horde. There was an explosion of fire, which barely struck the back end. About eight to ten zombies caught fire, slowly engulfing them.

"Going to have to get riskier," Missy mused.

"You just be ready with that extinguisher bomb," Tori replied, and readied another molotov, pitching it out.

This time the bottle landed about ten yards deep from the back, shattering on the head of a zombie. Flaming liquid shot out in every direction, coating dozens of corpses.

"There we go!" she exclaimed, punching a fist into the air.

The girls watched as the flames engulfed the monsters, the scent of burning rotted flesh reaching up to the window, causing them to gag a bit. Luckily, the fire stayed localized near the back half of the zombies. As the fire burned, they began to drop to the ground.

"Okay, one more," Tori said with a deep breath. "Going to go near the front this time." She turned to the man in the window. "And you, get ready, we may need you."

He nodded. "Just give the word," he said.

She got her molotov lit and lobbed it about ten yards from the building. It landed and creatures near the front erupted in flame, catching and burning in an outward circle through the ghouls. After a minute or so, the flames grew within a few zombies of the building.

"Extinguisher," Tori said, and Missy handed one over. "Okay, I'm tossing this out near the building," she called to the window man, "hit it when it's about ten feet above the crowd."

"Can do," he replied.

She counted down from three and then dropped it. They watched as it fell, and then a shot rang out. The jug exploded, sending extinguisher powder spreading over the front creatures. Almost in an instant, the fire snuffed out.

"Nice shot!" she exclaimed.

The three of them stared down at the zombies, easily still a hundred and fifty creatures still standing and pushing forward.

"How many cocktails we have left?" Tori asked.

"Two," Missy replied.

The blonde nodded. "Let's thin out the ones in the back a bit more, and let Harold and Jack pick off the stragglers with the impaler," she suggested.

Missy flicked her lighter. "Let's light 'em up!"

Missy and Tori came downstairs to see Zion trying out the impaler. He lined it up and fired, hitting three creatures in the head, letting out an excited yell in the process. He quickly yanked down the lever, reloading it far faster than Harold and Jack were doing together before rolling it over and firing again.

"This is so much fun!" Zion declared. "Can y'all make me a portable version of this?"

The boys shared a glance.

"Wheels wouldn't be practical," Harold said.

Jack shrugged. "Could make it like a steadi-cam, like they have for films."

"Like Vasquez's machine gun from Aliens!" Harold gushed.

Jack nodded vigorously. "Exactly what I was thinking."

"Forget the impaler, can you just make me one of those guns?" Zion cut in.

Tori shot them a playfully stern look as she approached. "I'm glad you boys are having fun," she said, "but can we go help Calvin out before you start coming up with diagrams?"

"Yeah, let's go," Zion replied with a nod. He peeked outside to the horde, seeing about forty or so remaining standing, with some still writhing on the ground. "While these two finish off the ones still standing, can you boys get prepped to clear out the burnt ones?" he asked, turning to the two gunmen that Tori had sent down. "Hunting boots and leg protections, just spike 'em and leave 'em be. We can clean them up tomorrow."

The two men nodded and ran off to gear up.

"Missy, why don't you stay here and keep an eye on the boys?" Tori asked, pushing her glasses up her nose. "Make sure they don't get into any trouble."

Her friend smiled and nodded, heading for the impaler.

Zion led Tori to the emergency exit, snatching up a piece of rebar on the way. "Just gonna borrow this," he said.

There was some light banging on the emergency door, sounding like just a few hands. Without being asked, Tori walked over to the nearest wall opening and smacked it a few times, yelling out to the creatures. Within a few moments, the banging stopped on the door and the zombies moved over to her, reaching through the opening with excited open mouths.

"Okay, did my part," she said, and Zion cracked a smile and snuck out of the emergency exit.

He stepped over to the first target and jammed the rebar into the back of its head, stabbing the next one through the eye as it turned to him.

Tori emerged from the garage, carrying a box with a few molotovs and extinguishers. "Just like to be prepared," she said.

Zion nodded in approval. "All right, let's go get your boy," he said with a grin.

They came around the wide of the building, seeing the smoldering mass of burnt flesh on the far side.

"Just to be safe," he said quietly, "let's cut through the trees."

She nodded. "Agreed," she said. "Death by barbecued zombie isn't on my list of preferred ways to die."

"Oh yeah?" He chuckled. "What *is* on your list?"

"Oh, you know, the usuals," Tori replied, pushing her glasses up her nose. "Death by orgasm, drowning in a sea of chocolate, death by stripper."

Zion raised an eyebrow. "Death by stripper?" he asked. "What, you want a bunch of Chippendales grinding you to death?"

"Did I say male strippers?" she asked.

He gaped at her, and she smirked back at him.

"Oh yeah," Zion said, shaking his head, "my boy Calvin has a live one."

She winked at him. "Yeah, he does."

The two of them made their way to the truck, heading slowly down the street. As they went, they passed several downed zombies, dotting the road like it's a trail so Calvin and Mateo could find their way back to the complex.

"Looks like we aren't going to have that many to clear out," Tori said. "Calvin is doing some work."

"He's also got our friend Mateo with him," Zion said. "We picked him up at Wendy's camp, and he's a madman."

She cocked her head. "Hope you mean that in a good way."

"In these times," he replied, "absolutely."

As they worked their way down the road, they finally caught up with the horde that had dwindled to about forty or so. Zion reached over to honk the horn, but she stopped him.

"No, keep them bunched up," Tori said, lifting a bottle. "Fire will work better."

He held out his hand, motioning to the monsters. "Have at it, then."

She lit up a cocktail and gave it a good heave, sending it right into the center of the horde, fire spreading quickly. Some of the flaming creatures turned and shambled towards her, but Zion stepped up and smacked them down with his wooden bludgeon.

As he lifted the bits of flaming flesh sticking to the end of his weapon, a grin spread on his face. "This gives me an idea," he said, and turned to her. "Think you can whip me up a flaming sword?" he asked as he smashed another creature.

"I don't think it would be the most practical weapon," she admitted, "but it'll look cool as hell."

Zion winked at her. "In that case, I'll only pull it out for special occasions."

"Consider it officially on the list," she replied.

He smacked down the last few zombies, and then sat Mateo and Calvin finishing the last few of their group, finally ending the threat.

As the two duos approached each other, Tori set down her box and ran to the sniper, throwing her arms around his neck. Mateo shot Zion a playful look, as if offering him a hug too.

"I don't care how good your grandmother's tamales are," Zion said, holding up a hand, "that ain't happening."

The quartet broke into a fit of giggles, exhausted and relieved that they'd managed to survive the chaos of the day.

"How we looking at the apartments?" Calvin asked as Tori stepped back from him.

"Building is a little singed," she admitted, "but other than that it's secure."

He inclined his head to Zion. "Think we should radio Wendy and tell them to come back?"

His companion shook his head. "Nah, let them go hang out down there for a bit while we get this place cleaned up," he replied. "A sea of burnt corpses isn't exactly the first impression I want to make."

"Good call," Mateo agreed.

As they headed to the truck, they stopped at the sight of two people running towards them.

"Oh hell, what now?" Calvin groaned.

It was Cheryl and Jack, both carrying guns, and out of breath as if they'd sprinted the entire way.

"Zion-" she gasped, skidding to a stop and trying to speak through her gasps.

He put out a hand. "Slow down girl, slow down," he said. "Now what's going on?"

"The…" She took a deep, ragged breath. "The horde on the interstate."

His brow furrowed. "What about it?"

"It's…" she huffed, "turned around."

He straightened up. "Calvin, Tori, with me," he snapped. "Rest of you get back to the complex and start fortifying that door with anything you can find."

"What are you going to do?" Cheryl asked breathlessly.

"Figure out how much time we have," Zion replied.

She motioned vaguely towards the interstate. "Jermaine is still down there keeping an eye on them," she said, finally catching her breath. "Said he was just short of the tunnel. He sent the rest of the crew back."

Zion nodded, and the trio got into the truck. He popped the vehicle into gear and peeled out, speeding towards the highway.

"How many zombies are we talking about?" Tori asked, pushing her glasses up her nose.

Calvin shook his head. "They took past ten thousand this morning, but there's fifty or sixty thousand more behind them," he replied.

Her face paled, and she looked down at her hands.

"Man, but what if we just say quiet?" Calvin asked hopefully. "Won't they just keep walking on the interstate?"

Zion gripped the steering wheel with white knuckles. "They might see the plume of smoke," he explained, "or hear the fire burning and come our way."

"And even if they don't," Tori added, "having that many zombies in this area would effectively mean we'd be prisoners in the complex. And we don't have the resources to sit there indefinitely."

There was a long silence in the cab.

Calvin finally groaned. "So, what do we do?" he asked.

"Don't know until we know how much time we have," Zion replied.

They raced down the interstate, going several miles before they spotted Jermaine waving them down on the side of the road.

"Hey," he greeted.

Zion jumped out. "How's it looking?"

He shook his head. "It's bad, man," he admitted. "The tail end of them, or hell, how I guess the front end of them, is about two miles up the road. I don't know what the hell went off, but it hooked every single one of those fuckers."

"They moving quick?" Zion asked.

"They ain't runners, if that's what you're asking," Jermaine replied, "but they're moving at a solid clip."

Calvin took a deep breath. "How long did it take you to get them from the exit up there?"

"I don't know man, five, maybe six hours?" came the reply.

The sniper groaned. "With where they are now, they could be at the crossroads in four hours," he said.

"Unless we find a way to slow them down," Zion replied.

"We have the bulk of the components made for the loppers," Tori piped up, "we just need the engines."

Zion cocked his head. "What do you say, Calvin?" he asked. "Feel like a trip to the mall?"

"I'm so glad you're into engines, and not jewelry," Calvin quipped, smiling at the blonde. "Makes shopping a whole lot easier."

She smirked. "Wouldn't say no to a necklace."

"But if we slow them down, then what?" Jermaine cut in.

Zion clenched his jaw for a long moment. "It gives us time to evacuate."

The four of them stood there in
silence, stunned and saddened, as a chorus
of faint moans grew louder and louder in
the distance.

END

Up next: Death is knocking on their
door, and Zion has no choice but to answer
in "Portland - pt. 5"

DEAD AMERICA: THE NORTHWEST INVASION
BOOK 2
PORTLAND - PART 5
BY DEREK SLATON
© 2020

CHAPTER ONE

Day Zero +22

The dull roar of a ten thousand strong zombie horde murmured in the distance. The situation was dire. After the bombs had dropped, all the hard work from weeks past was obliterated, coming back to haunt them as an army of the undead marched towards their home.

The clock was ticking. They only had four hours before the zombie mass overtook the crossroads, blocking their only means of escape. If that happened, the best case scenario for the apartment complex was that they'd slowly waste away from starvation. The worst case would be the horde overtaking them and breaking in.

Calvin swallowed hard. "So we're really going to evacuate?" he asked hoarsely. The wiry sniper fumbled with his pocket, pulling out a thin joint and jamming it between his lips.

"We don't have a choice," Zion replied, nodding and straightening his broad shoulders. "And if we don't slow them down, we're not going to be able to get everybody out safely."

Mateo rubbed his forehead. "Fire worked pretty well back at the complex, right?" he asked, hope in his lightly accented voice. "Why not give that a shot?"

"There isn't going to be nearly enough flammable liquid left to put a dent in them," Zion replied, poking his cheek with his tongue.

Calvin flicked his lighter a few times, finally managing to light up his joint, and took a deep, thoughtful drag. "What if we used it to thin out the crowd a bit?" he mused through a puff of smoke. "Wouldn't that help with the loppers?"

"It certainly couldn't hurt," Tori weighed in, pushing her glasses up her nose. The lopper her and her college friends had invented was a helicopter-inspired machine that had the potential to buy them some needed time. "We're just kind of making this up as we go, so we don't know how it's going to react to hitting numerous corpses at once. The less strain we can put on the loppers, the longer they'll last."

Jermaine linked his fingers together and rested his palms on top of his dark, bald head. "I can handle that," he piped up. "I'll load up everything I can and start thinning them out."

"When you do, throw them as far as you can, all around the horde," Tori instructed, curling a lock of blonde hair behind her ear. "We need to create some pockets if we can."

The moaning grew increasingly louder in the distance, pushing Zion into action. He took a deep breath and turned to Jermaine, who was wearing a digital watch.

"Mind if I borrow your watch for a little bit?" he asked, motioning to his companion's wrist.

Jermaine divested himself of the watch and handed it over. Zion fiddled with it for a few moments, finally managing to set a four-hour timer.

"Appreciate it," he said as he fastened it to his own wrist. "Let's head back to the complex and regroup. We got a lot of work to do, and not much time to do it in."

The group nodded and piled into the truck. Zion fired it up and sped back towards the complex. He glanced in the rearview mirror, thankful to see an empty road, at least for the time being.

As they pulled into the garage, rumbling over the charred remains of the ghouls who had tried to breach the parking deck earlier, he pulled up next to Tori's friends, who were hard at work on various machinery.

Tori jumped out and rushed over to them. "Drop what you're doing right now," she demanded, pushing her glasses up her nose, "we need to start working on the loppers."

Her friends blinked at her, confused, but concerned at the tense tone of her voice.

"What's going on?" Jack asked, brow furrowed.

Harold shook his head. "We don't even have the engines for those, yet."

"Well, you're about to get them," Zion replied as he caught up.

"Tori?" Missy asked, voice shaky.

The blonde glanced at Zion, silently asking permission to fill them in. He nodded his approval, and she clasped her hands in front of her, taking a deep breath.

"There's a whole lot of those things headed our way," she began. "If we don't slow them down, a lot of people are going to be trapped here. So I need you to focus, and start putting them together as quickly as you can, reinforce them as much as humanly possible, because they're going to take a beating."

The trio of students nodded firmly and then set to work like a hive of busy bees.

Tori turned to Zion. "I'm going to help them, but please come see me before you leave," she said.

He nodded. "Will do," he promised and then waved for Calvin and Mateo to follow him to the stairwell.

"My truck is on the exterior lot," Jermaine piped up. "I'll burn as many of them as I can."

"Thanks, bud," Zion replied, and held up his wrist. "And I'll take good care of your watch, too."

Jermaine chuckled. "I know you," he said, "if it doesn't come back with bloodstains on it, I'm gonna be disappointed."

They exchanged a fist bump before parting ways. Zion led Calvin and Mateo up the stairs quickly, headed for Cheryl's office. When they walked in, she sat in the corner at a radio, repeatedly trying to get Wendy on the line.

"Wendy, do you copy?" she demanded, voice frustrated as if she'd been at it for a while. "Anybody home? Anybody? Bueller?" She tossed the microphone angrily down on the table.

Zion crossed his arms. "Nobody home, I'm guessing?" he asked.

"No, they're either out of range or have their radios off," Cheryl growled.

He cocked his head. "They'll be to White Salmon soon enough," he reminded her. "You been able to reach them?"

"Nobody in Edward's camp is reading me either," she replied.

Calvin clucked his tongue. "Did you try Fingers?"

"No, just tried Edward's frequency," Cheryl said, pointing at him. "But that's a good idea." She swiveled around and fiddled with the dials before getting the frequency right. "Fingers, this is Cheryl from Zion's camp, do you copy?"

There were a few moments of tense silence, before the line crackled and Fingers' voice came through. "Go for Fingers."

"Hang on," Cheryl said back, waving maniacally at Zion, "I'm going to put Zion on."

He grabbed the microphone. "Have you heard from Wendy yet?" he asked.

"Wendy?" Fingers replied. "Who the hell is Wendy?"

"All right brother," Zion replied with a sigh, "I'm going to give you the nickel version cause we ain't got much time. Did you hear those bombs that went off a few hours ago?"

"Yeah, we were trying to figure out what in the hell that was," Fingers came back.

Zion leaned on the table. "They were missiles," he explained, "and they fucked our shit up good. We pulled survivors out of Wendy's camp and sent them your way."

"Whoa, whoa, sent them *our* way?" Fingers demanded. "Edward isn't going to be happy about that."

Zion's gaze darkened. "He's gonna have to get over it, because we're coming that way too."

"What the hell is going on there?" came the reply.

Zion took a deep breath. "We got fifty thousand of those things headed our way, and if we don't get our people out in the next four hours or so, we ain't getting them out," he said.

There was a long silence, and then Fingers finally said, "Fucking hell man." He let out a deep *whoosh* of breath through the line. "What do you need me to do?"

"For starters, when you get a hold of Wendy, you tell her to turn around and haul ass back here with those transport vehicles," Zion replied. "We don't have anything big enough to move our people."

"We're low on that too," Fingers admitted. "We trained all the diesel from the buses to power the generators. Wish I could be more help on that, but I can't."

Zion shook his head. "No worries."

"How many loads do you need?" Fingers asked.

Zion glanced at Cheryl, and she scribbled some numbers quickly on the back of a piece of paper. Once she was done, she held up three fingers.

"Three," he said.

There was another momentary pause. "You aren't going to be able to do that in four hours if they're coming all the way here." It was a statement, not a question.

Zion rubbed his forehead. "I remember that drive, and there wasn't really a whole lot out there," he said. "And I don't really feel comfortable leaving vulnerable people on the side of the road."

"Don't blame you there," Fingers agreed. "Those things are fucking everywhere, and by the time you really get going, it'll be nighttime. So even guards aren't going to help much on the side of the road." He paused. "But wait… wait…" There was a sound of papers rustling around through the radio, and finally he said, "Bridge of the Gods!"

Zion's brow furrowed, and he looked around at the others, receiving blank stares all around. "I have no idea what that means," he admitted.

"Bridge of the Gods, man," Fingers replied, speaking quickly. "It's about halfway between us. Toll bridge over the river, they turned it into a little tourist trap a while back. Not a whole lot there, but there is a decent sized hotel."

Zion nodded thoughtfully. "Which we can use to stash people while we get everyone to safety," he added.

"Exactly," Fingers said. "However…"

Zion groaned. "Fuck, what now?"

"I found a report on it from a couple of weeks ago," came the reply, "and it's overrun with those things."

Zion sighed. "You're killing me, man."

"Don't worry," Fingers said quickly, "if you can send me some people, I can sneak up there with a few party favors and help you clear it out."

Zion glanced at Mateo. "You think you can handle that?"

"If that's where you need me," his companion replied with a firm nod.

Zion smiled at him in appreciation. "All right, I'm sending you a few guys," he said into the radio. "Mateo is your point man. He's a bladed badass, so you can't miss him."

"Look forward to it," Fingers replied. "If memory serves, there's a little restaurant across the street from the hotel. Let's rendezvous there."

Mateo gave a thumbs up, and Zion nodded.

"He'll be there," he said. "Appreciate it, man."

Fingers took a deep breath. "Anytime, bud," he replied. "Anytime."

The line went silent, and Zion tossed the microphone on the table. "Cheryl, does that timeline even work?" he asked. "I didn't want to say anything with him on the line, as we don't have any other options."

She held up a hand as she finished scribbling some more math on the scrap sheet. "Okay…" she began, shaking her head. "Assuming that the horde is reaching the crossroads in four hours, and assuming Wendy gets back here within ninety minutes…" She scribbled some more. "Forty-five minutes each way to the hotel… shit. We need four and a half hours to get that last group loaded up and on the move."

Zion drew his bottom lip between his teeth and nodded slowly. "Thirty minutes," he said thoughtfully. "We can buy thirty minutes."

"Let's get those engines for the loppers and we'll be in business," Calvin piped up.

Cheryl swiveled to face them. "Engines?" she asked. "Wait, where are you boys going?" she demanded.

"Super Garden Center," Zion replied.

She shook her head immediately, letting out a deep sigh. "Well, if you're going to go there, you might as well get everything you possibly can," she replied, knowing there was no time to argue. "There's a moving truck place about a half a mile up on Weiss street. They should have some trailers you can hitch to the back of your truck."

"That's a detour worth taking," Zion agreed.

Mateo raised a hand. "What about me?"

"Cheryl, see if you can round up a few boys to help Mateo clear the hotel," Zion said.

She nodded and got to her feet. "Do you want some to go with you, too?"

He shook his head. "No, we're doing a hit and run to get this stuff," he replied. "And besides, we need to get people and supplies staged in the parking garage. Every second is going to count. We need to be ready."

She nodded and waved to Mateo. "Okay, if you want to follow me, I'll get you set up," she said, and then pointed to Zion and Calvin. "You two stay safe."

"Always," Zion replied as she left with Mateo in tow.

He and Calvin went back to the stairs in silence, walking with purpose towards their daunting task. When they reached the garage, the students were furiously at work on the loppers. They welded large metal poles together, sticking out like a multi-pronged helicopter blade.

As Zion and Calvin headed to their truck, the former noticed Tori approaching, and he elbowed his companion. "I think your girl wants some sugar," he whispered, and then hopped into the driver's seat.

Calvin shoved his hands in his pockets, nervous as she reached him.

"Time to go to the mall?" she asked, pushing her glasses up her nose.

He tried to act casual and suave, but came up short with his country boy twang. "Yeah, Zion and I are gonna go get what you need."

"Just remember, the bigger the better," she replied.

"I'll get you a big one, don't you worry," he said, and then they both paused before he blushed as she laughed at the double entendre. "The mower will be big… but I mean that's not to say I'm small… I-um…"

She laughed harder, and then Calvin joined in, unable to stop himself. He took her hand, pulling it up to his chest and stroking her knuckles gently. The laughter died away, and they stared at each other warmly. Tori licked her lips.

The horn blared, startling them both.

"Jesus christ man, will you kiss her already?" Zion bellowed from the driver's side window. "We got shit to do!"

The two blushed and smiled shyly, and then Calvin leaned in, brushing his lips against hers. It was short and sweet, but spoke more than either could put into words. He pulled away and darted into the truck, and Tori gave a little wave before rushing back off to work.

Calvin fumbled with his seat belt and then noticed Zion grinning widely at him. "What?" he demanded.

"Proud of my playa!" Zion exclaimed. "Yeah!"

His friend chuckled and shook his head. "Let's get moving," he mumbled.

"Yes sir, Mister Playa!" Zion declared, and fired up the truck. He shot Calvin one more wink before peeling out of the garage.

CHAPTER TWO

Zion and Calvin stopped about a block away from the moving place, the only light coming from a solar-powered street light above the parking lot. There were a few zombies milling about in the lot, only faint shadows of movement in the distance.

"Got a couple of 'em hanging out on the corner, but can't see much past that," he said.

Calvin looked around the side of the truck, making sure it was safe to step out. He popped out and raised his rifle, looking through the scope. As he peered into the darkness, he could make out several moving figures about fifty yards from the moving business.

"Can't tell exactly how many there are," he replied, "but it looks like it's more than we want to deal with."

Zion nodded. "We're gonna have to act quick, then," he said, and got out of the truck. He motioned for his companion to switch sides. "Come on, you drive."

Calvin closed the passenger door and jogged around to the driver's seat, and Zion hopped up into the truck bed. He opened the little back window.

"What do you want me to do?" Calvin asked.

Zion raised his trusty wooden weapon. "Drive up alongside them and I'll handle the rest," he said with a grin. "Then find the first trailer you can and back it up."

The sniper nodded. "I'll cover you while you get it hitched up," he said.

Zion smacked the hood and Calvin hit the gas, speeding off towards the moving truck depot. As he reached the lot, he quickly turned in, moving just to the left of the two ghouls. Zion leaned over and swung from the bed, catching one zombie on the side of the head before stabbing down into the top of the other one.

Calvin scanned the lot, finally seeing a ten-foot trailer beside the building. "Got one, hang on!" he called, and flipped the truck into reverse, flooring it.

Zion widened his stance to keep his balance, and then moved to the back of the bed, motioning left and right to help Calvin line up the hitch properly.

"We're good!" he finally called. "Cover me!" He hopped out of the truck and grabbed the heavy metal trailer. He lifted it and dragged it towards the hitch, straining under the weight. *Come on, come on,* he urged himself, and gave a great heave, lifting it up.

Calvin stood on the edge of the door, scanning the lot. One creature emerged from the darkness, rotted face illuminated by the spotlight. The sniper quickly aimed and put it down with a clean headshot.

Zion startled, arms still straining as he tried to line up the trailer. "We got incoming?"

"Just a straggler," Calvin replied. He glanced to the left and noticed several creatures staggering into the lot. "Okay, more than just a straggler," he amended. "How much time you need?"

"Just another minute," he grunted, and finally managed to line up the trailer over the hitch and drop it. He fiddled with it a bit as Calvin dropped a few of the closest zombies and then shook his head. "Fuck it, going to have to do," he muttered, and then clambered back up into the truck bed. "We're good, let's roll!" he yelled.

Calvin ducked back into the cab and floored it, moving away from the zombies and back down the way they'd come. When they made it a few blocks away to relative safety, he stopped so Zion could get back inside.

"How's it looking?" Calvin asked.

His companion shrugged as he jumped into the passenger seat. "Well, it's still behind the truck," he replied, "so I guess it's good."

"Good enough for me," the sniper agreed.

Zion jerked his thumb over his shoulder. "You good handling this?" he asked.

"Oh yeah, just like I'm back on the farm," Calvin assured him with a grin.

Zion returned the smile. "Then drive us off to the mall then, farm boy."

"I thought I was a playa?" the sniper asked, raising an eyebrow.

Zion chuckled. "Only when your woman is around," he said.

Calvin rolled his eyes playfully, and then turned down a side street, heading around the mini-horde. He drove slowly, making sure the trailer was properly attached. Finally, after several blocks, they reached the edge of the mall parking lot.

The City of Roses Mall was a mammoth structure that housed five anchor stores and another two hundred smaller ones. It was a two-story beast, state-of-the art circa 1995, with multiple entrances outside of the anchor stores. Now, it was home to a few thousand zombies.

The two men sat in the truck, staring at their target, the Super Garden Center, one of the newer anchor stores. Calvin popped the truck into park, and stepped out with his stomach clenched, raising his rifle.

His heart sank as he scanned the store through his scope. The interior of the store was dimly lit via several emergency lights, as were most areas of the mall. Solar powered and installed as an anti-theft deterrent, it was a boon and the only reason the boys had any chance of succeeding.

While the lights were vital, unfortunately they had the byproduct of attracting huge numbers of zombies. There were easily hundreds just at the garden center, with even more inside the mall. While there was tremendous movement inside the store, at least there were only a handful of ghouls outside.

Calvin scanned the doors, four sets of double glass, with several of them open. Rigid steel beams reinforced the frames.

"Well, the good news is," he began, taking a deep breath, "we have lights."

Zion pursed his lips. "And the bad?"

"It appears as though they've attracted every zombie in a five mile radius," the sniper replied, and sat back down in the driver's seat with a huff. They sat in silence for a moment, and then he glanced over at his friend. "How we looking on time?"

Zion checked his watch. "Three-twenty left on the clock."

Calvin scrubbed his hands down his face. "Ideas?"

"Kinda hoping you had one," Zion admitted.

The sniper sighed. "Originally I was thinking we just drive right in through the front door," he suggested. "But it would be a hell of a risk with those beams."

"Agreed," Zion said. "But if we can find a loading door entrance…"

Calvin nodded thoughtfully. "Attack it from the inside," he finished. "I like it. Let's see what we can find."

He popped the truck back into gear, and they drove around the outer edge of the lot, headlights off to avoid detection. As they drove, they stared at the mall, seeing some smaller entrances illuminated, with several zombies coming in and out of the building.

They had no luck until they reached the other side of the ball. One of the department store anchors had a gaping hole through the front of the store, mangled metal hanging from the top of the structure, with a ten-foot wide hole resulting from a crash. A few bodies lay scattered on the ground in front of the doors.

"Looks like somebody really wanted in," Calvin muttered.

Zion nodded. "Looks like they had a head of steam, too," he said.

"Let's see what I can see," Calvin said, and parked again. He hopped out after a cursory sweep and then inspected the hole with his scope. Several zombies roamed around it, but he was more interested on the inside. "Looks like whoever was driving was a speed demon, because they got pretty deep into the store."

Zion raised an eyebrow. "How deep?" he asked. "Can we get the truck and trailer through?"

"Deep enough that I can't see it," Calvin replied. "Shouldn't be a problem to get inside. Question is… then what?"

Zion shook his head. "Man, I only came to this mall once," he admitted. "Only thing I really remember is that it's a big ole bitch."

"Good to know we have enough room to drive, though," Calvin pointed out.

"That's not a problem," Zion agreed. "What is a problem, is going to be figuring out how to buy ourselves enough time to load the mowers into the trailer."

They sat in silence for a moment, contemplating.

"I got an idea," Calvin finally said, "but you're gonna think I'm crazy."

Zion chuckled, shaking his head. "I already think that, so you don't have to worry about your reputation."

"Well…" the sniper began, "I figure we can Blues Brothers it through the mall, park it beside the mowers in the Garden Center, then get to higher ground in the mall proper and draw them out of the store."

Zion nodded thoughtfully. "Those things aren't the most graceful creatures on god's green earth, so there shouldn't be too many of them on the second floor."

"That's my thought, too," Calvin said. "So we get in, fight our way to the second floor, draw them out and buy ourselves a few minutes to load up."

Zion's eyebrows rose at his friend. "That's a crazy fucking idea," he said.

"Yeah I know," Calvin replied sheepishly. "Just trying to think outside the box."

They sat in another contemplative silence for a moment, and then Zion looked at his watch again. Three hours and twelve minutes remaining.

"I hate to say it though," he admitted, "but it's the best idea we got."

Calvin blinked at him in shock, having a hard time comprehending that his dumbass idea was the one they were going with. "Just make me a promise," he finally said.

"What's that?" Zion asked.

The sniper held up a hand. "If we survive this," he began, "let me come up with another idea when we're doing a raid. Don't want this to be the best idea I ever come up with."

"If we pull this off," Zion replied with a grin, "this *will* be the best idea you will ever have, because it worked. You may want to retire from the idea business."

Calvin tilted his head back and forth. "Good point," he said. "So you ready to do this?"

"Let's do it," Zion replied.

They shared a fist bump, and Calvin popped the truck into gear. He crept along the parking lot, lining them up with the hole in the entrance. As they approached, several zombies began coming out of the hole, attracted to the noise.

"Hang on!" Calvin cried and punched the gas. The vehicle rapidly picked up speed, and he flipped on the headlights as they approached the entrance. Several more zombies emerged, creating a soft wall of rotting flesh.

The truck bounced as they hit the curb, sending it and the trailer flying a

foot or so off of the ground, landing hard
and slamming into the first creature. With
a rapid thump, thump, thump, they plowed
over the ghouls, sending them crumbling
underneath the vehicle.

As soon as they cleared the entrance,
Calvin made a quick left turn, running
over the clothing displays, one of which
cracked the windshield. He hit a couple
more before finding the walkway leading
through the department store.

Calvin got on it, looking straight
through the store to see the entrance to
the main part of the mall. Several zombies
still remained in their way, but they were
no match for the massive truck. They
cleared the threshold and reached the main
part of the mall.

The second floor was a rim around the
gigantic first floor, where hundreds of
zombies spread about like undead Christmas
shoppers. The engine revved, echoing
throughout the cavernous structure.

As Calvin navigated, doing his best
to avoid hitting too many ghouls and
kiosks, Zion fixated on the second floor.

"Shit," he growled.

Calvin didn't peel his eyes away from
his task. "What?!" he demanded.

"There's a whole lot of those fuckers
on the second floor," Zion replied.

The sniper glanced up, seeing a few dozen lining the rails, and then looked back to his task, gripping the steering wheel with white knuckles. The job had just gotten a lot tougher, but there was no going back now.

As they passed the food court in the center of the mall, they saw a horde of creatures walking between the tables, every one of them heading their way. Calvin sped up, attempting to put a little distance between them. Finally, they saw the Super Garden Center at the end of the hall, the entire front entrance wide open, and dozens of zombies in the way.

They sped past an escalator, about forty yards away from the entrance to the store.

"That's our way up to the second floor," Zion said, motioning.

Calvin glanced in the rearview, seeing hundreds of creatures all heading their way. "We're gonna have to haul ass, then, if we're gonna make it back in time," he said, and sped through the front entrance to the garden center.

He knocked several creatures to the ground and then skidded to a stop just inside the store. "Where are the mowers?" he asked.

They looked around frantically, and
Zion finally pointed to the display
towards the back right side of the store.

"There!" he cried. "To the right!"

Calvin didn't even look, just hit the
gas and headed that way, slamming through
a display before finding the walkway
again. As they raced towards the mowers,
there were two more zombies in the aisle.
He sped up, crashing through the two of
them before slamming on the brakes beside
the display.

Four large riding lawn mowers sat in
a row, sales stickers still displayed on
the front of all of them. The two men
quickly jumped out of the truck, and Zion
grabbed his bludgeon from the back while
Calvin quickly checked his rifle.

"Follow me through them," Zion said,
and took off running.

The sniper followed close behind as
they headed up the aisle, and zombies
began to emerge from the displays. Zion
stepped up to the first one, a former
Super Garden Center employee who had
numerous bite marks all over her body.
With one swing, he put her out of her
misery.

As the weapon hit, Zion saw another
eight zombies directly in front of him on
the walkway. He quickly darted off of the
path and into the displays, giving them

some minor cover. As they ran, the creatures adjusted course, reaching through the potted plants and tools, clawed fingers grasping at them as they went.

They tore towards the front of the store, reaching ten yards away when Zion spotted a mini-horde blocking the path at the entrance. He tossed his weapon behind him.

"Catch!" he cried, and Calvin managed to snatch the weapon out of the air despite his surprise.

With his hands free, Zion picked up a large metal display that stretched out in four directions holding gardening shirts. He put it in front of him as he ran, slamming the crossed end into several ghouls and clearing a hole for them to fly through.

Once they cleared it, he threw the metal rack aside, taking out even more creatures. They broke through into the main part of the mall, giving themselves about five yards of distance from the zombies at the entrance before they turned to follow their running meals. Hundreds headed towards them from the center portion, closing in on the escalator.

"Keep up, playa!" Zion barked, and they broke into a dead sprint, running straight for the escalator. Hearts

pounding, legs pumping, they ran as hard
as they could, ducking the outstretched
hands of the few creatures reaching for
them on the way.

As they reached the escalators,
Calvin followed Zion up one side, just
before the horde reached the bottom. At
the halfway point, several creatures from
upstairs started to come down their side,
filing one after the other.

Zion stopped, Calvin barely smacking
into the back of him. "What are we waiting
on?!" he demanded.

"Get ready," Zion replied, holding up
a hand, "cause we're gonna jump over to
the other side. When we do, haul ass,
because it ain't gonna take them long to
catch on."

The sniper slung his rifle over his
shoulder, looking at the three-foot gap
between the two sets of stationary stairs.
Zion remained focused on the creatures
ahead of them, shambling their way down.
When they were within five steps of them,
he made his move.

"Now!" Zion yelled, and the duo moved
in sync, leaping across to the other side
of the escalator. Zion landed perfectly,
but Calvin's foot caught on the median,
and he stumbled. His companion grabbed him
by the collar, yanking him up to a
standing. They quickly rushed up the

stairs, as the zombies reached from the other side, confused that their meal had escaped.

The creatures at the top that hadn't filtered down the other side had changed course, moving towards them. Zion snatched his weapon from Calvin's hand and whipped it in front of him, using it like a battering ram to send a couple of them flying back as they reached the landing.

The duo made a hard left towards the wall of stores before continuing towards the center of the mall. There were about two dozen zombies behind them, with a smattering of creatures in front.

"Anytime you wanna start shooting!" Zion barked. "We gotta get them out of the store!"

Calvin didn't wait to be asked a second time, aiming towards the center of the mall, selecting a target and squeezing the trigger. The blast echoed throughout the large space as one of the creatures dropped to the ground.

Zion turned his attention towards the escalator zombies that were following them. He delivered several quick, decisive blows that dropped them to the ground. Before too long, however, the ones on the escalator had cleared the stairs, and were quickly becoming too much for him to handle on his own.

"Let's head up!" he yelled. "Gotta keep 'em moving."

They took off about twenty yards, Calvin stopping and firing twice in rapid succession, keeping the noise up and the threat ahead at bay. As he aimed for a third one, he paused, drawing his companion's attention from the trailing horde.

"What is it?" Zion asked.

Calvin gulped. "We're in trouble," he said.

His friend looked ahead and saw about sixty zombies coming around the corner at the center of the mall. "Where the fuck did they come from?" he demanded.

"Doesn't matter, they're here!" Calvin cried.

Zion looked back, noticing several zombies had poured out of the storefronts, increasing the number pursuing them. He frantically looked around, seeing a clothing store with an open gate just ahead, a small chain with a door about twenty feet wide.

"There!" Zion pointed. "Into the clothing store!"

They tore towards it as the zombies began to close in from both sides. Zion ran in first, quickly working his way through the displays to make sure they were alone inside. There were plenty of bloodstains and overturned displays, showing that at one time there'd been a hell of a struggle in there, with someone not coming out on top.

While he did his sweep, Calvin grabbed the metal pole and used it to close the gate. He slammed it shut moments before the zombies reached them, securing it to the ground. He took a few steps back as dozens of creatures pressed up against it, scraping the flesh from their fingers as they tried to stick them through the small metal openings. Zion came up to join him.

"How we looking?" he asked.

Calvin swallowed hard. "Trying to remain hopeful that there is a back exit," he admitted.

"Haven't checked," Zion replied, "but we're alone in here unless something is in the storeroom."

They backed away from the gate, relieved that it was holding, but concerned they may be trapped. They went to the storeroom door, and Calvin put his hand on the knob as Zion readied his weapon and nodded.

The sniper threw open the door, and Zion burst inside, looking around at the horrific scene. A mangled bloody corpse sprawled on the ground, mostly eaten but still moving. He shook his head as he walked over to it, unable to tell at all what the person had looked like before they'd been attacked.

"Don't know who this was," he muttered, "but they were a hell of a fighter if they were able to lock themselves up with that kind of damage." He stood over the zombie as it gave a gurgled moan and tried to reach for his ankle. He brought his weapon down on top of its chewed-up head, destroying it.

The two looked around the darkened storeroom, unable to see much of anything without any lights. Calvin headed back out to the register, fumbling around the shelves underneath until he found a flashlight.

"Got a light," he said, returning to the dark room.

He flicked it on and scanned the room, and both men's hearts soared as they spotted a back door.

"Hope that's not just a closet," Zion said, and they approached it carefully. He unlocked it and then cracked it open, peeking through. There was a long cinder block hallway with several other doors, a dead end about forty yards ahead with a door. He gently closed it and backed up. "We got a way out," he said. "But first, I think we need to draw some attention our way, don't you?"

Calvin nodded, wiping his forehead. "Plus I could use a breather," he admitted.

"Weak bud, weak," Zion said playfully, shaking his head. "If you are gonna keep your girl pleased, you gonna have to work on that cardio."

The sniper chuckled. "You have such a one-track mind," he accused.

Zion clapped him on the back. "Come on, let's go cause a ruckus."

They headed to the gate and began yelling. Calvin stuck his gun through one of the holes and fired at point blank range, exploding a zombie's head and sending guts and brain matter everywhere.

"Whoa!" Zion cried, stepping back from the spray. "Watch it, there."

Calvin chuckled. "My bad," he said, and turned the rifle around. He used the butt to bang on the metal. After a few minutes of this, they backed away from the gate. Zion looked at his watch.

"Two fifty-eight on the clock," he reported. "We give this ten and we're back on the move."

Calvin found a spot behind the counter and plonked down on the floor, back against the wall. "I'll take every minute I can get."

Mateo drove Bryan and Michael towards the Bridge of the Gods. The SUV was silent, tense, everybody focused on the task at hand. The headlights pierced through the darkness as they drove along the interstate next to the water, providing a little ambient light. As they approached the exit, Bryan leaned forward from the backseat.

"This has got to be it," he said. He pointed to the water, and the metallic bridge shimmered in the distance in the moonlight.

Mateo nodded. "Now we just have to hope this Fingers fella is here."

"Almost afraid to ask how he earned that nickname," Michael said, earning a few light chuckles despite the somber mood of the car.

Mateo swerved lightly as a few zombies wandered onto the exit ramp from the woods. He hit the brakes.

"Clear 'em out," he said.

Bryan furrowed his brow. "Why?" he asked, shrugging his lean shoulders. "Just keep driving."

"We're gonna have our hands full as it is," Mateo replied. "Do you really want things sneaking up on us?"

Michael shook his head and looked at his friend before shrugging. The duo got out of the vehicle reluctantly, surveying the two zombies that looked badly damaged, the forest having taken its toll on them. They grabbed baseball bats out of the trunk and casually walked over, each smacking down a ghoul and returning to the vehicle unharmed.

"Happy?" Bryan drawled as he slid into the backseat.

Mateo pursed his lips, ignoring the man's sarcastic tone. He popped the vehicle back into gear and drove towards the meeting spot. As they crept through the tiny town, they looked down side streets, seeing movement on the far end.

"You want us to take care of them, too?" Michael asked, a touch of ice in his voice.

Mateo shook his head. "Let's see what Fingers has to say before we start clearing out the whole town."

They drove a couple more blocks before finding the hotel. It was a large five story building, with a few zombies in the parking lot. Bryan leaned forward again, tapping Mateo on the shoulder and pointing to a small restaurant on the other side of the street.

A man stood by the entrance, waving at them, and they realized he was missing a finger and a half.

"Going to go out on a limb and assume that's Fingers," Bryan quipped.

Mateo drove over, and they got out, carrying their weapons.

Fingers frowned at the trio. "This all you got?"

"All that could be spared," Mateo admitted, "they're really scrambling to get people ready to move."

He shook his head before motioning for them to follow him inside. "Well, it is what it is," he said with a sigh. "Come on, let me show you what I got."

They walked into the darkened restaurant, the only light coming from an industrial grade flashlight on a table near the back, away from the windows. As they walked, Michael stumbled over a corpse on the ground.

"Oh yeah," Fingers said, with a little laugh, "sorry, watch your step. Had to do a little handiwork to get this place secure."

They navigated to the back of the restaurant where there was a table set up. There were a few bombs, two large and one that would fit in the palm of a hand. There was also a hand-drawn map on the back of a kid's placemat, showing the hotel, bridge and immediate area.

"Have a seat," Fingers invited, spreading his arms. "We need to run through this quick." When they complied, he held up the map. "As I'm sure you saw on the way in, we have a potential shitstorm on our hands. We gotta clear out at least the bottom floor of the hotel and secure the doors. We also have a couple hundred of those fuckers roaming the streets that we need to deal with, too."

Bryan crossed his arms and leaned his elbows on the table. "Man, why are we worrying about the hotel when this place is clear?"

"Because there's too much glass," Fingers replied impatiently, "the back door is completely gone, and the hotel across the street is wide open, so it would just be a constant stream of those things that we'd have to deal with one way or another. Not to mention, if they are bringing six busloads of people here, it would get pretty cramped in here." He cocked his head. "Now are you gonna let me finish, or do you want to keep offering up ideas that are far beyond your pay grade?"

Bryan clamped his mouth shut and lowered his gaze.

"Good," Fingers said, and leaned on his palms. "Now, as I was saying. We have multiple problems and not a lot of time or resources to deal with them." He picked up one of the large bombs from the table, a pipe bomb that had been wrapped with a generous amount of nuts and bolts. "Now, I got six of these bad boys, which is how we're going to clear out street level. Which one of you boys is the fastest runner?"

Bryan and Michael both immediately pointed at Mateo, the only athletic-looking one of the bunch.

He shook his head. "Fuck," he muttered. "Okay, what do you need?"

"We got two streets where the bulk of them are," Fingers explained. "You get to run down, distract them, and bring them up to me."

Mateo nodded. "And where are you going to be?"

"On top of the building at the end of the street," Fingers said. "When they get close, I'm gonna detonate the bombs right over their heads. The blast should go a long way towards luring them out."

Mateo pursed his lips. "And what about the rest?"

Fingers glanced at the holsters on either side of the man's torso. "Here's hoping you're good with those," he said, inclining his head to the blades.

Bryan and Michael snickered and exchanged a fist bump, and Fingers eyed them with a calculating gaze.

"Not sure why you chuckle nuts are laughing," he drawled, "because it's going to be your job to start getting those things out of the hotel."

The duo sobered immediately.

"How do you suggest we do that?" Bryan asked.

Michael threw his hands up. "Yeah, and what are we supposed to do with that many of them?"

Fingers pointed to the ceiling in the center of the room. Four bombs dangled above them with a long fuse running out the front door.

"As far as what you're supposed to do with them," he began, "you lure them inside here and get out through the front before locking them in, and I'll handle the rest. As far as how, I really don't give a fuck." He spread his hands. "Yell, shoot, do an acappella version of Baby Got Back, whatever floats your boat."

The two men stared at each other, wide-eyed with terror.

Fingers laughed. "Amazing how quickly you tough guys fold," he scoffed. "Hope it's just you shitting your pants, and not you realizing it's hopeless."

They tried to respond, opening and
closing their mouths, but no sound came
out. Fingers grabbed the bombs from the
table and another bag from the ground. He
checked his watch and shook his head.

"Let's get a move on," he said
shortly, "we're gonna have guests showing
up in an hour or so. Probably best for
everybody if we're alone in this town."

CHAPTER FOUR

Zion and Calvin sat out of sight of the zombies at the gate, listening as they moaned and shook the metallic barrier. After a few moments with no conversation, Zion checked his watch.

"Two forty-eight," he reported. "Break time is over, brother. You ready to start causing a ruckus?"

Calvin stood, readying his rifle. "Let's do it," he declared. "You figure out the plan yet?" he asked.

Zion shook his head. "Out that door at the end of the hallway, you open fire, and we haul ass down the other side of the upstairs hall," he replied. "Just gotta hope that there aren't too many of them standing in our way."

"And if there are?" Calvin cocked his head.

Zion shrugged playfully. "Then it's been a fun ride."

The sniper chuckled and smirked at his friend. "You know, you might just have a future in motivational speeches."

Zion clapped him on the back. "Come on, let's roll," he said, and they headed into the back room. They crept to the back door and cracked it open, peeking out into the hallway. It was clear, so they stepped out, walking briskly to the end.

"Okay, when we get out to the main hall, you start picking those things off on the far side," Zion said quietly. "I'll cover you while you do."

Calvin nodded firmly. "How many shots you want?"

"You just focus on firing until I tell you to move," Zion said. "The more shots, the more of those things that are gonna head out of the store."

Calvin checked his ammo, making sure his rifle had been topped off. When he was ready, Zion peeked out the door, spotting a lone zombie about five yards away, with nothing else in his immediate view. He held up one finger to signal to his companion there was only one enemy.

He threw open the door and rushed out, swinging his bludgeon fiercely, striking down the ghoul as Calvin slammed the door behind him and did a quick sweep of their rear, finding several zombies far down the hallway towards the other anchor store.

"Forget 'em," Zion said, smacking his arm, "let's move."

They ran out to the main portion of the mall, straight towards a walkway over the large center area.

"Set up in the center," Zion barked, "let's do this!"

Calvin ran straight across, hopping up onto a bench and taking aim at the left side of the building. He quickly scanned, finding a zombie about twenty yards down. The first shot boomed, blowing the back out of the creature's head and alerting every zombie to where they were.

As he found his next target, Zion went into sentry mode, looking in every direction for something to bash. His first one came up from the rear, a teenager in blood-tattered pajamas, about fifteen yards away from Calvin. He rushed it and swung hard, sending the lightweight monster tumbling to the ground.

He turned and saw the group they had hidden from in the store was working its way up towards them. It was easily a thirty-strong horde at this point, too much to manage with just a bat.

Another booming shot rang out, prompting Zion to glance to the other side. Zombies began to pour out of the stores, with twenty to thirty stretching all the way down to the second floor entrance to the garden center.

"Gotta buy him more time," he muttered to himself, and frantically looked around, spotting a large metal trash can on the corner. He did a quick scan, seeing that nothing was close to them. He rushed over, set his weapon down, and picked up the can. It was heavy and cumbersome, so it took him a moment to get a handle on it.

Zion strained as he lifted it over his head. Once he had it secure, he started jogging towards the mini-horde as the shots from Calvin continued to echo. The zombies in front of him grew excited, seeing fresh meat coming their way. He stopped five yards short and threw the trash can as hard as he could.

The first three zombies in the center of the mass were crushed under the weight of it. The force of the impact knocked several more down, creating two columns of undead. Zion raced back to grab his weapon.

"Reloading!" Calvin called as the firing stopped momentarily.

Zion scanned the rear, seeing a handful of zombies coming up the other side of the aisle, still about thirty yards from the crossover. He looked at the aisle they had to run through, finding still about forty creatures out along the entire route of the run. There were a few really thick packs in their way.

"Thin out the big packs!" Zion cried. "Then get ready to go!"

Calvin nodded as he finished reloading and then took aim, firing some more. Zion turned to see the two columns of zombies were within ten yards of the crossover. He darted forward, swinging hard at the group closest to the railing. Instead of going for a headshot on the closest one, he swung deep and at an upward angle.

The thick wood caught three zombies under the arm, the force sending them lifting off of their feet and tumbling over the side railing. Zion didn't look, but he heard the thud below as they hit the floor. He quickly turned to the other column, which had broken rank and headed his way. He swung low and hard, taking out the legs from a few creatures, sending them to the ground.

He ran back to Calvin, who fired off another shot. He looked down the aisle they were going to have to run through, seeing dozens of zombies, but a lot more spread out.

"We gotta move," Zion said.

The sniper hopped down from the bench, both of them looking at the first floor. It was a sea of zombies, a lot of them pouring out of the garden center.

"You follow me and run as hard as you can," Zion instructed. "Just push 'em out of the way and keep moving. Escalator is at the center of the store. If we get separated, meet at the top."

Calvin nodded firmly. "Lead on."

They began their spring, launching from the spot. The hallway was about fifteen feet wide, and a hundred and fifty yards to the store entrance, with corpses both standing and laying dead along the path. Zion was five yards in front of Calvin as he approached the first pack. Three creatures shambled towards him.

He lowered his shoulder and barreled through them, clearing the path like a fullback for a running back. Calvin deftly hopped over the fallen corpses as they continued their run.

The next thirty yards were relatively easy, as the creatures were spread out pretty thin. Both men ducked around them, the outstretched claws never coming close to touching them. As they reached the next crowded section, there were two batches of four, staggered, leaving only a small section in the middle to break through.

"Go right!" Zion yelled. He broke towards the pack on the right, stopping just in front of them and swinging his weapon. The impact sent the lead two ghouls back into the others, all four slamming into the railing.

Calvin didn't wait for him to get moving again, just run right by him and the fallen zombies. As he approached the next group, trouble arose. He ducked underneath the arm of an older monster missing a limb. As he came about, there was a corpse on the floor with a massive bullet wound to the head. He saw it, but not quite in time, his foot clipping the lifeless leg and sending him stumbling forward onto the ground.

The zombie that had been reaching for him moaned in delight and moved in quickly for its meal. Calvin scrabbled to get up, knowing he was in a bad spot.

The creature's good arm reached out and grazed the fabric of the sniper's shirt, but Zion grabbed it from behind by the collar and belt. He let out an animalistic yell as he tossed the thing over the railing.

"Ain't no time to be lounging!" Zion cried, grabbing his companion by the arm and dragging him to a standing. The two men took off once again, despite the route ahead becoming more crowded, with about twenty zombies in the immediate vicinity.

Zion stared ahead, looking for a path through the mass of corpses that were standing nearly shoulder to shoulder and two deep. Calvin glanced to the rear, seeing the zombies they'd passed heading back in their direction.

"Whatever we're doing, we gotta do it now!" he cried.

Zion held his weapon horizontally across his body. "Stay close," he instructed, and took off running like a shot.

Calvin stayed hot on his heels as best he could, as Zion extended his arms at the line of zombies. He hit three at chest level with the wood, and pumped his legs hard, driving right through the corpses, knocking them back into the second row.

Both men leapt over the fallen creatures, as their friends reached out to grab them. By a hair's breadth, they made it through the line and continued sprinting hard.

The store entrance was just ahead, with only a smattering of zombies standing in their way. They navigated through them and rushed into the store.

"Escalators in the center!" Zion screamed.

They dashed through the store, going straight down the main aisle in the center towards the frozen escalator, which was on the other side of a massive wall. As they rounded the corner, a dozen creatures greeted them, congregating around the entrance. The duo skidded to a stop and blinked in disbelief for a moment at the sight.

"Just once today it would be nice to catch a break," Calvin groaned.

Zion looked around, spotting a shovel display just across from them. He grabbed one and held it out to his companion, who took it.

"Gotta stay silent," Zion said, putting a finger to his lips.

They stepped up, melee weapons in hand, and began their assault. Zion swung wildly, cracking skulls, as Calvin went for a more gory assault. He stepped up to a younger zombie, a young redhead wearing a bloodied Super Garden Center shirt. He stabbed the shovel forward, driving the tip of the makeshift weapon into the bridge of her nose.

The impact drove straight through into her brain, causing the zombie to convulse for a moment before slumping down. He kicked it in the chest, freeing the shovel from the corpse and allowing him to repeat the process on the next enemy.

After several moments of smacking and stabbing, the immediate threat in front of them had been put down, although the moans and footsteps coming from behind them grew louder and louder. Zion led them around the wall to the escalator, seeing one more creature near the top of the stairs, stumbling about trying to navigate to a fresh meal.

Rather than deliver a vicious blow, Zion gently shoved the monster with his weapon, sending it falling straight back off of the stairs. There was a loud crack as the back of its head impacted on the edge of one of the stairs.

With the path to the first floor clear, the two men headed down, treading as lightly as they could to minimize the noise. As they reached the bottom, they could see into the mall where hundreds of zombies lumbered around just outside of the store. They made the turn towards the truck, stopping at the sight of a handful of creatures still in the store.

"Run through them to the truck," Zion whispered. "I'll load up the mowers and you handle anything that comes our way."

Calvin nodded and held up his bloody shovel, approving of the plan. They darted out from cover, running as hard as they could down the aisle to the truck, passing half a dozen creatures browsing the various garden departments looking for brains. The footsteps alerted them to fresh meat, causing them to turn and head towards the duo.

Zion reached the truck and quickly dropped the back gate to the trailer, giving him a ramp. The first mower was a beast, forcing him to use every ounce of his strength to get it moving. Calvin glanced over with concern as he heard his friend grunt with the strain.

"Keep watch, I got this!" Zion hissed as he heaved the machine onto the trailer.

Calvin nodded and went back to sentry duty, watching the zombies they'd passed coming their way. He quickly checked side to side, to make sure there was no other threat, and then moved up to attack the first ghoul. With a quick swing of the shove, the first attacker was down. Rather than continue moving forward, the sniper retreated to the truck.

Zion got the first mower up, hopping off and immediately pushing the second one. Calvin watched the half-dozen zombies swell to about twenty in the main aisle. With the lead creature about twenty yards away, he swallowed hard, knowing this was getting out of hand quickly.

Before he could move up to attack, he heard movement from his right. A trio of zombies moved through the potted plants, knocking over long-dead plants with smashes and clangs. He frantically looked back and forth at the two front threats before dropping his shovel and retrieving his rifle.

"They're on to us, I'm going hot!" he barked.

Zion paused with the second mower and surveyed the situation, nodding. "Do it!" he cried, and continued to push.

Calvin aimed at the main aisle zombies, quickly squeezing off two shots, hoping that the fallen would trip up a few. He turned his attention to the plant section, the trio having grown to half a dozen and getting closer, within fifteen yards.

He quickly fired, taking out the closest two before frantically shifting back to the main horde, which had swallowed up the fallen easily. He fired two more times, but heard Zion struggling with a gigantic mower, far bigger than the previous two. It looked like an industrial sized one for mowing football fields.

Calvin glanced back at the oncoming threat, knowing that no matter what he did the enemy would be on them no matter what he chose to do. He broke from his defensive position and rushed back, throwing what little weight he had behind the mower. Despite his lean frame, it was just enough to get it moving up the incline. As soon as it was in place, Zion slammed the gate shut.

"You're driving!" he said, and they bolted for the cab.

They slammed the doors shut, breathing heavily as rotting flesh pawed at the windows. Calvin turned the key in the ignition, and both men let out a sigh of relief as the engine roared to life.

"Buckle up," he said. "This is going to be a bumpy ride."

He popped it into gear and they started moving, a little slower with all the weight they were pulling. The corpse hands slid against the windows as they pulled away, leaving trails of goop and slime in their wake.

The duo drove down the back aisle before making the turn on the opposite side of the store to head back to the mall. As they approached the entrance, they saw a horde of creatures in the hundreds standing in front of them.

"That is some densely packed trouble right there," Calvin said, swallowing hard.

Zion licked his lips. "All you can do is floor it and hope, brother," he said, extending his fist.

Calvin bumped it and then revved the engine a few times before punching the gas.

The truck gained speed, hitting thirty as they crashed into the front edge of the mass. Bodies flew about, a few embedding themselves into the front hood, brethren smacking off of their backs as the truck plowed through.

Zion looked back, seeing a couple of creatures reaching out, their hands shattered as the mowers slapped them on the way by.

"Come on baby, come on baby," Calvin muttered to himself, "you can do it."

The engine whined loudly under the strain, the constant mass of rotted flesh keeping their speed low. The truck bumped about as they ran over creatures, the sound of broken bones and moans coming from an undead carpet below.

As they plowed through, they could see light at the end of the tunnel, but the truck began to slow down. Calvin dropped the truck into four-wheel drive, giving them a little extra boost of power. Just before the edge, the truck groaned mightily, and the duo held their breath.

Calvin closed his eyes and mentally urged the vehicle forward, and then the truck finally punched through the other side of the creatures. They let out a sigh of relief, and Zion turned to make sure the mowers made it. They were all still on the trailer, although they were a bit bloody.

Calvin turned towards the entrance of the store so they could escape the mall proper.

"Gonna have to hose those things down when we get back," Zion said, facing front again, "but they're in one piece." He checked his watch. "And we still have two hours," he said.

Calvin shook his head in disbelief. "Holy shit, we might actually pull this off."

"We just gotta hope your lady is up to the challenge," Zion said with a smirk.

His friend laughed. "I'd put a lot more money on that than us pulling off what we just did."

Zion joined in and shook his head. "Ain't that the damn truth."

CHAPTER FIVE

Mateo watched Fingers climb up the fire escape ladder on the single story building on the corner. The building was large, covering the entire top of the block, reaching both streets with zombies congregating at the end.

Once Fingers was up, he motioned to Mateo, who picked up a large metal pole from the ground and handed it up to him.

"Okay," Fingers stage-whispered down to him. "Which side do you want to start on?"

Mateo looked around before motioning to the right, the street furthest from the hotel.

Fingers nodded. "Remember to duck at the alley so you don't get hit by shrapnel," he said.

Mateo nodded and gave him a less than enthusiastic thumbs up, clearly not thrilled with the plan. But there was nothing else to be done. He had a job.

He peeked around the corner, seeing about eighty zombies standing a hundred yards down. A few of them were banging on a small business door, leading him to believe that at one time someone had been alive in there.

Okay, this is easy, he thought to himself. *Just jog down, clank your blades together, and waltz back to cover… surely the seven-fingered man knows what he's doing.* He sighed, realizing his life was in the hands of a man who needed to use both hands to pick up a glass of water.

A moment later, a light whistle came from the top of the building, signaling that Fingers was ready. Mateo burst out from cover and began jogging towards the horde, pulling out his long knife and cleaver as he grew closer.

The bulk of the zombies were focused on the building, a small mom-and-pop shop, with a trio of creatures on the outer rim of the mass, about ten yards away. With the nearest ghouls focused on the horde, Mateo came up silently behind them, swinging the cleaver and taking the head clean off of the first one before quickly stabbing the next one in the side of the head with his knife.

The noise of the falling bodies alerted the third one, but before it could cry out it took a cleaver to the face. While it wasn't too loud, the crumpling of rotted flesh hitting the pavement peeled a few more zombies from the mass. They shambled forwards, clearing a few yards before their moans really started to amplify.

Well, if they're going to line up for me, then I'm going to take them out, Mateo thought to himself, and waited for the first creature to reach him. He lashed out quickly with his knife, directly into the ghoul's eye. Two more creatures came up, staggered a couple feet apart, and Mateo delivered another swing of his cleaver, slicing through the top part of its skull.

The moans and bodies hitting the ground alerted a dozen or so zombies, who had begun to move in his direction. Rather than continue the fight, he slowly began to back up, with the one remaining breakaway zombie keeping pace.

Mateo surveyed the situation. A pack of a dozen behind the lone zombie, with a gap between them and the rest of the horde.

Shit, he thought, *they need to be bunched up more if that bomb is going to be effective.*

Mateo continued to backpedal, glancing over his shoulder to keep track of his location and potential threats. The alley was now twenty yards behind him, and coming up quickly, the zombies still spread out.

Mateo glanced up on top of the roof, seeing Fingers standing there, waiting with the bomb attached to the end of the metal pole. He flicked his lighter a couple of times, letting him know he was ready to roll.

Mateo nodded and lunged forward, coming at the main breakaway zombie. He grabbed the beast by the shirt and shoved it back towards the dozen, causing a few of them to stumble, allowing the rest of the horde to catch up to them, though eight creatures still remained broken away.

Gonna have to do, he thought to himself, and jogged back to the alley.

"You think you can handle that tiny group?" Fingers called down to him.

Mateo looked down the alley, about six feet wide, butting up against another building that ran the entire length of the block. About two-thirds of the way down was a large dumpster that had been flipped over on its side, blocking the route to the next street.

"Yeah," he replied, "you just make sure you take those things out, though. I can handle eight. Eighty is another story."

Fingers gave him a thumbs up. "You just make sure you're clear of the street," he reminded him.

Mateo continued to stand at the entrance to the alley, waiting for the eight creatures to close in on him. When they were ten yards away, he slowly backed into the alley, readying his weapons. As he backed up, Fingers lit the fuse on the pole bomb and began to extend it off the corner of the building, positioning it over the edge of the next building, dipping it down so it was right beside the wall.

Mateo made it about halfway down the alley, zombies in pursuit, making sure he was clear of the blast. The first ghoul lunged towards him, and he stabbed it in the face with his knife, dropping it. The next two creatures were almost on top of each other, climbing on the other to get to their meal first.

He swung his cleaver from up high, blunt edge down. The metal weapon cracked the top of the skull of the first creature, and Mateo quickly swung back up, catching his partner underneath the chin, cutting straight through the front part of its face.

He continued to back up as the five remaining zombies navigated the alley and fallen creatures. Mateo grew tense, expecting a large boom to rattle his teeth, but it didn't come. He glanced up and saw Fingers shaking the pole frantically, but no boom.

Mateo's attention was refocused quickly when the moan of a zombie grew very loud directly in front of him. He snapped back just in time to face a creature lunging at him, forcing him to

react by instinct. He dropped his cleaver
and grabbed the zombie by the shirt,
shoving it hard against the wall before
jamming his knife through the bottom of
its jaw.

As it fell, he ducked down and
grabbed the cleaver, just as another
creature closed in. Mateo glanced back to
see he was only ten yards away from the
dumpster blockage, so he shoved the lead
creature back as hard as he could, giving
him some space. As it fell, he knocked
down the next couple of zombies, giving
him a view of the top of the alley.

The main horde was there, beginning
to filter in.

"Fingers!" Mateo bellowed. "What the
fuck, man?!" He looked up to see Fingers
pulling the pole back up towards him.

As the bomb got close to the
building, he cut the cord on it, dropping
it to the ground below. He pulled out the
small bomb and lit the fuse on it before
throwing it down into the alley.

Mateo panicked a bit, seeing a lit
bomb headed in his direction, eyes wide.

"Twenty second fuse!" Fingers yelled.
"Small yield!"

Mateo realized what he was doing as
the bomb clanged on the pavement between
him and the oncoming zombies. He dashed
forward, picking it up and tossing it

underhand towards the closest zombies, rolling it just past them. He immediately turned tail and rushed back towards the dumpers, tossing his blades up on top before quickly pulling himself up.

As he reached the top, the mini-bomb went off.

The echo of the blast in the alleyway was deafening, stunning Mateo momentarily. The bomb ripped through several creatures, sending blood and body parts flying through the air. Mateo grabbed his blades and rolled off of the dumpster, landing with a *thud* on the ground.

"Stay behind the dumpster and keep it in place!" Fingers yelled down to him.

Mateo nodded and watched as his rooftop companion secured another big bomb to the pole. He quickly lit it and lowered it into the alley, which was quickly filling with zombies. Mateo startled when the dumpster began to move due to the weight of the monsters on the other side, so he quickly pushed back.

He strained against it, trying to keep the barricade in place, hoping that this next bomb wasn't a dud as well.

"Come on, come on, come on," he muttered, the words like a prayer.

The bomb detonated with a blast exponentially louder than the smaller one, metal clanging like bullets ricocheting off of the dumpster. He flinched when several bits of the shrapnel crashed into the ground behind him.

The weight on the dumpster vanished, and he relaxed his shoulders, looking up at Fingers. The man on the roof glanced down into the alley and nodded. He looked over at Mateo and gave a thumbs up, prompting him to climb back up onto the dumpster.

The carnage was horrific, with dozens of bodies ripped to shreds in the alley, looking like they'd been pureed with a blender. Some of them continued to move, writhing around despite having no proper limbs to do anything with.

"I'll go ahead and tell you right now," Mateo said, motioning to the zombie stew, "I ain't cleaning this up."

Fingers chuckled, and then moans sounded at the mouth of the alley. There were a dozen creatures down there still remaining, excited to get to Mateo. They slipped as they stepped into the carnage, unable to stay standing as they attempted to shamble through the slick debris.

"They'll be fine there," Fingers said, "we need to worry about the other street."

Mateo nodded and hopped down from the dumpster. He readied his blades as he approached the corner, peering out down

the street. He was relieved to see that
this group was smaller, about forty
zombies or so, and they were all moving as
a single unit, no doubt attracted by the
bomb.

They were still about fifty yards
away, and closing in. Mateo jumped when
Fingers started talking, having moved just
above him.

"This group shouldn't be too bad," he
said.

Mateo shook his head. "That's what we
thought about the last group, so let's not
get ahead of ourselves."

"Yeah, sorry about that," Fingers
replied, scratching the back of his head.

"What the hell happened?" Mateo
asked, raising an eyebrow.

His rooftop companion shrugged. "It
was just a dud, man, they happen from time
to time," he explained. "But don't worry,
they don't happen that often."

"Well, if it's all the same to you,"
Mateo began, pointing a finger at the
street, "I'll wait for you to take out
this group from the comfort of the main
road up there. My days of luring shit down
alleys is over and done with."

Fingers chuckled and nodded. "Don't
blame you one bit," he agreed. "Just don't
go too far, because I'll need you on mop
up duty once this thing goes off."

Mateo gave him a thumbs up before making his way to the top of the street. He glanced back at the horde, thirty yards and closing slowly. "After taking out your friends, you ain't gonna be nothing," he muttered.

When he reached the top of the street, he looked back to see Fingers extending the bomb out of the crowd. He took cover behind the wall, resting comfortably against it, waiting for the blast to shred them.

Bryan and Michael knelt down on the edge of the parking lot by the street, taking cover behind some bushes. They surveyed the front of the hotel, a few dozen zombies lurking by the entrance. Bryan pulled his hunting rifle from his back and looked through the scope.

"What do you see, bud?" Michael asked.

His friend focused on the entrance, seeing the double doors propped open, creatures coming and going as they pleased. There were easily dozens more in the lobby.

"Fuckers are jam packed in there," he grunted. "Big place too, lobby desk looks like it's about twenty yards back from the door."

Michael sighed. "Can you see the stairs?" he asked.

"Too dark to find it on the wall," Bryan replied, shaking his head. "Can't see much past the front desk, since there's an emergency light over it. We just have to assume that it's wide open like the front door."

Michael scrubbed his hands down his face. "So how the hell are we doin' this?" he asked.

"One thing's for sure," his friend replied, lowering the rifle, "I'm *not* singing Baby Got Back."

Michael shook his head. "First good news I've heard today."

"We gotta figure out a way to get in there to secure the stairs," Bryan mused. "Or else we'll just have a constant stream of those things."

His companion looked over at a car at the far end of the lot. It was an older sedan with bloodstains all over the window.

"Come on," he said, waving his hand, "I might have an idea."

They stayed low while moving across the lot over to the car. They ducked down beside it, and Michael peered inside. He recoiled at the sight of a zombie in there, laying in the backseat, writhing around on the leather.

He pulled a knife, motioning for his friend to back up a bit, retreating to the back of the car. He readied his blade before yanking open the back door.

Thankfully, the creature was slow to react, giving him a chance to stab it in the top of the head.

Bryan came back from behind the trunk and crossed his arms. "Congratulations, you killed one that was already secure," he said dryly.

Michael rolled his eyes before patting the creature down, finally finding a set of keys in its pocket. He held them up and jingled them in front of Bryan's face.

"Are you kidding me?" his friend demanded, eyes wide. "I know where you're going with this, and I wish you the best of luck."

Michael smirked at him. "You aren't gonna rock, paper, scissors me for the honors?"

"You know damn well that only applies to riding shotgun, and who gets to hit on the hot girl at the bar first," Bryan shot back, pointing a finger at him. "Ain't nothin' in there about suicide runs."

Michael shrugged. "Fine, be a little bitch," he said off-handedly.

His friend glared at him and then waved him off. "Well, it's your ass," he drawled, "how do you want me to play it?"

Michael studied the hotel for a moment, and then looked back into the car, spotting a large jacket in the passenger seat. "I'm gonna plow right through the front door, and then lay low while you draw them out," he declared. "Once it's clear, I'll get out and secure the doors while you get them to the restaurant."

"Is that *really* how you want to do it?" Bryan asked, throwing up his hands.

His friend bit his lip nervously,
doubting his own plan. "We're real short
on time," he insisted. "So I say we go for
it."

Bryan nodded, and then both men
jumped at the sound of an explosion in the
distance. They glanced in the direction of
the blast, not seeing anything before
looking back at the hotel. The zombies
jerked their heads back and forth,
seemingly confused about the location of
the noise.

"If that wasn't the big one, then
we're in a lot of trouble," Bryan said.

Michael nodded and hopped into the
driver's seat, door still open, turning
the key and praying for good news. The
vehicle wheezed a few times before it
finally sprung to life.

"All right," he said firmly, "once
I'm in, pull them out as quickly as you
can. I'd rather not be a box lunch."

Bryan nodded just as another
explosion sounded, this one much bigger,
rattling the windows of the car. Despite
being several blocks away, the sound
resonated, and this spurred the zombies
into moving away from the hotel.

"Go!" Bryan said and slammed the
door.

Michael popped the car into gear and
sped towards the horde. He gained speed as

he approached the front edge of them, about thirty yards from the entrance to the hotel. Bodies bounced off of the front end, left and right, as he struggled with the car to keep it aimed towards his target.

The double doors were fairly wide, just big enough for a sedan to pass through if driven properly. Unfortunately, the zombies careening off of the vehicle caused Michael to have difficulty steering, and he clipped the right side of the door frame as he entered the building.

The headlights illuminated the lobby, an upscale marble floor open space with formerly high-end furniture now ruined by the undead.

As he hit the marble, he slammed on the brakes, sliding across it and smacking into a few more zombies before coming to rest just short of the front desk. He quickly killed the engine and then laid down, pulling the jacket over him.

He laid back, peeking out through the tiniest of openings, seeing a few zombies congregating at the window. They moaned, smacking their decrepit hands against it, seemingly unsure of what to make of the situation.

Anytime now Bryan, Michael thought, wrinkling his nose at the putrid scent of old, dead flesh in the car.

As if on cue, gunfire erupted outside. Four shots went off in rapid succession, and Michael watched as the creatures by his window slowly lost interest in the car, and wandered off towards the parking lot.

Michael sat silently for another minute, as the gunfire continued in the parking lot. He shifted in his seat so he could see out the passenger side, relieved to see nothing directly by the car. The lights reflecting off of the front desk illuminated the immediate area, but faded the further it got. He could barely make out the far wall, about thirty yards away, and he frantically scanned it for a door, straining his eyes.

He caught the faintest bit of movement, locking in on it and seeing a few more shadowy figures coming from the darkness, attracted to the noise outside. Finally the reflected light caught the flashy tennis shoes of a zombie, lighting up the area just enough that he could see a door frame.

Got it, he thought, and focused on what he could make out of the door, disheartened that it seemed to be wide open. The door opened inward into a stairwell, and his stomach sank when he realized he'd have to reach in to get at it. He watched for another moment, seeing

a steady but not overwhelming stream of
zombies coming out.

Before opening the door to the car,
he reached up and yanked off the top light
cover, smashing the tiny bulbs inside. The
last thing he wanted to do was attract
attention to himself by shining a light on
his face.

He slid out the door, taking a knee
beside the back wheel. He readied his
knife, and unattached the top of his
holster so his handgun was readily
available just in case he needed it. He
studied the situation, seeing half a dozen
zombies streaming from the door, spread
out about five yards or so from each
other.

A quick scan of the lobby showed that
it was the only source of the creatures.
He looked outside, seeing the parking lot
filled with them, the occasional gunshot
and muzzle flash in the distance.

As he psyched himself up to go, there
was another large explosion in the
distance, rattling the windows of the
building. *If they weren't coming before,*
he thought bitterly, *they will now.*

He immediately broke cover, moving to
the back wall by the desk and trying to
remain hidden by the darkness. When he
reached ten yards of the door, he broke

off, running over to it with his knife in
the air.

The footsteps alerted a zombie a few
steps away from the door, who turned and
moaned, struggling to find the source of
the noise. The lighting was just enough
that he could see the monster, so he
quickly stabbed it in the head.

More moans came from the door, as
well as behind him as the body hitting the
floor had drawn one of the zombies back.
He darted around, grabbing the retreating
zombie and throwing it towards the door,
hoping that the impact would be far enough
away that it wouldn't bring back any
others.

He stepped forward, stabbing the
fallen creature. As he pulled the knife
out, the first door zombie reached him,
grabbing onto his knife hand with its
rotted claws. Michael struggled to avoid
the bite, twisting his wrist as he went.
More moaning echoed in the stairwell,
multiple mouths calling out in unison for
a fresh meal.

"Fuck it," he grunted, and drew his
handgun with his free hand. He put it
right up to the forehead of the latched-on
zombie and pulled the trigger. The sound
echoed loudly in the small space, and back
into the lobby, immediately causing a
number of creatures to reverse course.

Michael didn't waste time, knowing he suddenly had significantly less of it. He immediately dropped the knife to secure the handgun for better aim and opened fire on the zombies in the doorway. It took several shots to put down the trio in and around the area, but he dropped them.

Moans and footsteps grew louder behind him, but he was more concerned with the echoing sounds in the stairwell. He darted forward, shoving the dead creatures away from the door so he could close it.

There were several zombies on the landing above, staggering towards the last set of stairs. The excitement got to them, and the front couple bounced down the stairs, face first, bodies creating cushions for their excited brethren to slide down.

Michael went into overload, shoving the corpses as quickly as he could before grabbing onto the door and pulling it shut. One of the fallen creatures reached out, grabbing the base of the door as he tried to secure it. He kicked hard, freeing the arm, the sound of the door slamming like music to his ears.

He whipped around to face the half-dozen zombies within a few yards of him. He raised his gun and fired three quick shots, dropping the lead ghoul. He aimed

at the next one, but when he squeezed the
trigger, there was only a dull *click*.

He looked around frantically for his
dropped knife, but couldn't find it in the
darkness. So Michael did the only thing he
could do, which was to try and escape. He
ran to the back wall, moving up against it
quickly to avoid being caught. The ghouls
followed his footsteps, snarling with
hunger.

When he reached the front desk, he
looked outside and saw a small wall of
creatures moving back towards him, drawn
by the handgun fire. He hesitated, knowing
he'd never survive fighting his way out.

He slid across the hood of the car,
landing a quickly throwing open the door
and leaping inside. He secured the locks
and hit beneath the jacket again. He
breathed heavily as one of the zombies
reached the car, hands smacking wetly
against the windows.

Okay buddy, he thought, *I did my
part, now hurry up and do yours so you can
come rescue my ass!*

Bryan watched his friend careening through the crowd of zombies in the sedan, disappearing into the lobby of the hotel. The bulk of the zombie horde in the parking lot began to turn around to follow the vehicle, prompting him to ready the hunting rifle.

He took aim, honing in on the back of a zombie's head and firing. Due to the distance and darkness, he missed badly, but it didn't really matter. What mattered was that the noise got the creature to turn around and head towards him instead.

"Come on bud, you can do better than that," he berated himself, and aimed again. This time his bullet punched through the zombie's face. He didn't stop to admire his handiwork, instead immediately firing at the next monster.

After four quick shots, he lowered his weapon to get a read on things. The majority of the zombies were heading towards him, dozens of them, all shambling across the lot, the closest being fifty yards away.

"Well, at least this part of the plan is working," he muttered, and fired a few more times before pausing to reload.

With his gun ready for action again, he stood up to begin retreating. He scanned the lot and made sure every single zombie in sight lumbered towards him. He ran across the street to the back end of the restaurant. The door had been completely removed, and it was a bit larger than a standard doorway because it was for deliveries.

He darted inside, did a quick sweep to make sure it was still clear, and then took up position in the open doorway. He aimed his gun and fired a few more rounds, making sure the undead knew exactly where he was. As he stood and waited for them to get there, another bomb went off in the distance.

"Hopefully they're getting the job done up there," Bryan murmured, and took a deep breath as the horde got within ten yards of the door.

He backed up, remaining in the hallway leading to the kitchen, to continue to make sure the creatures knew he was there. "That's it!" he called. "Come and get some!"

The first zombie made it to the doorway, with several others excitedly approaching behind it. Bryan walked slowly backwards into the kitchen, a large area that could have easily housed a dozen line cooks.

The monsters filtered into the building, and he fired off another shot to make sure the others kept on coming. The round hit a zombie in the shoulder, not slowing it down even a little.

Bryan reached the swinging doors to the dining room and kicked down the doorstop as he backed through it to make sure they stayed open. It took several minutes, but a few dozen creatures found their way into the dining room. He made his way over to the front door, waiting on the horde to get a little thicker before bailing out.

When they were within breathing distance, he turned to leave, but several zombies pushed against the glass from the outside. He snapped back, pulling up his gun and firing. The bullet shattered the window on the door, dropping the zombie, but freed up the space for several more to push into the gap.

Bryan stood there, petrified and dumbfounded, until a rotted hand grabbed him from behind. The grip was tight, but his reaction was to jerk away, narrowly sparing him from a lethal bite to the face.

He shoved the zombie back and retreated around the empty space on the side of the dining room. He frantically flipped tables towards the growing mass of creatures, buying him precious seconds. He

looked around, seeing zombies coming down
every available avenue of escape.

     He contemplated just making a run for
the fire exit near the kitchen, but there
were easily a dozen creatures blocking his
path. As he frantically looked around, the
zombies backed him into the corner.

     Panic set in as they grew closer. He
finally turned around and began firing
wildly at the windows. Three quick rounds
pierced one, shattering it, and he ran as
hard as he could towards it, putting his
foot on a booth cushion and diving
forward.

     The glass wasn't completely clear of
the window, several shards cutting into
his arms and stomach as he flew through
it. He landed hard on the ground, the wind
flying from his lungs, and he laid there,
gasping for air.

     At the sound of footsteps, he
struggled to flip over and aimed his rifle
from the hip.

     "Whoa, whoa!" Mateo cried, raising
his hands.

     Bryan dropped the rifle with a gasp
of relief, and Mateo and Fingers knelt
down to help him up.

     "Jesus, man, are you okay?" Mateo
asked as Bryan staggered to his feet.

     He looked down at his wounds and
winced. "It's not a bite," he said through

clenched teeth. "I took a header out the window and took some damage."

Mateo studied him for a moment, checking over his wounds just to be sure.

Bryan grunted and shoved them away, bracing himself on his knees to catch his breath. "Christ man, you can strip search me if you fucking want to," he spat.

Mateo raised his hands again, nodding. "It's all good, man," he replied gently. "Can't be too careful, you know."

Bryan nodded, his anger fading, as Fingers stepped away to the front of the restaurant. He shook his head at the huge hole in the door.

"Supposed to be a barricade, dumbass," he muttered, and pulled a lighter from his pocket. He found the fuse on the outside of the store, and lit it, watching it vanish into the building. He headed around where his companions still were and found the other two fuses. "You might wanna back up a little bit," he warned, and lit them.

The trio moved away from the eatery, heading towards the back and in the direction of the hotel. When they reached the rear, there were a few more zombies still pushing to get into the building.

Fingers waved for the men to join him behind some bushes. "We'll have a little cleanup to do," he said quietly, "but the bulk of them should be taken care of."

Mateo nodded. "Let's hope that this one isn't a-"

Before he could say 'dud,' a gigantic *boom* echoed from within the restaurant. Every window in the building exploded, and part of the roof caved in. A fire licked the sky, illuminating the area.

Fingers smirked. "You were saying?"

"Looks like that fire is gonna take care of our cleanup," Mateo replied.

Fingers nodded. "You're probably right, but just to be safe," he said, turning to Bryan, "do you mind staying behind and keeping watch?"

The wounded man cocked his head. "Where are you off to?" he asked shakily.

"Go see if Michael got his job done," Fingers replied, and waved for Mateo to follow him.

They headed across the street to the hotel parking lot. There were a few dead bodies on the ground as they approached the entrance, and five creatures banging on a car in the lobby.

"You think he's in there?" Mateo asked, motioning to the sedan with his cleaver.

Fingers shrugged. "I think regardless, we gotta take those suckers out." He drew his handgun and casually led the way into the lobby as Mateo clanged his blades together to draw the zombies' attention.

A few of them immediately broke away, shambling towards an easier meal. Mateo leapt forward and made quick work of them with his flashing silver. Fingers took the easy approach, walking up to the two creatures left that were still fixated on the car door, and executing them at point blank range with a bullet to the back of the head.

Mateo finished off the last remaining zombie on the passenger side and then peered inside.

Fingers knocked on the driver's side window. "Hey, anybody alive in there?" he asked.

Michael dropped the jacket, giving a smile and a thumbs up before opening the door. "Man, am I glad to see you guys," he blurted. "How we looking?"

"Just a few stragglers," Fingers said, "nothing more."

Michael nodded as he got out of the car. "Fucking A," he said with a sigh of relief. "I got the stairwell door secured, but I haven't checked any of the back rooms in the lobby yet."

"It's all good," Fingers assured him, "we'll take care of it together."

As they turned towards the back, honking echoed in the lot. They turned around just in time to see two shuttles arriving, stopping just short of the entrance. They stepped out to greet them, and a red-haired figure hopped out first.

"Are we good?" Wendy asked.

Fingers nodded. "Yeah, good enough to unload," he replied. "We got a couple of stragglers to deal with, but we can manage."

"Are you sure?" she demanded in her no-nonsense tone.

He nodded again. "Yeah, it's safe in the corner of the lobby," he assured her. "We'll keep Michael on them as we wrap up. Besides, you still got two more loads to do."

She turned away and threw her hand in the air, motioning for the buses to unload. "All right everybody, get a move on!" she barked as people began pouring out. "We're on a tight timeline here, people!"

Vulnerable civilians began to unload as quickly as they could from the buses, and Michael and Mateo corralled them into a corner of the lobby. Fingers stepped aside and sidled up next to Wendy, who turned to him with a stern expression.

"Do you think you're gonna make it?" he asked quietly.

She checked her watch. One hour and fifty-two minutes remaining. She pursed her lips. "Hopefully Zion is able to come through with a delay."

CHAPTER EIGHT

Zion sat on the ground just outside of the parking garage. There were a couple of emergency lights set up on either side of the entrance, shooting out into the distance to make sure there would be no unwanted visitors.

Hammering metal, yelling, welding, and grinding echoed from the garage as the students prepared the loppers to do their job. Zion looked down at his watch. One hour and eight minutes.

Come on Wendy, we need you here, he thought urgently. *Ninety-minute round trip, you should be back here loading up by now.*

He stared out into the distance, jaw clenched, and there was a rustle behind him as Cheryl approached.

"Mind if I join you?" she asked.

He motioned for her to sit down next to him, and she did so, the two of them leaning up against the wall. "So how we looking?" he asked.

"Just heard from Wendy, and they're getting close," she replied.

He checked his watch again, shaking his head as he did the math. "What about Jermaine?"

"He's still keeping an eye on the horde," Cheryl said. "Said he was able to break up a good number of them."

Zion rubbed his forehead. "Did he define good number?"

"He did not," she said shortly, shaking her head.

"Let's hope that brother is being modest," he said with a sigh. "We're gonna need a hell of a stand if we're gonna get everybody out of here."

Cheryl nodded, curling her knees up to her chest. "I know," she agreed. "Just to play it safe, I've been prioritizing the most vulnerable being evacuated first. The last bunch heading out are mostly healthy people, with a few of the trainees."

"What about the hardcore experienced guys?" Zion asked.

She shook her head. "Most of them went with the first load," she explained. "If Mateo and those guys weren't successful, I wanted to make sure those people had a fighting chance."

"Wendy say what the situation was down there?" he asked.

Cheryl drummed her fingers on her knees. "She didn't, but it must have been secure enough for her to feel comfortable about leaving those people behind," she mused.

"Good enough for me," Zion replied with a nod.

Tori poked her head out from the open garage door. "Sorry to interrupt," she said. "Just wanted to let you know that we need about ten minutes and then we'll be ready to go."

"Thanks," Cheryl replied with a smile.

"They looking pretty good?" Zion asked, raising an eyebrow.

Tori pushed her glasses up her nose and shrugged. "At the very least, it's going to be interesting to see them in action," she admitted. "Never seen what a spinning blade can do to the human body. So silver lining, I suppose."

Cheryl blinked at her in horror, but Zion simply smiled and chuckled.

"I can see why Calvin likes you," he said.

Tori held up a finger. "Speaking of Calvin, he said he could use your help," she said.

"Tell him I'll be right there," Zion said, and the small blonde nodded and headed back inside. He got to his feet and offered Cheryl a hand up.

She shook her head. "I'm just gonna hang out here for a minute," she said. "Just need to collect myself."

"All right," Zion said, lowering his hand. "Just one thing, though. I want you on this next load."

She immediately shook her head, eyes steely. "I'm a leader, which means I don't leave until everyone does."

"You may be *a* leader," he replied, "but I'm *the* leader. I'll be the last one out, which is exactly why you need to go now." He crossed his arms. "If this last load doesn't happen, or if I don't make it out, these people are gonna need you." She tried to open her mouth to argue, but he held up a hand. "Wendy's a warrior, same thing with my sister, but you got something they don't," he said.

She pursed her lips. "What's that?"

"You know how to bend people to your will," Zion explained. "I don't know how receptive Edward is going to be to everybody coming to town, but I do know that if you got your verbal talons into him, there's a damn good chance it'll work out."

She nodded, defeated. "I'll be on this trip," she promised. "You have my word."

Zion gave her a firm nod before heading into the garage. There was a hive of activity as the four kids worked hard on the mowers. Each of them had a tall metal pole sticking out of the front

engine block, with a few civilians helping
them out by holding stuff up for welding.
A few people brought in weights from the
gym, setting them on top of the mowers.

As Zion watched on, he noticed Calvin
waving at him beside the truck.

"Tori says we're under ten from
heading out," Zion said as he approached.

Calvin nodded. "Sounds about right,
but I need your help with something
first."

"Ain't no time to be playing
wingman," his friend teased.

The sniper rolled his eyes. "Well I
already got the girl, so I don't need a
wingman," he drawled. "What I do need is
your brute strength, and thoughts."

"Whatcha thinking?" Zion asked.

Calvin motioned for his friend to
follow him to the far corner of the
garage. There was a huge stack of
cinderblocks there, maybe forty or so.

"I was thinking, we got that rebar in
the truck that we were gonna use as a last
resort to stab these fuckers," he said,
"but what if we could trip some of them
up?"

Zion furrowed his brow in confusion,
shaking his head.

Calvin grabbed two blocks, setting
them down on the ground about six feet
apart, the holes facing each other from

side to side. "Now picture that with half a dozen rebar bolts through there," he said, motioning. "Stack them two high, put a few at the back to reinforce it. Probably ain't gonna last too long, but it could very well trip up several batches of them. Every minute counts, you know."

"That's true," Zion replied thoughtfully, "but the problem is that there's not going to be a way to secure them to the ground, so they're just gonna get knocked over."

Calvin's face fell. "No worries man," he said. "Just trying to think outside the box." He started to walk back, but Zion continued staring at the blocks.

"Hold up," he said, forcing his friend to stop. "Your original idea might not work, but we can still use these."

Calvin turned to him. "How so?"

"These things are heavy and rigid," Zion said, "so if I was to throw them off of the back of the truck, I could knock some of those things over."

The sniper grinned. "Zombie cinder block bowling?"

"Hell yeah," Zion replied with a chuckle. "Go get one of the trucks out of the main lot and bring it around back. We'll start getting it loaded up."

Calvin nodded and ran off. Zion perked up when he heard buses honking and

made his way outside as Wendy jumped out
of one of the shuttles.

"Here for the next load," she
announced.

Zion checked his watch. One hour and
two minutes. "Cutting this close, ain't
you?"

"Next time we'll have to steal
something that has more than a go-kart
engine in it," she snapped.

"I'm sure Fingers and Calvin can whip
something up," Zion replied. "Assuming
Fingers is still kicking, that is."

The redhead nodded. "He's good, as
are the rest of the boys," she reported.
"They did good down there."

"All right, let's move!" Cheryl
bellowed from the doorway. "Move your ass
like your people's lives depend on it!"

Civilians rushed out of the parking
garage, carrying bags full of possessions.
All they have left in the world.

Zion turned back to Wendy. "Now you
hurry back," he said. "We're gonna buy you
as much time as we can."

"It was eighty-eight minutes door to
door, including unloading at the hotel,"
Wendy replied. "Add three minutes to get
the next load on here, and five minutes to
get past the crossroads."

Zion wrinkled his nose. "If you want to speed a little, I won't complain," he said.

They shared a nod, and she retreated to the buses. He checked his watch again, clearing the timer and putting in ninety-six minutes, clicking start as they drove off. He stared at the ticking numbers, and his heartbeat quickened a little.

The final goal was in sight. They had to make it.

CHAPTER NINE

Two trucks sped down the interstate, ready to encounter the horde. They didn't have to go far before they ran into Jermaine, who was in the middle of the road, waving them down. They were about three-quarters of a mile away from the crossroads. Calvin and Zion manned the cinderblock truck, and the college kids drove the trailer truck.

"Man, I was starting to get worried!" Jermaine cried as they pulled up.

Zion leaned on the window. "You know I always come through," he replied. "So how far out are they?" he asked.

"About five hundred yards up," Jermaine said, pointing, "can't miss 'em."

Zion nodded and cocked his head. "You thin 'em out good?"

"Kinda," Jermaine admitted, scratching the back of his head. "There are some big packs in the front and some breaks, but they filled back in a bit. I used everything I had against them."

Zion held out his fist. "I know you did, man," he said, and after a firm fist bump, he got off of the truck. Calvin slid over into the driver's seat, and Zion sauntered over to the second truck, where Jack sat behind the wheel. "Okay, start getting set up here," he said.

Tori leaned over from the passenger's side. "I was thinking we set one up here, and retreat about a hundred yards before the next one," she said, and pushed her glasses up on her nose. "Gives us a chance to adjust our strategy if we need to."

"Have at it, girl," Zion replied, nodding. "Your boyfriend and I are gonna ride up ahead to try and slow 'em up a bit." He checked his watch. Eighty-seven minutes. "We need to keep them on this side of the crossroads for eighty-seven minutes. So do what you need to do."

Tori gave him a thumbs up as Jack began a three-point turn so that the trailer was facing the horde. Zion headed back to Calvin's truck and hopped up into the bed, waving his hand in the air.

"Let's move it!" he cried.

Calvin popped it into gear and drove slowly down the interstate. The headlights cut through the night, and it wasn't long before they caught a glimpse of the horde.

Thousands of zombies stretched across the northbound side of the road, with a few on the other side of the median, all moving as one. Zion shook his head when he saw there were only a few breakaway groups that had swelled in strength to several dozen each.

"Well, looks like those molotovs were a bust," Calvin called through the back window.

Zion clenched his jaw. "Hopefully the cinder blocks won't be," he said. "Get me in position."

His friend spun the truck around so that Zion faced the horde. The red brake lights illuminated the immediate vicinity, but didn't cut too far into the darkness, only about ten yards or so. He picked up a cinderblock and tested the heft in his hands, loosening his knees and waiting for the undead to get within striking distance.

The moans and footsteps grew louder with each passing second. After a moment, the first creature stepped into the light, ghouls bathed in a hellish red glow. Zion immediately lobbed the cinderblock at the first creature he saw, smashing it in the face and knocking it to the ground.

"Inch it up every few seconds!" he called back to Calvin.

The sniper complied, basically letting off the brake and allowing the truck to move a bit on its own in reverse. Zion chucked a few more blocks at the front edge of the horde, knocking down creatures and causing several more to stumble.

Gotta break these things up, he thought, and then began launching several cement blocks into the darkness, hearing the impact crunching bones he couldn't see. After several throws, he smacked the hood of the truck.

"Let's get back to the line," he said. "Gotta see how the lopper works before we use any more of these."

Calvin sped up, driving a couple hundred yards up to the first machine. Harold and Missy were there with Jack, making the last minute adjustments. The first mower was the smallest one they had, enough for a small home in the city. The most extended up from the engine, with two metal bars sticking out, one of which just cleared the seat and the other a foot above that. They were staggered, looking like a weathervane.

"Let's get this thing started up," Zion said, "they'll be here in just a couple of minutes."

Harold motioned for Missy and Jack to back up as he turned the key on the engine. It roared to life, idling nicely. He ducked down so he was below the seat before flipping a switch on the control panel. Then he crawled out of the way as the metal spokes began to rotate.

The three college kids hopped into the back of the truck with Zion as they watched the contraption pick up steam, rotating rapidly. They could hear the blades whipping through the air like a chopper.

Zion nodded in approval. "That's certainly going to leave a mark," he said, and smacked the roof. "Back us up, Calvin."

The sniper moved, and then they stopped about forty yards from the mower, turning the truck around so that the headlights could illuminate the battlefield. They anxiously awaited the arrival of the horde. It felt like an eternity for them to arrive, with Zion constantly checking his watch.

It was nearly ten minutes later before the horde came into view.

The lead zombie shambled towards the weapon and was quickly met with a metallic blow to the face. The impact tore off the front part of its skull, dropping the creature to the ground. More creatures met the same fate, blood and bone spraying everywhere, the moans drowned out by metal whirrs crunching bone.

The college kids let out whoops and began exchanging high fives, vibrating in their seats.

"Don't get too excited," Zion said tersely, "they're coming around the sides."

They sobered and turned to the mower, and while it did an admirable job of knocking down creatures in the center of the highway, hundreds of creatures walked past it as if it wasn't even there.

Calvin popped the truck into reverse and backed up a little as the ghouls got closer to them. As they moved, the mower began to rock back and forth from the constant impact of the blades. Within a few more seconds, it became completely unstable, flipping over onto its side, crashing to a halt.

Jack pressed his hands to his forehead. "My god, what did we get?" he groaned. "Fifty? Sixty?"

"That's not gonna do it," Missy added, crestfallen.

Zion checked his watch. Seventy-two minutes. He glanced at the crossroads, seeing it in the distance. He shook his head.

"No way in hell we're making this," he muttered. He looked back at the next mower in the middle of the road, about a hundred yards from their location. "Calvin, get us up to the mower," he barked.

The sniper complied, backing up as quickly as he safely could. They reached it and the college kids hopped out of the back to help Tori and Jermaine set up the next lopper.

Zion leaned out the window. "I need y'all to move that to the next lane," he said, pointing to the mower.

"I think it's more effective in the center," Tori replied, pushing her glasses up her nose.

Zion nodded. "Normally you'd be right, but we gotta do something drastic," he replied, and inclined his head to Calvin. "Get the truck across this lane," he instructed, pointing out the window.

"What?" His friend gaped.

"Get the truck across the lane!" Zion demanded. "Push it up against the end of the concrete median."

Calvin shook his head, but didn't question him, turning and nosing the vehicle against the concrete, nothing but grass on the other side.

"Make sure those blades have enough clearance on the truck," Zion said as he hopped out of the passenger's seat.

Jack scratched the back of his head. "A horde that size is gonna push through this truck in no time."

"Unless I'm up there keeping them off of it," Zion replied, and the group all froze.

"Are you crazy?!" Harold burst out,
eyes wide. "Those things will swarm over
you!"

Zion simply pointed to his watch.
"Sixty-eight minutes," he said firmly,
"and they're seven hundred yards away. I
know those things are slow, but they ain't
that slow."

"At least let us stay and fight with
you," Jack said helplessly.

Zion shook his head. "Nope." He
pointed at the kid. "You need to get the
big mower set up back by the crossroads,
and figure out some other way to slow them
down. I'll be alright."

Harold waved him over while the rest
of the group reluctantly piled into the
trailer truck to get ready to retreat to
the crossroads.

"Okay," the kid began, motioning as
he spoke, "when they start getting close,
you need to turn it on here, and flip this
switch. Just make sure you stay low,
because those things will kick right on."

Zion nodded and extended his fist for
a bump, and Harold awkwardly bumped him
back. The older man chuckled and waved for
him to run back to the truck. After a
nervous nod, he took off, and Zion stared
towards the coming horde, still a hundred
yards away.

"Looks like I'm gonna have to go all Gandalf on your asses," he declared. "You shall not pass."

221

Zion checked his watch. Sixty-one minutes. It seemed like an eternity when the forces of the dead were marching towards him.

"Seven hundred yards, give or take," he muttered. "Seven minutes per hundred yards, which means I still need to buy twelve minutes." He knelt down beside the mower as the ghouls crept within fifteen yards of him. "Let's get this beast started up."

He turned the key and hit the switch before rolling out of the way. Within seconds, the blades rotated rapidly, the breeze from the whipping metal blowing cold on his face.

He nodded, bouncing from foot to foot, psyching himself up for the upcoming battle before hopping up into the back of the truck. He inspected the cinder blocks, seeing about two dozen remaining, as well as a few lengthy pieces of rebar. He picked up the first block, looking at the coming horde.

Zion took a deep breath, pulled his arm back, and then flung it forward, sending the cement flying through the air. It went about four rows deep into the horde, cracking a ghoul in the face and dropping it.

He didn't waste any time, continuously grabbing blocks and lobbing them as far as he could, doing everything he could to create gaps in the crowd, trying to relieve the stress on the machine. After half a dozen throws, the first batch of zombies reached the truck, gently pressing up against it, reaching out for Zion's legs.

He stepped back as far as he could and threw a couple more blocks, creating little pockets within the mass. He picked up a piece of rebar and began using it like a spear, forcefully jamming it into the skulls of the zombies at the edge of the truck. The first few slumped over the edge of the bed, giving him a buffer from the reaching monsters behind.

As he did this, the first batch reached the lopper, delivering on the promise. Luckily the blades rotated away from him, so the body parts shot into the wooded area beside the road.

With the zombies directly in front of him taken care of, Zion went back to tossing blocks, this time focused on the groups approaching the mower. He lifted one over his head and threw it almost straight down, knocking over several creatures before they reached the spinning blade of death.

The process went on for several minutes, Zion taking a breather from throwing blocks to resume his rebar attack, thinning out his area so he had room to operate.

But eventually, enough of the thousand-strong horde pressed up against the truck that it began to move.

Zion threw more blocks, knocking over creatures closer to the truck than the lopper, which allowed for the ghouls to bunch up around it. There was a repeated sickening *thump, thump, thump* from the mower as a batch of zombies entered the kill zone all at once.

He glanced over to see it start to wobble, the pole causing the engine to smack up against the interior walls of the mower. Just as another group of creatures walked into it, he saw it failing, and knew it was time to abandon ship.

Zion leapt from the back of the truck, narrowly missing one of the blades that broke off and snagged the bed of the truck. He darted forward several yards before stopping to turn around. The machinery held back the bulk of the horde for nearly a minute, before the weight of the ghouls forced a hole between the mower and truck.

He looked at his watch. Fifty-four minutes. He nodded to himself, pleased with what he'd managed to accomplish.

Just need five more, he thought, *hopefully the big boy lopper can do it.*

He turned and jogged back to the line near the crossroads. It only took a few minutes to reach the college kids, doing some last-minute adjustments on the massive lopper in the middle of the road.

"Holy shit man, you okay?" Calvin blurted, approaching from the truck.

Zion nodded. "Yeah, that was not a lot of fun," he admitted, "but it did buy us some time." He glanced at the mower and noticed they'd attached six-foot chains to the bottom rung of the blades. "Is that gonna work?" he asked.

Missy shrugged as she checked one of the connections. "In theory," she replied.

"Good enough for me," Zion replied with a nod. He looked back at the truck and trailer, and inclined his head to Calvin. "How much rebar we got left?" he asked.

The sniper shrugged. "I don't know, fifteen sticks or so?"

"Let's hitch it to the trailer," Zion suggested, motioning as he spoke, "jam it through the sides so it sticks out as far as possible."

Calvin cocked his head. "What are you thinking?"

"We still gotta buy at least five minutes," Zion explained, "and even with the upgrades, I don't think the lopper is gonna be able to handle it."

His friend nodded, recognition dawning on his face when he realized what he was suggesting. "So you're gonna sacrifice the truck?" he asked.

"Don't worry, it's Fingers' truck, remember?" Zion asked with a lopsided grin.

Calvin opened his mouth, and then closed it, thinking for a moment before shrugging. "That's a good point," he admitted. "But, what happens if Wendy doesn't pick us up?"

"Then you gonna have to show a leg, cause we will be hitchhiking," Zion quipped. "But, if it makes you feel better…" He turned and cupped a hand around his mouth. "Jermaine!"

His companion ran over, cocking his head. "What's up?" he asked.

"I need you to go to the crossroads," Zion said. "When Wendy shows up with the transports, I need you to tell her we need a ride."

Jermaine gave him a thumbs up. "On it." As he ran off into the darkness, Zion clapped Calvin on the shoulder.

"Come on," he said, "we got work to
do."

There were eleven minutes left on the clock as Calvin slammed one more bit of rebar into the side of the trailer. Nearly a dozen spikes stuck out of both sides, with four feet of reach. Zion hopped in the truck and carefully pulled it around the lopper, setting it up in the middle of the road.

"All right, we're good," Calvin announced. "Save us a few pieces of rebar just in case."

Zion held out a hand to Jack as he hopped out of the driver's seat. "I need one of those weights," he said. "And a little chain if you got it."

Jack grabbed a twenty-pound dumbbell and a few feet of chain from the lopper, bringing it over to him. Zion used the chain to tie the wheel down so it remained in position. He looked up, seeing that the horde was within fifty yards of them.

"All right, stand back," Zion warned, and Jack took a few steps back.

Calvin, however, jogged forward. "Hold up a second," he said, and darted to the passenger side, opening the glove box. He pulled out a bottle of whiskey, and headed to the hood where he poured it all over the truck and then lit it up.

Zion nodded in approval. "Bonus fire damage, I dig it," he said.

Calvin jogged back, and Zion leaned into the truck, popping the engine into drive. He looked back at the rebar, seeing just how far he needed to get to avoid being torn to bits. He took a deep breath and then tossed the dumbbell onto the gas pedal.

The tires screeched as he dove back, narrowly missing the rebar as the truck sped by. The flames illuminated the path as the vehicle of death tore off towards the horde. It picked up speed rapidly, slamming into the front batch of zombies. It lost a little speed, but plowed through a good portion of them. The rebar on the side didn't deliver kill shots, however it was forceful enough to lop off legs, slowing the shambling dead.

Zion held up a victory fist, a few of the kids letting out hoots of excitement as the vehicle tore through the zombies.

"Harold, hit the lopper," Zion declared as the ghouls still standing ambled on.

Harold hit the switch before rolling out of the way, the extra length of chain making the machine extra dangerous. The group rallied behind the monstrous machine, watching as the truck vanished from view, overtaken by the dead.

The front edge of the pack slowly made its way to the lopper, the group holding its collective breath that the chain enhancement would work. The first zombies came into range, and the tip of the chain took off a ghoul's jaw, lopping it off into the woods. More creatures poured into the kill zone, losing chunks of flesh before their skulls cracked.

The heavier machine held its own, not losing its balance just yet, however even with the extended reach, there were still pockets where the monsters could slip through.

"Rebar!" Zion cried, and Calvin tossed him a piece.

He ran up to the coming zombies on one side, spearing one through the chest and driving it back into the reach of the chain, taking off the back part of its skull. He swung wildly, doing everything he could do to hold the monsters at bay.

Calvin pulled out his gun and began shooting on the other flank, picking off creatures one by one. "You four, get back to the crossroads!" he barked.

Tori clenched her jaw and stared at him with a worried gaze, but he shot her a wink before turning and continuing to fire.

The kids retreated, leaving the two warriors alone to stem the tide. The battle went on for several minutes, with Zion pushing hard to keep zombies from breaking the line. Eventually the lopper grew overwhelmed from turning the zombies into a puree and began to wobble.

"Watch it!" Calvin warned, and Zion glanced over, darting back just as the machine went haywire. There was a deafening blast of metal on pavement, shredding several dozen zombies as it gave its last bit of strength.

Zion ran back to Calvin, the duo standing forty yards from the crossroads, looking on at the coming horde. He looked down at his watch.

"Four minutes," he said, and raised his chin. "You think we got it?"

Calvin clapped him on the back. "Without a doubt, brother," he replied. "Without a doubt."

They shared a fist bump and prepared to make a final stand to hold off the horde. Once the creatures were within ten yards of them, honking cut through the air behind them.

Zion and Calvin looked back, seeing two shuttles sitting at the crossroads. Wendy flicked on the internal light, showing that everyone was aboard.

The duo didn't hesitate, turning and sprinting for the buses, leaving the horde in the dust. As they reached the door, the redhead put a hand on her hip at the top of the stairs.

"You boys need a ride?" she asked.

Zion grinned. "Fuck yeah we do," he replied.

Wendy pointed to the other bus. "I think your girlfriend is on the other one," she said. "She's cute, you should hang on to her."

"I intend to!" Calvin declared and then ran off to the other bus as Zion zipped up to join Wendy.

She patted the driver on the shoulder. "Let's roll."

The buses rolled across the crossroads safely, and Zion checked his watch. Two minutes left.

"You're early," he said with a smile.

She shrugged sheepishly. "We may have sped a little."

Zion flopped down in a seat in the front row, shaking his head. The reality of the situation fell down on his shoulders like a ton of bricks.

"I can't believe it's all gone," he said, scrubbing his hands down his face. "Everything we built, just obliterated. And all those people we left behind."

Wendy sat next to him. "Who, like Adam and his group?" she asked. "We got him well stocked up, so he can ride it out until we get back. Or whoever sent those damn missiles. Would be nice if they came and lended a hand."

"Nah, this is on us," he replied, eyes darkening. "God help whoever sent those missiles if they ever run into me."

She studied his expression, watching the quiet rage boil up in him. Rather than press the issue, she patted him on the leg gently.

"Monique is gonna be happy to see you," she said, hoping to defuse him. When he simply continued to stare out into the darkness, she got to her feet. "I'm going to go check on the others. It'll be okay, Zion. Just be thankful we got so many people out safely."

He nodded slightly, his chest burning with the anger building towards the people who destroyed his town, his community. *It won't be today,* he thought. *It won't be tomorrow. But soon, someone is gonna pay.*

END

Up Next: The invasion of Seattle begins as Sergeant Copeland leads a daring mission to the north of the city in "Seattle - Part 1"

DEAD AMERICA: THE NORTHWEST INVASION

BOOK 3

SEATTLE - PART 1

BY DEREK SLATON

© 2020

CHAPTER ONE

Day Zero +23

Captain Kersey sat in a small back office at the tiny regional airport at midnight. He studied several maps of the Seattle area, multi-colored marks flowing in various directions across them. The desk before him with the radio on it was buried in papers.

He took a deep breath. The responsibility on his shoulders was heavy. Even though he was just a Captain, and a newly promoted one at that, General Stephens, Adams, and the entirety of the presidential inner circle valued his on-the-ground experience so much that they'd given him command of barricade and diversion forces.

To the outside observer, that wouldn't sound all that impressive, however, to those in the know, it showed great confidence in the Captain. These three missions—the northern barricade, Mercer Island, and the downtown run—were all vital to the success of the mission.

Kersey pored over the maps as the noises outside grew louder. More men moved in, machinery came in and out. The moment was upon them, the biggest single operation since the invasion of Normandy.

Not only was this larger, it was arguably more important. That had been a battle for freedom, but this was for the survival of the nation, and possibly the human race.

As he contemplated, brow furrowed, the radio sprung to life.

"Captain Kersey, do you copy?" Stephens' voice came through.

Kersey picked up the receiver and stood up from the maps, refocusing his attention. "Yes, General."

"What's your status?" Stephens asked.

"The northern blockade team is gearing up," he replied. "They'll be airborne in fifteen. As soon as the planes return, they'll refuel and the Mercer Island squad will take off."

"Good," the General came back. "And the interstate team for downtown?"

Kersey leaned on his hand. "Last I heard, Corporal Bretz and his team were securing the trucks and awaiting dawn," he said. "With where they're going, they'll need the daylight."

"Understood," Stephens replied. "I appreciate the work you're doing for us."

The Captain nodded. "It's my job, General," he said. "And to be frank, you put your faith in me and I want to make sure you never think it was misplaced."

"I appreciate that as well," Stephens replied. "I'll never complain about being made to look good." They chuckled together and then he continued, "I do have one additional task for you, Captain."

"Of course, sir," Kersey said.

"As you know, ammunition is at a premium," the General began, "so in addition to the clear teams that will be trailing behind the main force, I need you to set aside some scroungers. They will need to look in every business that would carry guns and ammo, and even homes if they have time."

The Captain nodded. "Yes sir, I will make it happen."

"I know you will," Stephens replied confidently.

Kersey took a deep breath. "Sir, if there's nothing else," he said slowly. "I need to brief Sergeant Copeland and his team before they head off."

"Of course, Captain," the General replied. "I look forward to your updates."

The line went dead and Kersey took a beat before setting the receiver down and glancing at his watch. It was just past midnight.

"Okay," he said to himself, straightening his shoulders. "Game time."

He picked up a few of the maps of the northern area, the town of Burlington. It was a sleepy little villa just across the river from Mount Vernon, and if things went well, it would be a perfect choke point for the hundreds of thousands of zombies looming in the north.

He walked out of the room, maps tucked under his arm, and onto the airfield. There were six small planes lined up on the runway, pilots standing outside of them and biding their time. He made his way to the hangar at the far end of the field, currently bathed in light, both artificial and from barrel fires to keep the men warm. As he stepped in, Sergeant Copeland approached him immediately.

"Captain Kersey," he said politely, dark skin glimmering in the firelight.

"Sergeant," Kersey replied with a nod. "You boys about ready to go?" he asked, glancing past the burly bald Sergeant at the thirty-four other men prepping their gear for the assault. He pursed his lips, a look of concern crossing his face. "Looks like you're a little light on men there," he said.

Copeland sighed. "Yeah, tell me about it," he agreed. "Two of the planes conked out, so unless someone wanted to hang on to the wings, we weren't getting them there."

"No volunteers, I take it?" Kersey asked with a lopsided smile.

Copeland chuckled. "No, sir," he replied. "Although I'm pretty sure I could get Kowalski to do it on a dare."

Private Kowalski looked up from his pack. "I heard my name," he barked. "Whatever it is, I swear I didn't do it!"

"Must not be talking about any hot women, then," Private Wade quipped from beside him, grinning ear-to-ear.

Kowalski put a hand to his chest in mock offense. "What the hell, man?" he demanded playfully. "I thought us snipers stuck together?"

"If that were true, you wouldn't have cranked up the yacht rock the other day," Wade shot back, pointing a finger at his friend.

Kowalski smirked. "Eh, valid point."

Private Johnson began muttering obscenities behind them as he tried to strap on his parachute. Kersey and Copeland chuckled and shook their heads before the latter snapped his fingers at one of the other men.

"Corporal Dawson," he called.

"Yes, sir?" Dawson's short and stocky frame snapped to attention.

Copeland motioned to the struggling Private. "Can you please help Johnson there before he pulls something?" he asked.

Dawson laughed and turned to help the wild redneck, who was still grunting and huffing in frustration even as he lowered his arms to accept the help.

Kersey handed the maps out to Copeland, and the Sergeant flipped through them quickly. They were printed maps this time instead of hand drawn, with multiple locations circled throughout.

"Not bad quality," Copeland said.

Kersey wrinkled his nose. "Printer ran out of cyan before they all came out, so some of your boys will have to share," he said.

"First world problems, Captain," Copeland replied with a chuckle, shaking his head. "First world problems." He took one of the maps and then handed the stack to Private Mack, who began distributing them amongst the men. "All right boys!" Copeland barked. "Let's settle down. We got a busy-ass morning ahead of us, so we need to go over the game plan."

There was a shuffle as the men settled in, turning towards their Sergeant and holding their maps, a few bending over shared papers. Kersey stepped off to the side to watch the briefing.

"Our primary goal this morning is to block off the I-Five bridge over the river," Copeland began. "The bad news is, it's a four-lane road with thousands of

zombies to the north and south of it. The
good news is, the tools we need to block
it off are already there in the form of
concrete median barriers. Only thing we
need is to go find a way to move them.

"Our secondary goal is to block off
the town bridge to the east. Luckily, this
is only a two-lane bridge, and the
expected enemy push is going to be minimal
compared to the interstate area, so a few
trucks oughta do the trick." He held up
the map, pointing to the north. "There are
going to be three teams working together
to make this happen. Kowalski, Wade," he
said, pointing to the two snipers.

They perked up, sitting at attention
as their names were called.

"Your sniper teams are going to be
landing to the northwest of the river,"
the Sergeant explained. "Assuming you hit
your landing target, you'll be half a mile
from your position." He pointed to a large
shopping center between the interstate and
the surface road leading to the other
bridge. "You're gonna be set up here, in
two teams, one facing each road. Your
mission is to draw as many of those things
to you as possible, giving the bridge team
time to set up the barricade. When you hit
the ground, you start lighting them up,
cause we're going to need them away from

the bridge if we're gonna be able to do our job."

Kowalski's brow furrowed as he studied the map closely, focusing in on a dark section of the interstate. "Question, Sarge," he said, raising his hand.

"What is it, Private?" Copeland asked.

The sniper pointed to the blob. "Any idea what this dark patch on the interstate is?" he asked.

"We're hoping it's just darker pavement," the Sergeant admitted, shaking his head.

The snipers shared a concerned look.

"Hoping?" Kowalski demanded.

Copeland held up a palm. "Relax, Private, you boys are good at what you do," he said confidently. "You'll find a way to get across."

Kowalski and Wade preened with some pride at the praise, even though both knew it was a blatant dismissal of their concern.

"Corporal Dawson," Copeland continued, "your team is up next. While the population to the north in Burlington is around ten thousand, the population to the south in Mount Vernon is closer to thirty-five thousand. And it being mostly residential near the bridge, the sniper diversion teams wouldn't be nearly as effective." He grinned. "So we're gonna have to get a little more creative."

He held up the map, motioning at the landing zone to the southeast of the river, and the group all looked over their papers. There was a long line drawn down a highway running diagonally to the interstate, with a large circle just to the west of the road.

"You'll be landing with us to the southeast of the river," Copeland continued, "then huffing it. It's a three-mile hike through infested territory, but there's no other safe landing zone that's closer."

Dawson nodded. "We'll make do, Sarge," he assured his superior. "Just let us know what needs to be done."

"Good, because you got the most important mission of the day," Copeland declared. "Your target is a car dealership. You have a few mechanics on your team who are going to set the car alarm sensitivity to maximum, which means a stiff breeze will set it off. The rest of you will be spreading the cars out around town, hopefully attracting those things who will keep the cycle going by bumping into them. This won't be perfect, but hopefully it will keep the pressure off of my team on the bridges."

He took a deep breath, looking around at the men, who were nodding and staring down at the maps, murmuring quietly to each other.

Copeland looked to his squad. "You boys are going to be with me," he said. "Our first target is the Super Center just south of the bridge. According to the sat image, there are a few trucks parked in the back, which we'll use for the side bridge. For the main bridge, we'll need to secure some rebar or other pole from the store so we can move those barriers. We got a buttload of them to do, so if you see back braces in the store, grab some."

A light round of chuckles rippled across the men.

"Okay," Copeland continued, clapping his hands together, "let's talk load out. South teams, you got two hundred and ten rounds for your primary, thirty for your side. Sniper team, you've been authorized for double at four-twenty. We're gonna be relying on you to hold the northern front one shot at a time."

Kowalski raised a victory fist. "Don't worry Sarge," he piped up, "we're a competitive bunch, so you can be sure we'll be making every shot count."

"Double check your rations," Copeland reminded them, "and make sure you have a three-day supply, because we could be there for a while before reinforcements arrive. If you need a top off, they're handing stuff out in the next hangar."

Wade raised his hand, and the Sergeant pointed to him. "Who do we talk to about night-vision scopes?" the Private asked.

Copeland glanced over at Kersey, and the Captain took a step forward.

"I was able to score a handful of them, enough for the sniper squad, and one each for the others," he replied. "They'll be waiting for you at the planes."

The Sergeant nodded and then spread his arms, looking around expectantly. "Anybody else got questions?" he asked.

There was a moment of silence, and a few replies in the negative came from some of the men.

"Good," Copeland declared, and rolled a hand over his head. "Get loaded up, we're in the air in five."

Kowalski, Wade, and six other snipers packed tightly into a small aircraft. There was barely room to move between the men and the gear, all squeezed in like a sardine can.

Kowalski looked out over the darkness, catching the occasional glimpse of a building in the rural areas as the moonlight caught windows.

"Hey man, when was the last time you made a jump?" Wade asked, nudging his arm.

Kowalski tilted his head back and forth, unable to move enough to shrug. "I don't know, a year, maybe a year and a half," he said. "What about you?"

"About a week before all this began," Wade replied.

Kowalski blinked at him. "A week?" he asked. "Where the hell were you?"

"This little vacation spot in Colorado," his companion replied.

Kowalski raised an eyebrow at the tattooed sniper in disbelief. "You… you jump for *fun*?"

"Hell yeah I do!" Wade replied, excitement in his eyes. "Try to do fifteen to twenty jumps a year if I can. It's more of a rush than being in a mosh pit."

His companion shook his head. "Dude, this is going to be the first time I've

jumped out of a plane without being paid
to do so," he admitted. "At least I'm
assuming we're not getting paid anymore."

"You're missing out, man," Wade said.
"When we survive this, I'm gonna talk to
the higher-ups about setting up a jump
school."

Kowalski rolled his eyes. "Uh huh,
okay, well, if you need somebody to help
teach those people how to shoot once they
land, give me a shout."

Wade grinned and snaked a hand up to
give him a thumbs up. Kowalski simply
shook his head and leaned back, tapping
the pilot on the shoulder.

"How far out are we from the jump?"
he asked.

The pilot flicked on a small book
light and checked his map and then looked
over his instruments. "We'll be over the
zone in two minutes," he replied.

Kowalski patted his shoulder at an
awkward angle and then pulled his arm back
down to his side. "Okay, listen up," he
declared, getting everyone's attention.
"We're two minutes out. It's gonna be a
low drop, so don't wait too long on
pulling your chute. You all know the
landing zone. We rendezvous at the small
house on the east side of the field.
Questions?" When nobody said anything, he
nodded firmly. "Then let's get ready."

He shuffled over to the door, and waited by it, checking his equipment one last time as the throttle to the engine dialed back to reduce the speed. When the pilot held up his hand, giving the sniper a thumbs up, Kowalski threw open the door and began ushering his men out of the plane.

Right after Wade jumped, Kowalski waved to the pilot and then leapt out into the air himself. The wind rushed by his face as he hurtled towards the ground. His heart raced, blood pumping as fear and adrenaline coursed through him. Kowalski was not a fan of flying through the air.

When he finally pulled the ripcord on his chute, it opened without a hitch, and he finally allowed his body to relax a little. He looked around at the rest of his squad, gracefully floating to the ground. He looked down, checking the field within sight, only a minute or so away. From his vantage point he could also look over the interstate, the bridge, and their target shopping center.

"Holy fuck," he breathed, heart rate tripling at the amount of movement on the road and parking lot outside of the shopping center. "Guess that wasn't just dark pavement," he muttered, and then braced himself for his landing.

He hit the ground hard, stumbling forward and falling onto his hands and knees. Wade approached, chuckling, and helped him back up as he unclipped his chute.

"Need to work on that landing there, bud," Wade teased.

Kowalski grumbled. "Or, I could just *not* jump anymore," he replied.

Wade continued to chuckle as they headed off towards the rally point a few hundred yards away. "You catch the movement on the road?" he finally asked, sobering.

"Yep," Kowalski replied, voice level. "Gonna be a bitch to get around that."

His companion clapped him on the shoulder. "Well, good thing they sent the best of the best."

"Or the best that they could find," Kowalski shot back with a smirk.

Wade rolled his eyes. "Thanks for the morale boost there, bud."

"Anytime," Kowalski replied brightly.

They reached the farmhouse, a tiny rundown shack with a beat-up pickup truck in front of it. Privates Martin and Doyle came around from the other side, walking casually.

"Perimeter is clear," Doyle reported as they approached.

Martin shook his head. "Can't say the same about the road."

"No shit," Wade agreed, "I've seen major festivals that were less crowded."

"Where are the other four at?" Kowalski asked.

Doyle jerked a thumb over his shoulder. "We sent them up ahead to scout the shopping center on this side of the interstate and the road."

"All right," Kowalski replied, "let's go catch up with them and see what we're dealing with."

The quartet hiked across the field, nothing but empty, overgrown grass ahead of them. They were silent as they walked, the daunting task ahead weighing heavy on their shoulders. As they reached the end of the field, the four other snipers crouched near a giant tree, one of them scouting out the shopping center through his scope.

"What do we got?" Kowalski asked.

The sniper lowered his weapon and shook his head, face pale in the moonlight. "Nothing good."

Kowalski and Wade both took a knee, pulling out their rifles to survey the situation. About two hundred yards from their current position was the mid-sized shopping center with several outbuildings on the far end of the lot, close to the interstate. Past that was the interstate itself, and their main target across from that.

Both men's breath hitched at the hundreds of zombies in the lot, like a Black Friday sale gone crazy. The interstate was no better, jam-packed with ghouls. The two men put down their rifles before pulling the group together.

"Obviously the direct approach isn't going to work," Kowalski finally said, swallowing hard. "From what I could tell on the glide in, this group stretches up the road quite a ways."

Martin nodded. "Yeah, it would take way too long to try and circle around them."

"We need to draw them away from the road, create an opening we can slip through," Wade suggested.

Doyle shook his head. "Not gonna do much unless we pull some to the north, too."

Kowalski raised his gun again, looking through the scope to do a rough count of zombies, his mouth going dry when he realized it was in the thousands. He pushed down the anxiety and focused in on the shopping center, seeing a pathway to the back of the anchor store that was mostly clear.

"Hey, take a look at the center building there," he said, nudging Wade.

His companion complied, seeing a pathway through the field to the back of the store. "What am I looking at?" he asked.

"You think you can get to that ladder on the back?" Kowalski asked.

Wade studied the ladder in question, a metal structure with a protective cover that stretched eight feet up before the rungs were exposed. He scoped out the back of the store, seeing a dumpster about fifteen yards away, but also a half a dozen zombies in the immediate vicinity, with dozens more on either side at the far ends of the building.

"Ain't gonna be fun," he admitted, "but I think I can pull it off." He lowered his gun and turned to his companion.

Kowalski nodded. "Good," he said. "That's what I want you to do then. Get up on top and start causing a ruckus."

"What about the northern position?" Martin asked.

Kowalski pointed to two of the kneeling men. "I want you two to handle that."

Private Hurley spoke up from beside them. "That's gonna leave us mighty thin for the main target," he declared.

"Especially when we have two fronts to cover."

"True," Kowalski agreed, "but if we try to cross that sea of death without diversions, we're gonna be a whole lot thinner."

Hurley nodded in defeat. "Heard that," he agreed.

"How far up do you want us?" one of the snipers asked, getting to his feet.

Kowalski contemplated for a few moments, looking at the interstate and picking the crossing point. There was a spot about two hundred yards up from the edge of the parking lot, a short climb up a hill that led to the freeway.

"Two blocks," he said. "Find whatever structure you can get on top of, and start firing."

"What's your ETA?" Wade asked them as they nodded. "Don't wanna start firing too early."

One of the snipers shrugged. "If we're not firing consistently within ten minutes," he replied, "there's a good chance the shots you do hear will be our last."

"Ten minutes it is, then," Wade replied, clapping him on the shoulder.

Kowalski looked around at the group. "Okay, we good?" he asked, and when there was no response, he raised a fist. "All right, let's move."

The two snipers headed off towards the north, and Wade tore off for the shopping center. He stayed low as he moved across the field. The moonlight wasn't exceptionally bright, and while that was difficult for him to see where he was going, it provided him some cover at least.

After a bit, he reached the end of the field, taking a knee in the grass to get a look at the situation. The ladder was forty yards directly in front of him, with half a dozen zombies shambling about. To the left, fifteen ghouls hung out by a door about forty yards away, and to the right was the dumpster with about ten more monsters twenty yards past it.

Gonna have to go silent, Wade thought to himself, *at least initially.*

He pulled out a knife and unlatched the holster on his handgun, just in case. He focused in on the closest zombie that was directly in front of the ladder. He darted out from cover, using the soft ground to muffle his footsteps as he quickly closed the gap. He slowed to a cautious pace as soon as he hit the pavement.

The first zombie had its back to him, making the kill easy. He shoved the blade into the base of its skull, catching the creature as it fell. He gently laid it on the ground to the left of the ladder.

The other creatures milled about aimlessly, not alerted to his presence just yet. He turned his attention to the duo between him and the dumpster. They were close together, about three yards apart, looking away from him. He silently moved up, but his toe kicked a rock that skittered across the asphalt.

Shit, he thought, freezing.

The two closest zombies heard and turned around, immediately opening their mouths to moan. Answering moans erupted from behind him as well.

"Fuck it," Wade muttered and sheathed his knife, pulling his handgun. He popped off two quick rounds into the zombies by the dumpster. This set off a chorus of moans in both directions, so he rushed the bin and threw his weight into it.

It picked up speed, and he rammed it into a trio of ghouls headed his way. The front edge of the dumpster popped up in the air as it rolled over a rotted corpse. He pushed as hard as he could to make sure the back end cleared the obstruction.

The bin cleared the body, and he gave the metal beast a shove, stopping dead in his tracks to pop a bullet into the speed bump's head. He looked over at the two other zombies that had been knocked down, struggling to get to their feet. He aimed for a second but then quickly changed course, running towards the dumpster and pushing it against the wall by the ladder.

As the zombies closed the gap, Wade jumped up onto the bin, making sure to put the bulk of his weight onto the frame rather than the dumpster lid. With all the extra ammo and food weighing him down, he didn't want to risk crashing through the doors.

He stood up on the edge and watched the horde of creatures headed his way in both directions. He worked his way carefully around the outer edge of the bin before leaping up and grabbing on to the first exposed rung. He strained as he pulled himself up, using his upper body exclusively until he was able to swing his feet up onto the ladder.

Wade paused for a moment to catch his breath, locking his knee and looking below. Dozens of zombies clustered below, reaching up and moaning. He shook his head and took a deep breath, getting back to his task and climbing the rest of the way up to the roof.

As he hopped over the side, he dropped his heavy bag as he walked to the front of the building, carrying only his rifle. The sight below took his breath away.

"There's something you don't see every day," Wade muttered, and shook his head in disbelief as he gazed at hundreds of zombies. They were easily into the thousands on the interstate, just a sea of rotting flesh, none the wiser to his presence. He took in the sight for a few tense moments before remembering to breathe and readying his rifle.

He picked out his first target, looking through the night vision scope, seeing muted tones instead of bright and vibrant color. The first head that exploded could have been a watermelon, and nobody would have been able to tell due to the lack of color.

The gunshot echoed across the area, and within seconds the moaning increased exponentially. It was so loud that Wade paused, blinking into the darkness.

"Damn, looks like that got their attention," he muttered, and stared out at the death ocean for another moment before taking aim and firing again, hitting another monster in the head.

The zombies in the parking lot all began to move towards the anchor store he stood atop, and a small trickle of creatures began to filter in from the interstate.

He checked his watch, seeing it had been seven minutes since the other snipers had given him the ten minute timeline.

"Okay boys," he said under his breath, "you got three minutes to start firing. I know I can pull mine off."

CHAPTER THREE

On the ground, Kowalski led his squad of five into position to take advantage of the hole on the interstate. There was a fast food place just across from the field and directly in front of the crossing spot.

A trio of zombies roamed around the back, uninterested in the noise a block over that Wade was causing. Kowalski pulled out his knife, prompting Doyle and Martin to do the same. He inclined his head towards the ghouls, and they broke off in unison, each soldier jamming a blade into a zombie skull.

The group of five pressed up against the wall of the restaurant, keeping watch on their flanks as Kowalski crept up to the corner. He looked towards the interstate, seeing the path was still thick even though a few groups were working their way towards Wade.

"How's it looking?" Doyle murmured from behind him.

Kowalski shook his head and whispered, "Still too thick to pass."

"Why isn't Wade shooting?" Doyle asked.

Kowalski looked at his watch. "Probably still waiting on the northern group," he replied quietly. "Still got two minutes."

Martin stayed on the other flank, keeping watch. Three zombies came towards them, mouths opening with hungry moans. He clucked his tongue to get the attention of his team.

Doyle and Private Carver turned to deal with the threat, taking out the zombies as more moans erupted from the side of the restaurant. The former peeked around and saw a dozen creatures near the front of the store, looking around for the source of the noise that had dissipated.

He crept back to Kowalski. "We can't stay here much longer," he murmured.

His superior nodded and checked his watch again, seeing it tick down to one minute. "Come on, come on," he urged quietly.

A few tense seconds later, gunfire erupted to the north. Martin looked around the corner and saw the zombies near the front had lost interest in their skirmish and shambled off towards the new noises.

Wade opened fire right after, giving the zombies two different sounds to hone in on. Kowalski looked around his corner and watched the creatures breaking up, heading in one direction or the other.

After a minute of sustained fire in both directions, a pathway across the interstate began to open up, however several dozen zombies remained in the way, ping-ponging back and forth with every gunshot that went off.

"Okay, we gotta move," he hissed.

Doyle peeked past him at the zombies still in the way. "What about them?" he asked.

"Plow through them and get across," Kowalski replied. "Our target is the giant hardware store at the south end of the center. We're going around the back for roof access."

Doyle nodded and moved to the back of the line, letting the others know they were ready to go. Kowalski gave one more look to get his bearings and then broke from cover, the rest of his team hot on his heels.

He moved away from the wall and into the center of the drive-thru aisle to prevent any surprises around the corner. They broke out into the open, running across the parking lot as hard as they could. By the time they reached the frontage road, their footsteps had gained the attention of several indecisive zombies.

Rather than attack, Kowalski dodged the first few before lowering his shoulder into the next one, sending it to the side. He was the first to reach the grass and

quickly climbed the short incline, about
ten feet, with the rest of the group
behind.

He glanced back, seeing the others as
well as a few dozen zombies within twenty
yards shuffling towards them. He turned
back to the interstate, coming over the
crest of the hill and hitting the
pavement.

There were about forty zombies spread
out between them and the opposite side. As
he paused briefly to plot their course,
one creature about fifteen yards away
turned to moan at him, but then its head
exploded.

Kowalski cracked a smile as the rest
of the group caught up to him. "Straight
across, we got cover," he said.

They took off like a shot, running in
a straight line as Wade fired at a pretty
decent clip. One by one, the creatures in
front of them fell, clearing a path.

When they reached the median,
Kowalski hopped over the concrete barrier
first. As he did, several zombies
converged on his position, having been
unable to clear the barrier to get to the
gunfire noise.

"Move it!" Kowalski yelled. "The hole
is closing!"

Doyle, Martin, and Hurley cleared the
barrier, the latter barely making it past

the outstretched arms. Carver, a few yards
behind, hesitated, seeing the window
closing. He pulled out his handgun and
took aim, firing and hitting one creature
in the head. Another zombie on the line
fell in a spray of blood and bone from
Wade's bullet.

Kowalski skidded to a stop and looked
back. "Move it, Carver!" he screamed,
panic rising at his teammates' situation.

Doyle and Martin turned and squeezed
off a few shots with their handguns,
trying to thin the growing herd around
their friend.

"Fuck it," Carver said, and ran
towards the barrier, planting a foot on
the median and leaping forward with
everything he had. One zombie managed to
catch his ankle, stopping his forward
momentum and dropping him to the ground.

Before he could even register the
pain of his face meeting the pavement, a
dozen creatures dove at him, tearing into
him with claws and teeth.

As his screams pierced the air,
Kowalski grabbed Doyle by the arm. "He's
gone, we gotta move!" he cried, and shoved
him away from the carnage.

The quartet slid down the hill on
their side of the interstate, getting to
the frontage road with handguns drawn.
There were a few zombies on the road, with

more coming from the side streets and
business parking lots, attracted to the
gunfire and Carver's dying screams.

Kowalski stepped through the group,
leading them towards the shopping center a
few hundred yards away, at a brisk pace.
"Only fire if you have to, we gotta shed
some of this heat," he said.

His companions looked lost, ashen
faced and unsure of themselves.

Kowalski snapped his fingers, making
them look at him. "Carver's gone," he
said, tone harsh. "We'll have time to deal
with it on the roof. Now let's move!" he
demanded.

The snipers nodded and followed him
as he ran towards a side street, making
the turn towards the shopping center on
the right. Dozens of zombies littered the
side street, pouring out from the parking
lot.

Kowalski picked up his pace into high
gear, the others following suit. They
attempted to make it to the truck entrance
of the shopping center, but a throng of
zombies flooded out of it, drawn to the
noise.

He tore off of the street into an
overgrown field, trying to cut off the
horde. Halfway across, a hand grabbed his
ankle, and he instinctively fired down
into a zombie's head, just an inch away

from his foot. He stared down at it for a moment, stunned at the close call.

Doyle caught up to him and looked down at the corpse, missing its bottom half, and shook his head. "Way too close for comfort, bud," he breathed.

Kowalski nodded in agreement and then took a deep breath, continuing their trek. He looked to his left, seeing the zombies from the truck entrance were heading their way now, drawn to his gunshot, entering the grass.

"Gotta get to solid ground," he huffed, and tore towards the pavement behind the stores, relieved to be out of the tall grass where the undead could be lurking.

He glanced to the left, seeing dozens of creatures moving towards them, but still far enough away that they weren't yet a threat. To the right was mostly clear.

"Should be a couple hundred yards to the store," he said, and took off running.

His trio of companions followed him, guns raised and ready for action. As they approached the edge of the building next to a short driveway, they stopped at the sight of a hundred ghouls packed into the area, the back end fifteen yards from their corner.

"Shit, that's a lot of those things," Kowalski muttered under his breath.

Doyle looked over and saw the ladder on the back of the store, the same kind as the one Wade had used with the cover over the bottom eight feet of rungs. Unfortunately for them, there was no dumpster in sight.

"Well, there's our target," Doyle said. "But we're gonna need teamwork to get up there."

Kowalski peeked out again, but a zombie caught sight of the movement and moaned, shambling their way.

"Good enough for me, let's move!" he urged, and the quartet sprinted across the driveway. As they raced down the back of the store towards the ladder, moaning erupted in front of them. "I'll cover the front," Kowalski barked, "start getting up there!"

He stopped just past the ladder, pulling up his rifle and finding the target about thirty yards ahead with his night vision scope. He fired off several shots in rapid succession, buying them some time.

Meanwhile, Doyle crouched and laced his fingers together, giving Martin a boost up to the rung cover. After he was clear, he boosted Hurley up.

"Kowalski let's go!" Doyle cried, and his team leader fired one more shot before tearing back to him, practically flying up to the ladder.

Kowalski hooked an arm through the ladder rung and looked down at Doyle. "Grab my leg and climb up!" he called.

Doyle took a few steps back before running hard towards the ladder. He put a foot on the wall and launched himself up, grabbing onto Kowalski's leg. The sniper grunted at the extra weight, but it didn't take long for Doyle to secure himself and pull his weight from Kowalski's body.

"Free advice," Kowalski grunted, "lay off the carbs."

Doyle chuckled and shook his head as they climbed up to join the others on the roof. The duo took a moment to breathe deep, looking down at the creatures all reaching up to them from the ground. They exchanged a fist bump and then walked to the front of the store to join Martin and Hurley, dropping their bags and gear.

The quartet froze as they looked out over the sea of creatures in the parking lot, spreading back to the smaller bridge and road.

"What do you say we give them a reason to head our way, huh?" Kowalski asked.

The other men nodded and readied their rifles. Soon, the air was filled with high-powered rifle shots, booming off at a consistent pace. Kowalski took a deep breath and pulled out his walkie-talkie.

"Sarge, it's Kowalski, we're in position," he said into the radio.

CHAPTER FOUR

Sergeant Copeland reigned in his parachute as he looked around the field. Several men had formed a perimeter, keeping watch for the ghouls, while the rest of the men secured their gear. After a few moments, Corporal Dawson headed over to him.

"Your team good to go?" Copeland asked.

Dawson nodded. "Yes sir, fifteen of us ready to go," he replied.

"Okay, be safe, we'll see you on the bridge after a while," Copeland replied. The two longtime friends exchanged a fist bump before Dawson headed off to join his group.

A few moments later, Johnson approached, flanked by a group of ten soldiers. "Sarge, we're landed and ready to roll."

"Good man," Copeland replied, nodding. "So listen up everybody," he began, turning to the group. "We're gonna be moving quick. We got a mile and a half to cover, and we need to be there an hour ago. Unless you see me take a shot, nobody is to even draw their weapons, is that understood?"

There was a chorus of *yes, sir,* and he nodded again.

"One shot could give us away and undermine what our boys to the north and south are doing for us," he continued. "When we get to the Super Center, Johnson, Raymond, and Schmitt, you work your way to the loading docks and inspect those trucks. If they're not good to go, then we need to come up with a plan B. The rest of you will fan out in the store, clearing it of any hostiles and securing metal posts so we can build that barricade. If you see anything else that might be useful, make a note of it and we'll come back once our primary mission is complete." He crossed his arms. "Questions?"

There was a chorus in the negative this time, and he raised a hand. "Then let's move 'em out." He led the group off of the field and onto the street that ran parallel with the river. They moved faster than an average jogging speed, their footsteps echoing in the darkness.

As they moved, several zombies reacted to the noise, emerging from the neighborhood to the south. Copeland barely batted an eye at the emerging threat, instead picking up the pace to stay clear of them. As they reached the few blocks before the surface street bridge, he stopped the group at a crossroads.

Several moans erupted from the south of them, about thirty yards down the side street. Copeland glanced over, seeing it was about five zombies. He snapped his fingers and pointed, and five soldiers broke formation, pulling out knives and rushing the ghouls to take them out silently. Copeland focused back on the bridge as they returned to formation, leaving a pile of bodies in their wake.

"Johnson," the Sergeant said.

The Private approached. "Sarge."

"I need your night scope," Copeland said.

Johnson handed over his rifle with the night-vision scope, and the Sergeant looked through it to study the large congregation of zombies on the bridge that stretched almost to the road they were on. He let out a low grunt and handed the rifle back.

"Detour," Copeland said, "let's move."

He led the group down a block before turning back to the west towards the target. They reached the bridge road, and Copeland checked out the horde of zombies beginning about sixty yards up. He motioned for them to keep moving, but put a finger to his lips.

They crept across the road, keeping their footsteps as light as possible. When they reached the other side and moved behind cover, they picked up the pace

again, continuing to ignore creatures
stumbling out from the shadows.

After several minutes, they finally
reached the edge of the parking lot to the
Super Center. There were a few zombies
near the corner of the lot that Copeland
pointed to. The same soldiers that
dispatched the earlier ones repeated their
stealthy kills, ending the nearby threat.

The Sergeant took a knee, and the
rest of the squad followed. He held out
his hand, and Johnson gave him the night
vision scope again. The lot was dotted
with abandoned vehicles, as well as a
couple dozen creatures wandering about.
Copeland looked up towards the bridge,
seeing a mass of monsters on it.

As he looked, the first shots from
the northern group rang out, and some of
the zombies turned to shamble in that
direction.

"Those sniper boys don't waste time,
do they?" Johnson murmured from behind
him.

Copeland grunted, knowing that the
noise was going to quickly bring undead
reinforcements from the south. "You all
know what to do," he said, "let's move."

The Sergeant led the group across the
parking lot, spreading out as they went.
As they approached the front of the
building, various soldiers delivered knife

blows to creatures they encountered, clearing the way for them.

Copeland was the first to the front door, approaching it cautiously in case of undead company. He stood in front of it, motioning for Johnson to throw it open so he could breach.

As soon as the Private opened the door, Copeland rushed inside, delivering a vicious kick to the torso of a zombie, sending it flying across the entryway. He whipped around and jammed his blade into an eye socket of another, and Johnson swept past him to stab the one that was on the ground.

"Trucks, go," Copeland hissed.

Johnson, Raymond, and Schmitt rushed off down the side aisle of the store, pulling out flashlights to illuminate their path. As they reached the back of the store, they spotted five zombies standing in front of the loading dock door.

Johnson held the trio up, while putting his flashlight down to avoid the creatures coming their way. He glanced over, checking to see they were in sporting goods. He stepped into the aisle and grabbed an aluminum baseball bat, motioning for the other two to do the same.

Once properly armed, they rushed down the back aisle towards the creatures. Johnson delivered an overhead smash to the lead zombie, crumpling it, and held up the flashlight so the other two could swing away. After several batter-ups, the threat was eliminated.

Johnson motioned for them to follow him into the loading dock. He peeked through the small window in the swinging doors, seeing nothing close to it. They moved through and put up their flashlights, illuminating the entire area. There were three zombies at the far end, but nothing else in the sprawling area.

"You two, take them out," Johnson instructed, "I'll secure the back door."

The two soldiers walked down to bash some skulls while Johnson headed to his destination. He removed the bolt lock and gently opened the door a crack, listening for noise. When he didn't hear anything, he pushed it side open, seeing the back area clear. There were three transfer trucks backed up to the loading bays.

Something brushed up against his arm and he startled, whipping around, bat raised. Raymond and Schmitt backed up, hands out.

"Jesus jump-roping christ, don't do that!" Johnson hissed, his heart rate tripled.

The two men chuckled under their breaths, muttering *sorry* in unison.

He let out a deep whoosh of breath and motioned for them to follow him. "Come on, check the trucks," he said, "make sure the battery is good."

Each of the trio picked a truck, making sure that nothing was waiting for them beneath the vehicles. Johnson swept the area and then clambered up into his, turning the key and relieved to see the dash lights come on. He checked the gas meter and saw it was a half full.

"That should be good enough to get us four blocks," he said quietly, and then turned the ignition off and slipped out of the truck.

"My truck is good," Raymond reported as he approached. "Battery works and full tank of gas."

Schmitt shook his head. "Looks like I got gas, but the battery wouldn't cooperate."

"Two outta three ain't bad," Johnson replied with a shrug. "Come on, let's go find the Sarge."

The trio headed back into the main part of the store. There were footsteps, moans, and the sound of bodies hitting the floor echoing throughout the building. After a few moments, there were sporadic bellows of "*clear*", and then quiet.

"Sarge, what's your twenty?" Johnson called, cupping a hand around his mouth.

Copeland's voice echoed in the store. "Aisle fifteen," he replied.

The trio made their way over to the Sergeant, who was watching the soldiers running around the store. Some of them carried equipment to the front of the store to stage it, while a few others came up with various items of food and weaponry. Copeland gave a *yay* or *nay* to different items depending on need.

"Johnson, what you got?" he asked, as he gave a thumbs up to a case of tire irons.

The Private jerked a thumb over his shoulder. "Three trucks in the back," he replied. "Two are good to go, one needs a jump."

"Outstanding," Copeland said, nodding. "While we're getting prepped here, you hit automotive and see if they have one of those emergency battery chargers. Hook it up, leave it running, then get back here. As soon as Dawson starts pulling some of those things to the south, we're hitting the bridge."

Johnson saluted him. "You got it, Sarge," he replied and then headed off to automotive with Schmitt and Raymond in tow.

As they disappeared around the aisle, Copeland's walkie-talkie vibrated. He picked it up and clicked it on.

"Sarge, it's Kowalski," the sniper came through. "We're in position."

Copeland nodded. "Good news," he replied. "But I heard some gunfire earlier than expected."

"Ah, let's just say the interstate wasn't dark," Kowalski replied sheepishly. "Had to divert from the plan in order to get across."

The Sergeant stiffened. "Situation?" he asked.

"Three on the west side of the interstate, four at the designated target," the sniper reported.

Copeland sighed. Those numbers didn't add up. "Who didn't make it?"

"Carver," Kowalski replied, voice thick.

The Sergeant shook his head, taking a moment to process. "You don't lose anybody else," he finally said, firmly. "That's an order."

"Yes, sir," the sniper replied.

Copeland took a deep breath. "We're at the Super Center, gonna be ready to move as soon as Dawson gets to work."

"In the meantime, we'll pull them our way," Kowalski assured him.

"Heard," the Sergeant replied. "Copeland out." He put the radio away, crossing his arms as he watched his soldiers work. *Come on Dawson, get it done.*

CHAPTER FIVE

Corporal Dawson watched on as several members of his fifteen strong team stabbed and bashed in the skulls of a dozen zombies that had wandered out from a side street. It was the last one before the interstate, but the fourth major confrontation his squad had faced on the three-mile trek to the car dealership.

This worried him, because if they were encountering so much resistance on the residential streets, it not only made their job more difficult, but it made him wonder how bad the situation at the bridge was.

After the cleansing finished up, Privates Mack and Ross jogged back from the top of the road that intersected with the freeway.

"How are we looking up there?" Dawson asked.

Mack jerked a thumb over his shoulder. "Flat across the interstate, should be easy to traverse."

"Only about forty hostiles between here and there," Moss added. "Really spread out, too."

The Corporal nodded. "How'd the lot look?" he asked.

The Privates exchanged a look, concerning their superior.

"That good, huh?" Dawson asked.

"Couldn't really get a great look at it, but…" Moss trailed off, scratching the back of his head.

Mack winced. "There was some movement."

"Fantastic," Dawson drawled. "Looks like it's gonna be a long ass night." He turned to two soldiers taking turns curb-stomping a zombie into the ground. "You boys done?" he asked dryly.

The soldiers straightened up and moved away, falling back into formation.

"Final push gentlemen," the Corporal announced. "We got some light resistance on the interstate, and unknown hostiles on the lot. Mack, Moss, and myself make a beeline to the front door, and once you clear out the lot, you follow. Who has the night vision?"

One soldier with a rifle raised his hand in the back.

Dawson pointed to him. "I don't care how you do it, just get on that roof and keep watch on the interstate," he instructed. "I don't care about stragglers, but if you see a horde, you start shooting."

"Yes, sir," the soldier replied, nodding.

"Where are my mechanics?" Dawson asked.

Two soldiers off to the left raised their hands.

"You're with me," the Corporal said. "Until we get those car alarms modified, you stay back. Once we get that done, feel free to run into whatever shitshow you want to."

"Yes sir," they replied in unison, nodding.

Dawson appraised his team. "Then let's move," he said. "Hit teams, up front."

Two squads of four moved to the front of the formation as the group jogged down the last stretch of road. Their blood-stained blades and bludgeons sparkled in the moonlight, ready for action.

As they got onto the frontage road, the hit squads leapt into action to take out a trio of zombies. One squad of four rushed up, with the leader using his bludgeon to drive a zombie back staggering into another one. They fell to the ground and two other soldiers made short work of their skulls.

The rest of the squad moved to the interstate, several groups of creatures scattered about the pavement. The hit squads attacked in unison and formation, stabbing and bludgeoning, expertly neutralizing the threads.

They reached the other side of the freeway, not concerned with the zombies that were half a mile down the road. When they got into the lot, the infestation was a lot thicker than originally anticipated.

Dawson stopped short at the edge, staring at the dozens of creatures moving through the cars.

"Poor fuckers must have wandered in there and couldn't figure out how to get out," Mack murmured.

Dawson sighed. "We'll get 'em out real quick," he replied. "Hit teams, need a diversion on the flanks. Get that center cleared out for us."

The two teams of four ran down the outer edges of the lot on either side. When in position, one member from each team got up on top of a vehicle and started making a racket, jumping and yelling and banging their weapons, while the other three stood in front, waiting on the enemy to arrive.

Dawson and the remainder of the squad watched as the zombies staggered off towards the hit teams. They bumped off of vehicles, knocking into each other, but one by one, they stepped up to just get smacked down by the soldiers.

As the fight went on, the center of the car lot emptied out.

"Let's go," Dawson hissed, and led his team down the lot. They moved quickly but quietly, staying low so the cars would provide cover. As they approached the front doors, the Corporal stopped at the sight of several zombies pressed up against the glass, banging on them.

He stepped up to the door and pushed lightly against it, noting that it opened inward. At the bottom, someone had put door stops down to hold the ghouls inside. He pulled out his flashlight and shone it into the building.

There were numerous show cars as well as cubicles set up, but very little in the way of zombies outside of those at the front door.

"Okay, Mack, Moss," Dawson said, clicking off his light and turning to the soldiers. "I'm gonna get those door stops. From what I can see, it's just these three that we have to worry about."

They nodded and readied their blades. The Corporal crouched down in front of the doors, getting a good handle on the metal doorstops. He looked back to make sure they were ready, and when they nodded, he dove to the side, pulling the stops with him.

The trio of zombies burst out from the door, immediately going after Dawson who was closest to them. Mack lunged forward, plunging his blade into the side of the lead creature's head, and immediately throwing it back into the others.

Moss slashed a decisive blow to the face of the other zombie, while Mack jumped over the one he killed and booted the chest of the last one struggling to get up. He slammed his blade down into its eye with a vicious kill shot.

Dawson peeled himself off of the ground, dusting himself off. "Those fuckers came at me like a fat kid at a buffet," he grunted. "Appreciate the quick action."

"If we're gonna get promotions," Mack said with a smirk, "it ain't gonna be that way."

The Corporal chuckled and led the group inside. He pointed at the soldier with the night-vision rifle. "Get topside now," he instructed.

"Yes, sir." The soldier nodded and ran off.

"Rest of you fan out, we need keys," Dawson said. "And keep a watch out for zombies, those fuckers like to hide."

The group spread out, looking around for keys to the lot full of vehicles. After several minutes, Moss popped up from a cubicle.

"I think we're in business!" he called.

Dawson joined him and saw the Private fiddling with a large lockbox attached to the wall. When he opened it up, there were hundreds of keys, all arranged by parking lot number.

"Good work, Moss," the Corporal said, and pulled out his walkie talkie. "Sarge, you copy?" he asked.

After a short pause, Copeland came back, "Beginning to think you were going AWOL there, Corporal."

Dawson barked a laugh. "And leave all the glory of completing this suicide mission to you, Sarge? Never."

"What's your status?" the Sergeant asked, chuckling.

Dawson watched his soldiers work. "Dealership secured, keys located."

"How long until you can get me some distractions?" Copeland asked.

The Corporal approached one of the mechanics. "Once we pop the hoods, how long to get those sensors fixed?" he asked.

"Two minutes, tops," the mechanic replied.

Dawson lifted the radio to his lips. "We can have a party favor making noise in ten," he said. "Where do you want us to start?"

"Get me a pair five blocks south of each bridge," Copeland replied. "Those snipers are pulling their weight, so I want to pull the ones directly south of us away."

The Corporal nodded. "Understood," he replied. "From there, we'll spread 'em out."

"I'll let you know if we need to adjust the plan," the Sergeant assured him. "Copeland out."

Dawson clipped his radio back to his belt and whirled a hand above his head. "All right boys," he said, "get you a vehicle and let's roll."

CHAPTER SIX

Mack and Moss hopped into a bright yellow sedan, rolling down the windows as the car started up. The mechanic slammed the hood down and came around to Mack on the driver's side.

"Okay Mack, you're good to go," he said, leaning on the window. "When you get to your destination, take the keys with you, lock the door, arm the alarm, and give the car a good shove. That should pop it off for sixty seconds."

The Private nodded. "Is that going to give the zombies enough time to get to it?" he asked.

"No, probably not," the mechanic admitted, shaking his head. "Which is why you're going to have to find some shelter and keep hitting the alarm until some show up."

Moss rolled his eyes from the passenger seat. "You got some flares, too?" he drawled. "Might help them really notice where we are."

Dawson approached the window, crossing his arms. "No, but if you don't quit your bitching, I'm gonna have the mechanic here hook an alarm up to your ass and send you on a ten-mile run," he snapped.

Moss' sarcasm dropped quickly as the Corporal got his point across.

"And to confirm," Mack cut in, putting up a hand, "we're five blocks south of the surface street bridge."

Dawson nodded. "Correct," he confirmed. "Put it in an intersection a block off of the interstate, so that you capture the neighborhood crowd. Follow the mechanic's instructions, then haul ass back here, because we got a lot more cars to spread out."

Both privates replied with a firm, "Yes, sir," and Mack put the car into gear, punching the gas. They turned onto the frontage road before crossing underneath the interstate and heading up the opposite side.

"Why not take the interstate?" Moss asked, brow furrowing.

Mack shook his head. "Because if we run into trouble, we won't be able to hit a side road," he explained.

"Makes sense," his companion agreed.

They drove up a few more blocks before stopping. A horde of creatures milled about on the frontage road and on the interstate just above it, slowly making their way towards the bridge. The Privates listened closely and they could hear the faint sounds of gunfire in the distance. It wasn't rapid, just steady

with a shot popping off every couple of
seconds.

"Those sniper boys are lighting them
up," Moss said.

Mack shook his head. "Problem is,
they're drawing quite the crowd," he
replied dryly. "We're still a mile from
the bridge."

Moss shrugged as his partner turned
down a side road, driving a couple blocks
before turning north. They drove
relatively slowly through the
neighborhood, seeing the grass beginning
to get tall. There were a few paths
tracking through the yards where the
foliage was stamped down.

Moss wrinkled his nose as he
appraised the middle-class brick houses,
decaying after a month of neglect. "If it
wasn't for the zombies, this would make
for a nice town," he said.

"Kinda sad to think that this scene
is playing out in just about every single
town in the country," Mack agreed.

Moss swallowed hard. "Hell, the
world," he said.

They shook their heads simultaneously
at the thought.

"I can't imagine what those other
countries are doing to handle this," Mack
said. "We have more guns than people in
this country, and we still got our asses

kicked. Not sure a bunch of civilians
armed with knives and cricket bats are
faring much better."

Moss sighed. "So much for my European
vacation."

They headed up the side street,
stopping in the middle of an intersection.

"Is this five blocks?" Moss asked.

Mack shrugged. "Hell if I know," he
replied, "but I can see the dead end up
ahead."

Moss struggled to count the number of
cross streets between them and the end of
the road, but the darkness made it
difficult. "Well, it's either four, five,
or six," he said.

"Or in my line of thinking," Mack
replied, "close enough."

He made the turn back towards the
interstate, stopping the car in the middle
of the intersection. The two of them
checked their surroundings and got out of
the vehicle, doing an additional sweep of
the area.

"Clear," Moss said.

Mack nodded. "Same."

His partner cocked his head. "You got
the keys?"

Mack dangled them before pocketing
them. "So where do you want to hide out?"
he asked.

"Further away from the interstate, the better," Moss replied.

The duo looked around and spotted a two-story house one down from a place on the corner. The front door was ajar, and Mack nodded towards it.

"They left the door open for us," he said.

His friend scratched the back of his head. "Hope that's all they left," he quipped.

Mack shut the car door before fiddling around with the keys. He finally got the car locked and then paused. "You ready?" he asked.

"As much as I'm gonna be," Moss admitted.

Mack took a deep breath and looked around one more time before giving the car a good shove. It didn't take much, just his light touch, to set off the alarm. A loud horn bleated, echoing through the neighborhood, causing both soldiers to wince.

"Goddamn that's loud," Moss declared.

Mack waved at him. "Let's get to the house!"

They rushed to the two-story building, seeing some of the bushes across the street start to jiggle. They raised their assault rifles as they approached the house, and Moss took point, heading for the front door as Mack covered his rear.

He pulled a flashlight, holding it above the barrel of his gun before stepping inside. As he cleared the threshold, he spotted movement coming from the back of the room at the mouth of the hallway. He immediately fired, clipping a zombie in the face.

"Keep your fire down!" Mack hissed. "We want the car to attract them, not us!"

Moss shook his head. "Relax, as long as we got the alarm, we're-" Before he could finish his sentence, the alarm kicked off. "... Good. Shit." He kept his flashlight up and quickly drew his knife, waiting in the living room.

With the silence, he could finally hear footsteps on the second floor of the house. Meanwhile, Mack pulled out the keys and pressed the alarm button.

"Anytime now, bud," Moss urged.

His friend shook his head frantically. "I'm hitting it and nothing's happening," he replied.

"Might be too far away," Moss said, swallowing hard.

"Shit," Mack muttered. "Hang tight." He stepped off of the front porch and started walking towards the car, hitting the alarm button the entire way. When he got to the edge of the yard, it finally went off. As it blared, he turned to retreat into the house, but there were a dozen zombies coming around the side towards him. "Moss!" he cried.

He took off towards the house, pulling out his assault rifle. It was dark, and he was twenty yards away, but he opened fire anyway. His three-round bursts tore through the zombies, hitting mostly torsos but hitting one zombie in the head.

The gunfire alerted Moss, who quickly dashed out and opened fire himself, ripping the zombies to shreds at close range. Mack tore for the door, and his partner nearly fired at him, at the last second realizing who it was and stopping just in time.

"Christ dude, you all right?" Mack cried.

His friend nodded shakily. "Come on, let's clear this place out before the alarm stops," he said, and rushed back inside.

The duo pulled their flashlights and moved through the house quickly. Moss headed up the stairs, and as he approached the top, he spotted two zombies in the hallway, caught in a baby gate that had been wedged across it. They moaned and reached for him, and he quickly put them down with two precise shots to the head.

As they slumped over the gate, the alarm outside stopped. He listened closely for noise, but heard none. He tapped on the hardwood floor to draw any others out, but nothing came. As he descended the staircase again, Mack was just heading out the door.

"Clear upstairs," Moss reported.

His friend nodded. "Good deal," he replied. "I'm gonna get another blast going."

"We may need to hit the house next door," Moss suggested. "Not that safe for you to keep going outside."

Mack rolled his eyes. "What's this *me* stuff?" he drawled. "You're up next."

Before his partner could answer, the alarm began to blare on its own, and they shared an excited look. Mack shut the front door, and they hurried over to the living room window to look outside.

A few zombies hung out around the vehicle, banging on the doors and windows in reaction to the noise. Eventually the alarm stopped, and the duo waited with bated breath for a ghoul to hit it again.

"Come on, come on," Moss murmured, "you know you want what's in there."

A few seconds later, one of the zombies bonked into the driver's side, setting off the alarm again. This enraged its brethren, and they all began to smack the car with vigor. More zombies emerged from the side streets, a ton of them coming from the north.

"What do you think, give it fifteen minutes to make sure it's still working?" Mack asked.

Moss shook his head. "Hell no," he replied, checking his weapons. "We need to get out of here before it really draws a crowd. Then we find a house close to the dealership and hold up for fifteen minutes."

The two men shared a fist bump before heading towards the back door. They peered out at the smattering of zombies marching through the backyard. As they shambled past, Mack unlocked the sliding door and gently opened it. They silently crept across the back deck and hopped over the side, landing on the soft grass.

Keeping to the darkness, the duo pressed up against the house as more zombies came out of the neighboring yards. They froze when the alarm went silent, knowing that a single noise could doom them with this kind of gathering. A few seconds later, it began blaring again, keeping the attention of the nearby creatures.

They took the opportunity to bolt, running through a backyard and off into the darkness towards the dealership.

Copeland and the rest of his crew waited at the entrance of the Super Center, keeping an eye on the zombies on the bridge and interstate. Johnson stood beside him with the night vision scope, surveying the landscape.

The bridge began to clear out with the zombies moving to the north, attracted by the sniper fire. The ones on the interstate had either joined the bridge group, or had started being drawn south by the sound of car alarms, creating a mostly zombie-free pocket.

"Johnson, how we looking?" Copeland asked.

The Private continued to scan as he spoke. "The bulk is moving away from us," he replied. "Still gonna have a fight on our hands on the bridge, but I don't think it's worth waiting over."

The Sergeant motioned for Johnson to hand over the weapon, and he did. Copeland did a quick sweep with the night vision scope, and then nodded, handing the gun back.

"Okay boys," he said, turning to his team, "we're gonna move and move quick. Got four on the shopping carts, rest of us are on zombie duty. Drop 'em quick, drop 'em quiet, and get ready for some heavy lifting on the bridge. We get halfway down and I want everybody focused on that front line. We're gonna have to reinforce the rear eventually, but those things are way too close for comfort. Questions?" He didn't wait for an answer before continuing, "Didn't think so. Now let's move."

He led the group out, the eight on zombie duty carrying knives and baseball bats. Behind them were four soldiers pushing shopping carts full of supplies, like rebar, basketball goal posts, gloves, and such.

The run through the parking lot was smooth, with no resistance. A couple zombies on the interstate directly ahead had their attention drawn as the footsteps and shopping carts rattled on the pavement. There was nothing but a grass path keeping them apart.

Copeland led the charge towards the small pack of zombies, swinging hard with a baseball bat and cratering in a skull. Several other soldiers stepped up and did the same, while a couple stayed back to help the cart pushers traverse the grass, wheels wiggling.

The Sergeant stood on the interstate, patting one of the concrete barriers in the center. It was about eight feet long, solid concrete with the exception of two holes running through the top, about a foot away from each corner. He scanned ahead, watching twenty zombies between them and the center of the bridge.

These won't be a problem, he said. What concerned him was the thousands of zombies another hundred yards up that were congregating between the stores. He looked over to the rest of the men, who were standing and waiting for his move.

Copeland started walking up the interstate at a deliberate pace, not wanting to draw attention to them. The zombies were all focused on the gunfire in the distance, so one by one, he and the rest of his men stepped up to dispatch their enemies.

The group didn't take long to work their way up to the center of the bridge, moving quickly in tandem. The closest zombie on the bridge was fifteen yards up and walking away from them.

"Johnson, take two men," Copeland said quietly, "set up shop twenty yards up. Any trouble, you tamp it down."

The Private nodded. "On it," he replied, and pointed to Raymond and Schmitt. "You two, on me."

Copeland watched the trio head up to the zombies and take out the last few stragglers with ease, standing guard. He turned to watch the others come up with the shopping carts and stopped in front of him.

The Sergeant kept his voice low. "These bitches are heavy, so we're gonna be working in teams," he said. "Four men to a barrier. Get up to where Johnson is and start moving them back this way. One row, all the way across. We'll worry about reinforcing it later, but right now we just need something in case they lose interest in the snipers."

They got to work, throwing on work gloves, and grabbing up metal posts and heavy duty floor dollies, rushing their targets. Posts went through the two slots at the top of the barriers, and then there was a quiet countdown before lifting up. As the barrier reached a foot off of the ground, another soldier rolled the metal dollie underneath. Once on wheels, the two lifters could push it along the road, straining to roll the several thousand pound barriers.

The nose they made both straining and moving attracted a few zombies near the back of the pack, forcing Johnson and Raymond to step up and smack them down as quietly as they could.

"Keep watch," Johnson whispered to Raymond, who nodded.

Johnson jogged back to Copeland, who was helping to unload a barrier on the side of the road. He strained, but they finally got it into place with the two men rushing back to help with the next one.

"What is it?" the Sergeant asked.

"Moving that first barrier drew some of them back to us," Johnson explained. "It's loud. The gunfire is drowning it out a bit, but as soon as that goes away, we're in trouble. And at the rate they're going, it's gonna be awhile."

Copeland nodded. "Understood." He pulled out his walkie-talkie and dialed in before lifting it to his lips. "Kowalski, update," he said.

Several moments passed before the sniper came back, "We're holding our own, Sarge. Pulling a decent sized crowd from the city, but a little too far away from the interstate to do much. Satellite didn't show that many trees blocking the view."

"What's your ammo situation?" Copeland asked.

Another moment of pause. "The four of us at the target are down to about a thousand," Kowalski replied. "Can't speak for the others, as they don't have comms."

"Well, if you got three men just across the bridge, it's safe to assume they'll be at six or seven hundred based on the fire patterns?" Copeland asked, and there was a long silence before he growled, "Kowalski, I know you aren't smart enough to be doing math in your head, so talk to me, soldier."

"Wade is alone on the store just up from the bridge," the Private replied. "The other two, well, I assume two, at least one, are several blocks up."

The Sergeant grimaced, knowing that once they ran out of ammo, this bridge would become very active. "Well, here's hoping Wade sticks to a steady rhythm," he said, "because as soon as he's out, we're gonna have a fight on our hands." He looked up the bridge, seeing the men struggling with the next barricade before finally getting it onto the dolly.

"What do you want me to do, Sarge?" Kowalski asked.

Copeland paused for a moment, contemplating hard before answering, "If you feel like luck is on our side, then just keep doing what you're doing." He took a deep breath. "If you've been paying attention with how things have been going for the past month, I'd suggest coming up with more ways to stir up some noise." He stiffened as the men continued to strain, pushing the concrete barrier with everything they had. "Because, unless I'm mistaken, we're gonna need it."

Nearly ninety minutes had passed since the barrier building had begun. The soldiers had built a line completely across the bridge, running across all four lanes. They'd even created a rectangle in the center, stretching eight feet by eight feet, branching off the main line.

Copeland strained with several other men to get the large concrete block into place. Once it was in, the men leaned over it, breathing heavy sighs of relief.

"That's good work, boys," Copeland huffed. "Now we just got one more to build in the south."

There was a chorus of light groans from the men, and the Sergeant chuckled.

"Don't worry, that's not till later," he assured them. "Now, we get to do a suicide run on the other bridge."

One of the soldiers threw up his hands. "Finally, some good news."

Another ripple of tired chuckles rose, and then Copeland took a deep breath.

"I need four volunteers to hold this line," he declared. "And I'm not gonna lie, it could get messy. As soon as our sniper friend runs out of ammo, those creatures are gonna be looking for something new to focus their attention on, and it's going to be you. If those car alarms don't hold their interest, you're gonna be trapped in this little square of death fighting a two-front war. But we need to defend it, because if we get too many of those things pushing on it, the line isn't going to hold." He crossed his arms. "So, who's it going to be?"

All eight men's hands shot straight up in the air, and he shook his head, chuckling again.

"I'm going to assume it's because each and every one of you is dedicated to the mission," he said, pointing an accusing finger, "and not just because you want to get out of some heavy lifting."

One of the soldiers grinned. "Can't it be both?"

The group laughed again, and then Copeland pointed to the four on the left. "Okay, you four win the sweepstakes," he declared, and then motioned to one on the right. "I need you to go get Johnson and the others."

The soldier nodded and ran off up the bridge to retrieve the guards.

"Remember, limit your fire until you start getting overwhelmed," Copeland reminded the team staying behind. "We'll be back with reinforcements as soon as possible."

They nodded and started setting up their defenses, laying bats on the ground, knives, and some leftover metal posts. Johnson, Raymond, and Schmitt approached, the former patting the barricade.

"Well hell Sarge," Johnson drawled. "This is looking pretty good." He glanced at the eight-foot emergency barrier. "That, however, looks like nightmare fuel."

Copeland cocked his head. "Good thing you're going to be with me on the other bridge," he said.

"Which I imagine is a whole other brand of nightmare fuel," Johnson replied.

The Sergeant nodded. "Absolutely Private, wouldn't be any fun otherwise," he said. "Good luck, boys," he said to the soldiers staying behind, and they saluted him.

"You too, Sarge," one of them said.

Copeland led the group of eight back towards the Super Center, a chorus of car alarms bleating in the distance.

"Never thought I would say it," Johnson declared, "but I'm loving that car alarm sound."

Copeland grinned. "Hell man, it's making me want to go take a nap."

"A nap?" Johnson raised an eyebrow.

The Sergeant shook his head. "Didn't grow up in the best neighborhood," he explained. "This was my goodnight song for a number of years."

"And I thought my mother listening to Liberace was bad," Johnson said with a laugh.

Copeland joined him as they broke off of the interstate and headed back towards the shopping center. "Stay frosty," he finally said, "these bastards are sneaky."

He led the group into the center, checking corners to make sure they were still clear. One straggler had found its way in, but with a quick whistle and point, a soldier broke off and cracked it over the head.

The rest of the store was clear, much to the relief of the Sergeant. They had enough fronts to fight on, without dealing with backtracking. They reached the back of the store and into the back lot where the trucks were.

"Pile in and follow me," Copeland instructed. "CB radios on channel thirteen, let's move."

The soldiers hopped into the three trucks, the first two starting up without a problem. Copeland got into the third one with the recharged battery, Raymond in the passenger seat.

"Let's hope Johnson didn't fuck this up," he muttered, and turned the key.

To his relief, it sprung to life, and he quickly popped it into gear, leading the convoy out of the lot. They drove down a frontage road a few blocks to be able to cross under the interstate, and as they did, they encountered a handful of zombies meandering towards the car alarms in the distance.

Copeland adjusted his trajectory, making sure to slam into the ghouls as they went by, sending them flying into the grass. The other bridge was a half a mile away, and with each passing block, the dread in the Sergeant's mind grew.

Kowalski had said it was a packed house, but that was an hour ago, so hope began to creep in. As he made the turn for the bridge, Copeland's concern was realized.

There were upwards of a hundred zombies on the bridge, most of them towards the neighborhood, drawn by car alarms and not paying any attention to the constant gunfire from the snipers. Copeland studied the bridge, seeing two lanes packed with multiple large groups. He reached for the CB radio, flicking it to channel thirteen.

"All right boys, listen up," he said into the mouthpiece. "This is gonna be a bumpy ride. I'm gonna take the lead and plow through as many of them as I can, get up to the top of the bridge, and block it off. Johnson, you'll be up next, and I want you to wedge your truck across the road about halfway up. Schmitt, I want you ten yards behind Johnson." He took a deep breath. "With any luck, we'll be able to hold off any massive horde with this setup. Also watch your six, this is gonna be loud as hell, so we may have some company from the neighborhood."

He waited a moment to hear the affirmative responses and then glanced over at Raymond in the passenger seat.

"You ready to do this?" he asked.

The Private offered a grim smile. "If I say no, does it mean we're not going?"

Copeland smirked and popped the truck into gear, punching the gas.

The big rig jolted forward and began gaining speed. By the time Copeland hit the bridge, the truck was doing forty, which was more than fast enough to completely obliterate the first trio of zombies that it came into contact with.

Undeterred, Copeland floored it, the engine squealing drawing the attention of most of the creatures on the bridge, the next batch numbering close to two dozen.

"Hang on, Raymond!" Copeland bellowed, and braced as the truck smacked into the dense wall of rotted flesh. Both men surged forward as they lost momentum, bodies careening in every direction, some over the side into the water below. Some crunched straight back into the pavement, flattening underneath the truck.

With only fifteen yards to the next group, the truck didn't have much time to gain speed, so their momentum slowed significantly when they hit the next pack. They bumped up and down as the wheels crushed bone and flesh, jostling the soldiers around.

Copeland had trouble controlling the direction of the truck, darting to the left and scraping up against the concrete barrier. He quickly pulled it back to the

right, barely able to regain control,
heart pounding.

"Holy shit, we were almost swimming!"
the Sergeant declared, laughing
maniacally.

Raymond stared at him, mouth agape,
eyes wide as he clutched the handle above
his head with white knuckles.

Copeland hit the gas one more time,
gaining speed for the final group at the
top of the bridge. The horde was huge,
well over a hundred as the noise of the
zombie demolition derby had drawn them
away from the snipers.

"We got this, we got this!" Copeland
yelled, and they braced as they smacked
into the horde, grinding through bodies
and clearing the bridge. As soon as they
stopped, they were surrounded by creatures
on all sides.

Bloody, gooey hands slapped the side
of the truck, pawing it in vain.

Copeland did a three-point turn,
taking his time in backing up the big rig
so that it was on the surface street and
flush up against the bridge support
barrier on either side of the road.

"How am I looking over there, bud?"
he asked.

Raymond looked out the window, seeing
only a sliver of space between the truck

and bridge. "A supermodel couldn't fit through there, Sarge," he replied.

"We're in business, then," Copeland replied, and looked out the driver's side window facing the bridge. Half a dozen creatures stood right outside his door, moaning hungrily.

Down the bridge, there were thirty or so ghouls in various conditions spread out between him and the next truck, which Johnson was skillfully putting into place.

Copeland grabbed his walkie talkie, raising it to his lips. "Kowalski, you copy?"

"I'm here Sarge," the sniper came back immediately. "Was that you in the big rig at the top of the bridge?"

The Sergeant grinned. "Yes, it was."

"Gotta say, that was some mighty fine driving outside of scraping the paint job," Kowalski drawled. "Hope you got a low deductible."

Copeland chuckled. "Lucky for me, I borrowed it." He heard Kowalski laugh on the other end, and even Raymond cracked a smile despite his shell shocked face. "Hey listen, can you do me a favor?" he asked. "I seem to have some groupies hanging out by my door. Could you give me a hand with them?"

"You got it, Sarge," Kowalski replied. "Give me just a minute."

Copeland rested the walkie-talkie in his lap and relaxed in his seat. Raymond looked out the passenger side towards town and watched easily a couple thousand zombies spread out over the shopping center and streets. A few seconds later, several shots rang out, and blood splattered up onto the driver's side window.

The Sergeant looked out, seeing that three of the six zombies had dropped. More shots fired off, and the other three exploded, limp corpses falling to the pavement.

"Appreciate it bud," Copeland said into the talkie. "And if it's not too much trouble, we're gonna be making a run down the bridge, so if you want to cover us, I'm not gonna complain."

"Consider yourself covered," Kowalski replied.

The Sergeant smiled. "Appreciate it," he said. "One more thing, how is Wade doing?"

"He's still firing twice a minute, like clockwork," the sniper replied. "So unless he's found more ammo somewhere, he's gotta be running low."

Copeland shook his head, pursing his lips. "You figured out a way to generate some noise for me?" he asked.

"Got a couple ideas," Kowalski replied, dragging out the words. "Just not real thrilled with implementing them."

Copeland nodded in understanding. "Hopefully it won't come to that, but if it does…"

"I'll be ready," the sniper promised.

"I can see why the Captain likes you," Copeland said, sincerity in his tone. "Copeland out." He put his radio away and readied his assault rifle. "You ready to do this?"

Raymond nodded, steeled for battle as he checked his own gun. "What's the plan?"

"Run like hell back to Johnson's truck," Copeland replied. "Weapons hot, so don't hesitate to light them up, and hope Kowalski continues being a kick-ass shot."

"Good enough for me," Raymond replied with a nod, "lead the way."

Copeland opened the truck door and hopped down onto the pavement, quickly raising his weapon and firing a couple of shots towards the back of the truck. Several zombies fell limp, having been crawling out from under the back end of the vehicle.

Raymond immediately drew his weapon, eyes widening, but the Sergeant gently inched the barrel down with his hand.

"Couple of them crawling," he said, pointing. "Not sure if we knocked them down or they were actually crawling. Come on."

They took off running as soon as Raymond hit the ground, tearing across the bridge. They were careful to avoid the zombies on the ground, as even if their backs were broken they could still deliver a lethal bite.

Shots from the hardware store continued to go off, and still-standing zombies dropped like flies in front of them as they ran. They skidded to a stop in front of a group of eight, and raised their guns, side by side.

"I got the right," Copeland said, and then opened fire. Raymond followed suit, and they took down all eight with bullets to the face.

The truck was forty yards away, with only a few zombies standing in their way, easily dispatched with well-placed bullets. When they finally reached Johnson's truck, the Private stood casually against the hood.

"About time you got here, Sarge," he said.

Raymond's chest heaved, but Copeland didn't even look like he'd broken a sweat from their sprint.

"Status?" the Sergeant asked.

Johnson motioned to the truck. "Got this truck wedged in pretty good, as you can see." It stretched across both lanes, not quite touching the barrier, leaving only a sliver of space. "Schmitt got his too, just at the opposite angle. So if any of those things do squeeze through, they'll have to figure out to go to the other side of the bridge in order to get through." He grinned. "Frankly, I don't think they're that smart."

Before Copeland could reply, several gunshots fired from the southern part of the bridge.

"Let's move," he said, and the trio quickly crawled under the truck, darting towards Schmitt.

At the south end, five soldiers stood, taking aim and firing sporadically into the neighborhood where dozens of zombies poured out.

"Cease fire, cease fire!" Copeland barked.

The men complied, lowering their weapons.

"Best we can tell, Sarge, one of those car alarms stopped going off, so they got drawn to us," Schmitt explained, motioning to the threat that was still fifty yards away.

Copeland pulled out his walkie talkie and clicked to a different channel. "Dawson."

"What can I do for you, Sarge?" the Corporal replied.

The Sergeant kept an eye on the emerging zombies. "Need more decoys up here by the surface street bridge," he instructed. "Double it up, this time."

"Next two set of drivers that get back will head that way," Dawson promised.

Copeland nodded. "How many decoys have you been able to deploy so far?" he asked.

"Got thirty or so, spread out around the city, about six or eight blocks apart," Dawson replied. "We're filling in some gaps now to thin them out even more."

"Good," Copeland said. "Keep doing what you're doing, but be ready to move en masse. We might have a situation brewing on the interstate."

"Ten four," the Corporal replied firmly. "We'll be ready."

Copeland put the walkie-talkie away and readied his assault rifle. "Let's clear 'em out," he declared, and led the charge.

Everyone spread out in a firing line and unloaded single shots into the horde. The bullets found their targets, dropping the corpses quickly and efficiently. As they stood to admire their handiwork, the walkie-talkie buzzed against the Sergeant.

"Copeland," he greeted.

"Hey Sarge, Kowalski," the sniper said. "You might have an issue."

Copeland's brow furrowed. "What is it?"

"I've been keeping an eye on your truck," Kowalski replied, "and I've already seen a dozen or so of those things crawl under. They're on the bridge now and wandering towards you."

The Sergeant sighed. "Thanks for the heads up," he said.

"You want me to clear them out?" the sniper asked.

Copeland tilted his head back and forth. "If you're so inclined," he replied. "We have to take them all out eventually."

"On it," Kowalski said.

Copeland replaced his walkie-talkie and looked around at the houses on the other side of the bridge. Spread out over a block, he spotted several sedans, and then checked the crawl space under the truck. He turned to his team.

"You two," he barked, pointing at the two soldiers nearest him, "start clearing a path through these corpses. Rest of you, start pushing those cars over here, we gotta plug this hole," he declared. "Isn't going to be perfect, but when we start clearing out this part of town, it should limit surprises. Let's move."

Ten minutes later, Copeland watched as the final car wedged underneath the truck. It wasn't a perfect solution, as there were still a few small gaps, but it was extremely unlikely that even a handful of corpses would be able to squeeze through, no matter how much noise the soldiers made. If anything, they'd probably get stuck and add to the barricade.

Johnson and Schmitt stood in the middle of the road running parallel to the river, scanning for zombies. Johnson caught one with his night vision scope and fired, dropping it.

"Damn, I didn't even see that one," Schmitt muttered.

Johnson shrugged. "Yeah, when they get into the shadows like that, they can be tough to see."

Copeland's walkie-talkie vibrated, and he lifted it to his lips. "Copeland."

"Sarge, Sarge!" Kowalski cried in a panicked voice. "We got problems!"

The Sergeant's brow furrowed. "Settle down, soldier," he said as calmly as he could. "What is it?"

"Wade's out of ammo!" the sniper gushed. "And a lot of those things are starting to move towards the bridge!"

Copeland grunted in displeasure. "You make that noise," he instructed. "I don't care what you do, just do it quick." He put the radio away and turned to his team. "Our bridge boys are in trouble, so we're gonna double time it! If it isn't in your way, you ignore it." He waved at them. "Now let's go!"

He turned and took off at a brisk pace, all seven soldiers keeping up with him. They moved swiftly along the moonlit road, the light reflecting off of the water. It was a mile run to the bridge, and as they got closer, they heard a worrisome sound in the distance.

Gunfire. And lots of it.

If they're firing, then it's bad out there, Copeland thought bitterly, and pushed harder, picking up more speed and pulling away from the other troops. Despite giving it their all, they just couldn't keep up with the beastly Sergeant.

The group finally reached the frontage road, stopping before crossing it. As the rest of the men showed up, they found Copeland staring down at the interstate away from the bridge.

"What…" Johnson huffed, "what is it, Sarge?"

His superior just continued to stare, letting out another displeased grunt.

Johnson leaned over to see a few hundred
zombies coming up the interstate towards
the bridge.

Raymond clustered in behind them, and
his eyes widened. "Not sure we have the
ammo for that," he warned.

"We don't," Copeland confirmed, "but
we need to slow them down." He pointed to
a quartet of his team members. "You four,
on the interstate. Start picking them off,
thin them out as much as you can. Use
every shot if you have to."

They didn't even bother responding,
simply running off as the gunshots
intensified on the bridge.

"Anybody here know how to hot-wire a
car?" Copeland asked.

Raymond raised his hand. "I got you,
Sarge."

"Good," Copeland replied, and pointed
back the way they'd come. "Find the
sturdiest one you can in the Super Center
parking lot and get it ready to go. Bring
it to the front. Schmitt, you cover him
and make sure nothing sneaks up. Johnson,
you're with me."

The four of them tore across the
highway, glancing over at the bridge
barricade. There was a complete line of
creatures on the barrier, with the four
men frantically running back and forth,
using blunt objects to cave in heads and

occasionally firing off a shot if one or two toppled over the cement barricade.

Things were frantic, but the soldiers appeared to be holding their own.

Copeland and Johnson rushed into the Super Center, tearing in with reckless abandon. As they came around the corner past the front entryway, they encountered a trio of zombies. The Sergeant didn't even break momentum, just picked up the first one, pile-driving it into the other two and sending all three to the ground past the cash registers.

Johnson raised his gun and quickly fired, taking them all out in quick succession. When he looked up, he'd lost Copeland, and ran deeper into the store.

"Sarge?" he called. "Sarge?"

"Aisle eighteen," Copeland called back.

Johnson squealed around a corner and spotted the Sergeant looking at automotive accessories. He finally picked up a handful of road flares and held them out.

"I'm getting duct tape and a weight," Copeland said. "I need you to find the propane tank keys."

Johnson started to run up to the front, hoping that they were at the customer service desk, but stopped as he passed the hardware section. He checked an end cap and spotted a gigantic pair of bolt cutters, picking it up and smiling.

"This should do just fine," he said to himself, and ran outside, where Schmitt and Raymond were just pulling up in a giant eighties Cadillac. It was big as a boat and weighed twice as much. "Where the hell did you find this hoopty ride at?" Johnson drawled.

Schmitt just smiled. "Amazing what's still on the road, huh?" he asked.

Johnson waved for him to follow him. "Come on, gonna need help with the tanks." He led his partner to the tanks and peeled it open, digging out the canisters. They quickly hauled every single can they could to the car, packing it tight.

Copeland nodded as he approached, holding his tools. As they finished loading the trunk, he threw open the car door, climbing into the back seat and using his knife to carve out a hole in the back seat. He punched through to the trunk, leaving a three-inch wide hole.

"You get this car up to the road, and when you do, open up every canister in the trunk," he instructed. "Throw the road flares into the front seat, throw the weight on the gas, and let her rip."

The three soldiers exchanged worried glances.

"That…" Raymond began, "that doesn't seem safe."

Copeland pursed his lips. "It's either this or you grab a baseball bat and start whacking zombies."

Raymond shook his head, raising his palms in defeat.

Copeland nodded. "When you get it done, join Johnson and I on the bridge." As the boys drove off, the Sergeant turned to Johnson. "Come on, our boys need help."

As they sprinted, the Private spoke through gasps, trying to keep up. "What… what about… Dawson?" he huffed.

"Already called him," Copeland replied, as if he weren't even breaking a sweat. "He's on the way."

They reached the interstate and ran up towards the line, and the scene was chaos. The four soldiers had been forced to retreat into the center barrier, with a couple dozen zombies completely surrounding it. On the main line, ghouls lined up shoulder to shoulder, hundreds in view and easily thousands behind them.

It was a sea of moaning and flailing, the corpses trying to figure out how to traverse the obstacle in front of them to get to a fresh meal. Every so often, one would flip over, stagger to its feet, and then join the others at the center barrier.

Copeland and Johnson stopped about twenty yards from the action, with not a single zombie paying them any attention. The gunfire coming from within the barrier ceased completely.

"How many mags you got?" the Sergeant asked.

Johnson checked. "Five, fresh."

"Give me two," Copeland said.

The Private handed them over, and Copeland grabbed two of his own, putting all four in his giant hand before yelling, "Bridge team, ammo incoming!" He stepped up and underhand threw the four mags. They hurtled through the air, landing perfectly in the center of the ring. "We're on the flanks, don't shoot us!" he added loudly, and then he and Johnson broke to either side of the bridge.

They took aim and fired at the zombies closest to the main line, making sure no soldier was in the line of fire. As they continued to shoot, several zombies turned their attention away from the trapped men, and to the fresh meat.

One corpse, dressed in military gear, turned and spotted Copeland, and immediately broke into a dead sprint. The Sergeant aimed and fired, but the bullet tore into the creature's throat. Before he could aim again, the runner was on him.

Copeland dropped his rifle and pushed against the soldier, gripping its vest and whipping it to the side. He used the momentum to shove it towards the edge of the bridge. It snarled and bit, with far more vigor than an older zombie, and Copeland avoided it as best he could, slamming it into the concrete barrier. He lashed down and grabbed its leg and flipped it over the side.

As he turned around, he came face to face with four creatures that had broken ranks and closed in on him. One by one, they dropped to the ground, bullets ripping through the side of their heads. He blinked and saw Johnson standing near the middle of the road, aiming in his direction.

He gave the Private an approving nod and then retrieved his gun, the two of them going back to work. The trio in the center took careful aim and hit zombies at near point blank range to conserve ammo, while Copeland and Johnson delivered decisive strikes of their own.

After a few minutes of intense battle, grunting, and sweating, and hard beating hearts, the threat on the soldier's side of the barrier was wiped out. The three men jumped out of the barrier, and one immediately began tending to the line, keeping the creatures at bay.

The other two walked up, one limping and leaning on the other.

"What happened to you, soldier?" Copeland asked.

The young man, no more than twenty-two, turned his leg to reveal a large bite wound on his left calf. Johnson shook his head and swallowed hard, but then spotted a zombie tumble over the barrier, so he ran off to deal with it.

Copeland raised his chin. "Can you stand, soldier?"

The young man looked at his friend and nodded that it was okay. He leaned on his own leg and motioned for his companion to get back to the line. When they were alone, Copeland stared straight into the young soldier's pained eyes.

"You know what the standing orders are, don't you, soldier?" the Sergeant asked.

The kid nodded gravely. "Yes, sir."

"You tell me how you want it," Copeland said gently.

The soldier clenched his fists, letting out a frustrated grunt and then looking over at the line, watching his three companions fight hand-to-hand with the sea of creatures. "If it's all the same to you, Sergeant," he said, eyes blazing as he turned back to Copeland, "I still have a little fight in me." He glanced down at his leg. "What do you say we don't report this wound until we have the bridge under control?"

Copeland smiled at the young man, proud at his force of will. "I think that can be arranged, soldier," he replied. "Get on the line."

The kid saluted. "Yes, sir." He hobbled off toward the line, ready to fight. As he went, there was a large explosion on the interstate, startling everyone except for Copeland.

He simply turned towards it and smiled. "All right Dawson," he said as he readied his weapon, "the route is clear. Now we just need Kowalski to do his job."

Kowalski looked out over the interstate bridge battlefield, seeing the horde stretched across the four lanes and back hundreds of yards. Copeland had just given him the order to make noise, and now he had the pressure to draw enough zombies away from the bridge and towards the snipers safely on the roof.

He ran to the front of the store, looking straight down at the doors. Zombies pressed into the opening, disappearing inside.

"Damn, the door is open," he muttered.

Doyle shrugged. "Not sure why that's a bad thing, they can't get up here," he pointed out.

"Yeah, but I gotta get down there," Kowalski replied.

Martin blinked at him. "Man, you're crazier than we thought," he said.

"Got my orders," Kowalski replied. "And besides, if we don't do this, our bridge team is gonna get overrun, which means this whole day was a waste."

Hurley sighed. "So, how do you want to do it?"

Kowalski looked around the immediate area. "Okay, spread out," he instructed, "we have to find an access hatch.

Something that leads down into the store, and preferably something with a ladder."

The four men branched out, running around the roof, pulling on anything that looked like a doorway or hatch. Finally, after several minutes of looking, Martin yelled out from the back corner of the roof.

"Got something!' he called.

The other three soldiers dashed over to join him. He shone his flashlight down a ladder that dropped ten feet onto a catwalk.

"Doyle, you're with me," Kowalski said. "You two, get back to the front and keep shooting. Anything you can do to keep the focus on you and not me."

The duo nodded and ran back to their posts. Kowalski hopped onto the ladder and climbed down, with Doyle not far behind. They dropped down onto the catwalk and surveyed the sprawling network of metal walkways that spanned the entirety of the giant store. The darkness made it difficult to see exactly what they were up against.

"Christ, haven't these builders ever heard of ambient light?" Kowalski muttered.

Doyle shrugged. "You think they got paid enough to care?"

"Fair enough," his companion admitted.

They raised their night vision scopes and began to scout out the top part of the store.

"Gotta find anything that can get us to the ground," Kowalski said.

Doyle continued to search. "And then what?" he asked.

"Not a fucking clue," Kowalski replied dryly. They continued to look, and then he finally found a ladder at the far end. "Bingo, let's move," he said.

They crept as quietly as they could, even though they were a good fifty feet above the ground. It was always good practice to make sure the zombies below didn't know where they were. After a few minutes, they reached the ladder which went straight down into a mechanical room in the back.

Kowalski glanced over the railing down into the store, seeing several creatures shuffling around in the dark.

"Okay," he said quietly, leaning in, "it looks like this room is closed off from the rest of the store. Bad news is, there's a shitload of zombies in there."

Doyle swallowed hard. "What do you want to do?' he asked.

Kowalski pursed his lips for a moment, thinking hard. "What in here would make a shitload of noise?" he murmured. "Like noise that would resonate to the bridge?"

"Power tools ain't gonna cut it," Doyle replied. "What about an alarm system?"

Kowalski shook his head. "Home alarm system?" he asked. "Not even sure we'd be able to activate them."

"Hell, what about a regular alarm?" Doyle wondered. "Like an alarm clock? Before all this went down, I saw some infomercial about the supersonic alarm clock. Claimed it was loud enough to wake up a coma patient. These stores usually carry shit like that, don't they?"

His companion shrugged. "I don't know, but it's the best idea we got going," he replied. "So we'll need those, and batteries." He paused as an idea came to him. "Oh, and maybe air horns?"

"Couldn't hurt to look," Doyle agreed.

They looked out over the store, checking through their night vision scopes, seeing lots of creatures, easily in the mid-dozens.

"This is gonna be a bitch," Kowalski said with a sigh.

Doyle cocked his head. "You want me to stay up here and pick 'em off?"

Kowalski contemplated for a moment and then nodded. "Yeah, get to the center of the catwalk," he instructed. "You just follow my movement, hit what you can. Also keep watch and let me know if I'm walking into something bad."

"How do I let you know?" Doyle asked.

Kowalski smirked. "Just yell," he replied. "They can't understand you, and if anything it'll draw them away from me.

Doyle chuckled, shaking his head at his moment of stupidity. "Let's do it," he said, and extended his fist.

Kowalski bumped it and then began the climb down the ladder. He paused before he got to the bottom, using his scope to see where the door was. He had a hard time looking over the gun, so he removed it and slung his rifle over his shoulder, using the scope by itself.

He moved to the door, knife in hand, and took a deep breath. *Okay, you got this,* he thought to himself. *It's just like a Black Friday sale, only less chaotic.*

Before he threw open the door, he looked down and spotted a couple of large tool bags. He gently and quietly removed the tools and then slung two bags over his shoulder. He gently opened the door and inched out into the back aisle. As he moved, a moan rumbled behind the door.

He darted away and then froze at the sight of a blurry figure moving towards him in the darkness. A booming shot echoed in the store, and the figure slumped to the ground.

Kowalski looked through the scope, seeing the zombie dead on the ground, and then raised his hand to give Doyle a thumbs up for the assist.

The shot excited the zombies in the store, starting up a dull roar of moans and shuffling as they tried to get a read on where their future meal was. Kowalski moved as quietly as he could, using the scope as a guide.

I know batteries are at the front of the store, he thought. *So let's start there.* He looked around for a moment to get his bearings and then crept towards the front. A few aisle down, moans came from just around the next corner, and inched up to peek around it.

There were two ghouls there, shuffling dumbly, within striking distance. He motioned to Doyle, pointing to the far one, and then did a stabbing motion with the knife to show that he would be handling the closer one.

A second later, his guardian angel yelled out, "Okay!"

Kowalski counted down silently before striking. As soon as he lunged forward, a shot ripped through the far creature's head, causing the closer one to whip around towards the noise.

He slammed the blade into the base of its skull, and as it dropped, he marveled at his skill in delivering a perfect strike in the dark. *If I'm this good blind, no wonder I'm such a badass,* he thought, chuckling to himself.

He continued to the front of the store, getting to the top of the aisle and looking through his scope. There were a dozen or so zombies around the cash registers, but he scanned past them to find the battery display.

With the target in sight, he checked past it to the front door, which had been completely obliterated under the sight of the horde outside. Most of the creatures were focused on the snipers on the roof, but one wrong noise inside could trigger a tsunami of death.

He plotted his course, so he could stay low and use the registers as cover from the zombies at the front. But that didn't help him with the dozen between him and the batteries. He looked over at the shelf next to him, seeing some small bottles of bug spray. He picked one up, feeling the weight to it as well as a metal exterior.

Okay, so all I have to do is throw this close enough for the register zombies to hear, and far enough away that the mass at the front door doesn't sweep over me, he thought, and shook his head. *Yeah, I totally got this.*

Kowalski broke from the top of the aisle, moving up towards the registers. He knelt down behind the end cap display, about ten yards away from the closest ghoul, a thirty-yard dash to the batteries.

This may be your last throw ever, so at least make it a good one, he urged himself, and lobbed the metal bottle towards the center of the store, arching it high over the top of the shelving. A second later, it clanged on the cement floor, rattling around loudly.

The zombies at the registers moaned loudly and began shuffling off in that direction.

Holy shit, did that work? He shook his head in disbelief. *Really?*

His excitement tempered when he heard moans coming from the front entrance. He peeked around the corner and his stomach sank at the sight of a dozen or so ghouls attracted by the noise.

Gotta move, he thought frantically, *you gotta move!* He psyched himself up and moved from cover, quickly and quietly going from register to register, pausing at each end cap.

The footsteps and moans got louder as he got closer to the battery display. As he took a knee at the last end cap just before it, a shot boomed from above, and a corpse crumbled a few feet away.

Kowalski dashed past it to the batteries. *Fuck, what do these things take?* He used the scope to check all the battery types, finally shaking his head and opening one of the tool bags. *Fuck it, I'm taking everything.* He tore the packages from the shelf, grabbing every type of standard battery he could get his hands on.

Another shot boomed, and another corpse fell. This triggered moaning not just towards the door, but from the aisle he'd thrown the can down.

Good enough! Kowalski didn't worry about being quiet this time, running parallel to the front of the store. His footsteps excited the zombies behind him, drawing even more into the store and in his direction.

He sprinted about forty yards, holding the scope up to his eye so he had some rough idea of where he was going. He spotted a zombie in front of him, but within seconds the head exploded, so he ducked down behind the paint-mixing stand near the front of the store.

As he caught his breath, he looked through his scope at the main part of the store. There were still several zombies pursuing him, but they were a good thirty yards away and slowing as if they didn't have him in sight. He looked up at the aisle headers.

Hardware, door fixtures, cleaning… he read. *Fuck, where are these things?* He kept scanning until he stopped on one sign that read *Home goods*. Figuring that was his best chance, he checked, and then sighed when he realized that it was the aisle where the can landed.

Well, bad luck is at least a form of luck, he thought, *so the fates haven't completely abandoned you.*

He looked up to Doyle, who he hoped was watching him. He motioned to the aisle he needed, that was now filled with zombies.

A second later, Doyle yelled, "Are you insane?!"

Kowalski simply looked up at him, giving a big smile and a thumbs up. He imagined his companion sighing and shaking his head.

"Hang on, I got an idea," Doyle called back.

There was a moment of silence, and then bullets started flying. In addition to the boom of the gun going off, there were metal pings coming from the front of the store, and then a high-pitched hissing sound. Kowalski's eyes widened when he realized Doyle was firing at the propane tanks.

He had a moment of panic, though he told himself that without a significant spark those things weren't going to detonate. *Still, it's a risky move,* he thought, but it couldn't be helped. What was done was done.

At least the zombies from the aisle shambled towards the hissing sound, and he waited for several to go by before moving. As they staggered, one of the ghouls got its sleeve caught on a display, and no matter how much it shifted around, it couldn't break free.

Okay fates, I get it, I have bad luck, Kowalski thought bitterly. *Can you lay off now?*

He moved up quickly and quietly, hugging the top of the aisle, and darting across the openings in case something else was waiting for him. As he approached his target, another shot went off and the trapped zombie slumped on the display. Unfortunately the dead weight pulled down the metal structure, crashing loudly on the floor.

Kowalski froze, and then raised his scope, watching several of the zombies that had left turn around and head towards the sound. *Nice shooting, Tex,* he thought.

"Sorry, I got you!" Doyle called, and shots rang out at a rapid pace.

The returning zombies began to fall like flies, and Kowalski didn't wait, trusting his companion to have his back. Unconcerned with his noise due to the gunfire, he tore forward, sweeping the aisle to make sure it was empty, and then studied the shelves.

Halfway down, he looked around frantically, hoping the alarm clocks would jump out at him. He finally spotted something promising and picked up a box.

Supersonic alarm clock, he read to himself, *wakes the dead, or your money back.* He shook his head. *So that's what causes the apocalypse. At least they get to keep their money.*

He stuffed six boxes into the tool bag and closed it up. "Got them!" he called between gunshots. "Headed back!"

Kowalski ran down the aisle back towards the maintenance room, awkwardly looking through the scope as he went.

"Big crowd ahead!" Doyle yelled. "Get to the wall!"

Kowalski reached the center aisle and looked down towards the target wall, where several zombies came up from the back of the store. He put his head down and ran, trusting that his partner would do his job.

Blood splattered on his arm as he ran past a zombie, but he didn't stop. He made it to the side wall, staring at the maintenance room. Several zombies came towards it from the other side, so he took off at a sprint. He pumped his legs as hard as he could, the chorus of moans rising and echoing.

He pushed his body beyond what he'd ever pushed it before, beating the zombies by a couple of steps, and threw the door open, rushing inside. As he tried to pull it closed behind him, a set of rotted hands grabbed it from the back and pulled.

Kowalski strained, keeping the door as shut as he could, putting his boot against the doorframe. "Any time Doyle!" he yelled.

Another shot went off, and the hands fell from the door, allowing Kowalski to slam it shut.

"Holy fucking balls man," he muttered to himself as he made his way to the ladder. "I'm never doing that again." He climbed up, starting at the top when Doyle squatted there, waiting for him.

"You good man?" he asked.

Kowalski huffed. "Yeah, I'm good," he replied. "Just hoping I get a promotion from this."

"Does rank really matter at this point?" Doyle asked with a light laugh.

His companion smirked and shook his head. "Yeah, it means I would be able to delegate this to you while I set up here all comfy and shooting," he drawled.

Doyle chuckled and helped him up, and they made their way back to the roof. Once they emerged from the hatch, Kowalski let out a loud whistle so that the others knew they were back. Martin and Hurley gave a quick wave before going back to shooting.

Doyle and Kowalski walked to the back of the store, where the latter dumped out the tool bags. They quickly ripped open the boxes and battery packages, assembling them.

Kowalski fiddled with the controls on one of the finished ones. "All right, here goes nothing," he said, and then hit the alarm button. Immediately both men covered their ears as the 115 decibel alarm nearly blew out their eardrums. He switched it off. "Fucking hell, that's loud."

"If this doesn't do it, I have no idea what will," Doyle replied, and they scrambled to slam batteries into the rest of the clocks.

They brought all six to the air conditioner unit near the back of the store and aimed them towards the bridge, nodding while covering their ears as best they could before hitting all the alarm buttons.

The sound was deafening, blasting through the air in alternating beats. They backed away from the clocks and then went to the far end of the back of the store.

Come on motherfuckers, you know you want to know what this is, Kowalski thought, and both men raised their scopes, relieved to see that some of the creatures from the bridge at the back started to wander towards them.

"Hell yeah!" Kowalski cried, raising a fist. "Sonic doom for the win!"

The men exchanged a high five as they kept watch, surveying more and more creatures coming their way.

Kowalski pulled out his walkie-talkie, lifting it to his lips. "Hey Sarge, come in," he said.

A few seconds later, Copeland replied, "Not sure what that is soldier, but we can hear it down here pretty good."

The sniper grinned. "Sonic alarms," he said loudly, "and if you can hear it there, then you can only imagine what it sounds like up here."

"Question is," the Sergeant countered, "are they working?"

Kowalski nodded. "They're starting to," he said. "Already have several dozen peeling off and coming our way. Only a matter of time until the others join."

"Damn fine work Kowalski," Copeland said. "Damn fine work."

The sniper straightened his shoulders. "Thank you, sir."

"Copeland out."

The duo of snipers stood and watched as more and more creatures wandered off the bridge, heading towards the sonic distraction.

CHAPTER TWELVE

The alarms had been blaring for a half an hour, and the zombie horde at the barricade became smaller and smaller. The sun began to peek up from behind the horizon, illuminating the horrific carnage on the bridge.

There was a pile of bodies stretched across the interstate, easily three deep and piled three and four high in some spots. With the soldiers out of reach, and the alarms blaring in the stance, the stragglers on the bridge had lost all interest and wandered away.

Sergeant Copeland stood proud, nodding in approval of what his men had been able to accomplish. As he admired the scene, Dawson approached.

"Hell of a night, huh Sarge?" the Corporal asked.

"Understatement, soldier," Copeland replied with a sigh. "Understatement."

Dawson crossed his arms. "So, what's next?" he asked.

"I'm going to keep a skeleton crew here to do some reinforcements on this barricade," the Sergeant explained. "It barely held a couple thousand, so no way in hell it's holding back a hundred thousand. I want you to take the rest of the men and start clearing the neighborhoods. Those car alarm batteries aren't going to last forever, so we need to strike while we can."

"Any word on reinforcements or a resupply?" Dawson asked.

Copeland shook his head. "No, but I'm supposed to talk to the Captain in an hour or so."

"Good deal," the Corporal replied. "If you need me, I'll be on comm."

"Be safe, Dawson," Copeland said, and watched him walk away and begin to bark out orders for men to follow him.

Most of the group left, except for five standing at the barricade. Copeland took a deep breath and approached the young soldier who'd been bitten, standing guard as strong as ever. He sighed, showing a brief moment of reluctance as he knew it was time to do what he didn't want to have to do.

"Rest of you take five," the Sergeant said, "get some chow from the Super Center."

The four men shared glances, looking at him and then the young soldier. They nodded at him, silently paying their respects and thanking him for his service that night. As they cleared out, the kid stood firm.

"Is it time, sir?" he asked.

"It is, soldier," Copeland replied. "You've done a damn fine job. I couldn't ask for a braver soldier to be under my command."

The kid nodded, but remained stoic. "Thank you sir, that means a lot to me."

"Do you have any requests?" Copeland asked.

"Just one, sir," the young man said politely. "I would like to go out a warrior."

The Sergeant shook his head. "You don't have to worry about that, son."

"I do, sir," the kid replied. "If you… do what you need to do right now, it won't feel like I'm a warrior. It will feel like I'm being put down like an old dog."

Copeland nodded thoughtfully. "What would you like, then?"

The young soldier set down his guns and ammo and pulled his knife. "With your permission sir," he began, "I would like to hop that barrier and go slaughter as many of those things as I can before they overwhelm me. Using my knife only, so that none of the ammunition goes to waste. Even if there is enough to me to reanimate, I won't be a runner."

Copeland pursed his lips. "You know that goes against direct orders," he said.

"I won't tell if you don't," the soldier replied.

The Sergeant cracked a smile, impressed at the young man's quip. He contemplated for another moment, weighing his options, and then nodded.

"Happy hunting, soldier," he finally said, and saluted the kid.

The young man saluted him back, and then hopped the barricade, hobbling towards the zombie horde. Copeland watched, eyes shining, as he stabbed a couple of stragglers in the back of the head before moving up towards the bulk.

The Sergeant turned around and walked away from the barricade back towards the Super Center for a bite to eat.

END

Up next: The next phase of the operation. Corporal Herrera joins a team air dropping onto Mercer Island to create a diversion zone in "Seattle - Part 2".

DEAD AMERICA: THE NORTHWEST INVASION
BOOK 4
SEATTLE - PT. 2
BY DEREK SLATON
© 2020

CHAPTER ONE

Day Zero +23

Captain Kersey sat in his makeshift office, anxiously looking at his watch as the time approached one in the morning. "Those planes should have been back by now," he muttered, and stood up.

He paced back and forth, unable to stop himself from imagining the planes crashed and burning amidst a sea of undead runners wearing the faces of his soldiers. They'd left a little less than an hour ago to drop off Sergeant Copeland and the northern blockade group.

A knock at the door ceased his nervous pacing. "Come in," he said.

David, his civilian geek tech specialist, entered the office carrying a mug of steaming coffee. "Here," he said, "thought you might need a pick me up. These all-nighters can be a bitch if you aren't properly lubricated."

"Appreciate it," Kersey replied with a sigh, and took the ceramic mug, "but given how rundown this airport is, I'm a little concerned about the quality in this cup."

David chuckled. "Beggars being choosers, huh?" he teased.

The Captain shared his laugh and raised his mug in a cheers before taking a small sip.

"Don't worry, I pulled it from a gas station in town," David said, leaning on the desk. "Needed to stock up on energy drinks."

Kersey nodded and then took a deep breath. "Has… has there been any word on the planes?"

"As a matter of fact, just heard from the lead pilot," David replied with a nod. "They hit a headwind after dropping off the team, so they were delayed a bit. Should be landing in the next ten minutes or so."

Kersey's stomach lifted a little at the news. "How long to get them back in the air?" he asked.

"I have the refueling truck on standby," David explained, "so it shouldn't take more than ten, fifteen minutes or so."

The Captain checked his watch, shaking his head with a frown. "Barely an hour in and we're already twenty minutes behind schedule."

"Given that you've scraped together so much civilian aircraft and materials, it's a miracle these missions are happening at all," David pointed out.

Kersey tilted his head back and forth and then took a sip of his coffee. "This is true."

David pulled a can of his energy drink of choice from his deep pocket and cracked it open with a whzzztt, toasting the Captain before taking a long gulp.

"Do you have printouts for the Mercer Island mission?" Kersey finally asked.

David nodded as he swallowed his mouthful. "Yeah, I handed them off to the Sergeant leading that mission," he said. "He asked if he could give them a look over before you addressed them."

"Guess I should look busy, huh?" Kersey asked, scratching the back of his head.

David smirked and shook his head. "Nah, you're good," he replied. "Perks of being a Captain, they wait on you."

Kersey smiled and took another thoughtful sip of coffee. He took a deep breath, steeled himself, and then headed out of the office to the hangar where the team was ready.

"What do you want me to focus on next?" David asked, following him out.

"Corporal Bretz will be up at 0-three hundred," Kersey replied. "Please make sure we have all the maps and plans ready for him."

The tech specialist nodded. "I'll make it happen, Captain," he said, and then headed off briskly for his work area.

Kersey made the long walk across the airstrip, taking in the sight of numerous people moving in unison, making every preparation necessary. As he moved into the hangar, there was a group of men off to the side prepping their parachutes and gear.

As soon as he got close, Sergeant McCarty immediately hopped up from his kneeling position and rushed over. "Captain Kersey," he declared with a firm salute. "I'm Sergeant McCarty, ready to do battle for you, sir."

Kersey returned the salute to the upbeat man. "Thank you, Sergeant," he replied. "I really appreciate you volunteering for this mission."

"When I heard it involved a rough terrain landing, I knew I was the man for the job," McCarty said with a sharp nod.

The Captain raised an eyebrow. "Hopefully you can impart some of your experience onto this group," he said, motioning to the preparing soldiers, "because unless I'm mistaken, you're the only one who has made a rough terrain landing."

"Honestly, there weren't many of us to begin with," McCarty admitted. "One of

the fringe benefits of almost always
having an overwhelming force is that you
rarely have to get sneaky to land in a war
zone."

Kersey nodded thoughtfully. "Plus,
I'm sure it helped that the desert isn't
exactly known for its lush forests," he
added.

"Truth be told," the Sergeant replied
with a chuckle, "I'd much rather land in
the trees than suffer through another one
of those summers."

The Captain clapped him on the back.
"Well, today's your lucky day," he said,
"because you're getting your wish."

"Thank you, sir," McCarty replied,
straightening his shoulders.

"Why don't you go ahead and pass out
those maps," Kersey said, motioning to the
cluster of papers in his hand, "and we'll
get started."

The Sergeant nodded and turned to his
men, handing out the maps. "All right, all
right," he said as he moved, "listen up.
The Captain here is going to go over the
mission objectives, and then I'm going to
fill you in on everything else you need to
know." He stepped aside, motioning to
Kersey. "Floor is yours, Captain."

The soldiers turned their attention
on their superior, a few of them relaxing
to study the island maps.

"Thank you, Sergeant," Kersey said
with a nod, and then raised his chin.
"Good morning, men." He waited for the
murmured replies of the tired soldiers,
and then continued, "Today we have a top
priority mission that is vital to the
success of this invasion. What you are
looking at on the map there is Mercer
Island. Pre-war, it was home to twenty-six
thousand residents, most of them wealthier
than any of us could ever hope to dream of
being. While their wealth bought them big
houses in a secluded area, it didn't buy
them safety from the apocalypse." He
paused, clasping his hands in front of
him. "Satellite imagery shows that a
significant number of the twenty-six
thousand residents have not only been
turned, but they're out and about. And due
to some plane maintenance issues, there
are only going to be thirty of you going
in to take them on."

Hisses and whispers erupted
throughout the soldiers, and McCarty's
brow furrowed.

"Quiet down!" he barked. "Captain's
speaking!"

Kersey inclined his head towards him.
"Thank you, Sergeant," he said. "I know
the odds are stacked against you, and
frankly they're stacked against all of us.
This invasion is a gamble, and if we don't

take risks and pull it off, then
everything is over." He crossed his arms.
"I hope each and every one of you
understands that."

There was a ripple in the
affirmative, though the faces were still
concerned.

"The Captain did not year you!"
McCarty barked.

"Yes, sir!" the soldiers declared in
unison.

Kersey nodded to him and then
addressed the men. "If you will look at
the southeast portion of your map, you
will see a small forest circled," he
began. "This is your landing zone. People
in D.C. have been monitoring this island
for the last twenty-four hours, and this
is the only place where there aren't huge
congregations of zombies. Not going to
lie, it's going to hurt."

"A lot," McCarty added brightly.

Private Gilbert raised his hand,
scowling deeply. Corporal Herrera grabbed
his arm from beside him, trying to pull it
back down, but Gilbert tore his body away
and kept his arm staunchly in the air.

"What is it, Private?" Kersey asked,
tone clipped. He couldn't help but still
feel disdain for the ex-Sergeant that had
cost so many lives with his ego.

Gilbert lowered his hand. "Sir, with all due respect," he said, raising his chin, "why aren't we doing a water landing? Wouldn't that be safer?"

"Sergeant, would you care to take that one?" the Captain asked, cocking his head.

McCarty shot daggers at the middle-aged soldier. "Because Private, when you combine the amount of gear you will be hauling into battle with your complete lack of experience in water landings, half of you would drown while the other half would wish you drowned," he replied, and then glanced back at Kersey. "Sir."

The Captain raised an eyebrow. "Does that answer your question, Private?"

Gilbert frowned and lowered his gaze, nodding.

"Okay, just to the southwest of the forest, you'll see a building circled," Kersey continued, holding up his own map. "This is your rally point. It's a former country club, so the hope is that it'll be relatively deserted. First to arrive will secure the building, or if it appears to be too overwhelmed, secure a perimeter on the eighteenth green. From there, you will split off into two teams. The bridge team will be tasked with working their way to this shopping complex in the north." He tapped at the area on the map, holding it up high so the men could see. "To secure the trucks in the back of these two stores. It is a three and a half mile hike from the rally point, so this team will have to move and move quickly."

McCarty nodded. "I will be leading this team personally," he said, "so whoever is with me had better be ready to keep pace."

"You will have the standard layout of two hundred and ten rounds," Kersey added, "along with your melee weapons and sidearm, so avoiding detection is going to be key to this mission succeeding. Once the trucks are secure, you are to proceed to the I-ninety bridges to the east and west at the northernmost part of the island. You won't be able to plug them up completely, but the trucks should provide enough of a barricade to hold back the majority of the horde that will be coming from downtown and the suburbs."

Private Dixon raised his hand, his eyes one of the only sets that were bright at the ungodly hour.

Kersey pointed at him. "Yes… um…" He struggled to place the soldier's name.

"Private Dixon, sir," the young man replied.

The Captain nodded. "Go ahead," he said.

"Sir, why not just blow the bridges?" Dixon asked.

Kersey shrugged. "Because someone with a much higher pay grade decided they wanted to keep them up," he replied.

"Fair enough," Dixon agreed with a firm nod.

"Now, the second team has a two front mission," Kersey continued. "Their first task is to clear the high school to the southwest of the country club. This one is going to be dangerous, as the sports fields appear to be packed with zombies. The quieter you can do this the better, because this is going to be a rally point for the reinforcements arriving by boat." He held up a hand. "Which brings me to your second objective. About half a mile to the west are a string of docks that must be secured with the route to the school being cleared. As we speak, ship-based soldiers are departing for Vashon Island, which appears to be loaded down with the boats of people who were fleeing the outbreak in the early hours of this. Shortly after dawn, you can expect the first batch of soldiers to be arriving on the island, and they're going to need a place to stage." He raised his chin. "Once the sun is up, your orders are to begin clearing the island of any zombie not secure in a structure. When this happens, it's imperative that the truck blockade is in place, because that noise is going to attract a lot of attention."

Private Dixon raised his hand again, and Sergeant McCarty narrowed his eyes.

"Private!" he barked.

Kersey held up a hand to the annoyed Sergeant to calm him down. "It's okay, Sergeant," the Captain assured him. "I'm happy to answer questions. What is it, Private?"

"Sir, I think I speak for everyone here when I say we're going to do our job and whip zombie ass on Mercer Island," Dixon began, lowering his hand. "However, I think we'd all like to know exactly why we are going on what amounts to a suicide mission? I think knowing how we fit into the grand scheme of things would help to motivate us."

McCarty crossed his arms, eyes blazing. "Doing your job and surviving should be motivation enough, Private!" he snapped.

"Private Dixon is right," Kersey cut in. "It doesn't seem fair to drop you right in the thick of things, outnumbered eight hundred to one, and not know why. Plus, it's not like we have to worry about the mission details falling into enemy hands."

There was a ripple of chuckles, albeit nervous ones.

Kersey took a deep breath, clasping his hands in front of him. "In a nutshell, you are going to be turning Mercer Island into one giant decoy," he explained. "Once it's secure, we are going to be moving in hundreds of men and equipment to drum up as much noise as possible so that the zombies on both sides of the mainland will come to the waterfront. This is not only going to make life a whole lot easier when we start moving in the main force from the east, but will also greatly reduce the potential they get overrun by a massive horde."

The soldiers glanced at one another, nodding in approval.

"Knowing some of these boys like I do," Dixon piped up, "I can safely say we've all been called worse things than decoys before."

The room erupted into laughter, with even McCarty cracking a smile.

The roar of planes landing behind them cut through the air, and the Sergeant raised a hand, whirling it above his head, snapping back into work mode.

"Sounds like our ride, boys!" he barked. "Let's start getting suited up!"

Kersey straightened his shoulders. "Be safe out there," he declared.

There was a loud, emphatic chorus in the affirmative, and he gave them an appraising nod. He stepped to the side to allow them to get ready, but caught Herrera's eye and waved for him to come over.

"Yes, Captain?" the Corporal asked as he approached.

Kersey leaned in, lowering his voice. "Wanted to check with you and see how our problem child is doing?" he asked.

"Gilbert?" Herrera replied and shook his head. "He's still pouting a little from being demoted, but he's doing what I tell him to. Might have a little lip behind it, but he complies."

Kersey nodded, brow furrowed. "You know if you have any issues with him…" He let the insinuation hang in the air, and the Corporal playfully gave him a finger gun.

"Don't worry sir," Herrera assured him, "he's put his last person in danger."

The two men turned to see Private Dixon zipping around to the other men in the squad, helping them with their packs and giving words of encouragement, sometimes making them laugh.

"What do you know about Dixon, there?" Kersey asked.

Herrera shrugged. "Only been with him the last couple of days," he admitted. "Seems capable enough for a grunt."

"Looks like he has the trust of the men," Kersey pointed out. "Not an easy thing to get."

The Corporal smirked, a twinkle in his eye. "I don't know, I found it to be pretty easy."

"Well, not everybody gets to beat down a superior officer after they endanger the unit," Kersey shot back, and they shared a small laugh.

McCarty glanced over and pursed his lips. "Corporal, are you waiting on an invitation to join this excursion?" he demanded. "Because if you so require it, I can send a runner out to find a silver platter with which I can deliver one to you."

Kersey waved a hand at the creative Sergeant. "That's my bad, Sergeant," he admitted.

"Appreciate it, Captain," McCarty replied. "Corporal, you will be riding in my plane so that we may have a talk en route."

Herrera glanced at Kersey, who gave him a playful thumbs up in apology. The Corporal scratched the back of his head and then walked over to get geared up.

Kersey headed out of the hangar, looking at the planes being refueled before glancing back at the soldiers he was likely sending to their deaths. He took a deep breath, swallowing hard before heading back to his office.

The planes soared above the darkened landscape, carrying the soldiers heading to what could be the last battle of their lives. In the rear plane, McCarty shifted and adjusted his headset, picking up a second one and handing it across to Herrera so they could speak over the loud noise.

"Can you hear me, Corporal?" he asked when his subordinate slid the headset over his ear.

Herrera nodded. "Yes, sir."

"Good," the Sergeant replied. "Now from what I understand, you recently got a field promotion."

The Corporal nodded again. "Yes sir, a few days ago during the Spokane assault."

McCarty looked him up and down and then raised his chin. "Normally I like having experienced men as my second in command," he began, "but Captain Kersey seems to think you're up to the task despite your inexperience. I've heard other soldiers whispering about how you got your promotion, but I want to hear it from you."

"Not much to tell, really," Herrera replied, and inclined his head to Gilbert. "The former Sergeant here shit the bet,

got a few good soldiers killed, and I had
to step up."

"Is that all?" McCarty asked,
furrowing his brow.

The Corporal swallowed hard, and
lowered his gaze. "I… may have sucker
punched him and threatened to shoot him
after his ignoring of the orders killed a
couple of my friends," he admitted.

McCarty cracked a smile. "Well, I'd
like to think if I pulled the same kind of
nonsense he pulled," he said, "you'd deal
with me accordingly."

"You can take that to the bank,
Sergeant," the Corporal replied firmly,
meeting his superior's gaze.

McCarty nodded. "Good," he replied,
"I like having no nonsense people working
with me." He cocked his head and raised a
finger. "I am curious about one thing,
though."

"What's that?" Herrera asked.

"Why are you insistent on bringing
him along?" the Sergeant asked.

The Corporal took a deep breath. "Two
reasons," he replied, "One, I'm gonna make
damn sure he pays off his debts to the men
whose lives he squandered."

"And two?" McCarty raised an eyebrow.

Herrera grinned. "I get to push his
ass out of an airplane."

The Sergeant chuckled, shaking his head. "I look forward to seeing you in action," he said.

The plane suddenly throttled back, startling most of the men, Herrera included. McCarty checked his watch before changing the channel on his headset to speak with the pilot.

"There's no way we're already at the jump zone," the Sergeant said, turning to face the cockpit. "Why are we slowing down?"

The pilot shook his head. "Engine is running hot, so I gotta dial it back," he replied. "Don't worry, we aren't going to be more than four or five minutes behind the others."

"Four or five minutes is an eternity in a war zone, son," McCarty warned.

The pilot sighed. "So is the four or five minutes it takes to crash land when the engine catches fire," he shot back.

McCarty glared at him for a beat, and saw it returned, so he backed down, knowing that he was right. He nodded in defeat.

"So what you gotta do to get us there safe," the Sergeant conceded. "We'll make it work." He flipped the channel back to the Corporal. "We're good, just five minutes behind the others. Which means we're gonna have to haul ass."

Herrera nodded, and then pulled his headset down, leaning over to the man on his right to tell him the situation right into his ear. That soldier then turned and passed it to the man next to him, and so on. Soon, all the soldiers were nodding, accepting the news.

The plane fell silent of speaking, with the men looking out the window at the moonlit ground, contemplating the task at hand. As they approached the jump zone, downtown Seattle came into view on the horizon, standing up tall. The moon reflected off of the glass of the buildings, as well as the Space Needle.

Herrera noticed the concerned expression on McCarty's face, and his brow furrowed. He put his headset back on and asked, "You good, Sergeant?"

"Yeah," McCarty replied, shaking his head. "Just hoping this goes better than that debacle we had in Kansas City."

The Corporal felt his blood run cold. "You were in K.C.?" he asked.

"I was," the Sergeant replied. "Along with a lot of other boys who didn't make it out."

Herrera swallowed hard. "I'm sorry for your loss, Sergeant."

McCarty turned his gaze on the Corporal, all hint of concern gone from his stern expression. "Just means we're

gonna have to kick their share of ass,
too."

Herrera nodded firmly, giving him a
thumbs up, wisely deciding not to press
the issue further. Another few moments
ticked by, before the pilot tapped the
Sergeant on the shoulder.

"We jump in sixty!" McCarty barked,
voice carrying to the men clustered
around.

Herrera removed his headset and got
the men ready, looking out the window to
see the island coming up fast. It was big
and dark, with patches of clear field and
developments all around it. After a
moment, he found the landing zone, an
unmistakable dark patch on the southern
portion of the island.

The plane throttled back a little
more, allowing them a stable departure.
McCarty gave the signal, and the Corporal
threw open the door to the plane. He
stepped to the side, looking back at
Gilbert, who bounced from foot to foot,
psyching himself up to jump.

Herrera reached out and grabbed his
parachute shoulder strap, giving a heave
to throw him from the plane, prompting a
nod of approval from McCarty.

The other soldiers piled out of the
plane in short order, the Corporal and
Sergeant jumping last. They plummeted

through the air, hurtling rapidly towards the ground. At target altitude, they pulled their rip cords to deploy their chutes, the soldiers floating on the wind.

At the slower descent, gunfire could be heard popping off sporadically on the ground. Herrera's heart skipped a beat with each shot that went off, worrying about just how bad it was on the ground. What if the woods were infested with ghouls? They could become living pinatas.

Within a second or two, the hypothetical threat became real fear as the wind picked up, strong gusts blowing them off course. He held onto his straps, struggling to control the descent, but it was no use. The wooded landing zone quickly became unreachable, as well as the rally point.

The Corporal looked below to see the soldiers who'd leapt first heading to the high school, careening out of control. At a few hundred yards above the ground, he realized that the majority of the ground was moving.

He pulled as hard as he could on the parachute, trying everything he could to divert course. Two of the soldiers below were able to shift their descent to the right, crashing hard into the pavement of the parking lot. As they did, the dense mass from the field moved in their direction.

Two other soldiers weren't as fortunate, as the wind had blown them too far off course. Herrera watched helplessly as they landed right in the middle of the field, quickly vanishing under a swarming mass of rotted flesh.

Gunfire on the ground erupted, coming from the two soldiers from the parking lot who'd managed to avoid an instant death. With the ground rapidly approaching, the Corporal struggled to make the turn, getting just enough of it to land on the far edge of the parking lot.

He tumbled forward, landing hard on the pavement, his chute dragging him across the hard surface. Moans came from nearby, too close for comfort, and Herrera looked up to see a swarm dozens strong grasping at the chute, tangling themselves up in it.

He quickly pulled his knife and started hacking at the parachute lines, the horde growing closer and closer to him. Panic set in as they reached ten yards away, and he screamed as he sawed at the cords.

Gunshots rang out rapidly, striking several creatures in the head and dropping them. Herrera looked back to see Private

Choi and Gilbert running up to him, guns blazing.

"What the fuck you waiting on?!" Gilbert barked. "Get up!"

Choi continued to fire as Gilbert helped Herrera out of his parachute, the Corporal scrambling to his feet. The trio retreated a bit, putting room between them and the horde.

"You all right?" the ex-Sergeant asked.

Herrera nodded. "Yeah, fine."

"Where are the others?" Choi asked breathlessly. "Where's Sarge?"

The Corporal shook his head. "Two of them landed on the field," he explained. "I don't know about McCarty."

A moment later, rapid gunfire erupted in the south, on the outer fringe of the field. They quickly rushed towards the noise, keeping their eyes peeled for trouble.

About two hundred yards away they spotted muzzle flashes going towards a slow-moving mass of rotted corpses. As they got closer, they spotted Sergeant McCarty, tangled in his chute cords that had woven in with a horde of zombies.

They ran hard, raising their assault rifles as they went, and opened fire at fifty yards. The bullets weren't accurate, but they were desperate.

At thirty yards, the mass got closer and closer to the Sergeant, who struggled to free himself from the tangled mass of cords. He fired several more three-round bursts before his gun went dry, and the ghouls overwhelmed him.

Herrera skidded to a stop twenty yards from the Sergeant.

"What are you doing?" Choi demanded. "We gotta help him!"

The Corporal shook his head, knowing it was too late. Choi let out a frustrated scream as they watched McCarty reach into his bag, pulling out a grenade and jerking out the pin with his teeth just as the zombies piled on top of him.

The gruff Sergeant didn't even scream as the ghouls ripped into his flesh.

The trio of soldiers rushed away from the scene, not wanting to get caught in the shrapnel. As they cleared the area, a dull explosion sounded, countless bodies softening the noise of the blast.

The Corporal walked with determination into the neighborhood beside the school, the entire weight of the mission now on his shoulders.

Herrera, Gilbert, and Choi took a knee at the edge of a neighborhood, looking out over a golf course leading to the country club rally point. Choi kept a watch on the rear, as the fighting through the neighborhood had been tough and consistent.

"I'm starting to think nobody on this island survived this," he muttered.

Gilbert wrinkled his nose. "And apparently everybody was having a picnic, too," he spat. "Haven't seen this many of those things out in the open since Spokane."

"Still doesn't change the fact we have to get our job done," Herrera said firmly. He scanned the golf course, seeing small patches of creatures, making the plotting of the path through more difficult.

"I can't believe Sarge is gone," Choi groaned, scrubbing his hands down his face. "What the fuck are we gonna do now?"

Gilbert clenched his jaw. "We're gonna listen to the Corporal," he said. "He'll get us through."

Herrera blinked at the ex-Sergeant in surprise, and Gilbert gave him a confident nod. The Corporal wasn't sure what had brought it on, though in the back of his

mind he had a feeling the Private knew
they were in deep shit. If even Gilbert
could see that, then he worried they were
in the worst shape they could be. He shook
his head, assigning his brain to the task
at hand.

"We're on the move," he said, "follow
close, melee kills only. We don't know
what the situation is at the rally point,
and until we do, I don't want any more
attention to us than necessary." He stared
at them expectantly. "Good?"

Both Privates nodded and pulled out
their knives, and he led them out. They
ran to the golf course, hopping over the
waist-high chain-link fence and darting
onto the fairway. There was a group of
four zombies there, and Herrera led them
up, knocking several over as the trio made
short work of them with stabs to the head.

The country club building was half a
mile from their location, with the
moonlight doing just enough to illuminate
the rolling grassy hills of the course.
The Corporal led them through, darting in
between smaller groups of zombies when
they could, reaching a final duo of ghouls
in the way.

Herrera ran past them, letting the
Privates dispatch the undead so he could
get within view of the club. He knelt by a

tree on the hill, studying the area as the other two joined him.

"There's some movement inside," he murmured as he studied the shuffling beneath some artificial light source. "Looks like they've secured the rally point," he confirmed. "Let's get moving."

They moved quickly across the field, making sure to wave and zigzag a bit in case someone was keeping watch. The last thing they wanted was a friendly fire incident, especially when so many of their team had already been lost.

As they approached, a tall blond soldier waved maniacally at them. "We got friendlies!" he called back into the room. "Man, are we glad to see you," he gushed as the trio approached. "Thought you were goners."

"Some of us were," Gilbert replied.

Ayers looked them over, eyes widening. "Where's Sergeant McCarty?"

Herrera shook his head. "He didn't make it," he replied. "Lost two others, too."

Dixon came around from the other side of the room as Ayers' shoulders slumped. "What's going on?" he asked, and spotted the Corporal. "Where's Sarge?"

"He didn't make it," Herrera repeated.

Gilbert took a deep breath. "Went out like a beast, though."

"Holy shit," Dixon said, and then turned to the Corporal. "So, you're in charge, now?"

Herrera nodded, letting out a deep sigh. "It would appear that way."

"Well, I hope you're up to the task," Dixon replied, jerking his thumb over his shoulder, "because we got a shit-tastic situation on our hands."

The Corporal straightened his shoulders. "What's going on?"

"Well, for starters, whoever thought it was a good idea to land in the woods deserves to have their ass kicked," the Private snarled, "because it did not go well." He pointed to the far corner of the room where two soldiers laid on couches, several other men attempting to make a leg splint. "One split his leg so bad the bone was sticking out, and the other face planted into a tree so hard I'll be surprised if he remembers the last year."

"We should all be that lucky," Choi muttered as they came inside proper, Ayers closing the door behind them.

"On top of that, we still have seven missing," Dixon added.

The trio blinked at him in shock.

"Christ!" Choi blurted. "We're already down twelve men, and we haven't even gotten started yet?"

Herrera furrowed his brow. "Honest opinion," he began, "do you think any of them made it and just haven't found their way here, yet?"

Dixon immediately shook his head. "That forest was the stuff of nightmares, man," he declared. "If you were lucky enough to get to the ground in one piece, you had movement everywhere. That moon didn't do a damn bit of good either, lighting up just enough to scare you shitless. Frankly, I'm amazed that any of us survived it."

"Well I'm glad you did, because you're going to lead the docks team," Herrera said.

Both Dixon and Gilbert spat, "What?!" at the same time.

"Whoa, whoa, whoa, Corporal," Dixon blathered, putting up his hands, "I am not the man for that job."

"Corporal, I know we have our differences," Gilbert cut in, "but you know I can lead that assault."

Dixon motioned to the ex-Sergeant. "I tend to agree with him."

"Enough!" Herrera snapped. "Dixon, you're going to lead the dock mission." He put up a hand to stop Gilbert from speaking. "Take Choi and go help the injured to a secure room here. We can't take them with us, and we can't leave somebody to guard them. Make sure they have provisions, because it could be days before anybody gets back to them."

Gilbert wrinkled his nose, looking like he wanted to scream, but bit his tongue. "Yes sir," he mumbled, and headed off with Choi in tow.

Dixon's face was pale, his terror showing in droves on his face, staring wide-eyed at the Corporal.

Herrera stepped forward, putting his hands on the Private's shoulders to steady him. "Listen to me," he said firmly, "you can do this."

"I respectfully disagree, Corporal," Dixon replied shakily.

"When we were back at the airport," Herrera began, "Captain Kersey and I watched you interact with the men. The Captain marveled at how much trust the team had in you."

Dixon blinked at him. "Captain Kersey said that?"

"Yeah, and we were both impressed, because it's not an easy thing to get," the Corporal added.

The Private took a deep breath. "Corporal, I gotta level with you," he said, shaking his head, "I've never so much as led a boy scout troop, let alone a mission like this."

"Well, I just led my first mission less than a week ago," Herrera pointed out," and here I am being sent off in the first wave of this assault. If I can do it, you can. Just rely on your men and they'll pull you through."

Dixon nodded, his eyes slowly firming up as he bolstered his confidence. "So… so what do you need me to do?" he asked.

"Who do you trust the most in this group?" Herrera asked.

"Private Ayers," came the immediate reply. "We've been together since basic."

"Ayers, over here!" Herrera called, waving for him to come over.

The Private broke away from guard duty and approached them. "Yes, sir?" he asked.

"Private Dixon here is going to be leading the dock mission," Herrera said. "I need you to support him however he needs it."

Ayers smirked. "Look at you, getting promoted," he teased. "We're gonna wreck some shit." He held out his fist, and Dixon bumped it. "Frankly, it's about time they gave you more responsibility."

Herrera inclined his head. "See, you got the men behind you."

"Okay," Dixon said firmly, finally seeming to have accepted his fate. "So, we gotta clear the school, then the docks, right?"

The Corporal shook his head. "The school is a lost cause," he admitted, "especially with the numbers we have. You're going to have to find a new rally point a few blocks to the west of the school. And worse, you're going to have to be quiet about it."

"The school that bad?" Ayers asked.

Herrera nodded. "We lost three men, including the Sarge, just landing there."

"We'll figure something out," Dixon replied.

"Good," the Corporal said. "Now, with the men we have left, who knows how to drive a big rig?"

Dixon pursed his lips in thought. "Pretty sure Choi can handle one," he mused, "not sure who else."

"What about Eason?" Ayers asked.

Dixon turned to the other men. "Hey, Eason?" he called. "You know how to drive a big rig?"

A short kid that looked no older than nineteen stood up from the splinting. "In the eyes of the government?" he asked. "Nope." He held up a hand. "In reality? Hell yeah!"

Herrera gaped at him. "Is he even old enough to drive?"

"He's a country boy, so he probably came out of the womb on a four wheeler," Ayers replied offhandedly.

Dixon shook his head. "There's a mental image I didn't need," he muttered.

"I'll take him," the Corporal said. "Is there anybody else you can think of?"

Both Privates shook their heads.

"There were a couple more," Dixon said quietly, "but… they haven't shown up yet."

Herrera nodded. "Okay," he continued, "we're going to split up into groups of nine. Pick the seven other you need and send the rest over to me." He pointed to the table in the far corner. "Gotta do some planning."

"They'll be right over," Dixon replied, and headed off.

Herrera headed over to the table and pulled out a map of the island, spreading it out to study it. His original mission had been to take the docks, but now he'd have to adjust course and do the truck mission on the fly.

"Can I have a word?" Gilbert asked from behind him.

The Corporal didn't even look up from his map. "I know what you're going to say, and you can save it," he said flatly.

"I don't think you do," the Private
replied. "You know I can lead that
mission, and you're letting your personal
feelings endanger the whole operation."

Herrera shook his head and stood up
straight. "Wrong," he spat, and pointed to
the chair to his left. "Sit."

Gilbert sat, near pouting, and the
Corporal turned the map towards him.

"Three and a half miles of zombie
infested terrain to get to our target,"
Herrera said, pointing, and the Private
leaned forward to study the paper. "We
have half as many men as the mission
parameters called for, and only four
people capable of driving a truck, meaning
we're going to have to make two trips on
the bridges." He raised an eyebrow. "What
would you do?"

Gilbert studied the map carefully,
reading a few of the handwritten notes,
and then following several of the lines
going north with his finger. All of them
went through neighborhoods and paused at a
circled building halfway up with CHURCH
written beside it.

"Well," he drawled, "for starters,
given the resistance we found in the
neighborhood by the school, I would adjust
course right out of the gate."

Herrera nodded. "And go where?"

"I'd go right back through the woods where we were supposed to land, to get to this church rally point," the Private said with a shrug. "If we cross over some open areas, there are two more wooded areas that will take us all the way up to that church, leaving only a mile or so to the target."

The Corporal shook his head. "You heard Dixon, the woods are a nightmare," he said. "Dark and infested with zombies. You still want to go that route?"

"Absolutely," Gilbert replied with a nod. "We're going to face heavy resistance no matter how we go. At least in the woods, we'd have a fighting chance to lose whatever is pursuing us."

Herrera nodded as well. "I came to the same conclusion," he said. "What next?"

Gilbert continued poring over the map. "Looks like there's about six blocks of dense residential housing before the shopping center," he mused, "so since we're not going to have an overwhelming force to take them on, we'll have to improvise."

"How so?" the Corporal prompted.

"Diversion," Gilbert replied with a shrug. "Car alarms, blow something up, whatever it is, it'll have to be big enough to draw enough of them away so we can slip behind the lines and move up."

Herrera cocked his head. "What about the two trips?"

"There's nine of us," the Private replied, "so four drivers on the trucks, and five riding pickup duty."

The Corporal raised an eyebrow. "And if we lose people on the way?"

"We pick up some ten speed bikes and get our exercise in for the day," Gilbert replied.

Herrera nodded. "Now do you see why you aren't on the docks?" he asked.

"I really don't," the Private replied petulantly.

"Because blocking off those bridges is the most important objective," the Corporal said firmly. "If those docks don't get cleared, the landing party can handle it if need be, even if it takes a couple of waves. If we don't block those bridges, then they're going to get overwhelmed once the shooting starts. If something happens to me, I need someone capable who can pick up the reins and deliver."

Gilbert sneered. "So you're back to trusting me?"

"Fuck no," Herrera snapped. "Wouldn't trust you as far as a kindergartner could throw you. But you're experienced, and despite your major fuckup on the bridge, you're better equipped to see this through than anybody else in the room."

The Private chuckled, shaking his head. "I'll take it," he admitted. "When do we leave?"

Herrera checked his watch. "We're out in ten."

"I guess I should get prepped, then," Gilbert said, and shoved back his chair, heading off to check his weapons.

The Corporal picked up the map and stared at the wooded area they'd be heading into. "I really hope Dixon was exaggerating."

Herrera led the group of eight up to the edge of the woods. They stood there, listening to the light rustling and moaning coming from the trees.

"We sure this is the best way through?" Choi asked.

The Corporal nodded. "Surface streets are jam-packed," he replied. "You're more than welcome to try, but you'll be doing it alone."

"Guess I'll take my chances with you guys, then," the Private muttered.

"How do you want to do it?" Gilbert asked.

Eason took a deep breath. "Guessing eight of us going together in a big pack isn't a great strategy," he said.

"We go in two teams of four," Herrera declared. "Choi, you're with me, Gilbert, I want you to lead the other team along with Eason. If something happens to one team, at least there will be a truck driving tandem left."

Gilbert nodded. "Rendezvous at the church?"

"Yep," the Corporal agreed. "You all have a map, so you know where we're headed if you get separated from the group. If things go really south, or you can't make it to the church, fall back to Dixon's group and try again a different way." He pulled out his knife along with a retractable metal baton, jetting it out with a quick flick of his wrist. "We have to move quietly through these woods. One gunshot could doom us."

The men exchanged worried glances, clutching their guns with white knuckles.

"You heard the man, holster those guns," Gilbert snapped, putting away his own.

The soldiers complied reluctantly, switching their guns for blades and blunt objects.

"And one more thing," Herrera said. "Based on what Dixon told me about the rough landing, it's unlikely we're going to find any survivors out here. But we could have runners, so stay frosty."

The soldiers shared worried looks about the prospect of runners chasing them through the darkened woods.

"Let's head out," Gilbert cut in. "We'll see you on the other side, Corporal."

Herrera nodded and watched the ex-Sergeant lead his crew down the tree line a couple hundred yards before vanishing into the forest.

"Let's go," the Corporal said, and led his team into the trees. Choi came in behind him, Private Jacobs ducking in next, and Private Anton brought up the rear. They crept quietly and cautiously, knives and bludgeons at the ready.

The only light were small rays of moonlight piercing through the limbs to illuminate small patches of ground in the darkened woods. The leaves crunching softly beneath their boots sounded much too loud, but they didn't have much of a choice in the matter.

After a few hundred yards, Herrera stopped the group at the sound of significant movement up ahead. He motioned for them to stay put, and slowly moved as quietly as he could to the next tree, looking out into the darkness.

There was a moonlit patch between several trees with signs of tracks moving off to the side, as well as a few creatures milling about. He looked around on the ground, spotting a rock the size of his fist, and he picked it up, pitching it as hard as he could to the left of the lit area.

As soon as it landed, the zombies whipped around towards the noise, moaning and shuffling off towards it. The Corporal waited, holding his breath as a dozen creatures passed through the lit area. If they'd made a play for the visible creatures, they would have been overrun by the ones in the shadows.

When the immediate threat passed, he motioned for the others to follow him again. They continued to move, the path relatively clear for the next ten minutes or so, the group slow and steady. They worked their way north, only occasionally having to pause for a well timed rock throw or a quick jab to the skull of a lone zombie.

Herrera brought the group to a stop again, this time at the edge of a picnic area. He peeked out at a dozen or so creatures spread out over the fifty by fifty yard area, most of them hanging out by a gazebo and grill as if it were a family barbecue for the undead.

As he scanned the area, he looked to the left of the woods, seeing significant movement in the shadows, like a pack just waiting to be unleashed.

The Corporal pursed his lips and motioned for Choi to join him. "We have to cut across the open area," he breathed the words as quietly as he could.

The Private gaped at him, his eyes easily conveying, Are you fucking crazy?

Herrera pointed to the leftmost edge, and Choi squinted, his shoulders slumping when he spotted the massive amount of movement in the shadows.

The Private leaned in and whispered, "How do you want to play it?"

"Dead sprint, don't worry about noise," the Corporal replied softly. "Just get across and get back to cover, and we'll lose them in the woods."

Choi nodded and then stepped back to relay the message to the others. They clustered around behind their superior, ready to roll.

Herrera readied himself, giving another scan of the field. They were about fifteen yards away from the left edge where all the movement was, and twenty yards from the congregating barbecue zombies. He gripped his weapons tightly and then took off like a shot.

He broke from the tree line like a sprinter out of the blocks, his trio of men following several yards behind in a staggered pattern. There weren't as many leaves on the ground, but the heavy pounding of boots on the grass was enough to alert the zombies in the area.

He glanced to the right, where a few barbecue ghouls staggered towards him. To the left, dozens of creatures emerged from the trees, moaning and arms outstretched. He wasn't worried, as there was more than enough space between them. However, as they got halfway across the field, the collective noise of their boot falls had alerted more corpses in front of them.

He continued running even at the sight of half a dozen zombies shambling out of the woods ahead. They were spread out well, so it wasn't overwhelming. When he came within ten yards, three ghouls appeared right in his trajectory. Just before he reached them to attack, the sound of rapid footsteps made his heart rate triple.

A runner burst out of the trees, shoving past a slower zombie and tore towards the Corporal. Herrera didn't have time to attack, instinctively shoving the fast-moving ghoul to the left as it got close to him. He kept his momentum and slammed his knife into the zombie he'd originally been aiming for and then whirled around at the sound of Anton's screams.

The runner latched onto the poor Private's shoulder, and Herrera stared at the horrific mauling, eyes wide.

"Watch it!" Choi barked, and darted forward to tackle a creature within an arm's length of the Corporal's back. He hopped on top of the fallen ghoul and stabbed down repeatedly into its face, sending blood everywhere.

Herrera snapped back to reality and lunged for another nearby creature, bashing in its head with his baton. Both men returned their attention to Anton as

Jacobs managed to slam his knife into the runner's head as it tore another strip off of his friend.

"Jacobs, we gotta move!" Herrera cried, seeing the horde of creatures gaining ground past the bloodied duo.

The Private looked down at his friend, bleeding profusely from his shoulder wound. He reached down to help him up, and Anton immediately snapped off his vest, shoving it against Jacobs' chest.

"Take my ammo and go!" he demanded.

Jacobs stared at his comrade and then gulped, nodding and running off to join the others. Anton picked his weapons off of the ground, let out a primal scream and ran headlong into the crowd of zombies flailing wildly and trying his best to take out as many as possible, while making as much noise as he could.

Herrera led his two remaining team members into the woods, running as hard as he could through the trees, barely able to see what was ahead. He could hear the other two several yards behind him, but he tried to focus on clearing them a safe path.

As he approached a tree, a figure emerged from behind it. He grabbed it by the shirt, forced it back up against the trunk, and delivered a few brutal strikes to the head, dropping it to the ground. His chest heaved for a few beats, rage thrumming through him as he berated himself for shoving the runner aside and costing Anton his life.

"Come on Corporal," Choi huffed as they caught up, "we gotta keep moving."

Jacobs nodded. "He's right, we gotta move."

Herrera nodded, taking another few deep breaths to steady himself. "Choi, take point," he instructed, and the Private gave a thumbs up before darting off into the woods.

Jacobs patted the Corporal on the shoulder, giving him an encouraging glance, and Herrera gave him a nod before they followed their teammate.

CHAPTER FIVE

Dixon led his group up the road a few blocks to the west of the school. They'd taken the long way around, venturing south several blocks before crossing over, taking the Corporal's warning seriously.

The group of nine moved up the lightly packed street, with several soldiers rushing forward to dispatch zombies with their blades. With the route clear, Dixon led them to a house on the corner.

The road was filled with ten houses on either side of the street, a quaint little slice of American life. The road ran straight into a row of trees into a dead end.

"Ayers, Hurst, clear the house," Dixon whispered.

Both Privates complied, heading up to the house as the others fanned out to secure a perimeter around the building.

"Try the knob," Ayers suggested, and Hurst turned it, finding it unlocked. He nodded to his partner, receiving one in return, and then shoved the door open.

Ayers burst inside, his companion quickly following, and moved into the living room, where visibility was next to nothing.

He tripped over a corpse on the floor, and then immediately leapt back, slamming into the wall.

Hurst barked a laugh, earning a glare from his friend.

"What the fuck is so funny?" Ayers snapped.

Hurst pulled out a small flashlight and clicked it on, showing that the corpse on the floor was missing the top part of its head, a shotgun lying on the ground beside it. Ayers shook his head and finally conceded with a laugh, relieved that they weren't in any immediate danger.

"If you're finished shitting yourself, can we clear the rest of the house?" Hurst asked.

Ayers nodded and the two men glanced in the kitchen, seeing nothing, and then moved down the hallway. As they approached the back bedroom, there was clear moaning and smacking against the door.

The force of the banging intensified as they moved cautiously moved down the narrow hallway, readying their knives as they grew closer.

"I go low, you go high?" Hurst asked.

Ayers shrugged. "Works for me," he replied. "If you want to be at dead dick level, I'm not going to fight you on it."

"Well, I know how much you like to watch," his friend quipped, chuckling.

Ayers rolled his eyes. "Just make sure you hold the fucker steady."

"Just make sure you don't miss," Hurst shot back.

They reached the door, setting their flashlights on the ground, pointing up to illuminate the hall. Hurst took a knee, readying himself, and Ayers grabbed the knob. He turned it, and as soon as he did, Hurst gave it a great heave. It was heavy, but he was able to open it enough that a zombie wriggled through it.

He immediately shoved his hands up into the creature's chest, holding it at bay. Ayers stabbed downward, jamming his blade into the top of its skull. Before the creature dropped, however, a chorus of moans erupted from the room.

"He's not alone!" Ayers cried, and Hurst reinforced his grip, grabbing the creature's shirt tightly and holding it in place as a barricade against the several other zombies trying to paw through the door.

Ayers reached down and grabbed his flashlight, shining it into a duo of creatures pressing against their unmoving brother.

"When I tell you, lean it to the left," Ayers instructed. "Okay, now!" he cried, and Hurst moved the corpse, creating an opening for his companion to strike.

Ayers stabbed one of the zombies in the eye and then leapt back before one of the rotted arms could catch him. "One more, we got this," he huffed.

Hurst struggled to hold the ghoul up while his partner found the next target. A second later, a teenage zombie reached past the slumped ghoul, managing to grip his arm.

"Get this fucker off of me!" Hurst bellowed, and Ayers lined up his shot, stabbing right through the top of the dead teenager's head.

Hurst shook off the death grip, and both soldiers waited for a moment, listening to the moaning coming from the room, but not seeing the creature.

Ayers shone the light over the corpse's head into the room, and couldn't see anything. "I hear something, but don't see it," he hissed. "We're gonna have to go in."

"Gonna need a second to get up," Hurst groaned. "You ready?"

His partner nodded. "Go for it."

Hurst shoved the zombie barricade back into the room and scrambled to his feet while Ayers kept watch. The two men slowly entered the room, shining their flashlights all around. The sound of

clattering chains echoed, and they both
froze at the sight before them.

"Oh, that's just fucked up," Ayers
breathed.

On the bed was an older woman, easily
in her late seventies, chained by the arms
and legs to a bed, thrashing about. Her
mouth was bloody, but it was dried and
looked like it had been that way for a
while. Hurst shone the light onto the
zombies they'd taken out, seeing several
bite marks on them.

"Looks like they were caring for
Granny here when she turned," Hurst said,
grimacing. "Set off a nasty chain
reaction."

Ayers shook his head. "Might explain
why my living room assaulter blew his own
top," he said. "Can't imagine having to
lock my family away and listen to them
trying to eat me alive."

"Almost makes me glad I never had
much of a family life," Hurst added.

His partner sighed. "Thank god for
small miracles, right?"

Hurst chuckled darkly. "Come on,
let's finish her off and go tell Dixon."

Ayers took out granny with a well-
placed strike to the head, and then they
headed back out of the quiet house to find
Dixon. They found him using a flashlight

to study his map out front, standing with Private Shaw.

"Best I can tell, we're about three blocks to the west of the high school," Dixon was saying.

Shaw nodded as he stared at the map and then glanced down the street to the west, a block where there was a thick line of trees. "It's gotta be," he agreed, "because that tree line looks like this one on the map. So if we cut through there, we should be at the docks in another three blocks."

"Then this is where we're setting up camp," Dixon replied, lowering the paper.

Ayers clucked his tongue as they approached. "Man, you picked a hell of a house there, buddy," he declared.

"Find some new friends?" Dixon asked.

Ayers shook his head and ran a hand through his cropped hair. "Fuck," he breathed.

"Rabid Granny murdering the family situation in there," Hurst explained.

Dixon wrinkled his nose. "Not high up on my list of ways to go," he said. "You get it cleared, though?"

"Yeah it's cleared," Ayers replied with a nod. "Although we might want to put a sign on that back bedroom. Nobody else really needs to see that."

Dixon nodded. "Good work guys," he commended, "but we still got a lot to do."

"You got a plan?" Ayers asked.

Dixon motioned to the neighborhood and then pointed to the map. "Yep, and hope we find some ibuprofen in one of these houses," he said, "because we're gonna need it."

"Well doesn't that sound promising," Hurst said dryly.

"You know you wouldn't want it any other way," Dixon quipped with a small smile. "I mean, if you didn't get to bitch about a mission, did that mission actually happen?"

The quartet shared a laugh, even Hurst, shaking his head.

"Okay, so this is what we're doing," Dixon began, holding up the map. "This road dead ends at that tree line, which is going to be our backstop. We need to get the cars from the driveways and start blocking off this road. Start with one row from house to house, and reinforce if you can."

Hurst raised a hand. "What if we can't find the keys?"

"Remember the ibuprofen?" Dixon asked, raising an eyebrow. "Break the window, pop it in neutral, and start pushing."

"That's gonna be fun on grass," Hurst muttered.

"Once that's done, we need to do a sweep of the houses," Dixon continued, "making sure if a yard doesn't have a fence that we plug up the hole somehow. I don't care if it's another car or we start having outdoor couches like we're rednecks in rural Alabama. Anything and everything to slow these things down once we start making noise. Shaw, get the others and start making this happen."

Shaw nodded. "I'm on it."

"Ayers, Hurst, got another job for you," Dixon said as Shaw ran off.

Hurst laced his fingers behind his head. "Let me guess," he drawled, "more zombie killing?"

"No, just containment," Dixon replied, shaking his head. "We have an indoor area we can retreat to if things get bad. Now I just need you to make sure the rest of the houses are secure. We'll let those on the boats deal with them once they get here."

Ayers grinned. "I like the way you think," he said.

"Glad to hear it," Dixon replied, and waved them off. "Now get moving. Lots to get done."

CHAPTER SIX

Herrera, Jacobs, and Choi emerged from the woods a few blocks south of the church rally point. Their chests heaved from the running and fighting through the multiple wooded areas, still reeling from the loss of Anton.

"Church should be a few blocks to the north," the Corporal huffed.

As they stepped out onto the street, they looked to the west and spotted a small band of zombies, at least a few dozen, about fifty yards away. They weren't paying attention to the soldiers, so Herrera casually headed across the street into a neighborhood.

The group took a knee by the house, realizing they'd nearly doomed themselves by not paying attention. The Corporal was silent, motioning for the other two to follow him. He crept around the house, knife at the ready, reaching the backyard.

It was fenced in, as were the neighboring houses. There was movement from a few other yards, but none in their direct path. They hopped the fences and quickly moved through the neighborhood, seeing several clusters of zombies all around. When they reached the house across the street from the church, there was a

handful of ghouls hanging out in the front
lawn.

"Either of you know how to pick
locks?" Herrera whispered.

Jacobs raised his hand. "I'm not the
best at it," he admitted quietly, "but I
can get it done."

"You go straight for the door," the
Corporal instructed. "Choi and I will
handle the zombies."

Jacobs nodded and pulled out his
lock-picking tools while the other two
readied their blades.

"I'll take the three on the left,"
Herrera murmured, "you get the two on the
right."

Choi cocked his head. "I can take the
three if you want," he whispered.

"Nah," the Corporal replied, shaking
his head. "I need to get out some
frustration."

The Private nodded and waited for his
superior to move.

Herrera broke from cover, running as
hard as he could towards the trio of
zombies on the left side of the yard. He
jammed his blade into one creature's face
at full speed, the hilt smacking against
the forehead of the ghoul.

He shoved the beast away, preparing
to strike at the next two that approached
him shoulder-to-shoulder. He darted to the

side, grabbing one zombie by the shirt and shoving it into the other. He pumped his legs, driving the clumsy monsters back against the wall of the church. He stabbed one in the eye socket, and then ripped his blade free and gave the one in the back the same treatment, stepping back to watch them slide to the ground.

He turned to check on Jacobs, who was working diligently on the door as Choi finished off his second zombie. Past him, a dozen creatures shambled around the side of the church building.

"Fuck," he growled, and took off like a shot. "Choi!" he yelled.

The Private looked up, meeting Herrera's wild eyes as he ran, and then turned around to see the threat growing by the second. The Corporal joined him when the zombies were about fifteen yards away.

"Jacobs, you almost there?!" Herrera barked.

"Need another minute!" came the strained reply.

The duo stared at the ambling horde, shaking their heads.

"Not sure we can pull this off with knives," Choi said.

Herrera sucked his bottom lip between his teeth. "We're gonna have to," he replied. "If we start shooting, those

things are going to be on us before
Gilbert gets here."

"Fucking hell," Choi growled in
frustration.

They readied their weapons, falling
into loose fighting stances.

"Charge them, push them back," the
Corporal instructed, "and then start
stabbing the ones still standing. Go!"

They both rushed forward, a few yards
apart from each other. They hit the lead
zombies on either side of the horde at the
same time, shoving them back into the
others. Seven zombies toppled to the
ground like bowling pins, and then the
soldiers immediately began stabbing
creatures at the edges of the mass, trying
to bottle up the rest so they had a
fighting chance.

They dropped a few zombies each
before looking back at the ones that were
making it back up to their feet. Past
that, a fresh dozen appeared around the
corner, attracted by the noise.

"This ain't working," Choi warned.

Herrera shook his head. "We gotta
wait on Gilbert!" he cried.

The Private let out a frustrated
scream and prepared another attack. Just
before he leapt forward, several shots
exploded in the distance, ripping through
the zombies in front of them.

They turned to see Gilbert, Eason, and one other soldier approaching, guns blazing.

"Go hot!" Herrera cried, and he and Choi pulled their assault rifles, opening fire on the horde.

In a matter of seconds, their friends joined them, and the monsters all fell.

"About time you made it," Herrera said, clapping Gilbert on the shoulder as the last zombie crumpled to the ground.

The Private took a deep breath. "Dixon wasn't lying about those woods," he said.

"Yeah, no shit," Choi agreed.

Herrera's brow furrowed. "Down one?"

Gilbert nodded, his face pale. "Pack of runners."

"We had one too," Choi replied.

"Come on," the Corporal cut in, "we gotta get inside before their reinforcements get here."

The soldiers turned towards the door, just as there was a satisfying click.

"Got the door!" Jacobs announced proudly, and pushed on it.

Several rotted hands emerged, grabbing onto his shirt. He screamed and struggled as they pulled him inside, arms flailing.

"Jacobs!" Herrera screamed, and the five soldiers rushed to his aid, opening fire at the door, shooting wildly through it and hoping they scored a hit. The Corporal lowered his shoulder and smashed through it, the impact driving several zombies back onto the ground. He fired three precise shots, hitting the downed creatures in the head.

Gilbert entered next, taking out one remaining creature to the left.

"Gilbert, Choi, clear the building!" Herrera barked, and the soldiers in question pulled out their flashlights and took off into the main area.

Eason and Private Greer joined Herrera, who was standing over poor Jacobs, struggling to breathe through the bite wounds on his neck. He held the wounds uselessly, blood pouring out of him in droves.

"Help me pull him clear," Herrera said, and the two men dragged Jacobs clear of the door, securing it behind them. "Go make sure the rest of the building is secure," the Corporal demanded.

"Sir, I…" Eason said hoarsely.

"Go," Herrera snapped. "Now."

The soldiers hesitated, but finally nodded and ran off, pulling out their flashlights. Herrera took a knee and swallowed hard, pulling out his handgun.

"I'm sorry, Private," he murmured. "I really am." He stared down into the young man's fear-filled eyes, and immediately fired a round through his forehead in an attempt not to drag out the kid's suffering. The blast echoed throughout the cavernous structure, and he stared down at the dead soldier for a beat before taking a deep breath and refocusing on their task.

He walked into the main chapel of the church, a modest-sized area, big enough to house a few hundred people on a Sunday. As he entered, the four other soldiers stood by the pulpit, solemn after what they knew their Corporal had had to do.

"Report," Herrera said.

Gilbert stepped forward. "Building is clear," he said, "we're alone in here."

"We're secure, too," Eason added. "Nothing's getting in."

Herrera took a deep breath. "Good." He pulled out his map and spread it on the pulpit, motioning for the soldiers to gather around. He pointed to a school two blocks to the east. "This is our target, a school building. According to the intel, they have a propane cooking system for the cafeteria. We have to get there, rig it to blow, and then get back here before it does. Once it goes off, it should be loud enough to draw everything in the immediate vicinity to it."

"Thereby clearing the path to the shopping center," Gilbert added.

Herrera nodded and pointed to the shopping center to the northwest. "We're about six blocks away from it, as the crow flies," he said. "Hopefully this diversion is enough to make it possible for us to get through."

"How are we taking it out?" Greer asked nervously. "I don't know about anybody else, but I didn't bring anything that can be remotely detonated."

Herrera pointed to the back of the church altar, which housed several candles.

"Smart," Greer replied, as the soldiers nodded, getting the gist of the plan.

"We get to the school," the Corporal explained, "take out the pilot lights, light these puppies up, and haul ass back here."

Eason nodded thoughtfully. "School goes up," he said, "and they walk right past us."

"In theory, at any rate," Gilbert countered.

Choi raised an eyebrow. "You got a better idea?"

Gilbert shook his head. "Nope," he replied dryly, "in fact, this was my idea."

"That's true," Herrera agreed. "But if anybody has a better one, I'm all ears."

The three other soldiers glanced at each other and then shook their heads.

"Good," the Corporal replied, and clapped his hands together. "Everybody get candles and a wavy to light them. We leave in five."

CHAPTER SEVEN

Dixon watched from the front porch of the safe house as eight men scrambled to secure the makeshift rally point. Several soldiers pushed a car to the top of the road to fill the last gap in the metal wall spanning the space between two houses.

Another soldier stood guard on the opposite side of the wall, watching for trouble. A few moments went by, and he let out a whistle. Two men immediately broke off from pushing the car and ran over to him. They walked across the street to another house where a trio of zombies shambled out from the side yard. With three quick strikes, the threat was eliminated, and they went back to their jobs.

Dixon nodded in approval as Ayers and Hurst approached him.

"We may have an issue," Ayers said.

Dixon sighed. "Just the words every leader wants to hear," he replied. "What's up?"

"The side yards are secure, but the other side of the trees are going to be an issue," Hurst replied.

"You may just want to come see for yourself," Ayers added.

Dixon nodded. "All right, lead on," he said, and then whistled at the guys pushing the car.

They glanced up and he motioned that he was heading down the street, prompting them to give him a thumbs up that they understood.

As the trio walked, Dixon appraised the barricades between the houses. The men had used couches, playhouses, and all things in between.

"Good thing we picked a ritzy neighborhood to squat in," he said. "Lots of good stuff to pick from."

Ayers barked a laugh. "Ritzy doesn't even begin to describe it," he said. "Check out this house on the corner."

As they walked by the final house, Dixon picked up a flyer from the For Sale sign on the front yard. He recoiled at the price.

"Holy shit," he said, "you could buy my hometown for this."

Hurst shook his head. "You could probably buy most of it with just the property taxes."

"That's some serious first world problems right there," Dixon added, and the three men chuckled as they wandered over to the tree line.

It stretched about twenty-five yards before it reached the next neighborhood, which led directly to the docks. They walked into it and came across a fence halfway through. It was chain-link, and about waist high.

Dixon wiggled it a little. "This seems pretty sturdy."

"That's not the issue," Ayers said, and hopped over it. The trio approached the edge of the woods and took a knee at the edge of the woods.

"What am I looking at?" Dixon asked quietly.

Ayers pointed down the street a block or so, and he squinted at it. When it came into focus, Dixon's stomach dropped.

There were about a hundred zombies in the middle of the road, stretching to a house on the corner.

"Fuck me," Dixon breathed.

"Looks like something drew their attention, and it never got broken," Ayers said quietly.

Dixon shook his head. "What about to the north and south of us?" he asked.

"We went a block in each direction, and it's just stragglers with some small batches," Hurst replied, "nothing bigger than ten."

Dixon stared at the threat, wondering how in the hell they'd pull this off without drawing much attention to themselves. "Shooting is out, that's for sure," he muttered.

"Why?" Hurst asked. "We have more than enough ammo to take them down."

Dixon shook his head. "Because we run the risk of pulling the school to us," he explained, "and we certainly don't have enough ammo for that, let alone both."

"Hand to hand?" Ayers asked.

Hurst snorted. "Please, be my guest," he said. "I'm not holding them up this time."

"I mean, we can draw them back to the fence line here," Ayers continued. "We check a few houses, upgrade our weapons. Somebody has to have a baseball bat or something."

Hurst scratched the back of his head. "Great," he replied, "but how do we get them up here?"

Dixon glanced over at the yard closest to them, seeing a standalone shed. "Let's check in there," he said.

The trio darted out from cover, moving quickly and quietly towards the small structure. When they reached it, they found it locked with a cheap padlock. Hurst stepped forward and smashed it with the butt of his rifle. A few strikes later, and then the entire lock broke off.

They opened it up, staring around at the typical shed material, a few bikes, a lawnmower, tools…

"Now we're cooking," Dixon said, picking up a three-gallon can of kerosene. He shook it, noting it was about two-thirds of the way full.

He looked around for a dish, finding a small dog bowl filled with nails and screws. He grabbed it and dumped it on the floor.

"Okay, you boys get back to the fence line," he instructed. "One of you grab a few of the others and some more weapons, and I'll bring the zombies to you."

The soldiers shared a concerned glance.

Dixon rolled his eyes. "Don't worry, I'm a trained professional," he assured them. "I was doing Jackass-style stunts way before they even had a tv show. Now get moving, they'll be at the fence before you know it."

The two men rushed off, and Dixon took the goods and walked down the street towards the horde. There were over a hundred in the road, all focused on one house, paying him no attention at all.

He stopped about twenty yards away, staying as quiet as he could. He gently set down the dog dish and poured in some kerosene, filling it up. He looked up and saw a few of the ghouls had acknowledged him, turning to shamble in his direction.

"Oh good, I get a crowd for my performance," he drawled and then lit up the liquid in the dish.

It burned brightly, and he took a step back, picking up the can. He aimed the nozzle down and began to pour. As soon as the stream hit the fire, flames leapt up into it, and Dixon flung his arm side to side, sending plumes of flaming liquid into the horde. After a few good sprays, he reared back and lobbed the canister as hard as he could.

Flaming liquid spun wildly as the can floated through the air, coating every zombie it came into contact with. Soon, the darkness of the night was illuminated with flaming corpses.

"Damn," Dixon breathed, swiping his palms together, "that worked better than I thought."

He backed up slowly, watching as the bulk of the horde began to come after him. Some of the ghouls started to collapse from flame damage, and before long, the fire started to tamp down, but the zombies were sufficiently drawn towards him.

"Hope they're ready," he muttered, and turned, jogging back to the tree line, pushing through to the fence. When he reached it, Ayers, Hurst, and two others stood there armed with bats, hammers, and a sharpened pool cue.

Dixon hopped the fence to join them.

"I saw the tail end of that," Ayers declared. "I had no idea you were such a wild man."

Dixon smirked. "You should see me when I know I have an audience," he declared. The men shared a chuckle, and then he continued, "If you men got this, I'm going to go check on the others, and make sure we're good to go up there. Because once this is clear, we have to do the same thing all the way to the docks."

"We got you, man," Hurst assured him. "Go do what you got to do."

Dixon nodded and headed away from the line as the first few zombies approached. He listened to the sound of cracking skulls, smiling to himself in the knowledge that they were one step closer to success.

Herrera led his team through the neighborhood towards the school. They took out a couple of zombies hanging out in the side yard of a house, efficiently and quietly, as if they were more of a nuisance than a threat.

The group took a knee and looked out at the school, a mid-sized building smaller than the average Super Center. A decently sized pack of ghouls milled about out front, several dozen, it looked like. Towards the back, where the sports fields sprawled, there were almost a hundred monsters spread across. Near the back of the school was a smaller pack, no more than a dozen.

The Corporal pointed to the rear. "We get in through the back windows, then find our way to the cafeteria."

"What about the door on the side of the building?" Greer asked, pointing to a lone door along a brick wall in the center, looking flush with no handle.

"That looks like a fire door," Gilbert said quietly.

Herrera nodded. "That's our exit point, then," he confirmed. "Once we set this to blow, we're going to have to move quickly."

"Weapons?" Choi asked.

The Corporal held up his knife. "Melee only until we set the fire, then all bets are off," he replied. "Questions?"

The soldiers shook their heads.

"Let's move out," Herrera said, and then led the group away from the house, sprinting across the street to the school. Their footsteps were loud, attracting a little attention from the field zombies, who turned and began to shamble in their direction.

The soldiers ignored them, rushing straight towards the closest window they could find. As they reached the building, Herrera and Gilbert ran forward, jamming their blades into the two closest zombies. Meanwhile, Choi used the butt of his rifle to smash a window.

"We're in!" he hissed, and then knelt down, creating a step stool out of his thigh.

Greer boosted up first, diving inside and immediately hopping up to clear the small classroom. The door was shut, and he checked it to make sure it was secure, and then turned to help the others inside.

Herrera entered last, glancing over his shoulder to see that the field zombies were still a good distance away. He hauled himself up onto the window ledge and Eason pulled him in.

"Everybody good?" the Corporal asked.

There was a collective murmur in the affirmative, and he nodded, heading for the classroom door. He peeked out through the tiny window, seeing nothing but darkness, and pulled out his flashlight.

"Gonna have to risk it," he muttered, and then shone the light through the window.

There was nothing in the hallway close to the door that he could see, so he cracked it open and shone the flashlight down the hall, lighting up half a dozen zombies that immediately turned towards the disturbance.

"Six down the hall," Herrera said, "let's clear 'em out."

The soldiers walked out of the classroom, drawing their own flashlights as well. They stalked up the hallway, ready to throw down with the rival zombie gang. As they approached, Choi and Gilbert grabbed the first two ghouls and flung them up against lockers on opposite sides of the hall to take them out, clearing the path for the others to move up.

The rest stepped through the gap and quickly stabbed the remaining creatures, clearing the hallway. When they reached the crossroads, the Corporal shone his flashlight in each direction. The main hallway had a few stragglers towards the end, while the other two directions were clear.

He illuminated the wall, seeing a small sign reading LUNCH ROOM with an arrow pointing down one of the unoccupied hallways.

"Gilbert, Choi, stay here and make sure our escape route is clear," Herrera said. "Greer, Eason, you're with me." He waved to them, and they joined him as Gilbert and Choi kept their flashlights trained on the creatures at the far end of the hall. Thankfully, the zombies seemed uninterested in the light.

The Corporal led the other two down towards the lunchroom. He paused before entering, peering through the window, shining his light to see. There were a few zombies in the eating area, some of them tangled up in the chairs, thrashing about in a feeble attempt to free themselves.

"You two, clear the room," Herrera instructed. "I'll handle the kitchen."

They nodded as he breached the door. Greer and Eason immediately headed for the zombies, and the Corporal hopped up onto one of the long tables and ran down it, avoiding the tangled mass of chairs on the ground. As he hopped down, he bolted through the double doors into the kitchen, quickly sweeping it for threats and seeing none.

Herrera removed the candles from his
bag, setting them on the front counter and
lighting them up. Once they were blazing,
he rushed over to the stoves, flipping on
every single gas burner but not using the
igniter. The hiss of propane filled the
air, and he quickly caught a whiff of it.

"This isn't going to take long," he
muttered, and tore out of the kitchen.
"Fuse is lit, we gotta move!" he yelled,
and the two soldiers broke away from their
battle to run to the door.

As the trio burst out of the
lunchroom, Herrera hollered, "We're lit!
Weapons hot!"

Gilbert and Choi immediately drew
their assault rifles and fired a few
rounds downrange, striking a few zombies
that ambled up the hallway towards them.
As soon as the other three joined them,
the team sprinted towards the fire exit
door at the end of the hall.

Herrera reached it first, slamming
into it, but finding resistance. A few
rotted hands pushed their way in, grasping
at him.

"Get down!" Gilbert cried.

The Corporal dropped to one knee as
Gilbert shoved his assault rifle into the
door above his head. He fired off a few
three-round bursts, shredding the faces of

a few ghouls and easing the pressure on the door.

Herrera pushed hard, and Choi joined him, the two of them staying low so that Gilbert had a firing window. As the door opened far enough, the trigger-happy Private pushed his way through, turning quickly and firing behind the door.

"We gotta move!" he barked.

The rest of the men rushed out from the school, and the door slammed shut behind them. The field zombies had reached the building, and were closing in.

Eason and Choi began to fire, clearing out the ones that were closest. Herrera glanced at Gilbert, who was shooting into dozens of creatures from the front yard horde, closing in.

"Back to the church!" the Corporal yelled, and the group fired a few more rounds before sprinting away from the school.

When they hit the neighborhood across from it, several zombies emerged from around houses to investigate what the nose was. The group ignored them and kept running, even though their boot falls were gaining attention.

When they approached the church, there were a dozen or so zombies standing between them and the building. Herrera stopped short about ten yards away and readied his weapon. The other soldiers joined him to create a devastating firing line. As quickly as they began shooting, the zombies dropped, and the battle was over, with well-placed shots to the head.

Herrera opened the front door they'd left unlocked and ushered the soldiers inside before entering last and slamming it. He peered out the window, seeing zombies coming towards them in every direction.

"Sure hope this works," he uttered, and locked the door before retreating to the chapel.

The soldiers collapsed in the pews, chests heaving, and Herrera joined them, setting down his rifle and cracking his neck.

"That was fun," Greer said brightly. "Having PTSD flashbacks to my worst P.E. class."

Gilbert shook his head. "Only thing missing were the cheerleaders laughing at you," he quipped.

"That never happened to me," Greer replied, puffing out his chest a bit.

"Look at me," Gilbert replied, patting his belly, "might have happened a few times in my day."

A chuckle rippled through the men in a much-needed moment of levity.

Finally, Choi asked, "So, how long until that thing blows?"

"No idea," Herrera replied, shaking his head. "I put the candles on the far side of the room, so it might take a while for the room to fill up with gas."

"Wait, how big was the room?" Eason asked, straightening up.

The Corporal shrugged. "I don't know," he replied, "about the size of this one? Only with lower ceilings."

Eason looked around, the wheels turning in his head. "Yeah…" he said, swallowing hard. "We may want to get away from the windows."

The soldiers shared concerned glances and then slowly moved to the center of the room.

"It can't be that bad, can it?" Choi asked as he took a seat on the floor.

Eason scratched the back of his head. "Look at the bright side," he drawled, "we're going to get attention."

The group hunkered down, and then as if on cue, a loud BOOM rattled the building. The windows tittered, a few of them cracking, and the soldiers held their breath, hoping that they wouldn't shatter.

Luckily, the windows held, and they let out deep sighs collectively.

"Damn, they probably heard that at the docks," Greer said.

Herrera shook his head. "Let's hope not," he said, "we're going to have enough to deal with without more coming up." He headed for the window, staying out of sight as he peeked out.

The zombies that had been in pursuit of them had turned around and headed towards the school, a bright light in the distance. The Corporal nodded and smiled approvingly.

"Gilbert, set a timer," he declared, "for the next thirty minutes, we're on break."

The Private let out a deep sigh of relief and hit his watch before laying across a pew on this back. The troops spread out, stretching their tired limbs, and Herrera stayed at the window, keeping watch on the outside.

He watched the flood of zombies moving towards the explosion. "Come on, you know you bastards want to go to the bonfire."

CHAPTER NINE

Dixon led Ayers and Hurst toward the docks, stepping over charred remains of kerosene doused zombies as they went. Three others were in this portion of the neighborhood, using cars to block off side streets, while three remained back at the first blocked-off zone to make sure nothing would sneak up on them.

As they moved, there was an explosion in the distance. The force of the blast wasn't much, but it was bright enough to light up a small bit of sky in the distance.

"God damn Herrera," Dixon said, eyes wide with awe, "guess you aren't much for subtlety."

Hurst shook his head. "Please don't get any ideas," he begged, looking down at the charred corpses. "You've already done a good job of burning shit down."

"Don't worry," Dixon assured him, "I got out with my eyebrows still intact, so I'm calling it a win. Plus, if Herrera asks, we can always say we didn't see anything."

"If it keeps you restrained, then I'm all for it," Ayers quipped.

The three soldiers kept their rifles ready as they headed down towards the docks. They were two blocks away from the

426

water, and could already hear the lapping
of waves jostled around from the wind.

At the next intersection, they
stopped in the middle, looking both ways.
There was a small pack of zombies down a
block to the south, and a lone zombie to
the north.

"Don't see much of a threat here,"
Dixon said quietly. "Let's keep moving,
the others can handle it if these guys get
frisky."

He led them towards the docks,
stopping at the end of the road. The only
thing separating them from the water was
another row of houses.

"I can only imagine what these cost,"
Ayers muttered.

Hurst smirked. "Maybe if we all pool
our money together, we can rent it out for
a weekend."

"Nah, I'd rather just take it by
force," Dixon replied, and readied his
rifle. He led them across the street,
stopping at the front door of the nearest
house and peeking in the movement. There
was a little movement inside, towards the
back. "Two at the back," he said quietly.
"Ayers, you're with me, Hurst, you clear
the first floor."

They nodded, and he turned the knob,
pushing it in quickly. He crept inside
with Ayers right on his heels, aiming in

tandem and each taking out their targets with a single shot. Hurst swept the first floor, stopping at the stairs.

"Clear!" he declared.

"Hit the second floor," Dixon instructed, "we've got the back."

Hurst headed up as the other two walked to the back door. They opened it up, revealing a large patio. Dixon stepped out, looking straight out at the water. He couldn't help but admire the moonlit sand, and then Ayers grabbed him by the collar and yanked him back inside, quietly shutting the door behind them.

"What the hell?" Dixon hissed.

Ayers shushed him, and then motioned to the window. Dixon looked out, and then spotted several zombies to either side of the deck, stretching down several houses. He cursed himself for being so distracted by the water.

"Well, that's not going to work now, is it?" he muttered.

Another lone shot went off upstairs, startling the duo. They looked out at the zombies that were moaning and looking around for the source of the noise.

A few moments later, Hurst entered the room. "Not much upstairs, just-"

"Shhh!" Ayers hushed him, and Hurst blinked in confusion. His companions motioned to the window, and he peered out, wrinkling his nose. Dixon waved for them to follow, and the trio retreated to the living room.

"How do you want to handle this?" Hurst asked quietly.

Dixon pursed his lips as he reloaded his rifle. "Pop in a full mag," he said, "we pick off a few from the deck and bring 'em over to us. If there aren't too many, we bottleneck them up on the stairs and grab a meat tenderizer from the kitchen and do some work."

"And if there are too many of them?" Ayers asked, raising an eyebrow.

Dixon shrugged, holding up his rifle. "That's why we have the full mags." He led the group into the kitchen, stopping by the drawers and rummaging around until he found a large meat tenderizing hammer.

"How did you know they'd have one?" Hurst wondered.

Dixon smirked. "Place like this with a view like that," he drawled, "and you know they're grilling a lot."

"Remind me to check the liquor cabinet before we head back," Hurst replied. "Can't grill without a drink in the hand."

Dixon chuckled. "Just make sure you stash it well," he warned. "Don't want to be sharing any with those boat boys who have been lounging around at sea for the last month."

"What side do you want?" Ayers asked.

Hurst inclined his head. "I got right, you go left?"

Ayers nodded and slid the door open. The three men stepped outside, getting into position, with Dixon waiting at the stairs in the center.

The duo took aim and fired within a second of each other, quickly popping off several rounds, dropping ghouls on either side of the house. Moans rippled through the air as creatures on both sides emerged from the shadows. What had initially looked like a dozen swelled into three dozen, all of them hungry and coming their way.

"That hammer isn't gonna do much good," Ayers warned, and Dixon nodded, dropping it and stepping back.

The duo on the left did a good job of clearing out a dozen or so zombies in a short period of time, bullets ripping through skulls.

When they were down to about eight, Hurst bellowed, "Need a hand over here!" He panic fired, sending three-round bursts into a crowd of zombies.

Dixon dashed over, seeing several zombies had made it to the front of the deck. He hopped up on the banister, aiming straight down and opening fire in three-round bursts. The bullets ripped through the tops of the heads as well as the shoulders, depleting his mag. He reloaded as he surveyed the carnage, seeing most of the ones in the front had dropped.

Ayers approached as Dixon hopped back down from the railing. "My side is clear," he said, and then glanced over the side. "Damn man, you fucked 'em up."

"Never underestimate what a bit of panic fire can do," Dixon replied as Hurst resumed single shots into the smaller horde.

"Clear," he reported, lowering his gun.

The soldiers congregated on the right side of the deck, surveying the three dozen bodies sprawled in the grass. Dixon patted Hurst's shoulder a few times.

"Come on," he said, "we gotta find something to let the boys know where to land."

The trio headed inside and began rifling through closets, Hurst taking the garage. He entered the main house again, holding a stack of tiki torches.

"Hey, think this will work?" he asked.

Dixon inspected them, finding the fuel reserves full. "Lighting the way," he said, and took a long sniff of the

citronella, "and keeping the mosquitoes
away. Bonus. Let's get them set up and
we'll leave them a note on the sliding
glass door letting them know where we
are."

CHAPTER TEN

Herrera and his team hid inside a gas station across the street from the large shopping center. There were four large anchor stores, along with several hundred yards worth of smaller stores. There were easily a few hundred zombies that they could see from their vantage point, milling about in the parking lot area. The solar powered street lights were still bright, just as if it were any other night, except the glow illuminated rotted heads as opposed to Christmas shoppers.

The soldiers shared a lukewarm bottle of water and some salty snacks.

"Doesn't look like that school did nearly enough for us," Greer said dryly.

Choi swallowed a mouthful of chips and shrugged. "It got us this far, didn't it?"

"Hundreds passed by the church, and that was just from what I could see," Herrera pointed out.

Gilbert nodded. "HI would much rather face a few hundred than a few thousand."

"Yeah, that's true," Greer agreed, and then sighed. "Still, would have been nice if it was totally clear."

Eason took a deep breath. "So how are we doing this?"

"We're not going to bother going through the stores," Herrera replied. "We're just gonna head around back and go straight for the trucks."

Greer shook his head. "Man, that's one hell of a run on foot," he said dryly. "Especially if the back of the stores looks like the front. Really easy to get bottlenecked in there."

"I'm open to suggestions," the Corporal admitted.

"What about that pickup truck just across from us?" Gilbert asked, motioning to a shiny truck on the edge of the parking lot. "I mean, we're going to need transport from the western bridge anyway, might as well kill two birds."

Eason nodded thoughtfully. "If we're going to do that, wouldn't it be smarter to backtrack to the nearly empty neighborhoods, though?" he asked.

"Don't know about you, but all I saw were luxury sedans in the driveways," Gilbert pointed out. "If we have to plow through these fuckers, we're going to need something with a little more oomph."

Choi sighed. "Downside to being on a rich person's island," he said. "Heavy duty trucks aren't real popular."

"Corporal, what do you think?" Greer asked.

Herrera cocked his head. "Who knows how to hot-wire a car?"

Choi looked back and forth, and then hesitantly raised his hand.

The Corporal raised an eyebrow. "That didn't look very confident," he said.

"Because it isn't," Choi admitted, lowering his hand. "It's been years since I've done it."

Gilbert leaned forward. "Question is, can you do it now?"

"I think I can," Choi replied, though his voice didn't sound sure.

"We'll buy you as much time as we can," Herrera decided. "If it doesn't work, we say fuck it and make a run for the back, and we'll worry about transport later."

There was a murmur in the affirmative, and Choi nodded, rubbing his hands together to psych himself up.

"Okay," the Corporal continued, "we make a perimeter around the truck. Weapons hot, but only fire when it becomes necessary. As soon as that first shot fires, we're going to be the belle of the ball. Choi, when you get it started up, everybody pile into the back and you haul ass to the rear of the stores. First batch of trucks you see, we get to work. Greer, you'll be on pickup duty."

Greer nodded. "I'll handle it," he said, "but where are we getting the truck keys from?"

"A lot of these stores keep the keys in the back office in case of an emergency," Herrera replied. "We get in, find them, and move out. The interstate is due north of here. First two trucks take the inner loop, other two take the outer. CB channel eight, and we'll make the call on where to block the road based on conditions." He paused, looking at his team. "Ready?" At their affirmative, he said, "Let's move."

The Corporal led the group outside, everyone with their assault rifles at the ready save for Choi. They raced across the street, looking both ways and seeing a smattering of zombies in the road a ways down.

When they hit the shopping center lot, they raced for the truck. There were a few dozen zombies within sight, straight ahead and several stores up. Gilbert and Greer kept them in their sights, coming around the side of the truck.

Herrera and Eason turned to the right, looking down the other row of stores, seeing an alarming number of ghouls there, easily a hundred strong with the closest being only fifteen yards away.

"Steady," Herrera said quietly, "don't shoot until they move towards us."

Both men kept their aim true, waiting for the moment. Choi tried to open the driver's side door, but it was locked. He tried the passenger side, but it was locked too, so he pulled out his metal baton and gave the corner of the window a hard strike, shattering the glass.

At the noise, the closest zombie to the Corporal whirled around and stared at them, staggering forward.

"Don't shoot, I'll take it out," Herrera whispered, and pulled his knife, inching towards the ghoul.

Choi unlocked the truck and then slid over to the driver's side, opening the door to duck down beneath the dash.

As Herrera approached the zombie, it let out an excited moan, which gained the attention of several more ten yards behind it. In turn, they began to moan and shamble towards the truck, setting off a chain reaction.

The Corporal gulped, adrenaline spiking. "Start shooting, start shooting!" he cried, and raised his weapon. He hit the closest ghoul in the face at point blank range, dropping it. He and Eason began firing single shots, hitting the creatures one by one, but barely putting a dent in the horde.

Gilbert and Greer stood fast, keeping a close eye on the zombies in the distance as they, too, began working their way towards the truck. As the fire intensified behind them, Gilbert clenched his jaw.

"How's it going, Choi?" he barked.

"A lot better if you'd stop bothering me," his teammate yelled from below the dashboard. His speech was muffled by the flashlight between his teeth as he stared intently at the wiring. He picked and chose the wires carefully, finally shaking his head and thinking, fuck it. He stripped two of them and sparked them together, relieved as the engine came to life. He tied them together, the engine purring.

He dropped the flashlight and yelled, "Everybody in!"

The firing continued as the four soldiers backed up to the truck, and then clambered into the bed. Greer smacked the roof of the cab once they were clear.

"We're in, let's move!" he bellowed.

Choi popped the truck into gear and raced away, just as the horde reached them. A few zombies made a mad grab, but missed as the vehicle sped away from their outstretched hands.

They drove around the back of the stores, racing down the street in search of trucks. It wasn't long before they encountered six of them sitting at the giant loading dock for the Super Center. Choi put the truck in park and hopped out.

"Greer, you're up," he said.

"Gilbert, on me," Herrera said as he hit the pavement. "You two, start getting those trucks opened up and keep watch. We might have company soon."

Everyone got in position as the Corporal ran up to the back door. They got ready and threw it open before rushing inside, flashlights and guns pointed forward.

Herrera caught a glimpse of a couple zombies wandering about. He quickly aimed and fired, knocking them out. The soldiers stood quietly for a moment, waiting to hear moans, but nothing came. They scanned the loading dock for the office.

"Got it," Gilbert said, and rushed over to the small room. He burst in as Herrera stayed at the door, keeping watch. He heard the doors to the store opening up slowly, putting him on high alert.

"Hold up, I hear something," he hissed into the room, and Gilbert froze in his rummaging.

The Corporal stepped away from the office to get a better view of the doors. He shone the flashlight in that direction and saw half a dozen zombies pouring through. He immediately raised his weapon and fired.

"Find those keys, Gilbert!" he barked, shooting more ghouls, striking them with great accuracy, adrenaline pounding in his ears.

"Got 'em!" Gilbert yelled, emerging from the office with the ring in his hand.

Herrera fired off a few more rounds, and they raced to the back door, slamming it shut and securing it. "Find the trucks that match these, and let's hit the road," he said as Gilbert distributed the keys.

The soldiers all went to work, taking more time than Herrera was comfortable with locating the correct trucks. Finally, all four were inside cabs, starting them up and switching to channel eight on the CB.

"Okay, listen up," Herrera said into the radio. "I'm out first, Eason you're with me, and we're taking the inner loop. Gilbert, you and Choi are on the outer. Head west onto the bridge. We're going to go for at least a thousand yards. The further we can get the better, because it'll give us room to expand this blockade later. Now let's roll out."

He jammed the truck into gear and it lurched forward, taking a moment to get it moving smoothly. The rest of the trucks followed him out in a rumbling convoy.

As they made the turn onto the road to head north, several of the zombies from the shopping center parking lot poured onto the road. Herrera moved a little to the side to avoid the bulk of them, but still managed to crush a handful under his tires, bringing a smile to his face.

There was little resistance to the interstate, with the trucker tandems making their respective turns onto the proper interstate loops, smashing into a few straggler creatures as they went.

The interstate was mostly empty, with a few broken-down cars. The Corporal was amazed at the lack of debris everywhere.

"Is it just me, or is this interstate eerily creepy?" he asked into the radio.

Choi crackled through, "The airport here is a major hub, so if anybody coming out of Austin was flying international, it would have spread here quickly," he replied. "Doesn't look like a lot of people had time to react."

"Maybe," Gilbert cut in, "or maybe it could have been aliens!"

There was some light laughter across the radio.

"Aliens?" Choi scoffed. "Really, man? Don't tell me you believe in that nonsense."

"Dude, we're driving trucks so we can block off a bridge to prevent the living

dead from getting through," Gilbert
replied. "All bets are off at this point."

Eason chuckled and added, "Man's got
a point."

The playful banter cut short as
Herrera caught a frightening glimpse,
forcing everyone to slam on the brakes.

There were thousands of zombies on
either side of the bridge, all slowly
making their way across.

"Holy mother of god," Choi breathed.

"How far out are we, Corporal?" Eason
asked.

Herrera swallowed hard, mouth dry.
"Far enough," he replied. "Let's block it
off."

The four trucks did their best to
stretch across the entire four lanes on
either side of the bridge, with one truck
resting against the barrier and the other
doing the same on the opposite side,
doubling up in the center.

When in position, the men got out of
their vehicles and stood in silence,
seeing the mass of creatures headed
towards them.

Greer eventually snapped them out of
it by honking the horn. "Come on!" he
urged. "If there's this many on this side,
there could be a whole hell of a lot more
on the other."

Herrera and Eason exchanged a concerned glance, before turning to hitch a ride back. Before he went, the Corporal pulled out his handgun and fired several rounds into the large wheels of the barricade truck. As the air seeped out of them, they lowered another foot.

Shots went off on the other side as Gilbert caught on to what he was doing.

"What was that for?" Eason asked, scratching the back of his head.

Herrera shook his head. "Some of these things may climb under," he replied. "Don't want to make it easy for them."

Gilbert and Choi approached the gap between the bridges, which was only a few feet wide. They hopped up and jumped over the shot gap, meeting up with the others.

They clambered up into the truck bed and Eason slapped the roof, prompting Greer to turn it around and head back towards the Shopping Center.

Herrera watched through the gap in the trucks as the mass of rotting flesh came ever closer.

CHAPTER ELEVEN

Dixon, Ayers, and Hurst finished setting up the torches for the reinforcements' arrival. Hurst scrawled across the patio door with a permanent marker.

"What do you think?" he asked, taking a step back.

Dixon looked at the message: Up the road through the woods. And hurry cuz we got shit to do.

"Straight to the point," he said with a chuckle, "I like it."

Ayers furrowed his brow. "What if they send a higher up?" he asked. "They might not like that?"

"Get real," Dixon scoffed, rolling his eyes. "Why in the world would they send anyone of importance on this suicide mission"

"Hey now, I'm..." Ayers replied, holding up a hand, and then paused. "Well. Yeah, you're right."

The soldiers shared a dark laugh at their expendability and then froze at the sound of gunfire in the distance.

"You hear that?" Dixon asked.

Hurst nodded. "Sounds like somebody is panicking a bit."

"They really need to tone it down, unless they want to draw a crowd," Ayers said.

The shots intensified, multiple guns going off in three-round bursts. The trio shared a concerned look and then took off running.

"We gotta get to the line," Dixon said as they hopped off of the deck and sprinted as hard as they could back to the tree line. As they ran, they saw a few of the other men that had been fortifying the gaps between houses.

"What the hell is going on up there?" one soldier asked.

"Trouble!" Dixon barked. "Move it!"

The two soldiers joined them and all five raced towards the woods, quickly hopping the fence and tearing through the trees to the other side. When they reached the clearing, they skidded to a stop, frozen in horror at the scene.

Three men at the car barricade at the top of the road fired as rapidly as they could into a dense mass of ghouls that were quickly reaching the cars. A fourth soldier stood three houses back, standing in the gap and firing single shots at an unseen enemy.

"You two, help him," Dixon barked, motioning to the fourth man. "Ayers, Hurst, on me."

The group reached towards the fight, and he hoped that the situation at the top of the road was manageable. The hope faded the closer he got.

The schoolyard horde had made its way to their doorstep. Hundreds of creatures moaning and writhing, desperately wanting the fresh meat just out of reach. They were ten yards away from the cars, and in enough numbers to break the barricade.

As the trio reached it, two of the soldiers ran dry and had to reload. Dixon motioned wildly, and Ayers and Hurst rushed over to pick up their slack, sending round after round into the mass.

"How many rounds have you got left?" Dixon asked.

One of the soldiers shook his head. "Two full mags!"

Dixon chewed his lip as he stared out over the densely packed horde, easily hundreds strong. They wouldn't have enough ammo to take them out.

"We gotta reinforce the barricade," he said.

The soldier gaped at him. "How?!"

Dixon turned his rifle into single shot mode, and walked up to the zombies at the front of the line, carefully firing. The zombie slumped down on the hood of the car, providing an undead brick.

"Single shots, drop them at the cars," he said.

The soldier shook his head. "But they'll just keep pushing!"

"And with dead weight in front, it'll slow them down," Dixon replied, "which is what we need until we can come up with a plan."

The soldier nodded and started running up and down the line, firing single rounds into zombie heads. Dixon helped out, and the other four on the line sprung to action. As they went, a torrent of gunfire erupted behind them.

Dixon turned and spotted the trio by the houses fighting a three-front war. A few zombies had broken through at the first house, as well as two houses across the street, a few yards down from each other.

"Hurst, y'all hold the line!" he cried, and then tore off towards the others, who were firing in all directions at the dozens of zombies pouring onto the street. He flipped his gun into three-round burst, knowing he had to take a chance as the ghouls grew closer and closer to his men.

He stopped about fifteen yards from the closest group across the street. He opened fire, sending several bursts downrange, clipping several in the head and knocking others to the ground with the force of the shots.

Dixon continued firing wildly as more zombies emerged from between the houses, the makeshift barricades not able to stem the tide as another group shambled out from a different house. He fired off the rest of the bullets in his mag and quickly reloaded, noting that he only had two more in reserve. He looked up and saw about sixty zombies in the road, facing the woods.

Dixon looked over at the trio of soldiers who were not fighting back to back, firing in different directions, in danger of becoming overwhelmed.

"Back to the safe house!" he screamed, and the trio of soldiers began to retreat, continually firing the whole way.

They sprayed and prayed, hitting several targets in the head, but mostly in the upper torso. They broke off when they reached Dixon, and the four of them ran for the house on the corner.

He looked at the cars, seeing them begin to move in a few spots due to the eight of the horde, watching helplessly as Ayers and Hurst concentrated their fire on that spot.

Just as they reached the house, gunfire erupted from behind them, startling Dixon. He turned to see several men emerging from the tree line, taking aim and firing at the zombies in the streets.

"We got reinforcements!" Dixon yelled in excitement. "Everybody to the side!"

The soldiers broke from their position, moving to either side of the street, taking up positions by the houses to avoid the crossfire. They took aim, firing in a way that didn't endanger their reinforcements.

The next few minutes were filled with the deafening symphony of gunfire, bodies dropping in the street and a couple dozen reinforcement troops quickly moving in. As they approached the line, a gruff man began barking out orders.

Dixon recognized Sergeant Kipling from his tall, bearded frame.

"You men, shore up that line!" he bellowed. "I'm inspecting that line in five minutes, so it damn well better be secure!"

The men rushed off and started firing, thinning out the horde. Kipling stood in the middle of the road, looking side to side at the soldiers who had taken cover.

"Who's in charge here?" the Sergeant demanded.

Dixon emerged, heading over briskly. "Private Dixon, sir."

"Private?" Kipling asked, raising an eyebrow. "What the hell happened to your Sergeant?"

"Died in the jump," the younger man explained. "Corporal Herrera is up north blocking off the bridges. Which meant this fell to us."

The Sergeant looked around the makeshift safe zone before looking back at the eight other men who had rallied behind him. He nodded in approval.

"I was ready to rip you a new one for that message on the door," he began, "but seeing as how a bunch of Privates pulled this off, I'm inclined to give you a pass."

Dixon nodded, giving Hurst the side eye. "I appreciate that, Sergeant."

"Save your appreciation," Kipling snapped. "You got capable men here, and more on the way. Tell me what else needs to be done so we can get it going."

The Private straightened. "We set up here because the initial school target was completely overrun," he explained, and motioned to the horde. "Of course, they eventually found us, but we were able to stitch something together. Only have one house on the corner there cleared as a fallback, but the others are secure."

"Outstanding," Kipling replied. "We're going to shore this area up and when the next group gets in, we're going to take that school."

Dixon nodded. "Yes, sir," he replied. "Where do you want us?"

The Sergeant looked around at the carnage in the street and grinned. "I want you boys in the safe house for the next thirty," he declared. "Get some chow and recharge."

"Thank you, sir," Dixon replied with a relieved smile, and waved to his team. "Come on boys, you heard the Sergeant. It's dinner time."

The two trucks sped along the interstate towards the eastern bridge, which was significantly shorter than the western one. Herrera concentrated on the road, feeling the bumps as he ran over the occasional zombie. He finally spotted a sign reading Bridge - 1 Mile, and pulled up his CB radio.

"One mile, fellas," he said. "Stay sharp and let's get this done."

He glanced into the rearview mirror, seeing Greer in the pickup truck a few hundred yards back, swerving to avoid the zombies on the road. He looked back at the road, startled by one of the horns on the other side of the interstate going off.

He slammed on the brakes along with the rest of the group when they spotted the freeway packed with zombies. Not quite shoulder to shoulder, but it was damn close, and stretching as far back as they could see.

About half a mile past the front edge of the horde was the start of the bridge.

"Goddamn, that's a lot of zombies," Choi said through the radio.

Eason crackled through, "Can we set the blockade up here and call it a day?"

"Hang tight, everybody," Herrera instructed, and looked around, staring

down the interstate at the gentle slope
leading to the neighborhoods on either
side of the highway. "If we don't block it
off, we're going to get overrun," he
muttered to himself.

He rolled down his window and
motioned for Greer to come up, and the
pickup came to a stop right beside his
window. The Private slid out his window,
sitting on the sill to talk to Herrera
over the roof.

"That's a hell of a mess up there,"
he said.

The Corporal nodded. "Yep, which is
why you need to fall back," he said.

"To where?' Greer asked.

"I need you to get down to Dixon's
group if you can," Herrera instructed. "If
not, get as far south as you can and find
a safe spot to wait on them to move up."

Greer swallowed hard, staring up at
him with anxious eyes. "But what in the
hell are you going to do?" he asked.

Herrera hesitated, taking a deep
breath. "We're going to block this bridge
come hell or high water," he replied.
"When you make contact with Dixon's squad,
you're going to need to rally some troops
to come get us off this bridge."

Greer nodded, lips pursed and jaw
clenched.

"Go now," the Corporal said. "And above all, be safe. Because otherwise nobody is gonna know that we're here."

Greer gave him a thumbs up and then slipped back into the driver's seat. He made a quick three-point turn and sped off.

"Hey, where in the fuck is Greer going?!" Choi demanded. "He's our ride!"

"Wait, Greer is leaving?" Eason came through. "What's going on?"

"Everybody shut up!" Herrera barked and then waited to make sure everyone was quiet. "Now. We have to block this bridge," he said firmly. "If we don't, this whole island is going to be at the risk of being overrun. So it's either we face it now when we have a chance to stop it, or we fuck over not just us, but the entire mission."

There were a few moments of radio silence as his words sunk in.

"Okay, that's great and all," Choi finally said, "but how in the hell are we supposed to do it? These trucks aren't going to make it too far with that dense of a horde."

Herrera sucked his lip for a moment. "We do it the only way we can," he said. "Put the pedal to the metal and get as far onto the bridge as we can."

"Then what?" Eason asked.

"We sit back and wait for reinforcements," Gilbert replied.

Eason groaned. "Fucking hell."

"When your truck starts slowing down, do what you can to angle it on the bridge," Herrera instructed. "It isn't going to be perfect, but we're going to do what we can. Everybody ready?"

He didn't get a vocal response, instead the truck horns blared in unison, bringing a smile to his face at the bravery of his team.

"Let's hit it!" he cried, and all four trucks hit the gas, gaining speed as they approached the horde. Herrera was nearly at sixty miles per hour when they smacked into the mass.

The truck immediately lurched forward, losing speed as zombies splattered into the front grill. Soon after, the road grew bumpy as the wheels rolled over the fallen ghouls.

Herrera glanced over to the right, seeing Choi's truck experiencing the same level of bumping. He refocused on the front, seeing that the bridge was only another hundred yards away, however the truck was really slowing down, barely cracking twenty miles per hour.

"Come on girl, come on," Herrera urged. "You can do it."

He floored the accelerator, gaining just a small bit of speed that allowed him to get to the edge of the bridge.

He grabbed the CB. "Choi, make a hard left just after to get on the bridge, but let me pass first!" he said. "We're not making it much further."

"Heard!" Choi replied, and the Corporal gripped the steering wheel tight, holding the truck steady as he hit the bridge.

When he made it about twenty yards in, he pulled the truck hard to the right, coming to rest hard on the concrete barrier. He looked out the side mirror, seeing that the truck was at an angle, blocking most of the road.

"Gonna have to do," he muttered, and watched Choi, who was doing a good job of getting his own truck into position, leaving only a small gap for the zombies to work their way through.

"How am I looking, Corporal?" Choi asked.

Herrera shook his head. "Good as we're going to get," he replied.

"What about the gap?" Choi asked.

"We have enough ammo, we can create a zombie barrier once the sun comes up, and can aim better," Herrera replied.

Choi laughed. "Be like shooting zombies in a barrel," he said, "I love… oh shit!"

A loud crash boomed from the other side of the bridge, and Herrera watched as one of the trucks slid on its side, laying across the two lanes. Several zombies flailed in the wheel wells.

"Shit, they must have jammed it up," he grunted, and watched helplessly as the zombies pounded against the windshield. He pulled his rifle and tried to aim through the window, but couldn't get a good enough shot without potentially shattering the glass. "Whose truck was that?!" he demanded. But there was just silence. "Somebody answer me!"

"It was Eason's," Gilbert replied quickly. "I'm on it."

Herrera watched as Gilbert moved his truck into position, grinding it up against the back of the fallen truck and getting it into a decent position that blocked off the majority of the bridge. A few seconds later, the windshield went flying and Gilbert climbed out on top of the hood.

He jumped to the back of the fallen truck and raced down it towards the other cab. He leapt over the few foot gap and slid down to the front of the truck. He looked down at the front windshield,

seeing it was cracked and only being held
shut by Eason's feet pressed against it.

Gilbert quickly took out his rifle
and began firing straight down, clipping
several zombies on the top of the head and
dropping them. He knocked on the passenger
side window, motioning for his comrade to
cover his eyes before smashing it in with
the butt of his rifle.

"Can you move?" Gilbert demanded.

Eason nodded jerkily. "In theory,
yeah," he replied, "but as soon as I do,
these things are gonna bust through."

"We'll get you out of here before
that happens," Gilbert said firmly.
"Here's what we're going to do. I'm gonna
hit these fuckers one more time, then
reach in. When I do that, you move like
your ass is on fire and take my hand."

Eason nodded as he strained against
the weight of the ghouls. Gilbert quickly
hopped up, putting his rifle into three-
round burst, and taking aim. He squeezed
the trigger four times in rapid succession
and then tossed it to the side and reached
inside the cab.

"Let's go!" he cried, and Eason
reached up.

Gilbert pulled as hard as he could
while his comrade kicked off of the seat.
The dead zombies at the glass bought him a
precious few seconds, allowing him to get

above the windshield before it crashed into the driver's seat.

As Eason collapsed on top of the truck, Gilbert leaned over him.

"You okay?" he asked.

Eason nodded jerkily. "Yeah, just bruised up a bit."

"Come on," Gilbert said, helping him to his feet. "Let's get over to my truck."

They hopped over to the still-standing big rig and climbed into the cab. Eason propped his feet up on the dash, taking a well-needed breather, and Gilbert settled into the driver's seat.

"Gilbert, you copy?" Herrera asked through the radio. "You two okay?"

Gilbert picked up the radio and raised it to his mouth. "Yeah, we're good, Corporal," he replied. "How's life on the other side of the bridge?"

"We're alive and kicking, but still have a bit of work to do once the sun comes up," came the reply.

Gilbert nodded. "Won't be that difficult to get things squared away," he replied. "All in all, I'd say we did a pretty good job holding these things off."

"I think you're right," Herrera replied, and then took a deep breath. "And for what it's worth, you did a good job today."

Gilbert heard the reluctance in the Corporal's voice, and he couldn't help but laugh. "Let me guess… still haven't made amends?" he asked.

Herrera chuckled. "Hell no, not by a long shot," he replied.

"That's fair, I suppose," Gilbert admitted.

"Keep this up through the rest of the conflict, however, and we can talk," Herrera said.

Gilbert sat up straighter. "Rest of the conflict?" he asked. "You mean we aren't done after this?"

"Being a soldier is for life!" the Corporal replied, feigning shock. "Didn't anybody tell you that?"

Gilbert chuckled. "Pretty sure the only thing the recruitment guy told me was that if I signed that piece of paper, it would get me out of my hometown," he said.

"I mean…" Herrera drawled, "he wasn't wrong."

"No, no he was not," Gilbert agreed.

"Well, you boys get rested up," the Corporal said. "When the sun gets finished rising, we'll figure out all we need to do to secure this bridge."

"Good with that," Gilbert replied.

Herrera tossed down the CB and propped his feet up, taking a deep breath. He stared down the bridge to the east,

looking over thousands of undead heads all
struggling to get to him. A few minutes
later, the sun began to peek up over the
horizon, creating a beautiful view over an
ugly landscape.

He tried to reconcile those two
things meeting in the middle, knowing that
this was just another day in the
apocalypse.

END

Up Next: Corporal Bretz leads a
daring mission to block off the interstate
to the north of downtown in "Seattle -
Part 3".

DEAD AMERICA - THE NORTHWEST INVASION
BOOK 5
SEATTLE - PART 3
BY DEREK SLATON
© 2020

CHAPTER ONE

Day Zero +23

David walked across the crowded airport, still teeming with life despite the nearly five AM time. The planes from the Mercer Island mission had landed and were being refueled and checked in a few of the hangars.

He stopped on the runway as a large group of heavily armed soldiers walked across, pausing to give them space. Most of the men looked barely awake, still rubbing their eyes as they matched towards the commuter buses.

There were hundreds of soldiers dropping their gear by the side of the bus, stretching and taking a seat on the ground. David shook his head, worrying about what those men were heading in to, and how many more were on the way to join them.

Best trained military in the world. But they're really up against it this time, he thought bitterly. *If I'm going to have faith in anyone to pull this off, it's them.*

The last few soldiers in the formation passed, looking over at him with curious eyes. It was a strange sight to see a civilian in shorts and a t-shirt

carrying mugs of coffee casually int he
middle of a military zone. He nodded
politely, prompting friendly nods in
return. He couldn't expect all of the
general soldier base to know who he was,
considering most of his work with Captain
Kersey was behind the scenes.

He headed for the small office at the
base of the control tower. He checked his
watch, reading 4:58 A.M. He sighed,
knowing he was early. He didn't want to
bother the Captain even a second earlier
than he was supposed to, making sure he
got the proper recharge time he needed.

He turned around and continued
surveying the sights for a little bit,
sipping at his fresh coffee. He checked
his watch again, and when it clicked over
to 5:00, he carefully transferred both
mugs into one hand, juggling them to open
the door.

The office was dark, with only stray
rays of spotlights from the hangar
piercing through the cracks in the blinds.
He set the mugs down on a desk and gripped
the pull cord on the blinds, opening them
up fully, flooding the room with light.

He looked around, brow furrowed with
confusion, not seeing anyone around.
"Captain Kersey?" he called. "It's David."

A groan sounded from behind the desk, and the sound of cracking bones and shuffling.

"It's five A.M. and I have your coffee," David declared, "like you requested."

More groaning and a hand emerged from behind the desk, fingers curling over the wood to haul up the rest of its body. Captain Kersey peeled himself off of the floor and immediately flopped into his desk chair, rubbing his forehead.

"Five A.M. already?" he asked hoarsely.

David nodded and picked up the two mugs, approaching the desk. "Afraid so," he replied. "But I did bring you coffee." He wiggled the mug back and forth a little, the hot brew sloshing around inside.

Kersey reached out without even opening his eyes, and when the porcelain pressed against his palm, he took it and downed half the mug in a single gulp.

David blinked at him. "Be careful, it's fresh," he said, even though it was too late. "Might be hot."

"Nothing enhances caffeine like second-degree burns," Kersey replied, finally peeling his eyes open and even managing a small smile.

David cocked his head. "Are you sure you got enough rest?" he asked. "I can keep things rolling. I'm used to being up at this hour anyway."

"Nah, I got my thirty minutes of beauty sleep," the Captain assured him, shaking his head. "I'm good for the day."

His comm expert raised an eyebrow. "Talk about burning the candle at both ends," he said dryly.

"Forget that," Kersey replied, rubbing his cheek. "I'm pretty sure at this point I've just chucked that whole motherfucker right into the fire."

David chuckled as he watched Kersey down the rest of his coffee in a single Gulp and set the cup on the table.

"So, what's the status?" the Captain asked.

David took a slurp of his own brew, "The Mercer Island planes have returned and are getting prepped for when we need them next," he replied.

"Any word from the Mercer Island team?" Kersey asked.

His companion shook his head. "Not yet," he said, "but I really wasn't expecting to by this point. The first boats aren't scheduled to hit the island for another couple of hours. If they haven't made contact by then, I'll start reaching out."

"Good," Kersey replied with a nod, and swiveled in his chair towards the window. "So, how are we looking outside?"

David pulled a rolled up stack of papers from the side pocket of his pants. "The attack force for…" he paused to check over his notes, "the Redmond suburb on the far east side of things are gearing up. Buses looked primed and ready to go, so it isn't going to be long before they head out."

"Were you able to locate the people Corporal Bretz needed?" Kersey asked, taking another long sip of coffee.

His companion nodded. "Yes, but it wasn't easy."

"What is these days?" The Captain sighed.

"I was able to find three Privates, Hess, Short, and Kent," David explained. "All three have seen combat either in Spokane or the last week as we moved up here. And all three have truck driving experience."

Kersey nodded. "That's…" he paused, stifling a huge yawn and shaking his head to fight it off. "That's fantastic work."

"Captain," David said slowly, lowering his papers, "I know all the details of the mission for Bretz and his team. I would be more than happy to present it while you find your legs there."

Kersey stared down into the empty bottom of his mug and shook his head. "Yeah, let's find a refill and then go talk to him."

"Don't worry," his friend replied with a smirk, "I got the pot hidden."

The Captain laughed and wagged a finger at him. "I knew I liked you for a reason."

Corporal Bretz, Private Mason, and Private Baker fiddled with their gear as their three new team members approached.

Private Kent straightened, reaching them first. "Are you Corporal Bretz?" he asked.

The Corporal didn't look up from his gear. "Yep," he replied flatly as he packed up several days worth of MREs.

The three newcomers shared nervous glances as they set their stuff down, taken aback by the lack of acknowledgment.

"Oh, well," Kent replied, running a hand over his bald head, "I'm Private Kent. This is Private Short, and Private Hess. We were told to report to you by some assistant to Captain Kersey."

Bretz and his duo finally looked up, assessing the three soldiers that were easily in their early twenties.

"I wasn't aware we were babysitting on this mission," Baker said dryly.

Kent's gaze darkened. "Hey now, we've seen action just like you boys have," he snapped. "So drop the fucking attitude, will you?"

Baker clenched a fist and pointed a finger at the kid, "Now you listen here-"

Bretz put a hand out, smacking his palm into his subordinate's chest. "I think what my friend here is saying," he drawled, "is that he would feel a whole lot more comfortable knowing what kind of experience you have, since you'll be watching his back and all."

Short stepped forward, patting Kent's shoulder to try to defuse him. "I did a tour in the sandbox," he said.

Baker blinked, his annoyance melting away. "Wow," he replied. "A whole tour?"

"Yeah, as a transport driver," Short explained. "I'd be willing to bet I saw more IEDs go off in that one tour than you saw in however many you were there for. And if that's not a good enough resume for you, I was on one of the decoy teams in Spokane, and I somehow walked away from Kansas City as well."

Hess crossed his arms, voice level. "Two tours as a transport driver," he began, "line fire team in Spokane, emergency rescue team in Kansas City."

"Transport driver for a tour," Kent said, raising his chin with a sneer, "wasn't in K.C. but I was a part of the initial clear teams for the surrounding cities. Line fire team in Spokane."

Short spread his arms. "Let's put it this way," he said, motioning to his companions, "if these were normals times, the military would have moved all three of us up the ranks a notch or two for our experience. But given how everything is fly by the seat of your pants insane at the moment, promotions have kind of taken a back seat to merely surviving the day."

"So are we good enough for you?" Kent demanded. "Or should we go report to the grunt line?"

Mason and Bretz glanced at Baker, and he chuckled and nodded.

"Yeah, good enough for me," he said, and stepped forward to shake hands with the youngsters. "I'm Baker, that's Mason, and of course, that's Corporal Bretz, who will be leading us through his particular suicide mission."

Mason groaned. "I really wish you'd stop calling these suicide missions," he protested. "If they were really suicide missions, we would have died a couple of weeks ago."

"Not my fault I'm stubborn," Baker shot back.

Mason scratched the back of his head. "Actually, I'm pretty sure it is."

The group shared a laugh as they continued to organize their gear. There was a large pile of MREs on the floor, along with ammo and other various items.

"Make sure you pack up plenty of rations," Bretz instructed, "because if we pull this off, we're going to be on our own for several days."

Kent grimaced. "Oh good," he drawled, "nothing like our very own zombie-infested vacation."

"Not the worst vacation I've ever been on," Baker quipped.

"Oh yeah?" Short asked, raising an eyebrow. "Where was that?"

Baker sighed. "Cabo."

The trio of newcomers stared at him curiously.

"Cabo?" Kent asked. "How in the hell do you fuck up *Cabo*?"

Mason shook his head. "He refuses to tell us," he said. "Our best guess so far is that he got drunk, found a new friend, and brought back a souvenir that he didn't intend to."

"I keep telling you that's not it," Baker muttered, shaking his head.

Mason and Bretz both rolled their eyes.

"Nah, I'm with Mason," Kent said, motioning to his new friend, "it's definitely an unwanted souvenir."

Baker scowled. "Don't you start too," he warned, "or I might have to come over and teach you some manners."

"Is that what you said to your friend to start your evening to forget in Cabo?" Kent shot back.

"Naw, that's what his date said to him," Short added, smacking Kent in the shoulder. "Take a good look at him, don't he look like the discipline loving type?"

The group, minus Baker, erupted into loud laughter, just as Kersey and David reached them.

"Good to see everyone is getting acquainted," the Captain declared.

The three new recruits perked up to attention, while the other three just continued casually packing their gear.

Kersey waved his hand at the youngsters. "Please, guys," he said, "it's way too early in the damn morning for that. Keep getting ready." Another yawn escaped his mouth, and he covered it with his fist. "Oh man, sorry."

"You all right there, Cap?" Bretz asked, brow furrowing.

"Yeah, just," Kersey replied, and took a sip of his coffee, "lots I gotta be awake for. Which is why I'm going to have my friend David here walk you through the mission."

David's eyes widened as all six soldiers turned to him, looking like a deer caught in the headlights. "Oh, okay," he stammered, "just gonna jump on in." He pulled out his maps, fumbling the papers a little. "Okay, here we go." He spread out one of the immediate region, and one of a small town, on a nearby table. "Gentlemen, if you will please focus your attention on the small town map and we'll get started. What you are looking at is the town of Redmond, a quaint little suburb to the northeast of downtown Seattle. While you can't really tell from this crop, it is the first signs of civilization as you approach from the east."

Baker raised his hand.

David tongued his cheek for a moment, hesitating as he tried to remember his name. "Yes… Baker?"

"Yeah," the Private replied with a nod, lowering his hand. "When you say little, you wanna quantify that a bit more?"

David raised a hand, tilting it back and forth in the air. "Well, it's little compared to some of the other suburbs," he replied. "Pre-war, there were about seventy-five thousand people living there."

"You and I have very different definitions of *little*," Baker retorted.

The communications expert grimaced. "My apologies," he said, putting a hand to his chest. "The good news is, you aren't going to have to go very deep into Redmond to get what you're looking for." He pointed to a circled area on the southeast portion of town. There were several large white-roofed buildings making up a substantial shopping center. "According to our satellite imagery, the trucks you need to complete your mission are in this shopping center on the southeast portion of town. Now, the satellite imagery also shows a heavy zombie population, but you will be embedded with a moderate sized strike force who will be there clearing out the town."

"How big?" Short asked, without raising his hand.

David glanced at him. "We're sending a team of seven hundred and fifty to secure Redmond. A squad of a hundred will be tasked with escorting you to the site before rejoining the others. You are to get in, secure half a dozen trucks, and head out." He slid over to the larger area map. "Now." He took a deep breath. "This is where things get tricky."

"Pretty sure it's all tricky," Kent quipped, "but go on."

"With the trucks secure, you'll be hopping on highway five twenty south," David continued, "which will lead you to your destination. Unfortunately, it also means you have to go through the town of Overlake. It's smaller than Redmond, but the last images we have show a significant presence of zombies on the road."

"Can we go around them?" Mason asked.

David shook his head. "Wouldn't recommend it," he admitted. "A lot of the surface streets are covered in trees, but the areas where we can see the road appear to be crowded. You're going to just have to push through."

"And what are we supposed to do when those fuckers get wedged in the wheels?" Baker asked, throwing up his hands. "Or stall out the engine?"

Kent smirked. "You could always hitchhike."

"Would *you* pick me up?" Baker scoffed.

Kent winked at him. "Not after hearing your Cabo story."

Laughter rippled through the group again, and Bretz waved a hand to get them to settle down.

"The most difficult portion of this drive is up next," David said, raising his voice a bit to get them to focus, "the four-o-five interchange. The good news is, you'll be on the ground, so no risk of running off of a bridge. The bad news is, it's most likely going to be densely packed."

Mason leaned his hands on the table. "So, how are we supposed to get through there?" he asked.

"Air support," David replied.

The soldiers glanced around at each other and nodded, impressed.

"Air support, huh?" Baker asked, rubbing his hands together. "What we got?"

"Two Apache gunships," David replied. "They'll need a thirty-minute window to arrive, so you'll have to plan accordingly, but call them in and they'll clear a path for you here." He pointed to the stretch of road.

Baker raised his hand, and the communications expert reluctantly motioned to him.

"If we have Apaches," the Private began, "then why are we risking our lives to go block these bridges? Why not just blow them to hell and call it a day?"

David looked at Kersey, who appeared to still be half asleep.

The Captain startled when he realized everyone was looking at him and cleared his throat. "Because somebody way above our pay grade has decided that infrastructure like this has to be spared," he explained. "They feel like this city is going to have to be usable once we take it over, and we won't have the manpower or resources to repair the bridges." He took a long gulp of his coffee.

"Great," Baker said with a sigh, "so we're expendable, huh?"

Bretz patted his shoulder. "Nah, bud, just you," he said, "they're actually rooting for the rest of us to come back."

There was another light round of chuckles, and Kersey raised his mug to David to encourage him to continue.

"Okay," his friend said, "once the gunships clear the way for you, the first target is the five-twenty bridge over Lake Washington. Two trucks will need to block this off to protect our soldiers who are advancing from the east. The other four trucks are to keep going towards the main target, which is the I-five bridge just north of downtown."

They leaned over to have a look at the bridge, seeing a major interchange just south of it.

Bretz pointed to it, tapping his finger. "That interchange going from the five-twenty to the five looks problematic," he said. "Can we call in the Apaches to help us out there?"

"Unfortunately not," David replied, shaking his head. "They have a one-way ticket to the ships just offshore. In order to get more people on, they had to ditch a lot of non-essentials, like missiles and fuel."

Mason scratched his head. "So how are we supposed to get across, if we can't get to the bridge?" he asked.

David tapped an area on the map. "Just to the east of the target, there is a small surface street bridge," he explained. "This should let you get across so you can block it from the north. Once you do that, you just have to sit back and wait on reinforcements to arrive in a few days."

"And if they don't?" Baker wondered.

"Hope the water below is deep enough for a high dive," Mason replied.

Baker shook his head. "Comforting."

"Any questions?" David asked. When there was no answer, he took a step back, happy to concede the floor. "All right, Captain?"

Kersey took a deep breath and approached the table, a little more perked up as he set down his second empty mug. "I know this mission is dangerous as hell," he said, "but if we don't put some sort of blockade to protect our teams coming in from the north and east, this whole thing could be over before it even begins." He glanced at the younger soldiers. "I know you three don't know Corporal Bretz, but I spent several tours overseas with him as my right hand man. Saved my ass more times than I can count. You follow his lead, and he'll get you through to the other side. Understand?"

The three soldiers nodded and said, "Yes, sir," in unison. A moment later, the buses outside honked their horns.

"Good," Kersey said, straightening up. "And it would appear as though your rides are ready to go. Gear up, load out, and most importantly, be safe." He smirked playfully at Baker. "Well, not you, because you're expendable."

The group laughed, and Baker gave the Captain a mocking thumbs up. "Thanks Cap," he drawled, "always good to be reminded of where I stand." He cracked a smile, unable to contain his amusement any longer, even if it was at his own expense.

Kersey nodded. "Go get 'em, boys."

Bretz and Baker sat in the front row of the bus, looking out into the darkness as they drove along back roads towards their difficult target.

"What time is it?" Baker asked.

The Corporal checked his watch. "Around six-thirty," he replied.

"Good lord," the Private groaned, "how long of a drive is this?"

Private Kline turned from the seat across the aisle from them. "We still have another hour or so," he said, voice shaky.

Baker furrowed his brow at the kid that looked barely old enough to be out of high school. "Oh yeah?" he asked gently. "How do you know?"

"I… I talked with the driver earlier," Kline replied, clasping his trembling hands in his lap. "He said they had to take back roads to avoid… troubles on the interstate."

Baker cocked his head. "You all right there, soldier?" he asked.

"Y-yeah," the kid replied, nodding jerkily. "I'll be… okay."

Bretz wasn't convinced. "What's your name, soldier?" he asked, hoping to engage the kid enough to calm him down. "I'm Corporal Bretz, this here is Baker."

"Private Kline, sir," the kid replied.

"It's good to meet you, Kline," Bretz replied, offering a smile. "So talk to us. Why are you shaking like that?"

The young man's face flushed. "Just… just my nerves, sir," he said, shaking his head. "This is the first time I'm going to… see one of those things."

The older soldiers gaped at each other.

"How in the hell?" Baker breathed, leaning forward. "We're almost a month into this thing and you're in the fucking military. How have you not seen a zombie yet?"

Kline's flush deepened to almost purple as he struggled to contain his shaking hands. "Because I'm… Im a supply specialist," he stammered. "I was already stationed in Kansas when they started sending everybody to us, and since I was good at logistics and getting stuff to where it needed to be, they kept me isolated. Especially after… after most of my team fell ill."

Bretz swallowed hard and reached out to give the kid's shoulder a reassuring squeeze. "Sorry for your loss," he said solemnly. "Never easy to lose a comrade, especially when it just sneaks up on you out of nowhere."

"Thank you, sir," Kline replied, pursing his lips.

"I don't get it, though," Baker said. "If you're as valuable as you say, how did you end up on this charter bus to hell?"

The kid looked around, as if to make sure that nobody was eavesdropping. He leaned in, lowering his voice. "We're short on supplies," he said quietly. "Like, dangerously short. We had to abandon so much material during the evacuation, that finding enough resources for this invasion was almost impossible to do. I'm here because we need to know what's usable in this town. Guns, ammo, fuel, anything and everything." He shook his head. "There isn't time to fully secure the town and bring me in later. This stuff needs to get out to the front lines immediately."

Baker leaned his head back against the seat. "That's… disheartening," he said.

"Why are you telling us?" Bretz asked quietly. "This sounds like something that could create a hell of a panic if it got out."

Kline scratched the back of his neck nervously. "The driver may have let slip that we were waiting on some VIPs, which is why we were the last bus to leave," he admitted. "I don't know what your mission

is, but felt like it might do you some
good to know what if you see something you
might need, you should probably pick it
up." He sat back into his seat, still
trembling a bit.

Baker reached into his bag and pulled
out a pack of gum, holding it out to the
young soldier.

"I'm okay," Kline replied, offering a
weak smile. "Thank you, though."

Baker took the kid's hand and pressed
the packet into his palm. "Take two sticks
and keep chewing 'em, long after the
flavor is gone," he insisted. "When shit
gets real, just focus on the chewing.
It'll help calm you down. I get the sense
you're going to be behind the fire line,
so you don't have to worry about fighting
these things off."

Kline swallowed and nodded, fumbling
with the package and taking out two sticks
of gum. As he turned to face front again,
the older two soldiers leaned together.

"Haven't even fired the first shot in
this battle yet, and they're already
sending out scavengers," Baker said
softly. "That's not a good sign."

Bretz shrugged. "Wouldn't be the
first time we've had to scavenge to
survive," he pointed out.

"Still," his companion said. "I don't
know about you, but I'm adding some more

food to the shopping list. We may by out
there for a long ass time."

     The Corporal nodded silently before
turning back to the window, staring out
into the darkness. He blinked and tried to
put the new information out of his head,
focusing on the task at hand.

CHAPTER FOUR

Bretz' bus was the last one to arrive at the town, stopping on the outskirts. They parked behind three other buses unloading men onto the grass. The sun lit up the roadway with golden hues as it peeked over the horizon.

As they departed, sporadic gunfire echoed in the distance, coming from multiple directions. Bretz and Baker took a few steps away from the bus, the latter doing some stretches on the side of the road.

As the rest of the soldiers filed out, several squad leaders barked out orders, moving them all into groups. As this happened, the gunfire in the distance intensified.

"Man, the sun is barely up and already shit is going down," Baker groaned as he pulled his elbow back over his head.

Bretz shook his head. "And that's just a small suburb," he replied. "Can you imagine what it's going to be like when we get to downtown?"

"Since there's only six of us going in first, I'm going to assume we are going to have our choice of targets," the Private said.

The other men from their team headed over, setting down their gear and joining Baker in some stretches.

"Whole world at our fingertips, and the find the least comfortable bus to throw us on," Kent said, bending his leg and gripping his ankle.

Short shook his head as he leaned over to touch his toes. "Could be worse," he said, "at least it wasn't a school bus."

"Man, what does your country ass know about school buses?" Kent teased. "Did you even go to school?"

Short raised his chin as he straightened up. "I finished top of my class, thank you very much."

Hess snorted as he tilted his torso to each side. "Congratulations on beating the other four people in your grade."

"Hey now, it was more than that," Short shot back, and then hesitated as the others gave him a knowing look. "I mean, not *much* more than that. We did hit double digits."

Laughter rippled through the group, and then promptly ceased as a giant man stalked towards them. Despite his white hair, he didn't look frail, his six-foot frame broad and towering over most of the other soldiers.

"Are you boys my VIPs?" the beastly soldier asked.

Bretz nodded, stepping forward and saluting. "Yes sir, I'm Corporal Bretz."

"All right," the man replied, nodding at him. "I'm Sergeant Murphy, and I'm going to be leading you in. Hope you boys are ready to fight, because we're going in short-handed."

Baker raised an eyebrow, motioning to the pack of soldiers surrounding them. "There's like two hundred people standing here," he said. "Not sure that qualifies as short-handed."

"Good to know they're still teaching counting in basic," Murphy said, sarcasm evident as he stared down at the Private.

The group chuckled at Baker's expense, save for Bretz.

"What's going on, Sergeant?" the Corporal asked, brow furrowing.

"Our teams to the north are, for lack of a better word, getting their asses handed to them," Murphy explained. "They had to fall back to the high school, and they're kind of trapped. So we have orders to send three-quarters of our men up there to break 'em out."

Bretz nodded. "So we're going in with fifty?" he asked.

"Not including you six, that's right," Murphy replied, and pulled out a piece of paper printed from the satellite imagery. "According to the sat image, our shopping center target is looking relatively bare, at least in the parking lot. We should have more than enough firepower to get you to the target so you can secure your trucks."

The Corporal nodded again. "If you're confident, Sergeant," he said, "then I'm confident."

"Truth be told, it's more hopeful optimism than confidence," Murphy admitted.

Bretz shrugged. "It's more than I had in Spokane, so I'll take it," he said.

"All right, if you boys want to just hang out here by the bus, I'll send a runner when we're ready to move," the Sergeant instructed. "Shouldn't be more than ten minutes."

"We'll be ready," the Corporal replied.

Murphy nodded firmly and headed off, barking out orders at the top of his lungs as he went. Bretz turned to his team, noting their concerned faces.

"Six minutes into the assault and we're already getting our asses kicked?" Kent asked, shaking his head. "That doesn't bode well for things."

Baker took a deep breath. "Based on that, I think we should pick up some extra food before getting in those trucks," he suggested. "Might be weeks before they get to us at this rate."

"We stick to the plan as is," Bretz countered. "A lot of these soldiers haven't seen much combat, if any at all int he last month. And certainly not at the scale of this operation. Going to take them a minute to get their footing."

Baker jutted out his chin. "You don't actually believe that bullshit, do you?" he demanded.

Bretz cocked his head and gave a little shrug, not wanting to confirm or deny the Private's accusation. "All right," he finally conceded, "if you pass something while we're going through the store, grab it. But don't be going out of your way for stuff."

"That's a compromise I can get behind," Mason agreed, and the group fell into a tense silence as they readied their gear.

Bretz and his team followed the group of fifty led by Sergeant Murphy towards the shopping center. They stopped a block away, taking a knee by the side of the road. The center was the first bit of civilization they'd encountered, nothing but woods and fields up until that point.

Murphy pulled out binoculars and scanned ahead, focusing on the shopping center. It was a large complex, with two main anchors running along a five hundred yard long building, the back of which faced the group. Along the side to the left was a shorter building, about three hundred yards, with another major anchor.

While the driveway was only about thirty yards wide, he could see about eighty zombies or so in the lot, but it was impossible from that vantage point to see the majority of the area. He motioned for Bretz to come up beside him.

"What do we have, Sergeant?" Bretz asked.

Murphy tilted his head. "We have moderate resistance, just from what I can see," he replied. "I doubt we're lucky enough to have all of them to one side."

"Based on my experience, none of us are that lucky," the Corporal replied dryly.

The Sergeant pulled out a close-up satellite image printout of the shopping center, with two areas circled. One was on the main building on the far side, and the other on a shorter building closer to them.

"You need six trucks, right?" he asked.

Bretz nodded. "That's right."

"We got two target buildings here," Murphy explained, pointing to the circles, "neither of which are going to be easy runs if we're facing heavy resistance. I think in order to buy you the time you need, we're going to have to clear this lot and set up a firing line to the north in case we attract some visitors."

Bretz nodded. "If the keys are in the loading dock offices," he said, "it shouldn't take us more than ten minutes to get loaded up and head out."

"And if they're not?" the Sergeant asked, cocking his head.

The Corporal wrinkled his nose. "Could be thirty minutes or more."

"No matter how much time you need, we're gonna get it for you," Murphy said firmly, and let out a soft whistle, pointing to some men close by.

Four soldiers rushed over and took a knee in front of him.

"We gotta buy the Corporal here some time," the Sergeant explained. "Need two of you on each of the main buildings. Get up there, give us the lay of the land, then start picking them off. You got it?"

All four men made emphatic noises in the affirmative.

"Good," Murphy said, "get going."

The four men took off quickly down the road, moving faster than a jog. The Sergeant reached into his bag and pulled out a second set of binoculars, handing them to Bretz.

The Corporal took them with a brow furrowed. "You carry two sets of these?" he asked.

"My orders said I had to escort some VIPS," Murphy replied with a little shrug. "Just wanted to make sure I didn't disappoint."

Bretz smiled and nodded, then lifted the binoculars so he could watch the foursome approach the shopping center. When the boys got close, the teams broke off into groups of two, focusing on their targets. The duo to the left, heading towards the smaller building, took cover behind a few cars parked on the side of the building.

There were some zombies wandering about on the other side of the vehicles, looking around suspiciously at the noise of the footsteps. The Corporal watched the two men draw knives, readying to strike. One of them picked up a rock and heaved it over the enemy's head, and it smacked into the side of the wall.

"Smart move," Bretz murmured as the soldiers leapt over the hood of the car, dispatching the distracted zombies from behind with ease.

As soon as the duo disappeared behind the store, panicked gunfire erupted from the other side.

"What are those chucklefucks doing?" Murphy snapped, and they frantically searched for the other pair of soldiers.

Bretz finally found them as the gunfire grew more intense. "Got 'em, halfway down the building."

A horde of zombies swarmed around a spot on the ground, presumably where one of the men had been standing. One of the creatures' heads exploded, and then the gunfire went silent. Bretz' mouth went dry, and he scanned for the other soldier, finally spotting him climbing up onto a dumpster and collapsing on top of it.

It was clear that the soldier was clutching a wound on his neck. Bretz quickly pocketed the binoculars and readied his rifle.

"Sergeant, we have to move now," he
said. "We're about to have at least to
runners."

Murphy nodded, the implications not
lost on him. Runners were much harder to
deal with, and given that they were
already shorthanded, they'd need to be
dealt with fast.

"You're staying put, Corporal," he
said firmly. "My orders are to deliver you
safely, and I intend on doing just that."
He motioned to six nearby soldiers, waving
them forward. "Main building, eliminate
all targets with extreme prejudice.
Including our injured."

One of the soldiers' eyes widened.
"Sir?"

"Did I fucking stutter?" the Sergeant
demanded. "Those are the orders from the
top. Quick death for those who are bitten.
And when it's clear, two of you get
topside for diversions. Now move out!"

The group of six sprinted towards the
dead and injured, guns raised and ready
for action. As they made the turn on the
back of the building, Bretz and Murphy
watched through the binoculars as they
formed a firing line.

The soldiers fired quickly, striking
down several zombies in short order. They
mowed down the remaining ghouls and then
hesitated.

"Follow your damn orders," the Sergeant muttered.

"They will," Bretz assured him. "It's not easy, what's being asked of them."

Murphy's brow furrowed, and he lowered his binoculars. "You've been in their shoes, I take it?" he asked.

The Corporal shook his head. "Not pre-turn, but shortly after," he replied. "Even with my life in danger, it took longer than I would care to admit."

Several quick shots rang out, and they looked to see the job was done.

"Hope they've squirreled away some shrinks," Murphy said, "because a lot of us are gonna need some time on the couch when this is through."

Bretz shrugged. "Well, we are invading Seattle," he pointed out, "maybe Frasier Crane survived."

"One can only hope," the Sergeant replied with a dark chuckle.

They watched two of the men climb up onto the roof and scanned the other four coming back to the formation. They looked at the other building and spotted one of the men waving at them, prompting Murphy to pull out his walkie-talkie.

"What you got for me, soldier?" the Sergeant asked.

"Sarge..." the soldier's voice came back hesitantly, "I don't know how we're handling this."

Murphy sighed. "Well spit it out son," he barked, "what are we dealing with?"

"There's probably a thousand of those things in the parking lot," the soldier replied, "and there's another couple hundred up the road about half a mile."

The Sergeant lowered the radio, shaking his head and rubbing the bridge of his nose. He finally lifted it and held it to his mouth. "Standby," he said firmly.

"Yes sir," the soldier replied.

Murphy turned to his VIPs. "Well, if the other squad wasn't shitting the bed, we could clear this out no problem."

"We can still clear it out," Bretz assured him. "You got the six of us in addition to your crew. If we're smart, we can do it."

The Sergeant shook his head. "My orders are to get you to the trucks, and that's what I'm going to do."

"With all due respect Sergeant," the Corporal declared, "as soon as we fire up those trucks, we're going to be sitting ducks. And those back alleys are narrow. If we don't get a handle on the situation before we start those up, this mission is over before it begins."

Murphy pulled out his map. "You're right," he conceded as he spread it open. "So, we have a thousand zombies in the lot, and more up the road there."

"As soon as we start shooting, everything is going to converge on us," Bretz pointed out.

The Sergeant nodded. "The shamblers are slow," he said, "so we got what, ten minutes before the ones on the road join the battle?"

"About that," the Corporal agreed.

"So we need to clear the lot and get men over to the other side to fend them off," Murphy mused.

Bretz nodded thoughtfully. "I think if we send a few more men to the smaller building, they can provide enough of a distraction to buy us a little more time," he suggested.

"Agreed," the Sergeant replied.

"And if I'm overstepping my bounds, Sergeant, just say so," Bretz said firmly. "This is your operation, we're just along for the ride."

Murphy shook his head emphatically. "Your input is Welcome, Corporal," he replied. "Especially after your actions in Spokane."

Bretz nodded. "So how do you want to play it?"

"We get a few more men on top of each building, and pull as many of those things to the far end as we can," Murphy explained. "Put the bulk of our force straight ahead in the driveway, using the buildings as buffers."

Bretz handed back the binoculars. "I would also leave a few men on either side covering the back of the buildings," he suggested. "These things are sneaky, and the last thing we need is to be ambushed."

"Agreed," the Sergeant said, putting the binoculars back into his pack.

"I think once we set up the perimeter at the entrance, our focus should be clearing out the front of the main building," Bretz added. "That will give us more real estate to deal with the reinforcements."

Murphy cocked his head. "But if there's only a couple hundred coming up, wouldn't it make more sense to clear them out, first?" he asked.

"There are only a couple hundred that they can see," Bretz warned.

The Sergeant nodded thoughtfully. "Valid point." He whistled and pointed to six soldiers nearby. "Get up to the line, three on each building," he instructed. "Set up at the far end and start drawing them to you. Go."

They tore off across the parking lot, and then Murphy crossed his arms, turning back to Bretz.

"Okay Corporal," he said firmly, "here's the deal. You stay in the center of the action with me." He pointed a finger at him. "Understood?"

Bretz nodded. "Understood, Sergeant."

"Let's move out, then," Murphy said, raising a hand and whirling it above his head. "Those things aren't gonna kill themselves."

CHAPTER SIX

The gunshots from the rooftops went off at a steady clip. As Murphy led his team towards the shopping center entrance, they stared at the effects of it.

Most of the zombies that had been visible from their vantage point had since wandered in either direction, headed towards the far end of the buildings. This bought the group some significant space, fifty yards at a minimum, to set up their firing line.

They set up in a semicircle, no more than a yard apart from one another, one group kneels with the back row standing. They used the walls of the building for protection, fanning out to cover the entirety of the road.

"Okay men, listen up," Murphy said. "We're about to unleash hell on these things, and they're going to try to do the same to us. When you feel comfortable taking the shot, do so, but not before. The last thing we need today is to run out of ammo. Everybody ready?"

The soldiers murmured in the affirmative, and the Sergeant gave a sharp nod.

"Let's get it started, then," he said, and aimed towards a zombie fifty yards away, shambling towards the crowd at the far end of the smaller building. As he zeroed in on it, he squeezed the trigger, the head exploding in a spectacular fashion.

Soon after, several more soldiers joined in, firing off well-placed shots that dropped an entire line of zombies in both directions. The noise drew the attention of a lot of creatures on the fringes of the main horde, who began working their way back towards them.

The firing stretched out over the next few minutes, more soldiers joining in as the zombies got closer to their range. At twenty-five yards, the ghouls were thick, hundreds of them piled together shoulder to shoulder, swarming over their fallen, all headed towards a fresh soldier buffet.

The fire on the line became more erratic as some of the men began to panic at the closeness of the undead.

"Three-round bursts!" Murphy yelled, and the soldiers switched to a barrage of bullets, unleashing bursts of shots that ripped through the ghouls. While the fire rate increased, the additional zombies falling weren't enough to stem the tide.

Bretz glanced back as he heard gunfire coming from the teams guarding the back alleys. "Baker, on me!" he cried, and the two broke from the line, running back to the alley behind the main building. They found two soldiers standing there, frantically firing towards a group of monsters several dozen large.

The two men stepped up and immediately opened fire, sending single placed rounds downrange, dropping zombies one after the other.

"There's too many of them!" one of the soldiers cried.

Bretz shook his head. There *were* too many of them, and they were moving too quickly. As the other three men continued firing, he spotted a rolling full-sized dumpster about ten yards away, right in the middle of the no man's land between the zombies and the soldiers.

Without hesitation, he broke from the line, sprinting for the dumpster. It took Baker a moment to realize what was going on, and then he broke rank and joined him.

"Come the fuck on!" he yelled over his shoulder, and the other two tore after him. The trio helped Bretz move the large metal dumpster into the center of the alleyway, covering about a quarter of the area.

"Give me a boost!" the Corporal barked, and Baker linked his fingers together to make a step out of his hands. He propelled Bretz up on top of the canister, and the Corporal immediately opened fire, flipping into three-round burst mode and unloading on the enemy. The other three men set up on the sides of the trash can, opening fire as well.

The center of the zombie mass pressed up against the canister, moving it slightly back. Bretz widened his stance to keep his balance, still firing mostly at the zombies on the fringes, making sure they didn't make it around the barricade.

Once the threat of zombies making it around was gone, he focused on the creatures at his feet, making short work of them.

When the soldiers stopped firing, the gunfire coming from the main line was intensifying, with a lot of panic fire. Bretz hopped down and then opened the lid of the dumpster, finding it mostly empty. He contemplated for a few moments and then glanced at Baker.

"What do you say buddy," he said, tilting his head, "you want to go for a ride?"

Baker's brow furrowed in confusion before his eyes widened at the insinuation. He laughed and then shook his head. "Okay, but this is your one creative maneuver for this entire mission," he said playfully.

Bretz chuckled. "Fair enough, now hop in."

The two of them hopped into the dumpster, and the two other soldiers stared at them blankly.

"What…" one of them trailed off. "What are you doing?"

Bretz pointed at them. "You two are going to push us through the firing line," he said. "Get us as far out into the parking lot as you can."

The soldiers glanced at each other nervously.

"Do it now, that's an order," Bretz demanded, and when they still hesitated, he slammed his fist down on the edge of the dumpster. "Do it *now*, before their position is overrun!"

The two soldiers snapped out of their doubt and immediately began pushing the trash can. Baker knelt down, pulling the lid over himself. Bretz remained standing, holding up his side. As they grew closer, the Corporal yelled and fired twice into the crowd of zombies ahead, which were now within ten yards of the firing line.

Murphy whirled around and spotted the rolling force headed their way. "Clear the path!" he bellowed, and grabbed a few of his comrades to pull them out of the way.

The soldiers scrambled to make a hole for the dumpster to fit through, and Bretz lowered his lid, taking a knee. The duo pushing them gave a great heave as they pushed just past the line, stopping just a few yards shy of the front edge of the horde before retreating.

The heavy metal container rolled fast, slamming into zombies and knocking several of them down and out of the way. As soon as their momentum stopped, about five yards into the horde, Baker and Bretz popped up, throwing open their lids.

They took aim and opened fire in three-round bursts, sweeping the front line of zombies quickly at point blank range, spraying blood and rotted skull fragments everywhere. They pinned themselves at the back of the dumpster, using the lids as cover since the metal had landed on top of zombies, preventing them from being able to reach up and grab the soldiers.

They switched to single fire, taking deliberate aim and clearing out monsters one by one. Murphy nodded as the bulk of the zombies that had been headed towards them turned their attention towards Bretz and Baker, giving the firing line a little bit of breathing room. Several of the men stared, mouths agape, amazed at the sight.

"What are you waiting on them for?" the Sergeant barked. "Start shooting!"

Everybody took up arms again, firing into the mass, taking special care to aim clear of the two men in the dumpster. The added cushion allowed the soldiers to get a handle on the situation.

The battle was swift but brutal. With the bulk of the horde distracted, the firing line was able to inch forward, switching to single fire and clearing out the creatures with precision. Within several minutes, all the creatures in the main horde lay motionless on the ground, leaving only a nominal force in front of the anchor stores at the far ends of either building.

Murphy immediately began pointing at groups of soldiers. "You men, main building," he bellowed. "Rest of you, clear out the stragglers and then set up a fire line on the road."

A chorus of "Yes sir!" erupted before the majority of the soldiers ran off, leaving only Bretz' team with the Sergeant.

Murphy stalked towards the dumpster and crossed his arms. "That was a hell of a maneuver there, Corporal," he said dryly.

"Appreciate it, Sergeant," Bretz replied as he clambered out of the bin, reaching in to help Baker out.

"That wasn't a compliment," Murphy snapped, and then took a deep breath. "Okay, it was," he admitted, and then pointed a finger at him accusingly. "But

I'm not exactly thrilled with you at the moment."

Bretz shook his head. "Sorry Sarge, didn't really have time to get the okay."

"That was some quick thinking, I'll give you that," Murphy replied. "Saved us from getting overrun."

The Corporal shrugged. "I'm just glad it worked."

"Me too," the Sergeant admitted, and then he raised his chin. "But from now on, until I personally place you inside one of those big rigs, you are *not* to leave my side. Is that clear?"

Bretz nodded. "Yes, sir," he said firmly.

"Good," Murphy replied, satisfied. "Now, let's go see about getting you a ride."

CHAPTER SEVEN

With the last remnants of the zombie mass laying dead in front of the store, Murphy had a few men pry open the doors before carefully walking inside. The air was stagnant, the building having been sealed shut for nearly a month.

Bretz turned to head for the back, but Murphy put a hand on his arm.

"Not leaving my side remember?" he asked, and the Corporal nodded, halting.

The Sergeant let out a deafening whistle, and the team remained silent, listening for movement or moans. When nothing happened, Murphy motioned for the team to follow him and a trio of soldiers leading them through the store.

They made their way to the back, the other soldiers doing a quick sweep of the back storeroom, finding nothing.

"It's clear, sir," one of them reported.

Murphy nodded. "Good, hang tight for a minute," he said, and then turned to Bretz. "We've gotten you this far. What do you need from us?"

The Corporal motioned for Baker and Mason to investigate the back office, hoping that they would find some keys. "Hold that thought, Sergeant," he said, and then pointed at Kent, motioning for him to check out the back.

Kent jogged over to the door and peered out. "Got four trucks out back here, Corporal," he said.

"And what do you know, we have keys!" Mason declared as he and Baker emerged from the office.

Bretz raised an eyebrow. "Four sets?"

"Four sets," Mason replied with a grin, holding up the rings and jingling them.

The Corporal pointed to the door. "Get out there and get the trucks started up," he instructed, "make sure there's gas, at least a quarter tank."

Mason tossed two sets to Baker, and they headed outside with Kent and Short to get things up and going.

"For starters, we still need two more trucks," Bretz said, turning back to the Sergeant.

Murphy pointed to one of his three soldiers. "You, take a few men from outside, go to the other store across the lot, and make sure the route is clear," he said. "If you can locate the keys, even better."

"Before you go…" Hess piped up.

The soldier stopped, and everyone turned to Hess, surprised at the interruption.

"Yes, Private?" Murphy asked.

Hess looked to Bretz. "Corporal, we had talked about the necessity of acquiring more provisions," he said.

"I think we'll be okay, Private," Bretz replied.

Hess took a deep breath. "If it's all the same sir," he said politely, "wouldn't you rather change that think to a know?"

Bretz thought for a moment, and then finally nodded. "He's right," he admitted, turning to Murphy. "We could use some more food and water."

"We'll take care of it," the Sergeant replied, and motioned to the departing soldier. "Before you go, make sure each truck has a package of bottled water, as well as a large assortment of goods. Focus on trail mix, jerky and other long lasting proteins."

Hess grinned. "If they have any, perhaps some chocolate tasty cakes."

Both Bretz and Murphy cracked a smile.

"Well, you heard the man," the Sergeant said, "chocolate tasty cakes."

The soldier nodded and headed out as Mason jogged back inside.

"Corporal," he said, "we got all four running and there's plenty of fuel."

Bretz smiled. "Good deal," he said. "Make sure the truck containers are secure, and there's nothing int he back that's going to trip us up. Once that's done, we'll go inspect the trucks at the other site."

Mason gave him a thumbs up and headed back outside.

Murphy let out a low whistle. "So, you boys are really headed into the shit, aren't you?" he asked.

"That we are Sarge," Bretz confirmed, "that we are."

"Based on what I've heard about you and witnessed with my own eyes," Murphy said, "those dead fuckers aren't going to know what hit them."

The Corporal barked a laugh. "Let's hope you're right, Sergeant."

CHAPTER EIGHT

The trucks were all lined up in the shopping center parking lot, in an area clear of zombie corpses. Bretz fired up his truck before looking out the window at Murphy, who gave him a thumbs up.

"You have everything you need, Corporal?" the Sergeant asked.

Bretz nodded. "Food, water, and weapons," he replied, "everything a growing boy needs."

"My men said they threw in some books as well," Murphy replied, "give you something to do while you wait on us to come get you."

The Corporal looked over into the bag on the passenger seat that had been left for him. He fumbled through and pawed a collection of snacks before finding a stack of books. He picked up one up, chuckling at the shirtless muscled man on the cover holding a woman at a dramatic angle.

"The Rose and the Rapier," he read, shaking his head. "Well, it will be better than listening to zombie moans."

Murphy grinned. "You boys be safe out there," he said. "And I expect a full book report when I come get you." He smirked. "That's an order."

"You'll have it, sir," Bretz replied
with a laugh. "You watch yourself out
there."

The Sergeant raised a fist. "We have
your trash can maneuver," he declared, "so
nothing can stop us now."

The Corporal nodded and then pulled
down on the truck horn a few times,
letting out a deafening bleat. He picked
up the CB radio and raised it to his lips.

"All right, everybody on com?" he
asked, and waited as one by one, the other
five soldiers checked in. "Okay, here's
what we're doing," he began. "Heading out
to the north, the highway is about half a
mile up. Hit the outbound lane and haul
ass. I want a hundred yards between every
truck when we're out there. We have enough
on our plates without risking an accident.
Everybody clear?"

A chorus of "Yes, sir!" came through
the speaker, and he nodded.

"Let's move, then," he said, and
replaced the receiver to its holder. He
rolled out, the rest of the squad falling
in place behind him.

The drive to the highway was short,
with the road mostly clear. Bretz looked
out to the side at another shopping area,
watching Murphy's men get set up on the
rooftops, squeezing off shots to pull the
crowd towards them.

Bretz led the convoy up to the highway, making the turn onto the ramp, gaining speed as it went up. The road on the outer loop itself was mostly clear, with the occasional car left abandoned on the side of the road. The traffic on the opposite side was a bit more dense, with several people apparently trying to leave town as the mess had started and failing.

"That's a hell of a rush hour over there," Kent crackled through the radio.

"We don't have those sorta issues where I come from," Short piped up.

Kent laughed. "What is rush hour like in your hick town there, bud?"

"Only time we ever had traffic was when there was a cow break," Short replied.

"What in the hell is a cow break?" Baker cut in.

"There's hundreds of miles worth of fencing around the farms, and it wasn't always the sturdiest stuff," Short explained. "Those cows were tricky, always finding a way out. So it was a daily occurrence to see them wandering around the streets."

Kent barked a laugh. "Man, that is some countrified bullshit right there," he drawled. "I'm up in Chicago dealing with gangs, neighborhood pit bulls, rush hour traffic, lake effect snow and a thousand other things. Meanwhile, you're getting outsmarted by cows. How in the hell did we end up in the same unit?"

"I dunno," Short admitted. "Military brass probably saw you came from a town that thinks pizza is supposed to resemble a pie and thought you had a mental defect. Had to put you in with someone with a functioning brain."

Kent snorted. "Don't think I won't run your ass off the road for badmouthing deep dish pizza," he quipped.

There was a collection of laughter over the CB, and Bretz cut back in. "We're going to have to table this debate," he said, "because we're approaching Overlake."

The group calmed down, the seriousness of their mission taking hold once again.

The highway made a large turn around a bend, leading to Overlake, the next large suburb they'd have to pass through. As Bretz took the gentle curve, the road was packed full of zombies and cars up ahead, looking like a major pileup completely blocking the path. He slammed on the brakes, prompting everyone behind him to do the same.

The screeching tires were loud, squealing as the convoy suddenly came to a halt. A loud crash echoed from the back, and the Corporal's eyes widened.

"What in the hell was that?!" he demanded through the radio.

"Hess done fucked it up," Kent drawled.

"Wasn't my fault you slammed on the brakes in the middle of a goddamn curve!" Hess exclaimed frantically. "Couldn't see you in time!"

Bretz rubbed the bridge of his nose. "What's the damage?" he asked.

There was the loud wheeze of an engine trying to start, and then nothing.

"It's dead," Hess replied.

"Ten minutes into the drive and we're already fucked," Baker drawled. "Fantastic."

"Again, not my fault," Hess said through his teeth.

"Calm yourself," Baker shot back. "I wasn't assigning blame, just stating a fact."

Mason cut through, "Bretz, down the road."

The Corporal looked up the highway and saw the horde of zombies a few hundred yards away had started moving in their direction, shambling towards all the noise.

"Hess, grab your gear and get in the next truck," Bretz commanded. "We can't stay here."

"On the move," the Private replied.

Bretz stared down the highway, chewing over what their next move should be. There was an off ramp nearby, with another shopping center shortly past that. He stared at it, contemplating, and then finally raised the CB to his lips again.

"Okay, here's what we're doing," he said. "We're taking the off ramp and we're making an unscheduled pit stop at that shopping center."

"Bretz, you know I'll follow you anywhere," Baker said slowly, "but do you think that's wise? We still have five trucks."

The Corporal furrowed his brow. "And we need six," he replied firmly. "If we don't pull this off, our troops to the north are going to have way more to deal with than they can potentially handle."

"Yeah…" Baker trailed off, sounding nervous but knowing Bretz was right. "I'm with you. Let's do it."

"Got Hess aboard and ready to go," Mason cut in. "How are we doing this?"

Bretz took a deep breath. "We're just going straight for the back door," he replied. "Mason, can you and Hess handle it? Or do you need backup?"

"Should be a quick hit and run," Mason replied easily, "won't be any big deal."

The Corporal nodded. "Okay, the rest of you, follow me," he instructed. "We're going to spread out over the parking lot and hopefully keep the crowds around us down. Let's go."

He popped the truck back into gear and headed out, with the rest of the trucks behind him. They took the off ramp, rolling into a small neighborhood. The side streets were dirty and deserted, with some stragglers and cars dotting the road.

Bretz pulled the truck into the shopping center lot, a smaller center with a single anchor and some side stores. There were about a hundred zombies in the lot, all of which started moving towards him.

"Okay, pick your corner and go," he instructed through the radio. "And Mason, don't take too much time. That horde on the interstate is pretty thick. If they get down here, we're in trouble."

"In and out, Corporal," Mason replied firmly. "No problem."

Bretz watched the trucks move to the opposite ends of the lot, drawing the creatures in all directions.

"Come on Mason," Bretz muttered to himself, "let's make this quick."

The Private pulled his truck down the back alley, rolling over a couple of zombies as he went. There was a satisfying *pop* as the tire crushed a rotted head.

"Ah, that sound never gets old," he declared, shooting Hess a grin.

His passenger shrugged. "I suppose we have to enjoy the little things in life."

"These days it's about as good as it gets," Mason replied.

He stopped at the back loading dock of the store, where there were two trucks backed up. There were four zombies wandering around near the back door.

"Just leave the truck running," Hess suggested, "we're not going to be long."

Mason checked the gas gauge, seeing there was still three-quarters of a tank. He nodded in agreement and hopped out.

The soldiers hit the ground, assault rifles at the ready, and opened fire on the zombies by the door, quickly taking them out with precise headshots. They rushed to the back door, and Mason yanked on it, finding it locked.

"Shit, no good," he growled.

Hess looked down the loading dock and saw that one of the bay doors was open about two feet, enough to provide the workers with some airflow.

"Come on, we got a way in," he said, and waved for his partner to follow him.

The two men hopped to the ground and rushed over to the opening, Hess taking out a flashlight and shining it inside. There were several sets of feet in his line of vision, the closest being five yards away.

Hess went silent, pointing it out to Mason before motioning for him to boost him up. Mason laced his fingers together, giving his companion a heave up onto the dock.

Hess drew his knife and slammed it into the back of the closest ghoul, catching its body as it fell and gently setting it on the concrete to avoid making noise. He looked around, seeing the other zombies were easily fifteen to twenty yards away and hadn't noticed them yet. He quickly went back over to the loading dock and laid down to pull Mason up after him.

The duo readied their knives, wanting to remain stealthy, and headed towards the back office. There were a trio of creatures by the office door that would need to be dealt with, so Hess slid forward and stabbed one in the back of the head, catching the body as he jammed the blade into the temple of the second one.

In the darkness, he missed, glancing off of the creature's forehead and enraging it. It let out a furious moan and reached for him, and Hess dropped his

charge, stabbing the hungry zombie in the
eye socket.

Mason finished off the third ghoul,
but unfortunately the noise was enough to
alert the rest of the zombies in the room.
They turned in unison, moaning and
shambling for the soldiers.

"Find the keys!" Hess barked.

Mason rushed into the office, pulling
out his flashlight. Hess raised his rifle
and flashlight, finding targets and
shooting them one by one between the eyes.
After he squeezed off half a dozen rounds,
dropping that many ghouls, the swinging
doors to the store flew open under a fresh
swarm.

He froze in terror at the sight of
dozens of monsters pouring into the back
room. "Hurry up!" he yelled. "We're about
to get overrun!"

Mason frantically looked for the
keys, throwing stuff in every direction,
hoping to uncover them. Meanwhile, Hess
opened fire, carefully placing shots,
spreading out the carnage in hopes that
the ones behind the fallen corpses would
trip.

His fire intensified as more
creatures came in and grew closer and
closer, within fifteen feet away.

"MASON!" he screamed.

His companion opened the last drawer on the desk, relieved to find two sets of keys, and grabbed them both. "Got em!" he cried, bursting out of the office. "Let's go!" He shoved the keys in his pocket and raised his rifle, joining his companion in shooting to buy them time to get to the door.

Mason hit the release bar on the door behind him, but it didn't open. He shoved it a few more times, but the door wouldn't budge.

"We're stuck!" he cried.

Hess shot several more zombies before dropping his empty mag and reloading. He threw himself into the release bar, but the door wouldn't move. He looked down and saw a slot for a key.

"They must have dead bolted it!" he said.

Both soldiers fired off a few more shots as the zombies reached ten yards of them, the numbers still in the couple of dozen.

"Out the loading dock door!" Mason cried, and they inched forward, continuously shooting as they made their way to the loading dock.

As they grew closer, they saw that several zombies had been attracted to the noise and were now pressed against the opening.

"Fuck, what do we do now?" he demanded.

Hess clenched his jaw and shook his head. "We have to go through them."

"What?!" Mason cried.

"Get to the front of the store, and we'll circle around the back," Hess explained. They squeezed off a few more shots, dropping two more zombies. "Focus your fire on the center of the horde, drop as many as you can, and haul ass."

Mason swallowed hard, steeling his gaze, and the two men raised their weapons, flashlights illuminating the front line of the two dozen deep horde quickly closing in on them in the corner.

"Now!" Hess yelled, and they opened up in three-round bursts, sending as much lead downrange as they could.

The bullets ripped through the front edge of the mass, dropping several of them and cutting others to shreds, knocking them down.

Hess led them forward, both shooting rapidly as they went, clearing a path through the center of the group. When they got halfway to the door, his gun clicked empty. He clutched it tightly, extending it forward and using it as a battering ram.

He caught one ghoul in the chest, driving it backwards into the others while

Mason fired several more shots into the group.

"We're almost to the door!" Hess yelled, as the zombie he was pushing grabbed his arm, frantically snapping with its teeth to get a bite. He flung it side to side in an attempt to avoid the teeth.

Mason rushed up, lowering his shoulder and bashing into the last group of two zombies by the door. The impact sent them staggering backwards through the door and into the store. His momentum carried him forward through the door, and he stumbled before catching himself and whirling around.

Hess finally managed to throw his attacker to the ground and smash its face in, turning just in time to see a zombie leap on Mason's back, sending him face first into the linoleum. Hess drew his handgun and fired at the two zombies converging on his partner's position, tearing towards his fallen friend.

He grabbed it by the back of the shirt, but the ghoul managed to bite into Mason's shoulder, taking a chunk of him with it as Hess ripped it from his friend's back. He put the barrel to its head, watching it savor every bite of his companion's flesh before he blew its brain apart.

Hess looked down at Mason to help him up, but the blood poured out of him, the bite close enough to his neck that he struggled for breath, gurgling blood.

Hess scrubbed his hands down his face, brain still trying to process what had just happened. Moans erupted from the loading dock and he shook his head, snapping back to business at the looming threat of death.

"I'm sorry, man," he said, and swallowed hard before placing the barrel of his handgun on the back of Mason's head and pulling the trigger, setting him to rest. It was an undignified death, and Hess couldn't fight off the guilt washing over him, but he had no choice. He couldn't allow Mason to suffer at the hands of the zombies still here, and he couldn't risk a runner tearing free.

He dug into his fallen friend's pocket and grabbed the keys, slipping them into his own, and readied his assault rifle, slamming in a fresh mag and holding up his flashlight to illuminate any target he could find.

He moved swiftly through the store, coming around the corner into the center aisle and seeing several ghouls milling about. His first instinct was to light them up, to make them pay for the death of his partner, but he thought better of it.

The less noise and wastage of bullets, the better.

One of the creatures turned towards him, attracted by the light, and began shambling in his direction. Hess let out a huff and kept moving. He moved through the front half of the store, gun at the ready, but pocketed the flashlight as he got closer to the front glass with the sunlight pouring in.

There were a dozen or so zombies near the registers, and another few dozen just outside the front door, attracted to the rumbling of the truck just to the left of the entrance. Hess tried to plot a course through, but none of them looked viable as there were just too many zombies by the front entrance.

I have to signal whoever is driving to get out of the way, he thought, and looked around. There was a register just across from him with two ghouls standing next to it. *If I can get over there, I might be able to get his attention.*

He drew his knife, knowing he'd have to be quiet about it. He waited for the zombies to look in the other direction and then darted out. He rushed over and slammed his blade into the back of one monster's skull before immediately stabbing the second one through the forehead.

He quickly dropped to his knee, hiding behind the register for cover. He glanced out the window, seeing Kent sitting in the driver's seat of the truck, just hanging out.

Hess pulled out his flashlight and aimed it directly at Kent's face, clicking it on and off two times rapidly. His charge outside blinked, confused, looking around. Hess sighed and did it again, finally gaining the soldier's attention.

Kent looked straight through the window and saw Hess crouched there. When their eyes locked, Hess motioned for him to move the truck out of the way. He received a thumbs up, and Kent popped the truck into gear and moved back, the congregating zombies slowly ambling after him.

Unfortunately for Hess, the flicking light attracted several of the zombies at the front area of the store, and they wandered towards him, trying to find the source. He remained under cover, his knife ready in case one of them got too close. He watched as a couple of them wandered by the top of his checkout aisle, moaning, seeming to know that something was close.

He looked back towards the front, seeing only a few zombies inside the store and ten or so just outside of it, although a bit more spread out than before. As he went back into hiding, he inadvertently elbowed a travel mug that was underneath the register, sending it clattering to the ground.

"Dammit," he muttered as moaning erupted all around him. He sheathed his knife and readied his assault rifle. "Here goes nothing." He popped up from cover, aiming at the nearest creature and firing, dropping it fast as he turned and tore for the front of the store.

Zombies in front of him turned to screech at him, arms outstretched. He stopped and fired two quick headshots, and then leapt over the fallen, skidding into the front entryway and slamming the double doors behind him.

Ten zombies pressed up against the row of glass doors at the front, shoulder to shoulder and smacking on the glass. Hess raised his rifle, aiming at the first ghoul's head and swapping to rapid fire mode. He took a deep breath, and then pulled the trigger, running down the line, taking out a line of them in a matter of seconds.

As the corpses hit the pavement, he pushed his way out of the store and into the parking lot. As soon as he was out, somebody blared their horn, and he turned to see Kent's truck about forty yard away,

the bulk of the zombies on the passenger
side.

Hess broke into a sprint, running as
hard as he could for the truck. As he
approached, Kent flung open the door and
started firing from the driver's seat,
dropping the few zombies that were
directly in his running companion's path.

"Come on man, move it!" he yelled.

Hess reached the truck and clambered
up, crawling over the driver's seat and
collapsing on the other side of the cab,
chest heaving. Kent slammed the door and
turned to him, wide-eyed.

"Goddamn dude, you okay?" he asked.

Hess just nodded, still breathing
heavily.

"Well, let's get Mason and get the
fuck out of here," Kent said.

Hess closed his eyes, pressing his
palms into them momentarily before
clenching his jaw, staring helplessly at
his friend.

"Is he…" Kent trailed off, reading
the pain on his face.

Hess simply nodded, unable to form
words at the moment.

His friend swallowed hard. "Do you
want to tell Bretz?"

Hess shook his head, and finally
admitted, "I could use a minute."

Kent reached out and gave his shoulder a reassuring squeeze and then picked up the CB radio. "Corporal."

"What is it?" Bretz came back immediately. "Looked like you had some issues over there."

Kent took a deep breath. "It's Hess sir, he had to come out the front of the store," he replied reluctantly. "Mason… Mason wasn't with him."

There were a few moments of stunned silence.

"What the fuck do you mean Mason isn't with him?!" Baker suddenly burst over the line. "What the fuck did he do to him?"

Kent swallowed as Hess winced from the passenger's seat. "He didn't do anything to him."

"Bullshit!" Baker yelled. "This should have been easy, in and out. What the fuck?!"

"Put Hess on," Bretz said, solemn and low.

Kent chewed his lip for a moment. "Sir, I…"

"Put. Hess. On," Bretz said firmly.

The Private in question held out his hand for the receiver, not meeting Kent's gaze as he placed it in his palm.

"Hess here," he said hoarsely.

"Is he at rest?" Bretz asked.

Hess rubbed one of his eyes, blinking rapidly after. "Yes, sir."

"Okay," the Corporal replied calmly. "Is his truck still running?"

Hess nodded shakily. "Yes, sir."

"Kent, take him around to pick it up," Bretz said. "We've got to get moving."

Baker immediately cut into the line. "Bretz, we have to-"

"We have to keep moving," the Corporal said firmly. "We have to keep moving."

The devastated soldier let out another frustrated yell before the line went silent. Bretz sat in his cab, imagining Baker throwing the radio across his cab in anger. He knew how he felt. His chest ached with the loss of a good soldier, of a friend.

As he watched Kent drive around to the back, he rubbed his forehead. He'd decided to make this stop because they needed a sixth truck. Now Mason was dead, and they were down a driver, and they still didn't have a sixth truck. They'd have to complete the mission without the items they needed, and without one of their own.

"Hess has been dropped off, and he's ready to go," Kent's voice came through the radio.

The Corporal shook off his cloud of
what-ifs and guilt, knowing he needed to
focus on the mission, and get the rest of
them safely to the end of the line.
"Good," he said into the receiver. "Follow
me out and stay close, we're going to be
on surface streets for a while until the
interstate clears out."

"Yes, sir," Kent replied, and the
line clicked off.

Bretz popped the truck into gear and
started moving, his heart heavy. He took a
deep, steadying breath, and forced his
mind to focus on the mission.

CHAPTER NINE

Bretz led the convoy down the highway
towards the I-405 crossing, a major
interchange where the highway crossed
underneath the interstate. It was a couple
miles ahead, and he took it slow, only
driving about twenty miles per hour.

He struggled to focus on the task,
his thoughts about his decision getting
Mason killed pulsing in his brain. There
was some light banter over the CB between
the men, but it was just a low hum in the
background, his worries tuning it out.

There were a few zombies in the road,
which he drifted over a bit to clip, not
wanting to damage the engine, but wanting
to cause a little bit of pain just for his
own personal satisfaction. He continued to
zone out, but finally snapped into focus
as his name repeated on the radio.

"Bretz. Bretz!" Baker demanded. "You
gonna answer me or am I gonna have to ram
you"

The Corporal blinked a few times and
then picked up the receiver, raising it to
his lips. "What is it?" he asked hoarsely.

"Fucking finally," Baker snapped.
"Man, that's the fifth zombie you've made
a point to hit. You need to cut that shit
out. We've got enough going on without you
losing it."

"I'm fine," Bretz replied, voice a low monotone. "Just making sure my steering still works."

Baker scoffed. "Bullshit," he replied. "I know you're upset, god knows we all are, but you need to keep it together man, we still got a lot to get done today."

Bretz paused, letting the words wash over him and sink in. "Thanks, man," he finally said. He knew his friend was right.

"Anytime," Baker replied.

Bretz began to slow down as they approached the interchange. He came to a full stop half a mile from the bridge, Baker pulling up beside him and the other three trucks stopping behind them.

"Holy shit," Baker breathed through the radio, "how are we getting through *that*?"

There were easily a thousand zombies on the road in front of them, with even more on top of the bridge on the interstate. They were densely packed, shoulder-to-shoulder, with an untold number behind them on the other side.

"Not trying to be a Debbie Downer or anything," Kent drawled, "but now way in hell we're pushing through that."

"Is there another way around?" Baker asked.

Kent paused, and then came in, "According to the map, the only other route is on the interstate, and it isn't looking much better."

"Corporal, what are we doing?" Short asked.

Bretz stared at the horde, a deep sigh deflating his chest. This day kept getting worse and worse. "I think it's time to call in air support," he finally said.

"Fuck yeah!" Kent bellowed. "Light them motherfuckers up!"

"All right boys," Baker said, "let's back it up a bit. Don't want to catch some blowback."

As the trucks began to move in reverse, Bretz pulled out his satellite phone, dialing up Captain Kersey. It rang for several minutes, and then David answered.

"Captain Kersey's office," he greeted.

Bretz took a deep breath. "David, it's Corporal Bretz," he replied. "We need our air support."

"What's your location?" David asked.

The Corporal swallowed hard. "Four-o-five interchange."

There was a moment of silence, and then the communications expert replied,

"That's gonna be a no-go, sir. Orders are to protect major infrastructure."

"There's a thousand zombies underneath the bridge, and even more on top," Bretz insisted firmly. "Either we get air support to come in and clear it out, or this mission is over right here and now."

"Hold, please," David replied, and there was a *click* as the line went quiet.

After a few moments, Kersey came in, "Sounds like you're in a bit of a pickle there, Corporal."

Bretz sighed. "That's an understatement, Cap," he replied. "We need that air support if this mission is going to be successful."

"David filled me in," Kersey explained. "But tell me, how tall is that bridge?"

Bretz cocked his head, staring at the bridge. "Twenty feet, give or take."

"How's the road looking in front of it?" the Captain asked.

The Corporal shrugged. "Surprisingly clear," he admitted. "Only a handful of cars and most of those are on the other side of the road."

"I think we can work with that," Kersey replied, and then his voice muffled. "David, dispatch two choppers to Bretz's location." He moved his hand, and clearly said into the phone, "All right, you got incoming that will be there within a half an hour," he said. "Just make sure you're far enough back."

Bretz nodded, rubbing his forehead. "Way ahead of you, Cap."

Kersey paused, and then asked, "Everything going okay out there?"

"Mostly," the Corporal replied, grimacing. "Had some issues at the last stop and we're down to five trucks." His voice stayed monotone, not betraying any emotion.

"Okay," the Captain replied easily, "if there's a safe spot to pick up a sixth, you have clearance to do so."

Bretz clenched a fist, swallowing hard, trying to squash his emotions to stay focused. "Won't do any good," he replied thickly. "Mason's not with us anymore."

There was a long silence, as Kersey processed the information that his friend was dead. "Understood, Corporal," he finally said. "Do what you can with what you have. Call when it's complete."

"Yes sir," Bretz replied. "And Kersey…"

"Yes?"

The Corporal took a deep breath. "Thanks." He was glad the Captain didn't push the issue. He knew the information hurt Kersey as well, but he didn't want to talk about it, nor think about it, at the moment. They'd have time to grieve later.

The Captain didn't respond, and didn't have to. Bretz set down the phone, popping the truck into reverse and moving back to join the others.

The group sat a mile away from the interchange, yammering over the CB radio about nonsense. Bretz leaned back in the driver's seat, chomping on a granola bar and reading one of the trashy romance novels to attempt to get his mind off of things.

After a few moments of solitude, there was a knock at the passenger window, and he jumped. He looked up and saw Baker waving at him, so he unlocked the door.

The Private opened it and slid inside, closing the door behind him. "We're looking clear, so I thought I'd come over and check on you," he said.

"I'm fine," Bretz replied flatly.

Baker leaned over and looked at the book, raising an eyebrow. "You're reading the Rose and the Rapier," he said. "Even under normal circumstances, that would be a cry for help."

The Corporal didn't have the energy to laugh. He dog-eared the page and closed it, setting it aside with a deep sigh. "Now's not the time."

"I agree," Baker said, "which is why I'm here to talk about the mission. We're a truck short after all, and we need to figure out what to do about it. Thought you could use a sounding board without the newbies." He reached over and turned down the CB radio before pulling out one of the maps.

Bretz took a deep breath and nodded, feeling good about being in work mode. "Well, we need two trucks to block off the five-twenty bridge, and I think we should definitely do that."

"Once we get past this interchange, we're less than a mile away from it," Baker replied. "Are you thinking we drop two off as originally planned?"

The Corporal nodded. "I think we need to, don't you?" he asked. "We know for a fact we can complete this part of the mission, and based on what we saw in Redmond, our boys on foot coming in from the east are going to need all the help they can get."

"Every zombie we block is a zombie they don't have to fight," the Private agreed.

Bretz nodded. "Meaning it'll be more likely they'll get to us sooner rather than later."

"I'm all about that," Baker replied, and picked up the offending book, "especially if this is the level of entertainment quality we can expect."

Bretz chuckled, finally giving in to the levity. "It's not as bad as the cover makes it out to be."

"Okay, now I'm really worried about you," Baker said, shaking his head.

The Corporal shrugged. "I mean, a dude did get stabbed in the face in the first chapter," he insisted.

"All right," Baker replied, setting the book down. "Maybe it's not all bad after all."

They shared a laugh, both of them trying everything they could to avoid the elephant in the room. After a moment of awkward silence, the sound of helicopter blades came up from behind them.

"About damn time," Baker muttered.

Bretz sat up straight. "You should get back to your truck," he suggested. "Depending on what's on the other side of the bridge, we might not have much time to bust through."

They exchanged a fist bump and Baker jumped out of the cab. Bretz leaned forward, looking up to see how the chopper pilots were going to pull this off.

Two Apache gunships roared overhead, slowing down as they approached the bridge. The zombies underneath turned their attention to the flying fortresses, shambling out towards the road. The two war birds hovered about three hundred yards from the bridge before one of them descended, finally stopping about three feet off of the ground. It centered itself on the road and then opened fire.

The two mini-guns on either side of the chopper spun, sending thousands of rounds of hot lead down the road. The front edge of the zombie mass liquefied, vanishing in a spectacular spray of bone and blood.

It took a few moments, but the zombie mass started to melt away, like piping hot tap water on a block of ice in the sink. For a solid thirty seconds, the bullets flew, destroying everything in sight. Finally, the bullets ran dry, and Bretz could see through the mass to the other side.

The first chopper lifted up, moving away from the battle, while the second one dropped down and turned towards the trucks. It lowered down enough so that Bretz could see the pilot, who motioned for them to follow.

The Corporal grabbed his CB, barking, "We're on the move!" He popped the truck into gear and raced forward, the rest following behind.

He picked up steam to make it past the carnage on the road. While the zombies weren't a threat anymore, the puddles of gore on the ground could be an issue if their speed was too low. As he hit the front edge of the massacre, the truck fishtailed a bit, slipping on the liquified corpses.

"Watch it, the road's slick," he said into the radio.

Bretz pushed through, getting to the other side of the bridge just in time to see hundreds more ghouls on the road. They were spread out, but still a potential threat. As he pressed up the street, the gunship angled itself while moving forward, unleashing another torrent of mini-gun fire.

The pullets peppered the horde, ripping them to shreds and clearing a path for the trucks. The fire was sustained, shredding everything in their way.

The road took a long curve before leading to the bridge, forcing the pilot to maneuver some fancy flying. He continued firing as he made the adjustment around the bend, unleashing the last bit of ammo into the horde.

Unfortunately, there was a large pack of ghouls surrounding a small hatchback that couldn't be seen, and the hard fire hit it in just the right way to start a fire.

"Watch it, we got a burner!" Bretz barked, and sped past the car.

As Baker passed it, the car exploded, and he lost control of the truck, slamming it into the median before skidding off of the road.

Bretz immediately slammed on the brakes as all of the other trucks behind his friend were forced to stop. Several of the zombies still standing made their way towards the fallen truck.

The Corporal didn't hesitate, grabbing his rifle and hopping out of the truck, running as quickly as he could towards Baker. As he ran, he looked up and noticed the pilot frantically pointing towards the bridge. He glanced over his shoulder to see a pack of zombies in the dozens were a hundred yards away and closing.

He ran as fast as he could as the Apache flew off. There was another second or two of mini-gun fire, before it ceased and the chopper headed for the coast. Bretz remained focused on the current threat of the half-dozen creatures getting ever closer to Baker.

He opened fire, striking a few zombies in the side, doing little more than distracting them. "Yeah, that's it, come get me!" he yelled.

He ran towards the truck, skirting the ghouls and putting himself between the zombies and Baker, choosing his targets carefully. One by one, he aimed and fired, dropping the monsters in quick order. Once

they were reduced to a pile of bodies, he
whirled around and clambered up into the
truck.

"Baker!" he gushed. "You good?"

The Private was dazed, but conscious,
blood running down from his forehead, and
turned to look at Bretz with confused
eyes.

"Come on man, we gotta move," the
Corporal urged, holding out his hand.

Baker blinked a few times and then
reached up to wipe the blood from his
face, shaking his head as if to clear it.
"What the fuck happened?" he asked.

"Chopper boy blew up a car," Bretz
replied.

Baker grunted. "Nothing like a
friendly fire IED," he muttered.

"Get your stuff and come on," the
Corporal said, motioning for him to come.

Baker nodded and collected his gear,
including his freshly packed food bag.
They hit the ground and started running
towards Bretz' truck, as Short pulled up
behind it.

He unrolled his window. "Is Baker
okay?" he asked. "That was wild!"

"Yeah, he's just dinged up," Bretz
replied, suddenly realizing his heart had
been in his throat the whole time he'd
been fighting the zombies. The relief at

Baker being alive washed over him and he straightened his shoulders.

"What do you want us to do, Corporal?" Short asked.

Bretz motioned ahead. "Get up to the bridge and pick a spot to block off," he instructed. "Two trucks, don't care which, block it off fully. Just leave an opening so I can get through."

"We'll take care of it, Corporal," Short replied, and rolled out, bringing the CB to his lips to relay the orders to the others.

Bretz walked to the passenger side with Baker and helped him up into the seat. "We've been living off scraps for a month," he grunted playfully, "how in the hell are you still this heavy?"

"Just lucky I guess," Baker replied with a lopsided grin.

Bretz secured him and then slammed the door, running around to the driver's side. He popped the truck into gear and headed off towards the bridge. As he grew closer, there were still several standing zombies, which he bonked as he went by, unavoidable given how they were staggered across the road.

The bridge itself was mostly clear, with only the occasional straggler on it. As he grew closer to the blockade, Hess and Short stood standing outside, picking

off zombies within thirty yards of them.
There was a truck-sized hole between them,
and he easily pulled through. As soon as
he was clear, Kent moved his big rig so
that the two big vehicles blocked off the
entire highway bridge.

Bretz braked to a stop on the other
side and hopped down as the other soldiers
clustered around him.

"How's Baker?" Hess asked
immediately.

The Corporal nodded. "He's fine, just
got his bell rung when that car
detonated," he explained.

"I gotta admit," Kent drawled, "up
until that point those chopper boys put on
a hell of a show. Always wondered what a
mini-gun would do to a human body."

Hess motioned to the tires of the
parked trucks, which were coated in a dark
crimson goo. "Well, we're going to be
reminded of it until we get rescued,
because that stuff isn't coming off
anytime soon," he said.

"So who is staying behind?" Bretz
asked.

Hess and Kent both raised their
hands.

The Corporal took a deep breath.
"Okay, do me a favor though," he said.
"Take Baker. He's going to be okay, but
with the way the day is going, I need

whoever is going to be with me to the main target to be functioning."

Hess nodded. "Of course, Corporal."

"Wait," Kent cut in, raising his palms, "you're not still moving ahead, are you? There's only two trucks left! You can only get half the bridge with that!"

"Don't have a choice," Bretz replied firmly.

Kent's eyes widened. "Hell yeah, you got a choice," he declared. "Stay here and solidify this position. Make damn sure our boys to the east are good. And once they get here, we can move to the north."

"Wish I could, believe me," Bretz replied, shaking his head. "But even if it's only a partial blockade, it's going to be better than nothing. A significant portion of our troops are coming in from the north, and we need to secure as much of that bridge as possible." He turned to Short, raising an eyebrow. "Question is, are you game for it?"

"Yes sir," the Private replied immediately. "We'll get it done."

"Good, I like that attitude," Bretz commended, clapping him on the shoulder. "Hess, Kent, let's get Baker transferred over."

The trio moved to the passenger's side, and Bretz opened the door. Baker stared down at them, looking bewildered.

"Um…" he drawled, "is there something I should know?"

Kent smiled. "Yeah, you're bunking with us for a few days," he said, jerking a thumb over his shoulder. "So toss down your shit so the Corporal here can get a move on."

"Wait, no no no," Baker said, waving his hands in front of his face. "Bretz, you aren't going anywhere without me." He put his foot on the step, and slipped, grabbing the doorframe to steady himself. "I… I just need a few minutes."

"That's time we don't have," Bretz said gently. "I need you to get out of this truck."

Baker stared at him, shaking his head, pain in his eyes. "What in the hell are you going to do with only two trucks?"

"Yeah, we already tried that angle with him," Kent quipped, "didn't work. So come on, now."

Baker reluctantly climbed down from the truck, dragging his bag behind him. He turned and glanced at Short, who had been getting his stuff ready to get back to his own truck.

"You watch after him, you hear?" Baker said, as firmly as he could despite his shaky movements.

Short nodded. "I'll keep him safe," he said. "Now you go get some rest."

Baker patted him on the shoulder and then stumbled off towards the blockade.

"You ready to head out?" Bretz asked.

Short nodded and exchanged a fist bump with Hess and Kent.

"We'll see you boys on the other side," Kent said, clapping him on the back.

Bretz offered him a thin smile and then headed for the driver's seat, ready to face the horrors that lay ahead.

CHAPTER ELEVEN

Bretz and Short drove down the highway one behind the other, driving slowly to avoid any more wrecks. The closer they got to their destination, the more seemed to be littering the road. Abandoned cars were scattered about, and countless zombies roamed the streets.

The creatures were too dense to avoid, but in small enough groups that the trucks were able to just plow through them.

Bretz raised the CB radio to his mouth. "We have about a mile to go until we reach the interstate interchange," he said. "Once we hit that, we'll be less than a mile from the bridge."

"How far up do you want to get?" Short asked.

"With the way today is going, I'll settle for just making it to the bridge," the Corporal admitted. "Anything past that is a bonus."

"Hear that," Short replied.

They drove a little further before Bretz slowed to a crawl, and then squealed to a stop.

"You have got to be fucking kidding me," he muttered to himself.

"Everything okay, Corporal?" Short asked through the radio.

Bretz lifted the receiver to his mouth, shaking his head. "Why don't you pull up beside me and take a look for yourself?"

The second truck pulled up next to him, and then Short came through, "Some days it just ain't your day."

The interchange was a colossal clusterfuck. There was a major pileup, with overturned cars and transport trucks. To add to the mess, there were a few thousand zombies roaming about. They sat there, dumbfounded, before getting back to it.

"You got a map over there?" Bretz asked.

"Yes sir," Short replied.

The Corporal nodded to him through the window as he spread his own map over his lap. "Good," he said into the radio, "let's start figuring out how we're going to pull this off."

They studied the satellite imagery, tracing fingers over the numerous potential routes. After a few minutes, Bretz finally took a deep breath.

"I got one potential, and I'm not a huge fan," he admitted.

"Pretty sure we're on the same page, Corporal," Short replied dryly.

Bretz sighed. "Okay, that's the plan, then," he replied. "We'll backtrack half a mile to the previous exit, then hope to christ that surface street bridge is clear. We'll have to fight our way through some residential areas and get to the bridge on the north side. Or do you see something different?"

"Nope," Short replied with his own exhale. "That's what I had too."

The Corporal shook his head. "Looks like there's a break in the median a few hundred yards up," he said. "Let's get turned around."

"I'm on your six," Short replied.

Bretz accelerated slowly, carefully making the turn through the emergency crossover in the median. As he came about, there were several zombies in the way which Bretz just rolled over. He cut it a little tight, scraping the back portion of the trailer.

"Guess we need to add some pain to the shopping list," Short quipped.

Bretz found himself chuckling, glad for the levity. "Nah, scrapes build character," he replied.

He moved up the interstate a bit as he waited for his companion to take the turn as well. He looked to the side, watching the zombie infested neighborhood, the roads packed thick with them.

Every nook and cranny of this town is jam packed with these things, he thought bitterly. *Starting to wonder if we even have enough resources to pull this off.*

He continued to stare, just shaking his head in disbelief at the sheer number of them. He snapped out of his reverie as Short blared his horn behind him.

"Okay, follow close," Bretz said into the radio, "those surface streets look like they're going to be a nightmare."

"Lead on," Short said.

The Corporal hit the gas and they convoyed back towards the previous exit. As they descended the ramp, Bretz saw two cars at the bottom that appeared to have been involved in a crash at some point. It blocked most of the road.

He raised the radio to his mouth. "Lay off a bit, I'm going to have to clear this out," he said, and then hung up the receiver. He sped up, angling the big rig so that it would hit the back bumper of one of the cars. He smacked into it hard, sending broken glass and metal flying through the air. The jolt threw him around in the cab a bit, shaking him up.

The noise of course attracted some unwanted attention, and zombies began pouring out of the side streets, slowly filling the road ahead of them.

"Shit, that woke them up," he said into the radio. "We're going to have to haul ass or we're going to get trapped."

He hit the gas, truck picking up steam as the road to the bridge filled with more and more ghouls. There was a narrow path in the center of the road, and he aimed for it, silently praying.

As he pushed forward, hands smacked against the front grill as the undead reached for it. Soon the light smacks turned into thuds as bodies shambled out in front, and he punched the accelerator even more.

He glanced into his side mirror, watching as more zombies filled in behind him, getting into the way of Short's truck.

"You gotta keep your foot on the gas," Bretz said firmly into the radio.

"Trying to Corporal," Short replied, "engine isn't too happy about it, though."

Bretz shook his head, his stomach sinking at their situation. He perked up a bit at the sight of the front edge of the bridge a few blocks ahead. There were zombies there, but it was mostly clear, nothing like the streets they were currently on.

"Just keep pushing," he urged, "the bridge is just ahead."

Bretz floored it, giving the truck everything it had. He made it to the bridge, obliterating a group of zombies at the front of it, shaking the truck violently. The impact caused him to briefly lose control, smacking into the concrete barrier on the two-lane bridge.

He struggled with the wheel but regained control, breathing a sigh of relief at the close call. He slowed down a bit, as the bridge wasn't as packed as the street, Short doing the same thing once he was up.

Bretz checked the side mirror, seeing the front of the big rig covered in blood, several rotted limbs sticking out of the grill, and a few creatures jammed up into the wheel wells.

"How's your truck doing?" he asked.

"Not too good," Short admitted. "I don't know if she's going to make the bridge or not."

Bretz muttered obscenities under his breath and then looked in the mirror again, seeing smoke furling out from beneath the hood. "Dammit, no way that's making it to the bridge," he said to himself.

He made a westward turn towards the target, reaching a street along the waterfront. When he turned, he glanced to the right, seeing a college campus jam packed with zombies.

"How you doing back there?" he asked into the radio.

"With the way this thing is chugging, I'm going to be dead in the water in under a minute," Short replied, voice rising.

Bretz frantically looked around for some sort of solution. Finally he spotted a grocery store on the edge of campus.

"Get to that grocery store on the right," he barked into the radio. "Get as close to the building as you can."

"See you there," Short replied.

The two trucks veered off of the road and into the lot, with easily a hundred zombies strewn about. They turned, moaning, arms reaching for the trucks. Bretz drove down the outer aisle, smacking into the occasional ghoul before making the turn to the front of the store.

He bumped it up onto the sidewalk, scraping up against the wall and crushing some zombies as he went. He looked in the side mirror to see Short follow suit, parking just behind him.

Bretz rolled down the window, looking out to see outstretched arms less than a foot below him. There were a dozen creatures right there, with more headed his way. He carefully climbed out the window, pulling himself up onto the hood and climbing on top of the trailer. He strolled to the back, and watched Short kick out the front windshield to get out.

The Private stood on the front of the truck, a few feet away from Bretz's, and tossed over his bag and a container of water. The Corporal held out his hand to help him climb over the rotted chorus below.

"One last check for a truck, I take it?" Short asked.

Bretz nodded. "Figured we're here, might as well, right?" He spread his arm like a game show host, presenting the roof of the grocery store to his companion.

Short took a run at it, leaping the several foot height and pulling himself up. He turned around and reached down to help Bretz climb after him.

They walked towards the back of the store, the sun warming their skin as they strolled.

"I know we're almost in November…" Short began, and then paused. "Or heck, we might already be. Kind of lost track of days lately."

Bretz snorted. "No kidding."

"But this weather reminds me of being back on the farm," Short continued. "Bright sun, blue skies, and a nice breeze to keep it from getting too hot."

The Corporal cocked his head. "Spend a lot of time on the farm, did you?"

"Oh, yes sir," the Private replied. "Started helping my dad pick eggs up from

the chickens when I was four years old.
Every summer, every vacation and weekend,
I was out there bright and early with
him."

"Well, I hope you took good notes,
because when all this is over, we're going
to have a lot of mouths to feed," Bretz
replied.

"Dang, I hadn't even thought about
that," Short mused. "Gonna be a long
winter."

Bretz shook his head. "Can't have a
long winter unless we get to it, first."

They approached the back of the
store, looking down on the loading docks
and seeing nothing but empty pavement.

"Well, that's a bit of a letdown,"
Short said with a sigh. "Not sure how much
we're going to be able to block off with
only one truck."

Bretz shrugged. "Looks like we're
going to find out," he said. "Come on,
let's get back to the truck and head out."

As they walked, they passed by some
skylights that looked down into the store.
Curiosity got the better of Short, and he
paused to look down inside. There were
dozens of zombies roaming about, walking
up and down the aisles like undead
shoppers.

He let out a low whistle. "Man, it
looks like a bunch of folks took refuge in

the store," he said. "And it didn't turn out too good for them."

Bretz turned and joined him at the skylight, staring down. "I feel bad for the clear teams," he admitted. "Can you imagine how many buildings are going to look just like this after we clear the streets?"

"Thousands easily," Short agreed. "Probably in the tens of thousands. Those boys are going to be busy for months." He broke away from the window, but Bretz stayed put.

"Hang on a minute," the Corporal said, raising a hand.

"What do you see?" Short asked, rejoining him at the skylight.

Bretz pointed to a big display of vodka bottles.

Short raised an eyebrow. "I'm more of a bourbon man myself," he said.

"On that point, we're going to get along just fine," the Corporal said, pointing a finger at him. "But I do have an idea with the vodka. We may not be able to block off the other side of the interstate with a truck… but we can certainly take out a fair number of them as they try to cross."

The Private perked up. "Molotovs?"

Bretz nodded. "Molotovs."

Short grinned and then shook his head. "Wait, how we getting in, though?"

Bretz looked around and spotted a nearby hatch. He opened it up, finding a ladder into the top portion of the store. They quickly climbed down onto the catwalk, forcing their way to the end of it where there was an upstairs office overlooking the store.

Bretz climbed down the ladder, ducking his head into the office and shining a light, illuminating the small area and finding it empty with the door shut. He waved for Short to follow him down, and they descended into the office.

They stood at the small window overlooking the store, peering out. The skylights did a good job of lighting up the building, and the soldiers studied the two dozen aisles in the gigantic store.

"Okay, looks like the liquor section is directly below us, about two aisle over," Bretz said. "From this vantage point, it doesn't seem like there are too many of those things around."

"How do you want to go about it?" Short asked.

Bretz cocked his head. "The display looked like it had full cases of booze," he began, "so I say we get down there, each of us grab a case and haul ass back up here. If it works without drawing too much attention, we do it again. If we get too much heat on us, at least we can cause some trouble."

"I'm game, Short replied. "Unless you're feeling frisky though, I'd say we go silent." He pulled out his knife, and the Corporal nodded, revealing his own.

They quietly crept through the door, slipping out onto the enclosed stairwell that led down into the main portion of the store. When they got to the bottom, Bretz peeked around the corner, seeing that there weren't any zombies nearby.

He motioned for Short to follow him, and they darted out to head towards the alcohol. They stopped at the first aisle and he looked down it, seeing only a few ghouls. He motioned again, and they silently moved up, dispatching the two corpses and gently laying them on the ground.

When they reached the alcohol aisle and worked their way up, Bretz took a knee when they reached the end cap he'd seen from the roof. He flattened himself against the shelf, and Short followed suit.

Several zombies shambled by the aisle, moaning and dragging their feet as they went. Once they were past, Bretz moved up alone, looking out into the aisle and seeing fifteen zombies hanging out within thirty yards. He pursed his lips and then crept back to Short, speaking into his ear softly.

"Way too many of them to take out with knives," he whispered. "So it's going to be a hit and run."

Short nodded. "I got an idea," he whispered back. "Follow me."

He led them back towards the office stairwell, looking down every aisle as they went. After a few he stopped, giving the Corporal a thumbs up, and then pulled out a shopping cart.

"We load up as much as we can on the buggy, and get it back to the stairwell and unload it," he whispered.

Bretz nodded. "I like it," he replied quietly. "Question is, do you want to shoot or do you want me to?"

"Truth be told," Short admitted, "I ain't so good in low light."

The Corporal smiled. "I'll cover you while you load up."

They shared a nod and leapt into action. Short grabbed the cart, pushing it along until they got back to the alcohol. Bretz carefully stepped into the main aisle, looking both ways to make sure the zombies were only in one direction. He readied his rifle and then nodded to his partner.

Short grabbed the first case of twelve bottles, gently placing it into the cart. When he grabbed the second one, it rattled the display clinking a few bottles together. The noise gained the attention of a few ghouls, who began moaning and heading their way.

Bretz held off firing as long as he could, allowing Short to load in two more cases. Then he squeezed the trigger rapidly, taking out three ghouls in a matter of seconds.

"How many more?" he asked.

"Two more!" Short replied.

Bretz continued picking targets, dropping them as his companion loaded the cart with seven cases.

"We're full!" Short reported, and then began pushing towards the stairwell. They raced down the aisle, Bretz covering their retreat as they went, tearing around the corner towards the office. The noise had attracted a few zombies at the other end.

Short pulled out his weapon, but Bretz just pushed him forward.

"Get to the stairwell," he said, "I'll cover us."

The Private raced back to the stairs, stopping the cart and grabbing a case of vodka, tearing up the stairs to begin unloading. Bretz stood his ground beside the cart, aiming down both directions and firing, picking off zombies one by one as Short sprinted up and down the stairs.

"We're good to go, Corporal!" he cried as he grabbed the last one, and Bretz fired one more time, killing a zombie about fifteen yards away.

He cracked a smile before kicking the cart onto its side, blocking the stairwell and tearing back up into the office. Short slammed the door, and they pushed a desk against it to hold it secure.

"That went way smoother than anything else we've done today," Bretz declared.

Short grinned. "Speaking of smooth, bet you didn't catch my slick little move while running down the aisle, did you?" he asked.

Bretz furrowed his brow. "Apparently I totally missed it."

The Private reached behind one of the cases of vodka and pulled out a large bottle of bourbon.

The Corporal barked a laugh. "I mean, we are going to have a few days to kill," he said with a shrug. Short clapped him on the shoulder and they began hauling their loot up the ladder.

CHAPTER TWELVE

Bretz drove the two of them to the bridge, seeing zombies shoulder-to-shoulder as they approached. They were within a couple hundred yards, only a left at the top of the street, but there were dozens of zombies standing in their way.

"You ready for one last push?" he asked.

Short leaned forward. "Bigger question is, if this big beauty of a truck is ready for it," he said, and stroked the dashboard. "Okay girl, you almost home, just need you to push a little harder. Can you do that for me?"

Bretz raised an eyebrow.

Short shrugged. "I mean, trucks need encouragement too."

"Did you do that to your last truck?" the Corporal asked.

His passenger chuckled. "Well no," he replied, "probably why she didn't make it."

"Okay then," Bretz replied, and gave the steering wheel a tender pat. "Come on, you can do it."

Short laughed, and the Corporal joined in, the two of them a little loopy from the absurdity of the situation and what they were about to do.

"Regardless of what happens," Bretz said when he finally calmed down, "it's been a pleasure."

Short nodded solemnly. "Likewise, Corporal."

Bretz hit the gas, and the truck rumbled forward. He rolled over several zombies, and the noise gained the attention of the ghouls on the bridge. He floored it, gaining as much speed as he could, approaching the turn for the bridge. The sea of undead was dense, covering almost the entirety of the road on both sides.

The big rig chugged along, slowing with every impact. When Bretz reached the top of the road, he moved far to the right before making a hard left, hoping to keep up the momentum. The truck leaned to one side, several wheels coming off of the ground, crashing back down and crushing several bodies beneath. The impact sent bones jutting out of bodies, and a loud *pop* sounded as one of the tires blew.

The sudden loss caused the truck to jar to the right, but Bretz was able to correct it. The zombies on the bridge pressed up against the vehicle, covering it on all sides. The remaining tires squealed, struggling to gain traction between the blood coating them and the dense force of the dead in front of it.

"Come on!" Short yelled. "You're almost there!"

The front wheels crossed the bridge threshold, and as soon as it did, Bretz began to angle the truck. The tires whined as the truck inched along, taking nearly a minute of constant flooring it to make it to the edge of the bridge.

Bretz checked his side mirror, seeing that the trailer portion stretched across two lanes of traffic, with only a single lane left empty. He took a deep breath and cut the engine, patting the steering wheel.

"You did good, girl," he cooed.

Short shook his head in disbelief. "Hell, if I knew that was going to work, I would have been praising every vehicle I've ever been in," he said.

"What do you say we go check out the view?" the Corporal asked.

The two soldiers rolled down their windows, carefully crawling out to the hood before hopping up on top of the trailer. They looked down the bridge at the ocean of death. It was packed so densely that not a single inch of pavement was visible.

Bretz stood at the front of the truck, staring at the other side of the interstate that was just as packed. A decently sized crowd had stopped moving and staring up at him, arms outstretched.

Well, maybe everything isn't lost, he thought.

"Hey, Corporal, come check this out," Short said from the rear.

Bretz headed back to where his partner stood and cocked his head. Short pointed to the water in the distance, where there were a couple dozen small boats on the water, all headed towards Mercer Island.

"Looks like that island landing went well," Bretz said. "Hopefully they were able to secure it."

Short nodded. "Maybe there's some hope for this after all."

"Could be," Bretz replied distantly. "Could be." He reached into his pocket and pulled out the satellite phone, dialing it up. After a few moments, David answered.

"Captain Kersey's line," he greeted.

The Corporal cleared his throat. "It's Bretz, let me speak to the Captain."

"Hang on, Corporal," David replied, and there was a moment of silence before the line clicked back on.

"Your team at the bridge?" Kersey asked.

Bretz nodded. "The five-twenty bridge protecting the eastern force is secure," he reported. "God two trucks there with three men to pick off stragglers."

"And the main target?" Kersey prompted.

Bretz took a deep breath. "One truck," he replied. "Two men."

There was a moment of silence before the Captain asked, "Resistance a bit more than originally anticipated?"

The Corporal couldn't help but chuckle. "You could say that, bud," he said. "To be perfectly honest, we were lucky to get the one truck we did here. If it had conked out five yards earlier, we would have fallen just short."

"How's it looking up there?" Kersey asked.

Bretz turned and stared down at the undead ocean. "Like a shitshow and a half," he said. "Can't see any pavement at all."

"Hopefully the ones across the way will be more interested in you than our teams to the north," the Captain replied.

Bretz shrugged. "Well, if they aren't, we did manage to secure a few dozen molotovs," he said. "So we'll be able to stem the tide a bit."

"Hopefully that will be enough," Kersey replied. There was another tense moment of silence, and he quickly added, "And Bretz, I know you did everything you could to complete this mission. I have no doubt in my mind that nobody could have done it better."

The Corporal swallowed hard. "Appreciate that, Kersey."

"Sure thing," the Captain replied. "Well, you boys get comfortable, and we'll get to you as quick as we can."

Bretz nodded. "No rush," he assured him. "The young Private here managed to sneak us a bottle of bourbon while we were securing the molotovs. So we'll be good for a while."

"Did he get good stuff?" Kersey asked, sounding amused.

Bretz glanced at his partner. "Captain wants to know if you got the good bourbon," he said.

"Aww, hell yeah, Corporal," Short replied with a lopsided grin. "Top shelf all the way, none of that well bullshit."

Bretz chuckled. "He says top shelf," he said into the phone.

"Remind me to give him a promotion once you guys are back safe," Kersey replied.

Bretz laughed and gave Short a thumbs up. "He'll be pleased to hear that."

"Well, you two stay safe," Kersey continued, "I need to report to General Stephens and let him know what the situation is."

The Corporal nodded, tilting his head back to let the sun fall on his face. "If you need us, you know where we'll be."

"You got it," Kersey replied. "And again, great job today, Bretz."

"Thanks, Cap," he replied, and the line went dead. He pocketed the phone and scratched the back of his head, suddenly realizing the stench wafting off of the carpet of the dead was rather ripe.

"So what now, Corporal?" Short asked.

Bretz shrugged. "I don't know," he replied honestly. "You want to try out one of those molotovs to make sure they work? You know. For science?"

"Hell yeah!" Short replied, laughing. "I'll grab a bottle."

As the kid darted to the front of the truck, Bretz pursed his lips, struggling to keep his composure. The fight was over for the time being, which was a relief, but the future was uncertain. All he could do now was drink some bourbon with a country kid and toss some molotovs onto a horde of undead.

END

Up Next: The action shifts to the southwest as a single ship makes a desperate beach landing in an attempt to create a southern front in the war in "Seattle - Part 4".

DEAD AMERICA - THE NORTHWEST INVASION
BOOK 6
SEATTLE - PART 4
BY DEREK SLATON
© 2020

Day Zero +24

"What do you think, Jinx?" Private Davila asked, leaning on the railing overlooking the main cargo hold. "This the day we're finally getting off this boat?"

Corporal Eddie 'Jinx' Jenkins tongued his cheek. "That's the rumor going around," he replied. "Of course we're heard similar rumors for the last two weeks." He tilted his head, voice rising in pitch as he mocked, "Oh, we're getting off in Portland. Oh, we're headed for Hawaii. Oh look, it's Fantasy Island, I can't wait to party with that midget dude."

"Tattoo," Davila offered.

Jinx raised an eyebrow. "Tattoo?"

"Yeah, that was the dude's name, Tattoo," the Private explained. "He would always yell *Da plane, da plane!* How do you not know that?"

Jinx rolled his eyes. "How do I not know the name of a specific character from a seventies tv series?" He put a hand to his chest in mock offense. "I don't know, could be because I had a life before the end of the world. Better question is, how do you know the character name? What next,

you going to rattle off the crew of the
Love Boat?"

"Well, there was Captain Stubing,
Doctor Bricker, Isaac the Bartender,"
Davila replied, counting off on his
fingers.

The Corporal chuckled, shaking his
head. "Buddy, I'm going to tell you
something that someone should have told
you years ago," he said, clapping his
friend on the shoulder. "You really need
to get out more."

"Nah, it's not like that, man,"
Davila replied, sharing the laugh. "I
spent summers with my grandmother and she
loved those old seventies shows. Had
stacks of VHS tapes and would watch them
over and over again. Even still had the
commercials on them. I was so heartbroken
as a kid when I found out I couldn't get
New Coke."

Jinx grinned. "From what I
understand, you dodged a bullet there."

"Yeah, no kidding," the Private
agreed.

The loudspeaker in the cargo hold
flicked on with a light squeal and
fumbling mic noises before a booming voice
echoed in the room. "Attention, all team
leaders, please report to the briefing
room," it said. "Repeat, all team leaders
please report to the briefing room."

"Well, looks like the rumors were true," Jinx said, stretching his arms above his head.

Davila grinned. "Make sure you get us a good assignment," he said, pointing a finger at his Corporal. "None of this guarding a gas station nonsense. We've traveled this far and we're ready to light these things up."

"You know it." Jinx winked at him and they exchanged a fist bump. "Get the squad together at our usual table in the mess hall and I'll brief you when I'm done." He headed off towards the briefing room, glancing down at the floor below to see a few dozen men doing the same thing.

This is going to be a packed room, he thought. *Guess everybody is chomping at the bit to get off of this boat.*

Jinx worked his way down the narrow hallways of the ship, glancing in every room he passed to see them overcrowded with people and gear. When they'd left port nearly a month ago, there wasn't much time to load things like normal, which meant vital goods like guns, ammo, and food had been thrown anywhere and everywhere they could.

The USS Anchorage, a San Antonio class transport ship was state-of-the art, designed to carry all manner of man and machinery into battle. It was complete with a helicopter landing pad on the surface and a battery of weaponry that would put most other nation's Navy ships to shame.

Today, however, in the midst of the zombie apocalypse, the ship was vastly different. Instead of cargo holds filled with tanks and vehicles, it housed nearly a thousand soldiers on makeshift bedding. This effectively doubled the intended capacity for the ship, putting a strain on everything from the mess hall to simple things like plumbing.

The close quarters and constant deployment at sea had begun to take its toll on the soldiers, with numerous fisticuffs breaking out over the previous week. The stress of not knowing when they would get off made it even worse, coupled with the worries that what they would be facing was too much for them to bear.

Jinx, however, was not one of those soldiers. He was known for a wild streak and had gotten his nickname from his luck that bordered on the supernatural with how many times he'd escaped death in the field. He was itching to get off of this damn boat and dive headfirst into action.

He reached the briefing room, and it was already beginning to get crowded. About forty soldiers had squeezed into a room where twenty would have normally fit comfortably. Jinx looked behind him and spotted a handful of soldiers still working their way down the hallway.

"Yo man, let me slip by you real quick," he murmured, and when one of the men in the back turned towards him, he used the opening to slide in and work his way to the front of the room. He found a corner on the front row and knelt down beside the side door.

A few moments later, the door opened and Captain Odom entered the room. He was an older man, easily in his late forties, with rapidly graying hair. The men all stood at attention in his presence, but he waved them off.

"Everybody get settled, there's a lot to go over," he declared.

Another soldier entered through the door, carrying a large printed satellite image tacked to a cork board. He set it up beside the Captain so that the room could see. It was focused on a bay just off the ocean.

"Some of you have no doubt heard the rumors that our assault on Seattle began yesterday," Odom began, "and I can confirm those rumors are true. Multiple strike forces attacking numerous points on the north and eastern parts of the target launched operations just before dawn yesterday. They have been fighting throughout the day and have been making some progress against the enemy. Now, while the rest of our ships have been moving to the north to assist in the assault on downtown, we have been held back for a special mission."

He looked around at the cork board and found a thin pointer nestled in the bottom tray. He held it up and began pointing to different spots on the map as he spoke.

"This is North Bay, roughly fifty miles west of Olympia," he continued, "which is our ultimate target. For those of you unfamiliar with the layout of the Seattle Metro area, Olympia is to the southwest, and is the last pocket of major civilization. Our mission is to land and push forward towards Olympia to create another front for the enemy to fight us on. It's our job to distract as many as we can so that the ground forces can march in from the east."

He snapped the pointer against the area just to the north and east of the bay. "Before we can do that, however," he continued, "we have to pacify the town of Aberdeen. As you can see, the bulk of the town is situated between three rivers, the main one running along the southern border, and two smaller ones to the east and west. Our landing point is going to be to the harbor on the northwest of town, less than a quarter mile from a non-insignificant population area to the west of the river."

A hand shot up in the middle of the room, and the Captain sighed, reluctantly pointing to it.

"Sir, we have no landing craft on board," the soldier called. "How are we going to get ashore?"

Odom clucked his tongue. "I'm getting to that soldier," he said impatiently. "We have orders from the top of the food chain to beach the ship on shore so we can rappel down the side."

The stunned silence in the room was so pregnant, it was as if the soldiers weren't even breathing.

"Believe me when I say that I share every thought currently running through your heads," the Captain said firmly. "I even went so far as to share some of them with the General, who politely informed me that the enemy didn't have a Navy, so the mission is more important than the survival of our ship."

Murmurs broke out amongst the soldiers, some of them nodding, few still wide-eyed.

"Moving on," Odom said loudly, commanding attention once again. "Upon landing, we will be forced to rappel down the side of the ship. Thanks to the great resource purge, we will only have four lines coming down from the deck, so it's going to be a long process to get people to the shore. And with the noise we're going to be making, we're going to have quite the crowd before we're ready. This area had around twenty thousand people, so we are expecting a stiff resistance. To protect us from being overrun, I need three teams to volunteer for diversion duty." He paused, raising his chin. "I'm asking for volunteers because the likelihood of survival is… low."

Jinx's hand shot up into the air before anybody else, and Odom raised an eyebrow at him.

"Oh hell, is that Jinx?" somebody called from the back. "Gonna be a wild ride if it is!"

Laughter rippled through the men, but Odom didn't react, simply scanned the room for more volunteers. A few moments later, two more hands reluctantly went up, and the Captain nodded.

"Okay, that's our three," he declared. "Need you to stay behind, the rest of you get your teams together and see my assistant on the way out for your landing assignments."

The soldiers began to filter out, varying noise levels of chatter as they went. Corporal Spence and Sergeant Dickerson approached the front of the room.

"Yeah, I thought that was you," Dickerson said with a lopsided grin as he stepped up next to Jinx.

Odom cocked his head. "You two know each other, Sergeant?"

"Oh yes sir," Dickerson replied. "Corporal Jinx and I go back a ways. Had a few misadventures in the sandbox."

The Captain raised his chin. "Is this going to be a problem?"

"Oh, not at all, Captain," the Sergeant assured him, raising his palms. "The Corporal and I get along real well. In fact, I'm kind of relieved to know he's on this suicide mission."

Odom clucked his tongue. "Oh yeah?" he asked. "And why's that?"

"Because the only way he could be any luckier is if he shoved a rabbit's foot in places best left to the imagination," Dickerson replied.

The Captain gaped at the soldiers, shaking his head. "*Luck?*" he asked. "You're excited to have him along because he's lucky?" He blinked and then turned to Jinx. "So you're lucky, huh?"

"In a single tour, my team and I walked away from four IEDs, a dozen ambushes, and a whole host of other

situations that have since been erased
thanks to the hard work of bourbon
destroying those brain cells," the
Corporal declared proudly.

Odom clucked his tongue again. "Lucky
indeed," he replied dryly. "Let's hope
that keeps up." He motioned for the trio
to cluster around the map.

He removed the top sheet to reveal a
tighter shot of the city of Aberdeen. He
used the pointer to motion to the area on
the west side of the bridge.

"Once you're on the ground, you need
to push forward across this area," he
said. "It's ten blocks of mostly
residential housing leading up to the
bridge. Once you're across is when the
real fun begins." He motioned to the
north. "This area to the north is a
shopping center that should provide cover
to draw the enemy up there." Odom pointed
to a specific spot in the south by a
river. "Same thing with this spot in the
south. I need a team to go to each one,
set up a diversion, and hold the enemy's
attention while we get a foothold."

"Sir, my team can take the southern
target," Spence piped up.

Dickerson nodded. "My team will take
the northern target."

The Captain turned to Jinx. "Then
that leaves you with the big job." He

pointed to a shopping center on the far east of town, practically on its own little island with two bridges leading across to it. "Corporal, your team will have three primary goals. The first is to get to the target and draw as many of those things as you can. The second is to escape via the river within a stone's throw of the building, circle back, and block off the bridges with whatever you can find. And the third is to cause as much havoc on the way there as you can. Set up traps, set things on fire, whatever you need to do to distract the enemy and eliminate them."

Jinx nodded. "My team and I can handle that, sir," he said, and then raised a finger. "But I do have a question."

"Go for it," Odom said.

"If we're blocking off the bridge on the east side of town to trap these things," the Corporal began, "then why don't we just block off the bridge into Aberdeen and call it a day?"

The Captain took a deep breath. "We considered that," he admitted, "but with the amount of enemy forces in town, the higher ups felt like we could end up in a surge situation. If the barricade failed, our landing zone would be overrun and

there would be little we could do about
it."

"That works for me," Jinx replied
with a nod. "Like a lot of the soldiers on
this ship, my team and I are ready to get
into the action. Lot more fun rampaging
through the streets than babysitting a
barricade."

Odom raised his chin. "Well,
Corporal, you and your team have free rein
to do whatever you deem necessary," he
declared. "This isn't a strategic target,
so once we clear it, it's unlikely anybody
is going to be back here for quite some
time."

"Burn the city to the ground, got
it," Jinx replied with a playful smirk.

The soldiers chuckled, and Odom shook
his head.

"Not sure I would go that far," he
replied with a playful shrug. "But if it
comes to it, then it comes to it. Now, go
brief your teams and get ready to move.
We're grounding this ship in thirty, and
your teams are the first over."

"Yes, sir," the soldiers replied in
unison as the Captain headed out of the
room.

Dickerson smacked Jinx on the
shoulder. "You ready to get after it?"

"Just another walk in the park," the
Corporal replied with a smirk.

"What channel are you going to be on?" the Sergeant asked.

Jinx winked at him. "Lucky number thirteen, as always."

"Same as it ever was," Dickerson replied, chuckling and shaking his head. "You give me a call if you need a hand."

The Corporal nodded. "Likewise," he said, and then turned to Spence. "Same goes for you. We're running headlong into the shit, we got each other and not much else for a while."

"See you two topside in thirty," Spence replied with a firm nod, and the three men exited the room, splitting off to seek out their respective teams.

Jinx entered the mess hall, which was crowded as usual. Soldiers were everywhere, trying to get whatever bits of food and drink they could before it ran out. Rationing had been going strong since they'd set food on the ship, but even with that food was beginning to run out.

"Yo Jinx, over here!" Davila called, waving his hand in the air.

The Corporal approached the table, giving a nod to the shorter latino soldier. "Hope you are getting your rations in, because we're about to go raise some hell," he declared.

"Do tell, Corporal!" Private Stein drawled, leaning his broad shoulders forward.

Jinx took a seat. "Oh, just the normal shit, storm the beach head and distract the enemy so the bulk of the force can get a foothold," he said.

Private Burch's eyes widened. "Beach head?" he asked. "What are we doing? Swimming to shore?"

The Corporal shook his head with a devious smile. "Nope," he replied. "We're crashing the ship right onto shore."

Private Jarvis furrowed her brow. "Have I been in a coma?" she asked, pointing her fork at him. "Because I totally missed when they promoted you to Captain."

Jinx barked a laugh. "Surprisingly enough, it wasn't my idea." He put up his hands in surrender. "I mean, let's be honest, if it was, there would be more explosions."

"This is true," Jarvis agreed.

"So, is that all we're doing is running around, blowing shit up?" Private Rollins asked, the fluorescent lights shining off of his dark, bald head.

"You say that like there's anything else to do in life," Burch quipped.

Rollins shrugged. "I mean, I can work with it, but it would be nice to have a solid objective," he admitted.

"Don't worry, we got one," Jinx assured them. "Long story short is that we have to get to the other side of town, pull a whole mess of zombies across some bridges, and then block them off. Nothing we haven't done before."

Jarvis shook her head. "Again, coma," she said. "When in the hell did we lure zombies somewhere?"

"How many men have you lured back from the bar in your day, Jarvis?" Davila asked innocently.

She shot him a sheepish smile. "I withdraw the question."

The table erupted in laughter, and Jinx got to his feet.

"Where you off to, Corporal?" Burch asked.

His superior inclined his head to the door. "Going to see if I can procure us some extra provisions," he explained. "As for you five, finish up, grab your gear, and be up on deck in twenty."

His team nodded, and he headed off to make some last minute preparations.

Jinx led the group up to the deck, joining the other two teams standing at the top. Odom stood there with them, along with a few other troops who were making preparations on the rappelling lines that were being connected to the railings.

Jinx raised an eyebrow at the line, which was made of chain link. "Sparing no expense for us, Captain?" he asked.

"So much stuff was cast overboard to make room for more soldiers that this is all we could scrounge up," Odom explained. "Four chains."

The Corporal raised a fist. "Don't worry Captain," he said firmly, "we'll buy you all the time you need to unload."

"That's what I'm counting on," he replied.

The soldier by the railing made the final check before turning and giving him the thumbs up.

"Looks like we're good to go, here," Odom said.

Jinx nodded. "We're ready to rock-and-roll too."

The Captain nodded and pulled out his walkie-talkie, raising it to his mouth. "We are ready to go up here," he said.

"Yes sir, moving out," the soldier from the bridge replied.

Odom put the radio away and turned to
face the three groups, each of them six
strong. The boat began to move from
position towards the bay entrance.

"Everybody listen up," he declared.
"Just gave the order, so we'll be on shore
in a matter of minutes. We have a handful
of snipers on board, so once we make
landfall, they'll be covering your
descent. You all have your assignments."
He raised his chin. "Be safe out there."

There was a chorus of "Yes, sir!" as
the Captain headed back inside the ship.

Jinx approached the railing and stood
next to Stein and Burch, staring out at
the bay as it grew closer and closer.

"What do you say, Jinx?" Burch asked.
"You think we got a chance of pulling this
off?"

The Corporal grinned. "Yeah, it'll be
a walk in the park," he said, spreading
his arms. "A giant, zombie filled park."

"You able to find us anything fun?"
Stein asked.

Jinx smirked. "Oh yeah," he said,
"but if I tell you about them, it won't be
a surprise." He winked and then headed
over to Spence and Dickerson, who were
prepping their teams. "If you gentlemen
don't mind," he said to catch their
attention, "I'd like my team to be the

first over the side. We have the furthest to go, so I'd like to get a jump on it."

"Fine by me," Spence replied. "My team isn't too happy I volunteered them for this, so pretty sure if I made us go first, I'd be in line for a friendly fire incident."

Dickerson chuckled. "Look forward to following in your carnage-filled footsteps."

"Come on Sergeant, that was *one* time," Jinx drawled, rolling his eyes.

Dickerson shook his head. "One for me," he corrected. "I've heard stories from others who have followed you into battle."

"What can I say?" Jinx replied, puffing out his chest. "I take pride in my work."

The trio shared a laugh and then exchanged fist bumps.

"You stay safe out there," he said, in a rare moment of seriousness. "We'll swap stories on the march to Olympia."

"Back at you," Dickerson replied.

The Corporal headed back to his team, all of which stood, looking out over the water. The ship was passing through the entrance to the bay and making the turn towards the landing zone. The beachhead was another thousand yards away and closing quick.

"Okay, we're first over the side," Jinx announced. "So, as soon as we stop moving, get those chains over and start climbing." He looked around. "Who has binoculars for me?"

Rollins reached into his bag, pulling out a pair and handing them over. Jinx looked through them to the beach, seeing several dozen zombies wandering about, some of which were looking towards the beastly ship.

"Damn, we're going to be coming into a crowd," he muttered. He looked past them at the thick line of trees about a hundred yards behind. It was hard to see, but he spotted movement within the branches. He continued to scan, finally focusing on a small shack at the far end of the beach. "Got movement in the trees, too."

"Any idea how thick the woods are?" Burch asked.

Jinx tilted his head back and forth. "Twenty, thirty yards max," he said. "Edge of town is on the other side of it, which is where the real fun begins."

"If there's this many on the beach, we could be coming in for one hell of a welcoming party," Jarvis said dryly.

Jinx nodded. "Which means we're going to have to move quick," he said. "As soon as your boots hit the sand, make your way to the shack on the far end of the beach. That's the rally point."

"And the zombies?" Rollins asked.

The Corporal handed back the binoculars. "Clear the landing zone for the other teams and let the snipers handle the ones coming from the woods," he instructed. "We got a double load out, but four hundred and twenty rounds is gonna go quick. Questions?"

The team shook their heads, making noises in the negative.

"Let's get ready to roll, then," Jinx said.

The soldiers geared up, loading up their ammunition and gear bags, and checking their files. Burch leaned over and looked at the chains, inspecting the thick gauge metal with large chunks welded to it every few yards for hand holds.

"This is some Frankenstein bullshit right here," he muttered.

The deck teams lined up on the railing, bracing themselves as the ship hurtled towards the shoreline. As they reached the hundred yard line, the PA system crackled to life.

"All hands, brace for impact!" the Captain bellowed.

The ship began to run aground as it approached the shore, hitting the low part of the sea floor. Everyone lurched forward as the momentum quickly stalled. There was a horrific loud sound of metal vs rocks as the ship skidded along the sand.

The strike teams rattled around, holding onto the railing. Jinx's eyes were wide, a massive grin on his face as if he were on a roller coaster. A few members of his team looked excited as well, prompting a few of Spence's team to stare at him with furrowed brows.

Jinx flashed them a hand with his pointer and pinky fingers extended in the iconic devil horns sign, letting out a whoop.

Finally, the ship came to a stop on the shore, the front end of the ship about ten yards onto the beach.

"Chains overboard!" Jinx barked, and his team moved fast.

The soldiers shoved the heavy chains over the side of the ship. It took two people on each one to get it going, but soon the metal plummeted to the ground below.

Jinx looked over the side, all four lines close together, no more than five yards apart, landing on the sand below. One of the chains smacked a zombie on the shoulder, ripping the arm clean off.

"So close Davila," the Corporal cried, "you almost had a headshot!"

Davila chuckled and tapped his gun. "Don't worry, I'll make up for it."

"Davila, Jarvis, Rollins, on me," Jinx said, "let's move!" He hopped over the railing and grabbed onto the chain as his three teammates did the same.

He looked down the forty yards to the ground, watching the dozen zombies directly below them, and a few dozen more on either side of them on the beach, and headed their way. He climbed down quickly, hand over hand with his feet walking down the side, moving faster than his soldiers. When he was about ten yards from the ground, he stopped, looking at the dozen zombies reaching up for him hungrily.

Jinx wrapped his off-hand around the chain, enough to support his weight. He pulled his handgun, and then opened fire, one by one popping rounds into rotted foreheads, dropping them.

A few seconds later, the other three members of his team were level with him, joining in the execution of the ghouls.

"Landing zone is clear!" Jinx said, holstering his gun. "Move!"

The four troops dropped the rest of the way to the ground, quickly finding their footing on the sand and raising their assault rifles.

"Jarvis with me," Jinx said, moving his hand in quick flicks of his wrist. "Rollins, Davila, other side."

He moved to the left of the ship, taking aim at the twenty or so zombies that moved towards them, the closest five yards away. The duo acted as a single unit, moving forward and executing ghouls with precision, stepping over the fallen corpses to reach the next one in line.

The entire firefight was over in a matter of moments, with the two soldiers mowing through the crowd with ease. As Jarvis shot the last remaining zombie in the face at nearly point blank range, she turned and gave her Corporal a high five.

"Fucked 'em up, Jinx," she declared.

He nodded. "Yeah, we did," he agreed with a grin. "Lot more waiting on the same treatment, let's move."

They rushed back to the ship as Stein and Burch hit the ground.

"Let's go," Jinx called, "rally point."

The four soldiers moved across the beach, headed towards the old shack at the far end. As they went, they saw a trail of death from Rollins and Davila who'd cut through the immediate group of zombies.

When they spotted the shack, fifty yards away, there were several zombies emerging from the woods. As they ran, gunshots boomed from the ship, and the zombies began to fall as the backs of their heads exploded.

Rollins and Davila took a knee on the side of the shack as the other four caught up, and the shorter man nodded to the Corporal.

"Off to a good start," Davila said.

Jinx nodded. "Yeah, we navigated through your handiwork on the beach," he said. "Nice job."

"So what's next?" Rollins asked, keeping watch on their flank.

Jinx looked out from behind cover towards the woods, which was about fifty yards away, running for hundreds of yards in both directions. There were dozens of rotted corpses emerging from the trees, and they were starting to make headway to the ship, the numbers greater than what the snipers could keep up with.

The Corporal pulled out a satellite image of the area on their side of the bridge. "Bridge is on the south part of town, so let's stick as close to the south as we can," he said, running his finger along the paper. "The woods are going to be a bitch with as many of those things, so we need to push through. Rally point is this wrecker yard looking place. Teams of two, watch each other's backs, and let's move."

He and Jarvis broke off first, Davila and Rollins shortly after, leaving Burch and Stein as the final team.

The three mini-teams broke out into the open, spreading out about ten yards apart from each other and racing towards the tree line. There were a few dozen zombies ahead of them, with more coming out of the woodwork as they grew closer.

"Knock 'em down and keep moving," Jinx said.

The duo reached the first few who were a few yards apart. Both soldiers lowered their shoulders and rammed into a zombie each, sending the flailing corpses tumbling to the ground. Their presence drew the attention of numerous zombies around them, who quickly changed their target from the ship to them.

Jinx and Jarvis made it to the woods, seeing the trees packed full of the dead, but at least broken up thanks to the thick trunks. They darted to the left, hoping to put a little distance between them and the other two teams.

The Corporal led the way, his partner a few yards behind. He drew his handgun for close encounters, as they were far too many creatures to simply push through. He came around a tree, quickly popping a zombie in the head before shoving the lifeless corpse aside.

There was a torrent of gunfire coming from the other two teams, and he furrowed his brow in concern, wondering how bad it was on the other side. He had to concentrate on himself, however, as he came around a thick trunk and spotted half a dozen creatures blocking his path.

"Jarvis!" he barked.

She stepped up with her assault rifle, peppering the zombie group with some three-round bursts, dropping most of them. The Corporal put a bullet in the last remaining creatures for good measure.

"Five outta six, not bad," he said, and she wrinkled her nose as she followed him deeper into the woods.

They avoided the outstretched hands of several ghouls continually drawn to their noise. Soon, the daylight at the far end of the woods peeked through to them.

"Keep pushing, almost there," Jinx said.

He took out a few more zombies, making their run a bit easier. They pumped their legs hard, darting around a couple more trees before emerging into a field on the other side of the woods. There were a handful of corpses in the field, but they were spread out fairly well.

"Looks like the first wave of those things aren't too bad," Jinx mused.

"Snipers and those other teams should be able to clear them out."

He glanced to the right, hoping to see his teammates emerging, but they hadn't yet. Instead, all he heard was more gunfire in the woods. He took a deep breath, and then glanced at Jarvis, whose eyes were hard to mask her own concern.

"They can handle themselves," the Corporal assured her, "let's get a move on."

Jinx and Jarvis moved briskly across the field, avoiding the spread out zombies as they went. Soon, they hit a road and started moving to the south. A quarter mile later they spotted the driveway to *Eddie's Scrapyard*.

"Stay alert," he said quietly, "silent kills if possible."

Jarvis nodded and slung her rifle over her shoulder, drawing her knife as they jogged down the dirty driveway. As they grew closer to the small building, they spotted numerous broken down cars stacked up along the side of the road.

The sounds of moaning and flesh smacking against metal erupted from the other side of the wall of cars, but it didn't seem as if the creatures could get through.

Jinx rushed up to the window of the small dilapidated building that looked like it would collapse if someone punched it in just the right place. He peered inside, seeing a darkened messy office, but no movement.

"Let's get inside," he whispered, and turned the knob, but it was locked. He studied the door for a moment, the weathered wood with peeling paint, and then gave it a forceful straight kick. The entire frame shattered, and the door hung open. "Knock, knock," he murmured.

They stood at the entrance, waiting patiently for something to come out, but nothing did. Just to be safe, they did a quick sweep of the building, finding it empty.

"See if you can find anything useful and wait on the others," Jinx instructed.

Jarvis raised an eyebrow. "Where are you off to?" she asked.

"Going to check and see what's coming up," he replied, and then headed out of the building. He checked the satellite image of the area, noting a short line of trees to the north of the junkyard. On the other side of that was the main residential area that stretched on for several blocks before the bridge.

He readied his knife, not wanting to draw attention to himself, and walked through the woods. There were only a couple of zombies milling about, both of whom had become entangled in roots and branches, writhing in anger at being unable to free themselves. They got agitated when they spotted a fresh meal, moaning and thrashing about.

"Was going to let you slide," the Corporal muttered, "but you had to start making a racket." He stepped up and executed two swift knife blows, slumping the creatures over in their entangled mess. He cleaned his knife off on one of their shirts before sheathing it.

Moans erupted from the other side of the woods, and he moved slowly and silently. He inched to the edge of the trees, stopping about ten yards before exiting, which was close enough to see out without giving up his position.

He swallowed hard at the sight of a small army of zombies, easily hundreds of them, closer to a thousand than zero. All of them moved up the street towards the gunfire coming from the ship, faint but still loud enough to attract attention.

Shit, he thought bitterly, *if this group makes it to the beach they can forget about gaining a foothold. We're gonna have to do something.*

CHAPTER FOUR

Jinx ran back through the woods, getting to the rally point as Davila and Rollins walked up the driveway. They turned and saw the Corporal running towards them, which made them stiffen for a moment before they realized nothing was chasing him.

"Holy shit, you scared the fuck out of me," Davila said, letting out a deep whoosh of breath. "Thought we had a runner."

Jinx shook his head, chest heaving. "It's worse than that," he replied. "Come on, let's get to the others."

They picked up the pace, reaching the building where the other three members of their team stood waiting.

"What did you find?" Jarvis asked.

The Corporal took a deep breath. "There are a thousand of those things on the other side of the tree line, and they're all headed towards the ship," he said. "If we don't distract them, there's no way our guys will get a foothold."

Jarvis cocked her head, smiling as she held up a set of keys. "It's a good thing I found these, then," she declared, jingling the keys.

The boys all shared confused glances, and she smiled even bigger, waving for them to follow her. She led the pack out the back door towards the personal parking lot. As the lot came into view, the soldiers stopped short and stared at the sight.

"That…" Burch gaped. "That is a big ass truck."

Standing before them was a souped up pickup truck, with a major lift kit and oversized wheels. It wasn't quite a monster truck like one would see at rallies, but the front bumper was almost four feet off of the ground. It was jet black, with tack fire decals running down the side of it from the front wheels.

"Did we hit a teleporter and end up in Alabama?" Stein asked.

Burch barked a laugh. "You tell us," he said. "Do you have the sudden urge to fuck your sister?"

"Nah, wouldn't want your sister to get jealous," Stein shot back.

Davila snorted. "Please, you couldn't get Burch's sister with a stack full of fifties."

Both men paused and stared at their shorter friend.

"Not sure if you were insulting me or Stein," Burch admitted.

Davila shrugged, giving them a sheepish smile. "It's the rare two for one deal."

Jarvis jingled the keys again. "If you boys are done," she prompted, "which one of you is coming along for the ride?"

"Burch, you're with Jarvis," Jinx said as he pulled out the satellite image again. The soldiers clustered around him to have a look as he pointed to the areas of interest. "If you head due north of here, you'll run into the main road," he began. "Get up there and start heading towards the water, look for something to blow up. Lay on the horn the entire time, shoot, do whatever you can to draw the crowd your way."

Davila raised an eyebrow. "Where are we headed?"

"The bridge is seven, eight blocks due west of here," Jinx replied. "Mostly through residential areas. When that crowd starts moving north, we haul ass towards the bridge."

Jarvis nodded. "Rally point?" she asked.

The Corporal shook his head. "No clue," he admitted, "but it'll be on this side of the bridge. We'll be on the lookout for you, so we'll signal when you are getting close."

She nodded again and turned to Burch. "You want shotgun, or in the back?"

"You're not going to let me drive?" he asked, putting a hand on his chest in mock offense.

Jarvis put a hand on her hip. "I've seen you in the shower, and unless you have a boyfriend you aren't telling us about, it's obvious you have no experience handling anything big," she quipped. "Now come on."

Burch simply shook his head as the others snickered, unable to come up with a viable comeback. He climbed up into the passenger seat as the engine roared to life, rumbling loudly before settling into a nice rhythm.

"We'll see you at the bridge soon," Jarvis said through the window, and then popped the truck into gear and peeled out. She did an impressive burnout as she drove the behemoth out from the lot and onto the road.

"Okay, we give them five minutes, then we move," Jinx said, folding up the map and putting it back in his pocket. "In the meantime, we gotta give the other teams a heads up." He pulled out his walkie talkie.

"Let's just hope they are in a position to hear it," Davila said. He pointed into the air, signaling the constant stream of gunfire in the distance.

Jarvis drove up to the main road, zombies streaming out from the main part of the neighborhood. "Need you to keep your eyes peeled," she said.

"For what?" Burch asked.

"Anything we can use to draw these things away," she replied as she reached the top of the street. She barely paused as she cut the corner tight, and the truck rolled over the edge of the sidewalk, taking out two zombies easily.

Jarvis let out a satisfied yell as the creatures flew backwards onto the grass. The main road was littered with ghouls, all moving towards the ship. There were about a hundred or so stretching out several hundred yards, with more coming out from the side streets. She put the pedal to the metal, prompting Burch to hold on to the 'oh shit' handle at the top of the door.

"This is gonna get bumpy," she warned, and began weaving back and forth on the road, cutting a path through the spread out zombies.

Bodies flew everywhere, some crushed beneath the gigantic tires. There were so many smacks on the vehicle that it sounded like a high school band drum section that was horribly out of sync.

Burch looked down every side street as they went, seeing they were fairly packed as well. When they crossed the fourth road, he straightened up.

"Stop stop stop!" he yelled.

Jarvis slammed on the brakes, skidding to a halt and smacking into a few more zombies. "What is it?" she asked.

"Back it up!" Burch instructed.

She threw the truck into reverse and went back until he held up a hand, and they were parallel with the side street.

"Half a block down," he said, pointing. "Down on the left."

Jarvis peered past him down the road, and a smile broke out on her face. There was a gas station on the left side, right across from the neighborhood. A few dozen zombies stood between them and the target.

She nodded slowly. "How much time do you need to light it up?" she asked.

"There's no power, so going to have to use brute force to get into the gas line," Burch replied. "Probably some fuel left in the surface line, or I can open up the load valve on the ground and drop something in."

Jarvis pursed her lips. "Once the gas is out, how long?" she asked.

"Thirty seconds?" he replied. "Got to set a little bit of a fuse, or else we're going up with it."

"All right," she replied, and laid on the horn, getting the attention of the ghouls near the station. "Anytime you want to start shooting," she teased.

Burch grabbed his assault rifle and hung out the window, popping off a few rounds towards the station. He aimed at the ground and a car on the side of the road, resulting in some nearby noise for the ghouls. Finally, the bulk of the creatures were heading their way.

Jarvis punched the gas and pushed through the crowd that had gathered in front of the truck, taking a few moments to pick up speed. She glanced in the rearview, seeing that only about twenty percent of the horde was following them.

She made a hard right turn on the next street, still plowing through zombies on the road.

"Where are you going?" Burch asked.

"Taking the scenic route to buy you time," she replied, heading up two blocks before turning back towards the station. She circled back onto the road.

The diversion had worked somewhat, the bulk of the zombies walking towards the main road, however about ten ghouls were stubbornly hanging out near the station.

Burch readied his weapon, but Jarvis shook her head.

"Put that away," she said, "your only job is getting the station rigged to blow. I'll cover you."

He nodded before pulling out his knife and reached down to grab an old ratty tank top from the floor below. He cut it into a long strand and held it up. "Let's do it."

Jarvis hit the gas, speeding up the road. As they grew close to the gas station, she swerved, hitting two zombies and sending them flying back onto the road, smacking their heads wetly against the pavement.

"Move it!" she barked.

Burch leapt out of the passenger seat, stumbling as he fell the four feet to the ground. He regained his footing and then tore for the fuel pump.

Jarvis opened her own door and stood on the step. "Come get some, motherfuckers!" she yelled, and carefully aimed and fired, striking a few zombies in the head and drawing the majority of the others towards her. Two ignored her and shambled towards Burch, so she reached back inside and slammed on the horn.

Burch startled, glancing back towards her. She pointed to the two zombies, and then tried to pick them off, but it was a difficult shot from the truck at that distance. He waved her off, and she nodded, turning back to fending off the rest of the zombies near her.

He tried the first pump, tugging at the fuel line and finding nothing. "Shit," he muttered.

He tried two more, but there was nothing left in the line. He looked around for something heavy, finally seeing a slim metal sign sitting between the pumps. He rushed over and picked it up, using it as a battering ram on the pumps.

Jarvis laid on the horn again, and he glanced over, the two zombies much closer. He pulled his handgun and quickly dispatched them, and then watched as his partner fired off a few more shots from the truck, clearing the immediate threat to them.

Burch smashed the pump a few more times before throwing the sign down in frustration with a clatter.

"What the fuck are you doing?" Jarvis yelled.

He shook his head and turned to her. "The lines are dry," he called back, "but if I can get into the pump, the internal lines lead straight down to the main tank."

She looked up the road at the hundred or so zombies that had been attracted to their gunfire and headed their way. She looked back at Burch, who had run over to

the far side of the parking lot,
struggling to undo the metal cap to the
refueling tank.

Jarvis hesitated for a moment,
contemplating her next move. She glanced
in the rearview mirror, seeing another
large group of zombies headed their way
too.

"Fuck it," she muttered, "if it
doesn't work at least it'll be
spectacular." She honked the horn a few
times, but Burch ignored her, struggling
with the cap. She backed the back end of
the truck up and lined it up with the
outermost pump, and revved the engine,
honking the horn again.

Burch didn't break his concentration.

She shrugged, giving up and flooring
the vehicle in reverse. The tires
screeched, and the truck sped backwards
towards the pump. The back bumper hit in a
vicious strike, knocking the pump clear
off of the moorings. Gas spewed out,
filling the parking lot with flammable
liquid.

She moved the truck up, vaguely able
to hear Burch screaming obscenities as he
ran towards the truck, his ranting coming
out in an unintelligible fast stream.

"What's that?" she asked, putting a
hand to her ear as he jumped into the

passenger seat. "Can't hear you. I was too busy fixing your problem."

Burch shook his head. "You're a crazy fucking bitch, you know that?" he asked breathlessly.

"Why do you think I fit in with this unit so well?" she asked.

All he could do was smirk, knowing she was exactly right.

"So, light this puppy and let's get the fuck outta here," Jarvis said, jerking a thumb over her shoulder. "We got a lot of company headed our way."

Burch looked up and down the street, noticing the horde coming from both directions. He balled up the shredded tank top and lit it on fire, tossing it out the window. The fireball landed about five yards from the ever expanding pool of gas.

"Might want to get a move on," he urged, "we don't want to be anywhere near here when that thing goes off."

Jarvis peeled out of the parking lot, headed away from the main road towards the smaller pack. As she started to plow through them, there was a gigantic explosion behind them. They checked the rearview mirrors, seeing a fireball engulfed in smoke rise a hundred feet into the air.

"That oughta get their attention," Jarvis declared.

Burch laughed. "If Captain Odom asks, it was Jinx's idea," he suggested.

She shook her head vehemently. "Hell no!" she declared. "He isn't stealing credit for this one."

Jinx led the group of four through the neighborhood, taking shelter in a house to examine where they were. He studied the map with Davila looking over his shoulder as the other two kept watch out the front and back of the house.

"Pretty sure we lost that pack," Rollins reported. "A couple of them just wandered by and didn't even so much as look our way."

Jinx nodded. "Good," he replied, "let me know if that changes." He studied the map, tracing his finger along the route they'd taken to get to the house. "Did we go five or six blocks?" he asked.

"Pretty sure it was five," Davila replied.

"Okay, that puts us here," the Corporal said, pointing. "Just a block away from the shopping district and three away from the bridge."

Davila nodded. "We didn't have that much resistance getting up here," he said, "so hopefully the bridge isn't too bad."

"The gunfire from the ship isn't too present up here," Jinx replied, "so hopefully it won't alert too many of them."

Davila raised an eyebrow. "And if it is?" he asked.

"Then let's hope Jarvis keeps that truck in one piece," the Corporal replied, folding up the map and returning it to his pocket.

"Speaking of them, any idea how we're going to signal them?" Davila asked, stepping back as his superior got to his feet.

Jinx nodded. "I say we get to the shops the next block up and see what we see."

"Stein, how we looking on the backside?" Davila asked.

"Yard is clear and haven't seen anything on the next street," came the reply. "Could be hiding behind the houses, but none of them have walked by."

Jinx checked his weapons. "All right, let's get moving," he instructed. "We have a half block of houses until the stores. If it's crowded, find the first place with multiple exits we can get into. If it's not, let's find the most useful."

He headed for the back door, his team in tow. They readied themselves, doing one last sweep of the yard.

"Silent if possible," he said. "Light them the fuck up if not."

The soldiers nodded as the Corporal opened the door and led them out. They rushed through the backyard to the next set of houses by the first row of shops across the street. Jinx paused at the first house and looked out.

There were half a dozen standalone shops, none of them in mini-mall style buildings. They were mostly a few small consignment shops, all of which were built into existing homes.

"Ain't this all nice and quaint," Stein murmured.

"Yeah, just dress up the zombies in formal wear and it can be a real tourist trap," Rollins added.

Jinx held up a hand. "Come on, let's move up," he said quietly.

He led them across the street, moving swiftly so that they didn't draw too much attention to themselves. They sidled up next to one of the businesses, and he noticed one of the zombies had seen them and wandered towards their position.

"Rollins, hang back and handle it when it gets here," Jinx instructed quietly. "Davila, let's see what we're working with."

The duo moved to the back side of the building, which butt up against another. They inched their way up to the corner, peering out over the road.

There were a few dozen zombies on the roadway and in the parking lots of the businesses. They were spread out well, covering about a hundred yards. Across the street was a large grocery store, and on either side were mini-malls packed full of random stores.

"What do you think, grocery store?" Davila asked.

Jinx shook his head. "No, too many of those things around," he murmured. "We need to stay mobile."

On the right they saw the front edge of the bridge, but the bulk of it was blocked from view by the buildings.

"Stay here," the Corporal said quietly, "I'm going to scout the bridge."

Davila nodded as Jinx carefully moved out in front of the building, creeping along the wall as close as he could. He darted down a few buildings before ducking down the alley, taking cover. He scanned the area, happy to note that none of the corpses had taken notice.

From this vantage point, Jinx could see the bridge, and that it was sparsely populated with zombies, maybe fifty or so running the entire length of the structure. At the far end was the main shopping district, and there was a lot of movement down the street and on the side street running along the bridge.

If we can get to the other side, we can push through and start causing some trouble, he thought to himself. Pleased with what he'd seen, he worked his way back to the others. His footsteps attracted the attention of a few zombies on the road, and they turned, moaning and shambling towards them.

Jinx reached the others just as Rollins jammed a knife into the skull of a zombie. Davila kept an eye on the two that were giving chase to the Corporal, relieved that it was only a duo and not more. Stein joined them as Rollins kept watch on the back end.

"How did it look out there?" Davila asked.

Jinx leaned in. "Bridge is spread out pretty good," he replied, "and the other side has some significant resistance, but I think we can push through."

"Especially if Jarvis has that truck still purring," Stein added.

Jinx nodded. "We still need to find a way to signal them."

"I got that under control," Davila said, and pointed to a small fireworks stand off to the side of the parking lot. "Get their attention, *and* give us some more firepower."

The Corporal grinned. "I like it."

All of a sudden, a gigantic explosion in the distance rattled the windows of the buildings beside them.

"What in the fuck was that?" Stein gaped.

Jinx raised his eyebrows. "Looks like Jarvis is having some fun," he said.

Davila glanced out and saw the two zombies that had been heading their way had changed their trajectory and were moving towards the explosion. They leaned against the building, watching as they shambled by harmlessly.

Jinx raised a fist. "They're going to be here soon," he said. "Let's get over to the fireworks stand."

The soldiers looked out, noting several of the zombies in the street turning towards the explosion in the distance. Jinx waited until there was a significant opening, twenty yards between groups, and then broke cover.

He led his team across the street towards the grocery store, running hard. A few of the zombies spotted them and changed course to follow, but only a handful.

"Keep moving," Jinx instructed, "we'll worry about them later."

They reached the parking lot and rushed the fireworks stand. It was a small building, a converted mobile home. The three others stood guard as Jinx worked on the door. A dozen zombies wandered towards them, but none were closer than forty yards.

Jinx jiggled the door handle, finding it locked. Rather than worry about picking it, he drew his knife and shoved it into the mechanism. The cheap material shattered as he gave the handle of the blade a good hard smack.

"We're in," he said, and then opened the door cautiously, keeping the knife at the ready. He stepped inside, finding the building abandoned. Sunlight pierced the cheap curtains hanging over the windows, revealing a treasure trove of consumer grade explosives.

Jinx looked around and found some roman candles, grabbing a pack and tossing it to Davila. "Start lighting them up to signal Jarvis," he suggested.

The private ripped the packaging opened with excitement, brandishing his lighter and sparking up the end of one of the candles. "Man, this shit makes me miss the fourth of July," he said.

The fuse ignited, quickly vanishing into the handheld device. He aimed it high and towards the road, and soon the first colorful ball of flame shot out. It arced high, landing on the road and burning for several seconds.

"Ten bucks says you can't hit one of the zombies," Rollins said.

Davila smirked. "Shit man, make it twenty."

"Done," his friend replied.

Davila adjusted his aim, the next ball flying just over the head of one of the zombies coming their way, still twenty yards from them. "Shit, double or nothing," he said.

"Done," Rollins repeated with a lopsided grin.

Davila lowered the trajectory as the next colorful ball jetted out. It flew through the air, landing on the shirt collar of a bloody corpse in business attire. The bright blue flame stuck to the clothing, quickly setting it ablaze.

Davila and Stein cheered, while Rollins muttered obscenities under his breath.

Jinx poked his head out the door. "What in the hell are you doing out here?" he asked.

Davila held up the empty candle. "Just won a bet against Rollins," he declared, and pointed to the flaming zombie, how fully engulfed in fire.

"Nice shot," the Corporal replied. "But can you guys clear them out? We're going to have stuff to load in."

Rollins raised an eyebrow. "Doing some shopping?"

Jinx grinned. "Just seems criminal not to use this stuff."

Davila inclined his head towards the small pack of zombies still ambling towards them. "Come on, let's go clear them out," he said, and lit up another roman candle, aiming it towards the road as they headed towards the pack.

He hung back as Rollins and Stein made quick work of the ghouls, stabbing them in the head and dropping them. As they wrapped up, an engine roared in the distance.

Davila lit up another candle, keeping the flames going to the road. A few moments later, Jarvis rolled into view, making the turn into the parking lot. She skidded to a stop in front of her smiling friend.

"Where the hell did you find a roman candle at?" she asked through the open window.

Davila jerked a thumb over his shoulder. "Fireworks stand," he said. "Jinx is over there and says we need to load up."

"We're gonna have to hurry," Jarvis replied. "Getting a good number of them coming from the bridge."

Davila nodded as she sped off towards the stand. "Rollins," he said, "let's go check it out."

The duo headed towards the road as Stein jogged back to help load up the fireworks. As they approached the main road, a few more zombies came into view, a new group appearing from the shops across the street. They were more than twenty yards away, so the soldiers didn't pay them any mind for the time being.

"Yikes," Rollins said as he looked towards the bridge. "That looks like a shitshow."

There were a few dozen zombies emerging from it, shambling towards their position.

"Well, it doesn't look like we need to worry about attracting attention to ourselves anymore," Davila replied. He pulled out his handgun, took aim at the trio of zombies headed their way from the store, and opened fire. In three quick shots, they lay motionless on the ground. "Come on, let's get back," he said.

As the duo approached the stand, Stein was just shutting the tailgate. Davila hopped up to get a look at the bed.

"Holy hell, clearing them out, aren't you?" he asked with a laugh, and looked closer. "Man, there's mortars, high end rockets, bricks of firecrackers. We're going to have a good ole time, aren't we?"

Jinx nodded. "We have to do whatever we can to keep them on that side of the bridge, and nothing brings them in like an explosion," he said.

Jarvis raised a hand. "I can attest to that," she said proudly.

"Yeah, what the hell was that, anyway?" Rollins asked.

Burch grinned. "Just your local gas station."

"Wonder what Captain Odom is going to have to say about that?" Stein raised an eyebrow.

Jinx shrugged. "As long as we complete the mission, not much," he said. He tossed in another handful of firecrackers before hopping over into the back of the truck. "So let's get a move on, and we won't get chewed out."

CHAPTER SEVEN

Jarvis revved the engine as Jinx, Rollins, and Davila clambered up into the truck bed, laying down on top of the explosives. The Corporal smacked the side of the truck to let her know she was good to go. She peeled out of the parking lot, Stein and Burch jostling to the right as she turned onto the road leading to the bridge.

There were easily a hundred zombies standing between them and the target, and she stopped, opening up the window behind her. "What do you think?" she asked.

Jinx sat up and looked out, cocking his head as he studied the densely packed horde. "This thing got some juice to it?" he asked.

"Oh yeah," Jarvis replied, nodding. "Could probably clear one of those hybrid cars if I picked up enough speed."

Jinx gave her a thumbs up and laid back down. "Lead on, then!" he called, and they held onto the side of the bed tightly.

Jarvis revved the engine, prompting everyone to be ready. She floored it, picking up speed quickly, and within moments the truck smacked into the front edge of the pack, sending zombies flying every which way.

The men in the back watched bloody rotted limbs sailing around, corpses and crushed bodies landing on other zombies, creating a total mess. The momentum of the truck slowed as they pushed through, but the lift kit kept the vital components of the truck out of harm's way. Soon they were through the other side, driving onto the bridge.

Jinx raised his head to look through the back window, watching the daylight between them and the next batch of zombies at the head of the bridge. There were a few dozen spread out across it, all shambling towards them.

"Hold up here," he called.

Jarvis stopped the vehicle and Davila sat up.

"Yo, we're not drawing that big of a crowd back here," he reported.

Jinx looked back and saw that the zombies they'd plowed through were mostly turning and walking away, with only a few coming towards them. "Well, why don't you do something about it?" he asked. "Just don't blow us up."

Davila grinned, looking around through their stash for something to use. He finally settled on a large mortar device, a two-foot tall metal tube with balls of explosives in the package. He grabbed it and jumped down onto the bridge.

"Cover me, guys!" he declared, and then knelt to get set up.

Jinx and Rollins each took a side of the truck, readying their handguns. As they did so, a few corpses staggered by, headed towards their friend. They both aimed down, firing at near point-blank range to drop their respective enemies.

Davila gleefully opened the package like a kid at Christmas, positioning the mortar tube at a low angle, almost horizontal to the ground. He propped it up with his foot while he lit one of the explosives and shoved it in.

"Fire in the hole!" he barked, and a few seconds later the mortar went off, rocketing across the bridge just a few feet above the pavement.

The aim was true, striking a zombie directly in the back, exploding in a grand display of colorful flames. Davila let out a celebratory whoop before loading up another one. The second shot was on target as well, striking a turning zombie in the chest and knocking it back, setting a small fire on its blood-stained shirt. The noise and the fires attracted most of the zombies that had been wandering away from them.

Davila glanced over his shoulder just in time to see Rollins fire off a few more shots, taking out the last of the would-be attackers.

Jinx grabbed a large brick of firecrackers. "All right, saddle up," he said. "I think that's as good as we're getting with those."

Davila tossed the mortar device back into the truck and climbed up as Jinx lit the firecrackers and tossed them out onto the asphalt. He smacked the roof of the truck, and Jarvis took off again.

As they picked up speed to ram through the next batch of zombies, the firecrackers went off, loud sustained snapping filling the air.

"Hey Jarvis, once we're through," Jinx called through the window as he exchanged a fist bump with Davila, "stop at the next safe area so we can keep this up."

CHAPTER EIGHT

Jarvis drove the truck around slowly as the boys were on the ground, setting up fireworks to go off. There were a few hundred zombies on the main road headed towards them, but nearly a football field away.

Rollins aimed his assault rifle down the side street, firing off a few shots and taking out some nearby zombies that were attracted to the noise.

Davila and Stein set up a row of mortars on the roadway, lighting them up at the same time to send up a barrage of explosives, hoping that the combined noise would draw more zombies in.

Burch found a metal dumpster in an alley, running up to it and throwing in a brick of firecrackers. A few moments later, there was a loud metallic echo reverberating through the alley. When he looked back, he saw smoke rising from the dumpster, and Jinx approached, chuckling.

"Well, if that isn't a metaphor for the last month," he said.

Burch snorted. "No shit."

Jarvis honked the horn to get everyone's attention, coming to a stop. "All right, really starting to draw a crowd up here," she announced. "Let's get moving to the next site."

Jinx walked up to the window, and she handed over the satellite image of the area, where she'd put several red X marks on the map, showing locations to the west of the bridge.

"So where we at?" he asked as he surveyed it.

Jarvis pointed to the locations as she spoke. "About six blocks due west of the bridge," she explained. "I think we need to put some significant distance between us and the bridge this time."

"Agreed," the Corporal said. "If there are any on the other side of the bridge, they aren't going to care about the noise we're making this far out. We need to focus on keeping the ones here occupied."

Several gunshots erupted from the other soldiers as they cleared out nearby ghouls coming from alleys and stores. Neither Jinx nor Jarvis even flinched at the noise.

"If we can find someplace we can rig to blow like that gas station, that would be ideal," the Corporal mused.

Jarvis shrugged. "I haven't seen any yet," she admitted, "and from the looks of it, we're about to get into some residential areas for a bit."

"Couple of house fires, maybe?" he asked. "Might get lucky with them having gas instead of electric."

She shook her head, smiling. "You were totally a little arsonist as a kid, weren't you?" she asked.

"Yeah, pleading the fifth on that one," he replied.

A few more gunshots went off, and then the rest of the team clambered hop into the truck. Jinx used the back tire as a foothold and hopped into the bed with Davila and Rollins.

"So, what we doing next?" Davila asked.

Jinx jerked a thumb over his shoulder as he sat down. "Start a few house fires," he replied, "see if we can't get a gas explosion."

"Hell yeah," his friend replied with a grin, "I'm in."

Jarvis drove the group a few blocks up, smacking into several clusters of undead on the road while the fireworks in the background attracted more ghouls from every nook and cranny on the roadside.

The neighborhood was middle-class, with nice brick homes stretching along the tree-lined streets. Jarvis drove up to an intersection, with houses stretching in every direction, and slowed to a stop. As the boys hopped out, she hung out of the window.

"Hey Jinx, I got an idea," she said.

He approached her. "Let's hear it," he said.

"We got plenty of those fireworks, right?" she asked, motioning to the back of the truck. "We should set some of them up by the windows and doors of the houses you're setting on fire. It'll be like an extended fuse on 'em, so we can get a little more bang for our buck."

Jinx nodded and whirled his hand in the air. "You heard the lady," he declared, "let's set us up some extra party favors!"

Davila and Rollins grabbed large handfuls of fireworks out of the back and followed the other three up to the nearest house. As they set them up along the windows, the Corporal led the way inside.

He smashed open the front door, assault rifle raised. There were two zombies in the kitchen, staggering towards them, and he quickly put them down.

"Burch, check the stove, see if it's gas," Jinx said. "Stein, keep watch."

The men leapt into action as the Corporal pulled a blanket off of a shelf and stretched it over the couch. He pulled out his lighter, but then Jarvis' horn sounded.

"Everything okay?" Rollins called.

Jinx furrowed his brow. "Not sure," he replied, and then looked out the window.

Jarvis stood in the driver's side door, frantically waving her arms to get him to come over.

"You boys finish this up and get the fire going," he instructed. "I'm going to go see what the problem is."

He headed out the front door and walked casually towards the truck. Jarvis hopped out and ran over to him, unable to wait for him to reach her at his slow pace.

"Christ, what's up?" he demanded.

She held out the walkie-talkie, thrusting it at him. "It's Dickerson," she said.

Jinx immediately raised the device to his lips. "Sergeant, it's Jinx, what's going on?"

"Thank Christ," Dickerson gushed. "We're pinned down and in need of immediate backup."

The Corporal's brow furrowed. "What do you mean, you're pinned down?"

"We ran into a shitload of these motherfuckers and got driven into a house," the Sergeant explained. "We're completely surrounded and there's hundreds of these things. Don't know how much longer we can hold out." There was deafening gunfire before he let go of the button.

"We're on the way," Jinx replied immediately. "Where are you?"

"North side of town, three, maybe four blocks due east of the hospital," Dickerson replied. "Don't have an address, but when you see the shitstorm, we'll be in the middle of it."

Jinx nodded firmly. "Hang tight Dickerson, we're on the way." He lowered the radio, jaw clenched.

"I know we need to help them," Jarvis said slowly, "but what about our mission?"

The Corporal shoved two fingers in his mouth and let out a piercing whistle, his team immediately rushing out of the house.

"What's up?" Davila asked as they approached.

Jinx took a deep breath. "Sergeant Dickerson and his team are in a heap of trouble," he replied. "We're going to go bail them out. Davila, Rollins, can you two handle the house fires?"

"Absolutely," Davila replied immediately.

Jinx held out his hand. "Map."

Jarvis reached into her pocket and grabbed the paper, slapping it into his hand. He unfolded it and quickly studied it, seeing a large white-roofed building in the middle of the green residential area.

"Okay, I want fires every half-block, alternate sides of the street," he began. "Pull out the fireworks that you can and use them." He pointed to the white-roofed building. "Rendezvous at whatever this building is ten blocks to the west. Given the location, it's probably a school or community center. If it's too dangerous, meet one block to the west in the corner house. Now let's move."

Davila nodded and pointed at his teammates. "Burch, Stein, help us unload the fireworks," he said. "Just dump them in the street and we'll find a wheelbarrow or something to get them moved."

The four soldiers rushed off to do so as Jinx and Jarvis studied the map.

"We're six blocks south and a few blocks to the west of the hospital," the Corporal mused as he pointed to the map. "So they're somewhere in this area. I think if we come up to this road, we should be able to find them."

Jarvis nodded, but cocked her head. "And what do we do once we find them?" she asked.

"Haven't thought that far ahead," Jinx admitted, and shoved the map into his pocket. "Now let's move."

CHAPTER NINE

The drive to the north side of town was tense, the soldiers on edge, worrying about what they were going to find. Jarvis slowed down as they reached the neighborhood and slowed to a stop after Jinx smacked the side of the truck.

"We should walk from here," he suggested, "we have to be close and don't want attention on us until we're ready for it."

The quartet readied their weapons, and the Corporal made sure to grab the walkie talkie and stuff it into his pocket before leading the group away.

The neighborhood had a handful of zombies milling about, all of them headed northward. There was sporadic gunfire in the distance, but it was muffled, sounding like it was from inside a building.

"That's gotta be them," Jinx said.

The soldiers moved quietly, creeping quickly but as lightly as they could. They got off of the main road, walking between the houses, letting the grass soften their footsteps. Jinx made sure to be cautious, stopping at every corner of each house, not wanting to end up surprised with a bad situation.

After a couple of blocks, the Corporal finally spotted the target house across the street. He motioned for the team to be silent, leading them to the back porch. He pulled out his knife and slid it into the lock, slamming down on the handle with his hand to use brute force to open it.

He moved inside, motioning for Jarvis to cover the other hallway. As soon as she set foot on the carpet, a zombie lumbered out from a bedroom, and she kicked it in the chest, knocking it to the floor. She shoved her boot into its throat and stabbed it in the forehead, then finished her sweep before rejoining the others in the main room.

"We're clear," she said.

Jinx waved to the team from the front. "Window," he said.

They moved to the front window, standing on either side of it so they could see out without being visible. The situation across the street was dire. The entire front of Dickerson's house was covered with zombies, stretching twenty-five, thirty ghouls deep.

"I've played concerts with fewer people," Stein murmured.

Jarvis shook her head. "That's what you get for playing in a shitty band."

"Hey now, I…" Stein began, but then shook his head. "Yeah, you're right, we were shitty."

Jinx pulled out the walkie talkie, raising it to his lips. "Dickerson, do you copy?"

"Jinx, where are you?" the Sergeant replied immediately. "Not sure how much longer we can hold out. The front door is starting to crack under the pressure."

The Corporal peered out at the crowd. "We're across the street."

"All right," Dickerson replied. "First order of business is going to be moving some of these fuckers away from the door. Too many are pushing on it, and we can't hold it up much longer."

"Ten-four," Jinx said. "Give me a minute to come up with a plan."

"Understood," the Sergeant replied. "We ain't going anywhere."

The Corporal lowered the radio, studying the area. "Ideas?"

"We got some fireworks left, we can try and peel them away," Burch suggested.

Jinx shook his head. "Too many of those things are engaged, they aren't going to break away for some firecrackers," he said.

"We could fire the roman candles into the crowd?" Stein piped up. "Start lighting some of them up?"

Jinx pursed his lips for a moment. "That's a plan of last resort," he replied. "On the one hand, it might work, but on the other hand it might set the house on fire."

"With our luck it would be the latter," Stein muttered.

"I could plow the truck through them," Jarvis suggested. "If I build up enough speed I should be able to make it from one side to the other, cut their numbers in half."

Burch shook his head. "But that would only be temporary," he said. "Plus, if you don't make it across, we'd have to walk back, and I'm already getting enough exercise for the day."

"So you don't want to do my plan because you're a lazy fucker?" She raised an eyebrow.

He shrugged. "And because it's a temporary solution."

Jinx studied the landscape, paying special attention to a large thick tree on the other side of a fence that was parallel to the horde and just up from the front of the house. "I like the idea," he said.

Burch blinked at him. "Really?" he asked. "You want to risk the truck?"

"Nope, and we're not going to," the Corporal replied, shaking his head. "But I like the idea of cutting their numbers in half."

Jarvis raised an eyebrow. "So if we're not going to use the truck, how are we going to do it?"

Jinx smirked and pointed towards the giant tree he'd spotted. "Who wants to be a lumberjack?"

Jarvis put a hand to her forehead, laughing in exasperation. The other two shook their heads in disbelief.

"All right," Burch finally said, smacking his thighs as he stood up. "I'll check the garage."

Stein jerked a thumb over his shoulder. "Pretty sure we passed a work shed on the last block, I'll go check that," he said.

"I'll let Dickerson know what the plan is," Jinx said.

Jarvis snorted. "That should be a fun conversation."

The Corporal chuckled as he lifted the radio to his mouth. "Dickerson, come in," he said. "We have a plan."

CHAPTER TEN

"Are you out of your fucking mind?!" the Sergeant demanded.

Jinx shrugged. "Might have been accused of that from time to time," he drawled. "Nothing was ever proven, though."

"Jokes. You got jokes," Dickerson snapped. "That's great."

"Look, there's only four of us with limited resources," Jinx shot back. "We're in a serious ticking time bomb scenario right now, and I have the only pair of wire cutters, as it were. If you have a better idea, I'm all ears, but unless I'm mistaken, if that idea takes longer than ten minutes, you and your boys are toast."

There was a long pause on the line before the Sergeant finally asked, "Have you even ever cut down a tree before?"

"No," Jinx admitted sheepishly, "but I watched a lot of those lumberjack competitions at two A.M. on ESPN Two back in the day. Pretty sure I got the angle concept down."

There was a torrent of gunfire from the house, and then Dickerson came back. "Fuck it man," he said. "Do what you gotta do."

"We're on the move, good luck, Sarge," Jinx said.

"Same to you," Dickerson replied.

The Corporal put the walkie talkie away and he and Jarvis stood up. As they walked to the back door, Burch entered, hands empty.

"Nothing?" Jinx asked.

Burch shook his head. "Not even a lawnmower," he replied. "Guess whoever lived here was livin' high on the hog and hiring someone to cut the grass."

"Good life if you can get it," Jarvis added.

Stein came busting in through the back door, holding a giant chainsaw above his head. "Leatherface bitches!" he cried. "Yeah!" He waved it around for a moment and then lowered his arms when he realized nobody was reacting. "I mean… Texas Chainsaw Massacre? Nobody?"

"Chainsaw killers are a lot more effective when the saw is actually on," Jarvis said, crossing her arms.

Stein's shoulders slumped, and he held out the weapon to Jinx.

"Okay, we're moving three houses up, cutting across the street, and working our way back," the Corporal said as he took the chainsaw. "From this vantage point, the yard looks pretty clear, as that fence is holding them back. That's probably going to change real quick once I fire this thing up." He motioned to the

645

soldiers as he spoke. "Jarvis, you cover our rear, Stein and Burch, you clear out as many of those things beside the house as you can. If this thing lands right, we may only have a short window to get them out. Everybody clear?"

At the affirmative, he nodded and led the group outside. He ran up several houses as quickly as he could, adrenaline pumping with the clock. He peered around the corner of the third house, seeing that the road and yard straight across was clear.

Jinx darted out, carrying the chainsaw upwards while the others kept their assault rifles aimed and ready. They got across the street without any problems and moved across the front yards of the houses, working their way back to the tree.

When they reached the target yard, they hopped the four-foot tall wooden fence, landing safely in the private yard. As Jinx rushed over to the tree, the others did a quick sweep to make sure the area was clear.

The Corporal took a knee, readying the chainsaw, waiting for his team to get in position. Once they gave him the all-clear, they all braced to unleash fury.

Jinx pulled the starter cord on the saw and it roared to life, but then fell

silent. The noise was enough to attract
the attention of several of the zombies on
the other side of the fence. They turned,
moaning and pressing themselves against
the wood. Jinx pulled the cord a second
time, failing again, and Stein and Burch
opened fire, popping off in three-round
bursts, dispersing hot lead in a wide arc
and dropping several of the ghouls.

"Come on, you piece of shit," Jinx
muttered, and gave the cord another hard
pull. This time, the engine snarled to
life, and he hit the throttle a few times,
revving it up to make sure it stayed on.
As soon as it was steady, he picked it up
and put the hammer down.

The blade pierced the bark of the
tree, and he cut straight down, creating a
large notch in the front of it. Then he
got to work on the base.

Jarvis kept a watch on their rear as
the Corporal worked, popping off a few
shots as some zombies started trying to
come over the fence at the top of the
yard. As she fired, the other two
continued to unload on the horde, both of
them clearing out a full mag each and
reloading, leaving a pile of corpses
beside the house and directly in front of
it.

Jinx managed to get the saw most of
the way through the tree and noticed it

starting to collapse into the notch he'd cut out. He turned the chainsaw off and stood up.

"Timber!" he yelled.

Burch and Stein sprinted away from the falling tree, leaping to either side as the big thing sailed into the neighboring yard. Jinx had been hoping for it to fall diagonally across, but his cutting wasn't up to par, and it tumbled straight across.

"Oh shit, oh shit, oh shit," he muttered as he watched it fall across the fence into the other yard, crushing through a row of zombies no more than five feet from the front of the house.

The gutters at the far end of the house ripped clean with the branches, but no other major damage was done to the house.

"Oh hell yeah!" he bellowed. "Just like I planned!"

The zombies were only two deep in front of the house, and the trunk was large enough to create a decent barrier from the rest of the horde.

Jinx pulled out the walkie talkie. "Dickerson, get a move on!" he yelled. "Move to our position!"

Burch and Stein concentrated their fire on either side of the tree, which had damaged the wooden fence a bit, thankfully not so much that the zombies could push through.

"Jarvis, clear in front of the house!" Jinx barked.

She turned her attention towards the house, aiming straight down the line and opening fire in single shots, picking off one ghoul after another like a carnival game.

The Corporal smirked, starting the chainsaw back up and leaning over the fence on the roadside. He stretched over, working his way towards the road, cutting into rotted necks with the blade, sending gore and blood everywhere. This was short lived, as the chainsaw quickly got mucked up with bone, stalling out.

Jinx dropped the saw, having enjoyed the small pleasure, and then glanced over at the door to see Dickerson emerge with his troops. Torrents of bullets cleared a path, and they hopped down into the gully between the house and tree, racing towards the fence.

Jinx and Jarvis reached over to help them over one by one, and the six soldiers escaped certain doom, hopping over to relative safety.

"Come on, our truck is a few blocks away," the Corporal said, waving them over.

Dickerson nodded and he and his team followed the group out of the yard, hopping over the fence on the other side. The ten soldiers raced through the neighborhood, running through yards and quickly losing the horde that had been in pursuit.

After several minutes of hard running, they arrived at the truck, thankfully with no zombies around. The soldiers all caught their breaths, letting out some disbelieving laughter at their luck.

"I gotta say Jinx," Dickerson huffed, "you don't disappoint."

The Corporal grinned. "Glad I could be of service, Sergeant," he replied. "Everybody make it out okay?"

"All six of my team are safe and sound," Dickerson replied, straightening up.

"And I got to check off a bucket list item," Jinx declared. "So it's a win-win."

The Sergeant chuckled. "Yeah, I've always wanted to carve up zombies with a chainsaw, too," he admitted.

"No, I'm talking about being a lumberjack," Jinx said with a wink. "Could never get a full beard to grow in, so I had to abandon that dream."

Dickerson lost it, laughter exploding from his belly. "You're a fucking wild man," he gasped, smacking his friend on the shoulder. "Never change."

"Can we drop you boys off somewhere?" Jinx asked, patting the side of the truck.

The Sergeant shook his head. "I think we can take it from here," he said. "You get back to doing what you were doing." He extended his hand, and the men shook hands. "I won't forget this. I definitely owe you one."

"Given the shit I get myself into, I can all but guarantee I'll need to call that in sooner rather than later," Jinx replied.

"Be safe," Dickerson said. "We'll see you on the march to Olympia."

Jarvis hopped up into the driver's seat and started it up, the rest of Jinx's team clambering into the back. The Corporal smacked the side, and she took off, leaving Dickerson waving to them as they peeled out.

CHAPTER ELEVEN

Jarvis drove down the residential streets towards the rally point. As they went, the soldiers could see large plumes of smoke rising in the distance, with the occasional firework or brick of firecrackers detonating as well.

They looked down the side streets, seeing straggler zombies, but none of them in packs greater than five, wandering towards the noise and smoke.

As Jarvis reached the turnoff road, she looked both ways. Back towards the bridge there were a couple hundred zombies, all moving across the road into the neighborhood. Hope flared in her chest that the distraction was working.

The other direction was a little more sparse, as the noise from the distractions were waning a little at that point. She made the turn, speeding off towards the rally point. After several blocks, she stopped at the corner of an intersection.

Davila and Rollins waved at them from a playground swing set in front of the school. They were the picture of relaxation, swinging lightly back and forth. They hopped down and headed for the truck as their teammates exited the vehicle.

"Looks like Operation Arson was a roaring success," Jinx said as he hit the pavement.

Davila grinned. "Yep, got a lot of those fuckers burning," he declared. "Made sure the houses we picked didn't have overhanging trees to try to limit the damage to the neighborhood as a whole."

"Good thinking," the Corporal replied, cocking his head. "Any houses with gas?" he asked.

Right as the words left his mouth, there was a gigantic explosion in the distance, and they all turned to look at a fireball shooting up into the air over the trees.

"Just one," Rollins said.

Jinx nodded in appreciation. "If nothing else, I have timing," he said.

"How did it go with Dickerson?" Davila asked.

Burch raised his hands above his head. "Jinx saved the day by going full lumberjack."

"Bucket list item," Davila replied with a smirk, "I like it."

"Day's not over yet," Jinx cut in, "you still got time to make some off your list."

Burch barked a laugh. "He just burned down an entire neighborhood worth of houses," he said, "he should be good."

"Hey now," Davila piped up with mock offense, "why would you think that's on my bucket list?"

Burch rolled his eyes. "We've all heard you talk about the horrors of suburbs," he pointed out."

"Eh, fair," Davila admitted.

"Hop in," Jinx said, motioning to the truck, "we gotta get to the main target. We should be close enough to it now to draw any zombies on this side to it."

The soldiers climbed up and Jarvis drove through the back half of the residential area, Davila and Rollins lighting fireworks and tossing them over the side in an attempt to pull the ghouls in their direction.

After several blocks, the residential area turned into retail, with small shops dotting the landscape alongside a few mini-malls. Zombie infestation was moderate in that area, the parking lots only having groups of twenty to thirty.

Jinx motioned for them to stop throwing out fireworks, as the truck noise seemed to be attracting enough that they could handle. There was a huge vacant lot on the far south of town, and Jarvis pulled into it. It was a corner lot, with the main river to the south and the smaller river running to the north. There was no resistance nearby, with the zombies on the bridges or congregating around buildings.

As soon as the truck came to a halt, Jinx, Davila, and Rollins quickly hopped out, rushing towards the five zombies in the lot and quickly dispatching them with their knives.

The Corporal was particularly vicious, running at full speed towards the first one and jamming his blade through its eye and shoving it straight out the back, breaking the skull open. He moved in a single motion, stabbing into the forehead of the one behind it.

With the lot relatively secure, the group rallied in the back of the truck. Jinx pulled out the satellite image of the immediate area and pointed to it as he spoke.

"Okay, listen up," he began, "to our south here is the bridge going over whatever major river that is. To be blunt, that's someone else's problem. To our north are two commuter bridges that cross over into what looks like Super Center island, because that's all that's there. We have to get over there, create a hell of a ruckus, pull as many of those things over as we can, and escape via the water. We also have to block off the bridges with whatever cars we can find."

Jarvis pointed to another bridge over the river that looked darker than the obvious commuter bridge. "Any idea what this thing is"

"Best guess is a rail bridge," Jinx replied with a shrug. "Not exactly conducive for zombies to get over, but could be our ticket across the river."

Davila nodded thoughtfully. "So what do you think?" he asked. "Two teams? One on cars, one on diversion."

"Works for me," Jinx agreed. "Jarvis, why don't you play escort around the town?"

Burch grinned. "Not the first time she's been an escort around town."

"One more word," Jarvis said, pointing a finger at him, "and I will bend you over the back of this truck."

Jinx laughed. "I'll give her the time too, just to see it happen," he offered.

"I withdraw the previous insult," Burch replied, raising his palms in surrender.

The Corporal shook his head. "Well Burch, I think for your own safety, you'll be coming with me and Davila to the Super Center," he said with a chuckle. "Jarvis, you drive Rollins and Stein around to find some cars. Stash them across the street from the bridge so we can move them

quickly once we get enough of those things
over the bridges. Questions?"

"Yeah," Jarvis said, "where are we
meeting once we get this done?"

Jinx pointed to the map. "Just across
the southern bridge, there is some sort of
store," he explained. "Get inside and get
to the roof. And I don't know about the
rest of you, but I'm ready to relax, so
let's knock this out."

"All right boys," Jarvis declared,
clapping her hands together, "hop in,
we're going car shopping." She got into
the driver's seat and shot Jinx a salute.
"See you soon." Once the other two were
secure, she did a burnout, kicking up dirt
as she sped off towards the retail area in
search of cars.

The three remaining soldiers coughed,
waving their hands in front of their faces
to avoid breathing in the dust.

"That's on you, Burch," Davila
gasped.

"Yeah I know," he replied, "just
couldn't resist."

Jinx whirled a hand above his head.
"Train tracks, let's do it," he said, and
led his team across the vacant lot to the
property line.

They looked out towards the Super
Center, the massive store sitting no more
than thirty yards from the water, which

ran on both the back and left side of the store. Two hundred yards to the north was the rail bridge, a rusted out truss bridge stretching over the water. There were a handful of zombies on their side of the bridge, which was a far cry from the transportation bridges half a mile further to the north.

Jinx pulled out the binoculars and scanned, letting out a low whistle as he did. "That doesn't look like fun," he muttered, and handed off the device to Davila.

The Private peered through the binoculars, checking out the bridges packed with hundreds of zombies each, easily close to a thousand between the two. "Yeah, that rail bridge is a good call," he said, lowering the device. "But how are we going to pull them off of it and over to the store?"

Jinx smirked and reached into his bag. "Remember how I said I got us a few things for the mission?"

"Yeah?" Davila raised an eyebrow.

Jinx pulled out a hand grenade, tossing one over to his teammate.

A grin broke out on Davila's face. "Oh now we're cooking," he declared.

"Figure it should be loud enough to draw them over to us," Jinx said, "maybe take out a fast food joint or two in the process."

Burch nodded. "Find one of those flame grilled places and set off the gas, too."

Jinx rubbed his hands together. "Let's go see what kind of trouble we can get into."

CHAPTER TWELVE

Jinx led the trio across the bridge, Davila playfully walking along the rail like a kid balancing. The other two strolled across the beams, enjoying the brief bit of quiet before the coming battle.

"Man, I used to do this all the time when I was younger," Davila said as he moved gracefully across the rail. "My brothers and I would walk for miles on the tracks, even going over to the next town some days."

Jinx shook his head. "I had the benefit of growing up in a neighborhood where I was the youngest kid by about five years," he said. "So when the rest of the kids hit high school, my only options were to wander around alone or play video games."

"What did you pick?" Burch asked.

"If Jinx ever bets he can beat your Galaga high score," Davila cut in, "just save time and hand over your money."

The Corporal shrugged. "On the plus side, my hand-eye coordination is next level."

"What about you, Burch?" Davila asked, stretching out his arms to keep his balance. "Happy-go-lucky childhood, or sad glowing screen childhood?"

Burch shook his head. "Neither," he admitted. "Been working since I was fourteen and haven't stopped since."

"Christ that's sad," Davila said with a sigh. "Yo, Jinx, can we pick him up a Gameboy or something at the Super Center before we head out? Hell, it'll even be my treat."

Burch barked a laugh. "Nah, don't need a Gameboy," he assured his friend. "But if you come across a bottle of scotch…"

"That's a man with priorities," Jinx declared, snapping his fingers. "I dig it."

They went quiet when they reached the end of the bridge, seeing a couple of zombies wandering by, stumbling over the side of the rail. Jinx motioned for the other two to move up to take them out quietly, while he covered them with his rifle.

The duo broke rank, rushing forward with their knives and stabbing into the zombie's skulls as the creatures tried to get up. Jinx walked to the end of the rail bridge, sweeping the area carefully. There were a couple dozen zombies spread out in the area leading up to the Super Center.

They took a knee in the field across from the parking lot, surveying the situation. Jinx pulled out the binoculars and scanned the lot, honing in on a flame-grilled burger restaurant at the far end near the road, with forty to fifty zombies in their path and a couple hundred more on the road leading to the nearby bridge.

"Gonna be one hell of a run," the Corporal murmured. He passed the binoculars to the others, who took turns looking at the scene.

"Maybe we can get into the Super Center and find something useful in there," Davila suggested.

Jinx pursed his lips. "Hold that thought," he said, and broke rank, running up to the building and hugging the wall.

He crept along it and peeked around the corner, checking out the thirty or so zombies milling about the front entrance. He grimaced and then darted back to his team.

"Well, that idea's out," he said quietly.

Burch cocked his head. "How bad?"

"Thirty, maybe a few more," Jinx replied. "Won't be any problem to take them out, but if we do, the ones from the road will swamp the restaurant."

Davila held out the binoculars. "So, straight to the restaurant then, huh?" he asked.

"Only play I see," Jinx agreed. "We run up, hit 'em hard, and get inside. In and out in sixty, then run like hell to the front entrance of the Super Center."

"We should be bringing enough noise that it'll pull them away from the entrance," Burch pointed out.

Davila nodded. "You'd hope, at least."

"Get inside here," the Corporal said, "blow the windows, and pull the fire alarm."

Burch's brow furrowed. "The power has been out for weeks now," he reminded his superior.

"These Super Centers have to fire backup power supplies for fire systems," Davila explained. "We just have to hope that the backup battery hasn't gone dead."

Burch pursed his lips. "And if it has?"

"I'm not opposed to blowing more shit up," Jinx replied.

Davila grinned. "One track mind," he said, "love it."

"Okay," the Corporal said as he pulled his rifle from his back, "three-round bursts, don't stop moving to aim, go right up the center of them. Burch, you're on burner duty, get that gas flowing. Davila, you sweep the room. I'll take care of the exit route. We good?"

The trio readied their guns and then Jinx broke cover, his teammates a few yards to either side of him. They moved quickly, almost at a full sprint, running towards the group of zombies near the restaurant. They were about forty yards between the first zombie and the eatery, moderately packed in.

Jinx fired first, clipping two ghouls in the head, and they pushed through. Davila opened fire, aiming slightly to his left to attack a trio that had turned their attention towards them. Burch let rip on his group just to the right, doing his part to keep the alleyway open.

The gunfire was intense, with all three soldiers releasing trios of shots one right after the other. The zombies began to move towards them, arms outstretched and mouths open with excitement, and the gaps began to close.

When they were within twenty yards of the restaurant, the pack started to get closer together, shoulder to shoulder as Jinx approached.

"Everybody forward!" he barked.

On his command, both Davila and Burch aimed forward and the three of them sent a couple dozen rounds towards the front facing group. The bullets ripped through the decrepit flesh, sending a large number of them tumbling to the ground.

Several still remained standing, so the Corporal lowered his shoulder and plowed through, creating an opening for the trio to rush in.

The side of the restaurant was ten yards away, and only a couple of ghouls remained in the way.

"Cover the rear!" Jinx yelled, and his friends turned to fire at the creatures now chasing them.

Jinx stopped, aimed, and fired a burst towards the two zombies in front of him, blowing the backs of their heads clean off. He turned his attention to the large window on the side of the building, sacrificing another three bullets to shatter it to pieces.

"We're in!" he cried, and tore through the window. The other two soldiers joined him in rushing inside.

Burch immediately rushed to the back, and as soon as he saw it was clear, he made his way to the gas grill burner. He flicked on the switches and quickly blew out the starter flame before taking a quick sniff.

"Oh yeah, we're hot," he declared, and darted back out into the main room.

Davila finished his sweep, and Jinx stood at the window opposite the broken one, looking out at the Super Center.

"Gas is flowing," Burch said, and then jumped as a few zombies smacked into the open window.

"The Super Center crowd is headed our way and looking pretty thinned out," Jinx reported. "You boys ready for another run?"

Davila nodded. "Lead the way."

The Corporal fired a single round at the corner of the window, shattering it. The three soldiers hopped down into the parking lot, doing a quick sweep. The closest zombie was thirty yards away, about halfway between them and their target.

"Fire in the hole, boys!" Jinx yelled, and pulled the pin from the grenade, chucking it back through the window towards the kitchen.

The trio immediately sprinted for the Super Center, firing as they tore through the lumbering mass. Jinx fired two bursts, with the third pull of the trigger resulting in a click. He lowered his shoulder, driving himself into the closest zombie and driving him back.

As he did this, the grenade detonated, igniting the gas. The entire building went up in a spectacular display, sending plumes of smoke and fire into the air. As it happened, Davila moved up to cover for the Corporal, firing several bursts into the zombies ahead, clearing up room for them to move.

The three men did more ducking and diving, narrowly avoiding outstretched rotted hands as they approached the front of the building. The soldiers quickly reloaded, and Jinx grabbed the door handle, finding it open.

"Open twenty-four seven," he said with a grin, and then slipped inside cautiously.

Davila flicked the lock closed behind them, and the trio crept forward into the front of the store. It was well lit, thanks to the large windows at the front. Jinx moved for the register row, checking every aisle for zombies. He had to fire a few shots here and there, switching to single burst mode, picking off the occasional stray that broke away from the pack. When he reached the end, he saw no other zombies nearby, and headed back for his team.

Burch and Davila looked out the front window, watching the raging fire that had once been a restaurant, and a couple hundred zombies coming from the road towards the inferno.

"How's it looking out there?" Jinx asked.

Burch shook his head. "Seeing that restaurant burn like that is really making me miss grilling," he said.

"One day chief, one day," Davila said wistfully.

"Come on let's clear out our path to the back, we're not out of this yet," Jinx said, raising his rifle.

The three men broke away from the window and began moving swiftly through the dark in the store. They had their flashlights out, aiming them down every aisle they came across, luckily finding nothing. After a quick trip, they get to the loading dock doors.

Jinx gave a silent countdown from three, bursting through the door on one. They quickly swept the back area, seeing nothing but bare concrete flooring with several boxes stacked up.

"Burch," Jinx said, "check the door and make sure we're good to go. Davila, find us a fire alarm."

The two soldiers rushed off to do their assigned tasks, while Jinx looked out the double doors leading to the store. He shone his flashlight around, making sure no ghouls were headed in his direction.

Burch opened the back door, looking out to see only a few zombies wandering around the back of the store. He gently shut it and came back over to the Corporal.

"Coast is pretty clear," Burch said, "we can get back to the rail bridge."

"What about the water?" Jinx asked.

Burch shook his head. "We can go that route if we need to as well."

"Just worried about that southern bridge," Jinx admitted, furrowing his brow. "With all this noise, we're going to be pulling zombies up from the south."

Davila approached from the back. "Got us a fire alarm switch."

"Good, so here's the plan," Jinx said, waving them towards him. "I'm going to take a position by the front windows, you're going to pull the alarm, then I'm gonna open them up. That will draw those things in and make it more difficult for them to wander back out. We get out the back, swim across, then wait for the other troops to do their jobs."

Davila nodded. "I'm ready when you are."

Jinx readied his gun. "Let's give it a few more minutes," he said, "give Jarvis time to locate some vehicles. We move in five."

Jarvis drove Rollins and Stein around to some of the businesses a few blocks away from the main road. The zombie resistance was minimal back there, as most of the ghouls had opted to stay on the main road.

"Got one over there," Rollins said.

Jarvis slowed to a stop as Rollins pointed to an SUV sitting in front of a shop.

"This will make what, three?" Jarvis asked.

He nodded. "Yeah, that should be enough to fill in the gaps on the first bridge," he mused. "A few may be able to wander out, but not enough to make a difference."

"Stein, cover him," she instructed.

The two men hopped out of the truck and raced over to the SUV. Rollins immediately began patting his hand underneath the back wheel well.

"Come on, come on, no whammy," he muttered, and then let out an excited whoop when he felt a small metal box connected to a magnet. He pulled it out and slid it open, revealing the key. "Oh, how I love trusting, naïve people." He clicked the unlock button, and the SUV beeped. "Come on Stein, let's roll."

His partner headed over to the passenger side and opened the door, immediately jumping back. There was a badly decomposed corpse inside, belted into the seat. The flesh had started to melt away from the body due to the extreme heat in the car over the previous month.

The zombie slowly shifted, letting out a low gurgling moan, struggling to even move without most of its body mass.

"Yeah, this one is all you, buddy," Stein said, wrinkling his nose.

Rollins looked in through the driver's side and sighed, shaking his head. "Can you at least stab it in the head for me?" he asked.

"Don't say I never do anything for you," Stein retorted. He pulled out his knife and jammed it into the zombie's temple, ending its miserable existence.

"All right, watch out," Rollins said, and reached in to unbuckle the corpse. He gave it a shove and the mass of gunk flopped out onto the road. Melted goo slapped everywhere, and Stein sighed as a bit sloshed onto his boots.

"Dude, really?" he whined.

Rollins shrugged. "I told you to watch out," he said as he got into the driver's seat. "Now you getting in, or what?"

Stein stared down at the slimy passenger seat. "I'll hitch a ride with Jarvis," he said, jerking a thumb over his shoulder.

Rollins shrugged and started up the SUV, opening all the windows. "Baked zombie, ugh," he muttered as he nearly gagged on the putrid stench in the car.

He popped the vehicle into reverse and pulled out, Jarvis and Stein following close behind. As he drove, there was a gigantic *BOOM* in the distance. As he parked in the lot a few blocks down from the bridges, he spotted a giant plume of smoke rising on the horizon.

"Jinx certainly doesn't disappoint, does he?" he said to himself and got out of the vehicle. The zombies on the bridge began to wander towards the noise, the nearby ghouls in the store parking lots joining them.

"Quit yapping to yourself and come on," Jarvis barked from the truck. "We need a couple more cars for that other bridge."

Rollins leapt out of the SUV, leaving the key in it, and hopping up into the back of the truck. Jarvis peeled out of the lot and headed back towards the residential area.

"Where are you going?" Stein asked.

"A few blocks further back," Jarvis replied. "That explosion is going to get everything closer all riled up."

She went for six blocks, reaching a cozy tree-lined street. They looked around, trying to find vehicles to borrow.

Stein pointed to a house with two sedans sitting outside. "That's our winner," he said. "Two cars, meaning they probably never got out. Just gotta find the keys and we're rolling."

"Good enough for me," Jarvis replied.

She parked the truck in the driveway and all three got out. They rushed up to the front door and Jarvis nodded to Rollins. He gave the door a forceful front kick, rattling it pretty well but not opening it. He tried again, but the door stayed fast.

"Jesus Christ," Jarvis muttered, "let me at it."

She shoved him out of the way and gave the door a good boot, which freed it from the latch. Stein chuckled.

"I loosened it for her," Rollins insisted.

His friend shook his head. "Yeah, I'd totally go with that."

"Move," Jarvis urged, and the duo snapped back to it, quickly moving into the spacious bungalow. They took up position in the living room, keeping an eye on the hallways. They could hear movement at the far end of it, sounding like several hands banging on a door.

"Company down the hall," Stein reported.

"Watch that," Jarvis replied. "Rollins, kitchen."

He moved into the kitchen, scanning the walls for any key ring holders. She did the same in the living room and finally found two sets of keys hanging by the front window.

"We're moving!" she declared, and grabbed the rings, tossing them to the boys.

They went back outside and the boys each picked a car, checking thoroughly for any unwanted passengers inside, and thankfully finding none.

Jarvis hopped back into the truck and led the caravan back towards the bridges, stopping at the rally point. Most of the zombies had moved across the bridge, but there were still a few dozen making their way towards it. The trio sat in their vehicles with the windows down so they could hear each other.

"How long do we wait?" Rollins asked.

Jarvis took a deep breath. "As long as we can."

"We got five minutes at best," Stein said.

Jarvis cocked her head. "What makes you say that?"

He pointed towards the southern bridge, half a mile or so away. There were easily a couple hundred zombies moving across it towards them.

"Fuck, okay," Jarvis said. "We need to move now."

Rollins furrowed his brow. "And just leave them on this side of the bridge?" he asked.

She shook her head. "It's going to take time for us to do this," she explained. "We block off the northern bridge and they can still cross on the southern one."

"Fuck it, good enough for me," Stein agreed. "There were a few broken down scars on the bridge already, so we just have to fill in the gaps."

Rollins waved his hand. "Well lead on then."

Stein popped it into gear and started driving, with Rollins behind him and Jarvis bringing up the rear. There were several zombies in the roadway, some of whom turned towards the noise. She gave a single honk of the horn and then floored it.

The increased speed sent Jarvis flying around the other two soldiers, pulling in front. She sped up, smacking into the zombies in the road and crushing them, clearing the path for the other two.

The bridge had a few dozen zombies on it, most of which were on the far side of it, moving towards the restaurant fire. There were a few cars broken down, having gotten into a crash at some point several weeks ago. There was a gap on either side of the wreck.

Jarvis stopped in the middle of the street about thirty yards from the wreck, and the other two drove around her, one on each side.

Stein skirted a few dozen zombies and pulled gently into his opening, leaving just enough room to open the door and get out. As he hopped out, he readied his assault rifle, firing a few shots at the throng of ghouls standing between him and the truck.

Rollins pulled his car into the gap on the other side, squeezing between the wreck and the side of the bridge. As he started to open his door, he had to shut it again quickly as a zombie from the window of the wrecked car lunged out, smacking against the glass.

He clambered into the back seat, opening the back door, but it was wedged up against the wreck, making it impossible to get it wide enough.

"Fucking shit, man," he muttered, and looked out the back window. There were thirty or so zombies growing ever closer to him.

Stein noticed that Rollins was stuck, and cupped a hand around his mouth. "Shoot the window!" he yelled.

Rollins gave a thumbs up and drew his handgun, firing a few shots into the back window, shattering it. Stein continued to fire at the coming zombies, attempting to cover his friend as he struggled to get out of the busted window.

"Goddamn it," Jarvis muttered, and hit the gas, speeding towards her friends.

Stein dove to the side to give her a wide berth to do her damage. She drove into the middle of the back and cut the wheel sharply, flooring it. Within seconds she was doing donuts on the bridge, sending zombie bodies and smoking tire debris flying through the air.

This gave Rollins enough time to clear the car, and immediately started firing, clearing out the ghouls in his path. After a few full rotations, Jarvis hit the brakes.

"Come the fuck on!" she bellowed.

There were still a handful of creatures standing, moving in various directions, but the soldiers were able to avoid them as they raced to the truck.

They hopped into the back, smacking the back window of the cab, and Jarvis punched the accelerator to get them out of there.

She sped several blocks away from the bridge, skidding to a stop in the residential neighborhood. She opened the back window, eyebrows raised.

"Holy shit, that was wild!" she declared. "Everybody good?"

Rollins made an *a-ok* sign with his hand. "Might need a change of pants," he joked, "but other than that, I'm golden."

The three shared a relieved laugh, and then sat back and relaxed for a moment, giving time for the other pack of zombies to make their way to the bridge so they could block it off.

CHAPTER FOURTEEN

Jinx readied himself by the front window, looking out at the zombies pressed against it. There were dozens of them, and hundreds more in the parking lot, all attracted by the gigantic blast at the restaurant.

He checked the ammo on his assault rifle, making sure it was full. When he was satisfied, he let out a two-fingered whistle that echoed throughout the building. A few seconds later, the ear piercing sound of the fire alarm filled the air.

He winced. "Christ, it might be less damaging just to be on fire," he muttered, and flipped his rifle into three-round burst mode and aimed at the big windows.

He unleashed half a mag's worth of bullets, peppering the windows with them. The impact did little more than put a few holes in it.

"Fucking safety stuff." He shrugged and reached into his bag, pulling out two grenades before walking back behind the registers. He pulled the pins on both and lobbed them over to the windows, and then turned tail, sprinting back towards the loading dock.

A few seconds later, another earth-shattering *BOOM* filled the air. Jinx didn't bother to look back, since if the blast hadn't opened the windows, nothing he had would have. He tore for the loading dock.

"What happened to just shooting them out?" Davila asked wryly.

Jinx shrugged. "Safety glass, so had to go big," he explained.

Burch opened the back door and stepped out, immediately raising his rifle and firing several shots as the other two piled out behind him. By the time the trio reunited, the zombies lay on the ground in a heap.

"Let's get to the water," the Corporal instructed, and led his companions across the back of the lot. They pushed through the waist-high grass, splashing down as they reached it. They sloshed out into the water, seeing their target on the other side of the southern bridge.

"Man, that was a good call to go on the water," Davila said.

Burch nodded. "No kidding."

The southern bridge was covered in easily a couple hundred zombies, all moving across it towards the noise. Jarvis plowed through some of them with the truck, sending bodies flying every which way.

"Fuck, we gotta move," Jinx urged. "She's going to attract a crowd."

The soldiers swam as hard as they could towards the southern bank. The current of the river wasn't strong, but they still had to fight against it to make sure they didn't end up downstream. As they paddled across, gunfire erupted from the building up ahead, a lot more sustained than was comfortable.

The trio pushed even harder and faster.

After a few minutes of intense swimming, they finally reached the other bank, just below the store. Gasping for air, they staggered forward, pulling their rifles from their backs.

"Suck it up boys," Jinx huffed, "we gotta get up there."

They climbed the grassy hill, struggling to reach the top with their slippery boots and heaving lungs. When they finally crested the hill, they saw their three teammates standing in the back of the truck firing down at a small army of zombies, easily sixty or seventy strong.

"Clear 'em out!" Jinx barked, and the trio raised their weapons, hitting the ghouls from the side.

The mass of rotted flesh was twenty yards away, which was an easy distance for

headshots. A few of the creatures nearest
the new source of noise turned to move
towards it just in time to take a bullet
to the face.

The soldiers burned through mag after
mag, sweating and breathing hard, focused
on the battle raging around the truck.

Finally, the battlefield fell silent,
the last of the corpses fallen, and the
soldiers lowered their weapons. Jinx
looked back towards the bridge and top of
the driveway. There was a smattering of
zombies staggering their way, but they
were still fifty yards and moving slowly
in the heat.

"Get the bridges squared away?" the
Corporal asked.

Jarvis hopped down from the truck.
"Not a hundred percent, but the ones on
the other side are going to have a hell of
a time getting back," she said.

"Good enough for me," Jinx replied.

Burch took a knee to catch his
breath. "So now what?" he asked.

Jinx jerked his thumb over his
shoulder at the grocery store. "Let's go
clear that out, get comfortable, and wait
on help to get here."

CHAPTER FIFTEEN

The sun hung low in the sky, bathing
the front of the grocery store in a golden
glow. The reflections on the nearby water
caused the front window to sparkle.

Sergeant Dickerson led a squad
several hundred strong across the southern
bridge, ignoring the stray zombies his men
took care of for him. He looked at the
grocery store across the way, looking
beautiful in the evening light, and
spotted the truck that Jarvis had been
driving earlier in the day.

He shook his head at the mountain of
dead zombies around the vehicle. "I think
we found them," he said.

"Sir?" the soldier next to him asked.

"Come on," Dickerson said, "let's go
make sure they're safe." He motioned for a
few soldiers to follow him as the rest of
the force moved into the southern portion
of town.

They carefully stepped through the
sea of corpses on the way to the front
door, and the Sergeant's heart leapt into
his throat at the sight of smoke coming
out of the seams. He rushed up and banged
on it.

A moment later, Burch appeared,
waving smoke away, and when he locked eyes

with Dickerson he grinned and opened the door, a flood of smoke billowing out.

"What the hell is going on in here?" the Sergeant asked, walking inside.

Burch held up a metal spatula, motioning to the charcoal grill behind him. The others waved, kicking back in chairs with their feet propped up on checkout lanes.

Dickerson laughed, shaking his head.

"Sergeant!" Jinx bellowed, spreading his arms. "Welcome. Can we get you something? Lukewarm beverage? Something from the grill?"

Dickerson put a hand to his forehead in disbelief, still laughing. Right in the middle of the biggest invasion in U.S. history was a cluster of soldiers having a cookout.

"Jinx, it's been nearly a month since this place had a fresh delivery or power," he declared, "so I'm afraid to ask what you're cooking up."

Burch used a pair of tongs to hold up a slice of canned meat, grilled to perfection. "This stuff takes forever to go bad," he said. "Pretty sure the secret is to coat it in a metric ton of salt." He slapped it down onto a tortilla that looked slightly stale and handed it to Dickerson.

The Sergeant reluctantly took it. "Guess I should enjoy this now," he conceded, "since it's going to be awhile before I have anything like this."

"That's the spirit!" Jinx exclaimed. "We work hard, we play hard, right?"

Dickerson took a bite of the food and nodded in surprise at the decent flavor. "Well, just don't play too hard," he said after he swallowed, "because the Captain is going to be here within the hour."

"Is that your way of telling us to take it easy for a bit?" Jinx asked as his friend gobbled down the rest of the taco.

The Sergeant shrugged, wiping his mouth. "I do owe you one for earlier today," he admitted. "We'll finish clearing it out, just do me a favor, will you?"

"Sure thing," the Corporal replied, curling his hands behind his head comfortably.

"Save another one of these tacos for me," Dickerson said. "I'll be back soon."

Jinx raised a plastic cup filled with an unknown substance to his friend as he headed out the door. "Everybody, listen up," he said to his team. "Each and every one of you did a hell of a job today. We keep this up, we might just live to see this thing through." He raised his cup high. "On to Olympia!"

The others raised their own cups and bellowed, "On to Olympia!"

END

Up Next - Private Janey Watts finds herself trapped behind enemy lines when a mission to the north goes horribly wrong in "Seattle - Part 5".

www.ingramcontent.com/pod-product-compliance
Lightning Source LLC
Chambersburg PA
CBHW071417190726
48292CB00001B/21